PRAISE FOR
RACHAEL HERRON'S
WORK

"A celebration of the power of love to heal even the most broken of hearts." - NYT Bestselling Author Susan Wiggs

"A superlative architect of story, Herron never steers away from wrenching events, and yet even moments of deepest despair are laced with threads of hope." - Sophie Littlefield, author of *A Bad Day for Sorry*

"Rachael Herron tells the kinds of stories that make you want to lean in closer." - Erin Bried, author of *How to Sew a Button*

ALSO BY RACHAEL HERRON

FICTION:

PACK UP THE MOON

CYPRESS HOLLOW NOVELS 1-4:
HOW TO KNIT A LOVE SONG
HOW TO KNIT A HEART BACK HOME
WISHES & STITCHES
CORA'S HEART

MEMOIR:

A LIFE IN STITCHES

Fiona's Flame

A CYPRESS HOLLOW
YARN

RACHAEL HERRON

Fiona's Flame / Rachael Herron. -- 1st ed.

ISBN: 1940785154
ISBN-13: 978-1-940785-15-8

DEDICATION

For the Rachaelistas, my darlings.

ACKNOWLEDGMENTS

As always, thanks go to Susanna Einstein for believing in me and for being my friend as well as the best agent in the world. Deep, heartfelt hanks to Beverley Cousins and the whole crew at Random House Australia (especially Lex Hirst, Kirsty Noffke, and Elena Gomez) for helping me build Cypress Hollow, where every man looks good in Wranglers. Many thanks to Robin Leone for curling my quotes and catching the bits that fell through the cracks. Thanks to John Spitlor for the small-town mayoral advice, to Todd Thomas for Snowflake's nickname, to Kenneth Ely for untangling my sailing lines (any error is my own), and to Lorajean Kelley. Every author has a perfect reader she writes for, and Lorajean is that reader. Even when she breaks up with me temporarily.

And for Digit, the worst cat who ever lived. He was alive when I wrote the book. I knew he might not be around when it came out. I love you always, you big stupid jerk.

CHAPTER ONE

Knitting warms a body twice. – Eliza Carpenter

Fiona leaned back and crossed her black cowboy boots over each other. If anyone had to make their way down the aisle, she'd draw her legs back, but right now this was the best seat in the house. No one in the City Hall council chambers was going anywhere.

She should have brought popcorn.

On the stage, Mayor Finley's face was turning a deep purple, a stark contrast to her perennial all-yellow outfit. She spluttered, "Elbert Romo, this shouldn't even *be* an issue. Nudity is something one indulges in on the way from one's bedroom to the shower. Not at the corner of Main and Third."

Elbert Romo, his face as creased as his overalls, said, "You're right, Mayor. But it's the damn tourists."

Old ranchers like Elbert didn't ever say the word *tourists* without prefacing it with *damn*. Fiona figured it was probably something they learned in the back room at Tillie's, where they hung out most mornings drinking coffee and gossiping.

The mayor said, "The tourists aren't the problem here. What we're talking about is outlawing public nudity on our public beaches."

Elbert clapped his hands together. "But they're the ones that *started* this. They come, they decide Pirate's Cove is the best place around to drop their skivvies. Then they put it on the internet! On those, you know, those *websites*."

Fiona watched the mayor take a deep breath and push the errant gray strands of hair back from her temples. "Make your point, Elbert."

"Once it went online, we got famous. Those sites even tell you where to park, did you know that? And they tell where the rope to climb to the bottom is hidden. You kidding me? That rope used to be a Cypress Hollow secret. You could get horse-whipped for givin' that info to the wrong person. Now we got nudies comin' from all over the state, just to get our sand stuck in their cheeks. And I ain't talking about the ones on your face."

"We already know all this. That's why we're discussing the ban tonight."

Elbert said, "I *know*. But no disrespect, ma'am, the thing is—a lot of us have found out how right the damn tourists are."

A light laugh rippled around the room. Daisy, Fiona's best friend, leaned over the arm of her wheelchair and whispered in Fiona's ear, "Best show in town."

The mayor, even redder now, said, "Would you care to explain that, Elbert?"

Elbert stuck a thumb under the strap of his overalls. "There are more'n a couple of us, ma'am, who've kind of seen the light, as it were, and it took the damn tourists pissing us off for us to figure it out. Pete Wegman, Jesse Sunol, and me, we went down the rope one day to shoo 'em off for good."

That must have been something to see, thought Fiona. Three old men, climbing down that rope, kicking away from the cliff-face, dangling over the sand. It was something Fiona hadn't done in years, and she was an easy forty years younger than the youngest rancher in question.

"When we got down there, one nekkid damn tourist dared us to take off our clothes."

A light laugh went around the packed council chambers. Everyone else was enjoying this as much as Fiona was.

Elbert shrugged. "Don't knock it till you've tried it, is what I always say. And I'm here to say, the body is a beautiful thing." He unclipped one strap of his overalls. "And to feel the sun where it don't normally shine, to feel the ocean breeze caress your...well, lemme tell you, it's nice." He unfastened the other strap. Gasps rose to meet the sound of giggles in the room.

RACHAEL HERRON

Fiona whispered to Daisy, "He wouldn't."

Daisy just shook her head.

Elbert's overalls hit the polished wooden floor of the city chambers. His faded, blue engineer's cap was next to come off, his gray buzz cut standing at attention underneath. Then he started undoing the buttons on his blue, button-down shirt.

One by one, the buttons opened. His chest hair was as gray as the hair on his head.

Daisy held her hand over her eyes. "I can't. I just can't."

Fiona poked her in the shoulder. "You have to."

Elbert was now in front of the crowd, wearing only tighty-whities which were no longer either tight or white. His skinny, wrinkled body was surprisingly tanned. He held himself proudly and tucked his thumb into the elastic of his underwear.

The mayor gripped the podium so hard it rocked on its base. "*Mr. Romo.* We will have our community discussion without visual aid assistance, thank you very much!" The microphone squealed with feedback.

Elbert shook his head. "It's a point I gotta make. We voted, and the boys picked me, seein' as I have the biggest package."

Next to Fiona, Daisy squeaked, her hand still over her eyes. Someone did a drum roll with their fingers on the back of a chair.

And then Elbert Romo dropped his last remaining piece of clothing.

Chaos erupted. Some stood—others remained in their seats, immobilized by laughter. Some cheered, others clapped.

Both hands over his head, Elbert turned in a slow circle. He waited for the room to quiet and then said, "My point is, well. Look at me. Eighty-nine and a half. And thanks to a life of good hard work and a bit of time in the sun, I'm looking fit as a fiddle. I'm *proud* of my body, ladies and gentlemen, and being in the great outdoors with it is probably gonna let me live forever. Down with the ban on public nudity." He drove his fist up in the air. "*Naked is good! Naked is right! Naked is good! Naked is right!*" He marched down the middle aisle, chanting, pumping his fist. By the time he hit the back door, he'd been joined in the chant by so many people that the overhead rafters shook with the noise.

Fiona's stomach hurt from laughing.

It took Mayor Finley ten more minutes of gavel-rapping to get order restored, and even then it was clear she knew she'd lost. She directed her words to the line of city council members sitting to the left of the stage. "We don't even need to put it to a vote, do we?"

Laughter was the answer she got.

"Fine. Public nudity—at Pirate's Cove, and *no place else*—will not be prosecuted. Moving on." She ignored the applause. "That's enough for tonight. Grace, thanks for doing the minutes. They'll be up on the website tomorrow, folks. In two weeks, we'll be talking about the lighthouse."

Fiona stopped clapping. She glanced at Daisy and then back at the mayor.

"Fiona Lynde, I'm looking at you."

Fiona gasped. She tugged on her earring, schooling herself not to take it off. What she really wanted was the soothing warmth of the metal between her fingers. But instead she folded her hands in her lap.

"Yes, you," continued the mayor. "I want to hear about that plan you keep pestering me about, the one to bring down the lighthouse and put in an accessible public garden."

It was just an *idea*. She hadn't pestered the mayor about it. Not officially, not really. She might have mentioned it a couple of times. In person and in email. That was all.

"And who was it talking about turning it into a museum? Abe Atwell, was that you?"

Fiona's stomach lurched. *Abe Atwell?* She turned in her seat and scanned the room.

God, there he was.

A man playing cat's cradle.

She would have bet that game couldn't be sexy. Right? But if anyone could make something childish like that sexy, it would be Abe Atwell, damn him. There was just *something* about the rugged harbormaster, slouched back in his chair, boots kicked out ahead of him, his hands moving with that white piece of string—he could have been making nets or tying ropes. It looked right. And it made her heat up inside, in an embarrassing, alarming way.

Concentrate, she told herself. This was about the old wooden lighthouse. About making things right. Not about the way her heart raced when she watched his fingers. He kept his eyes down, his face thunderous. He obviously wanted to be called upon as much as she did.

Daisy whispered, "Maybe you'll finally talk to him now."

Fiona shook her head once. Hard. No way. She hadn't managed to have an idiotic crush without speaking to him for years for nothing. She couldn't ruin her track record. She cleared her throat and said as loudly as she could, "It was only an idea."

The mayor didn't hear her. "Fiona, what was that?"

The room's chat quieted. Fiona could feel Abe's gaze on the back of her head. Had he ever even looked at her before?

"It was just an idea," Fiona said. She bit her bottom lip and said more quietly, "It's a good idea, though."

"Great. Put together a proposal and present it at the next meeting. Abe, do the same." She lowered her yellow-framed glasses and looked around the room. "They're the only two so far who have approached me about the Coast Guard turning over the lighthouse to our local government, but the forum will be open. The council will decide in closed session after that meeting what we're going to do with the building. That's all, folks. Please keep your clothes on, at least until you get past the security of your own front door, and have a good night."

Fiona felt Daisy clutch her forearm. "You'll be great! You can rehearse your pitch with me, and you'll finally get that eyesore torn down."

Fiona, though, just drew her black cowboy boots back out of the way of Mrs. Luby, who stepped over them with small, pinched steps. What if people hated her idea? What if they ended up hating *her*? She tugged off her earring and worked the metal between her fingers.

And the idea that Abe might also be presenting?

The hook of the earring snapped between her clenched fingers.

CHAPTER TWO

*When asked if a knitter should plan her knitting, I always
say, "Yes! Make a spreadsheet!"
And then I laugh and laugh and laugh. – E. C.*

"Ready!"

Abe's coiled line played out over the post as
the *Rising Hope* bumped alongside the dock.
Zeke, excitable as always, grabbed the line and pulled,
almost hurling himself off the dock into the water.

Abe reached for the second line. "Easy there! No, use
that cleat. Buddy, I got it, in case you've got better places
to be."

Zeke rubbed his hands together and then tugged
down the tiny, blue, knit beanie that wasn't even
beginning to cover his head. He waved at the seven
disembarking tourists. "I know. I know. I don't mind,

though. I want to help, want to make sure she doesn't go anywhere you don't want her to." He turned to a startled-looking woman wearing a red coat. "Hello. Good afternoon, how are you? Did you see any whales while you were out? You're looking lovely today, aren't you? Good captain, isn't he? Good old Abe. Yep, I just think he's the best."

The woman in the red coat started to answer him but Zeke ignored her as he stepped onto the boat's gunnel. "Permission to come aboard, Captain? What say you? Can I come up? Walk the plank?"

How many times had Abe told Zeke he didn't need to ask? His vessel wasn't part of the damn navy and he wasn't going to deny him access just for the hell of it. But it gave his friend such a thrill, Abe only told him to knock it off every other time or so. Today wasn't that day. "Permission granted."

"Nice day, nice day." Zeke rubbed his hands together again—one of his many tics—and nodded hard. "Need a little help?"

Zeke often helped out on Abe's fishing charter vessel. An ex-pro linebacker turned jack-of-all-trades, Zeke was good at just about everything he did with his hands. He made his living doing odd jobs, since he'd long-since blown the big football money he'd made. Abe often got him to help out, either at the dock or on the sport-fishing and whale-watching trips he led.

Today, though, Abe didn't need the help. He was back from the only trip planned so it was an easy day, which was good since the pile of paperwork in his harbormaster office was threatening to topple over if he looked at it wrong. Winter was Abe's slowest time—he ran the 53-foot yacht-fisher every day he could, but due to weather or lack of tourists he didn't always go out. Only squid and crab were being caught now, the salmon and rock cod trips wouldn't start till spring. Apart from the whale-watching trips and the occasional, chilly coastal viewing trips to the Farallon Islands, he was down to one run every couple of days.

"I thought you were supposed to be working at the bait shop this afternoon," Abe said to Zeke.

Zeke snapped his fingers with a loud crack. On such a huge man, any small movement was large. "I don't go in until tomorrow morning, but that's gonna hurt, 'cause I've got karaoke at the Rite Spot tonight." When Zeke had started hosting his Tuesday karaoke nights, there had been complaints from a group of regulars who liked to have prayer meetings in the back pool room of the Rite Spot. Tuesday nights had been their chance to pray for the lost souls of Cypress Hollow over a pint or two and maybe a quick smack of the pool balls. Karaoke, they said, wasn't conducive to the prayerful setting they'd been hoping for, and they had taken it over the head of the bar owner, Jonas, all the way to city council. Mayor Finley had rapped her gavel three times briskly (it was rumored she used it at home to call her husband to the dinner table), declared that any usage of Jonas's bar was up to him and didn't even let it go to a vote. Jonas had responded by buying Zeke an extra microphone and adding a gospel CD to Zeke's machine. Now, on any given Tuesday night, the preacher from Baptist Memorial could be heard freestyling "Baby Got Back" before adding his own quick prayer in the last couple of lines.

Zeke said, "I won't even get home till after 2 am and then I'll have to be up early to sell bait. Joni wrote the schedule wrong. Can you *believe* that?"

Abe could, actually. Perpetually distracted, Joni could be told flatfish and write down albacore. He moved toward the bow, picking up the trash his passengers had left behind. "So what are you up to now, then?" There was always something left behind—paper coffee cups, Snickers wrappers, broken pencils. Once he'd even found a used condom in the head—he'd tried very hard not to revise his image of the two middle-aged school teachers from upstate New York who had been on that trip. Hey, if people felt the need to get their freak on while whale-watching, at least his boat was getting some action. It sure wasn't seeing it from him.

"Just came by to talk to you about the city council meeting. Whatcha think, huh?" Zeke bobbed up and down in his size fifteen sneakers. Even after all the hits he'd taken as a professional football player, there was nothing wrong with Zeke's mind. It was his body he couldn't seem to control at times. "Elbert Romo sure was something."

Abe shook his head. "Something I never wanted to see, that's for sure."

"I always meant to climb down to Pirate's Cove, but I thought if I did I'd see cute, naked girls playing volleyball," said Zeke. "Maybe girls who needed help with their sunscreen. You know?"

"Instead, now you're picturing smearing the lotion on Elbert's back?"

"Dude," Zeke said. "Okay, so you gonna do that proposal thing the mayor said? For the lighthouse?"

"I don't know."

"Seriously?"

Abe felt the scowl crawl across his face. "They should know better anyway. The lighthouse *does* have historical merit. Old thing like that deserves to be saved. What's a city council for, if not for that? They shouldn't need a proposal."

"Bull. You just hate getting up in front of people."

He hated it worse than a local oil spill. Zeke was on the mark, but damned if Abe was going to let on. "Waste of time, that's all those meetings are. Full of the same people, yammering about the same things, all of them trying to change Cypress Hollow." They were trying to take it from almost perfect and change it to a Silicon Valley suburb community. The very thought of a certain Seattle coffee-clone pushing its bossy way in next to Tillie's was enough to make Abe's blood boil, and at least once a meeting someone suggested trying to lure the coffee giant. *But we have no extra-hot triple-vento mochaskinnychoos! Tillie's just has plain old coffee!*

"That's not why you don't want to talk to them, though. Why *do* you hate public speaking so much?"

It wasn't the speaking, really. What he hated was being in front of people. He liked to be behind the scenes. Behind the steering wheel. Not lecturing people about something they should already want to do, like saving a landmark that meant something to everyone.

"Is it because Rayna might be there?"

"No." He hadn't even thought about her. Hell, yes, speaking in front of her would make it even worse.

"Is it because you think Fiona has a better idea than you?"

"Who?" Abe reached around Zeke—no easy feat given the man was as big as a tugboat—and put away the last vest.

"That girl who owns the gas station. You know, the one who always wears that beat-up black cowboy hat. She wasn't wearing it at the meeting, so you probably didn't recognize her."

Oh, yeah. The woman who owned Fee's Fill. The one who wanted to tear down the lighthouse. "You think her idea is better? I think it's crap."

"So you better argue against her. Right?"

The thought of getting up there in front of the town made Abe feel seasick, something he never felt. Maybe he could blame it on the gathering storm. "Shit." Abe looked up. The mass of grayness above wasn't fog—it was a cloud bank lowering ominously. It would rain tonight. He might have to cancel tomorrow's tours. Not that he minded going out whale-watching in the rain, but tourists generally complained too much to make the money worth it. "It's gonna pour."

Zeke ignored him. "You have to do something if you want to save the lighthouse."

"I *know* that." Abe snatched at a tarp that was about to sail over the edge in the cool wind.

"What about talking Fiona out of her idea, then? You think you could? Would it be better to talk to just one person? Get her to listen to you? Huh?" Zeke bobbed and swayed.

It was a thought.

Maybe it was a good thought. "Do you know her?"

"How do you *not* know her? She's got the only gas station in town. You know she lived at the lighthouse for a couple of years a long time ago, right? You'd think she'd be into saving it."

It wasn't like he didn't know who she was, he just never talked to her. Abe always used his debit card at the pump. The fewer people he conversed with, the better he liked it. "Do you think she'd listen to me?"

"Give her something in return." Zeke looked around the dock. "Offer her a fishing trip."

"If she was a fisher, I'd know it."

"A whale tour, then."

"Whale tours are for tourists."

"Yeah, well," said Zeke. "So's nudity, apparently."

Maybe it could work. Abe could try sweet-talking her. Not that he'd ever been any good at that. But he could try.

CHAPTER THREE

*Sometimes we think we want to knit a sweater
when all our hands want is a simple scarf.
It's okay to cast on for socks while you decide. - E. C.*

I t rained the next day. Fiona spent the first part of
the morning fixing three broken tiles on the roof.
She could have sent Stephen up to do it—he'd
offered—but they weren't busy, and she wanted to get
her hands dirty. Stephen was more than capable enough
to handle doing both the Honda's paint job (just a side
door ding) and running the register at the same time.

And even though the steady, cold rain kept dripping
down her neck every time she tilted her head, Fiona
enjoyed being on the outside of her business, looking in.
On a dreary day like today, when the clouds were
weighted and the light was dull, the view into the well-lit

windows of the filling station was cheerfully warm. People had laughed at her when she'd done up the inside with hanging plants and welcoming couches. *Like some kind of day-spa*, they'd said. *Not like old Roy had it, nope.*

Not like Roy. And unlike when he'd run the place—when it had only smelled of grease and gasoline—people actually enjoyed coming in to Fee's Fill. The interior of the store still held the usual gas station things: water, soda, snacks, oil and antifreeze. But they were semi-hidden, tucked away in the dark wooden bookcases that the old library had been throwing out when they moved. The coffee Fiona sold was locally roasted and freshly ground, unlike the stuff Roy had peddled straight out of the bulk generic bucket. She swore she'd once seen him get paint transfer off with the oily brew.

Peeking in from the ladder, Fiona saw the geraniums and begonias that lined the walls, hanging from hooks in the rafters, next to the wind chimes that Hazel Montrose made from driftwood. The African violets that lined the tops of the bookshelves were Fiona's favorites—thanks to the skylights she'd put in a few years earlier, she could coax them to bloom all year round.

Even the garage itself, a space only she and Stephen worked in, was clean and well-lit. They couldn't work on more than two cars at a time, but doing body-work in a town as small as Cypress Hollow wasn't where the money was. The real cash came from tourists stopping and filling up with gas, picking up a locally-made kite and some salt-water taffy at the register. The bestsellers in the shop were the pieces of jewelry Fiona crafted from scraps of auto-parts. The price of a steel bracelet tripled if she could mark it as part of a vintage Mercedes.

Fiona finished climbing down and put away the ladder. She shed her jacket and dried her jeans the best she could with a shop towel. Then she waved at Stephen, who smiled back at her over his paint respirator mask. "I've got the register now," she called and he nodded.

Fiona took a long, deep breath as she hung her jacket on its hook. The smell of good coffee and Cora Sylvan's cinnamon candles, mixed with the occasional acrid scent of diesel drifting in from the garage bay, was as comforting to Fiona as the smell of chicken soup. This was home. The last big decision—whether or not to repair the old neon sign that read *Fill Here*—had been hers to make, hers alone. She reached behind the shelf of maps to flick on the outside lights in the dim afternoon, and heard the buzz she loved. It had turned out the old sign had been too expensive to repair. The new one was still big and curved and old-fashioned, but now the words *Fee's Fill* arched over the top of the building. Though she couldn't see it from inside the station, she could see its red glow blinking reassuringly against the steel-fronted gas pumps.

Home was just steps away, in the backyard on the other side of the herb garden, in the rundown cottage she'd spent the last three years redoing by hand. Home was here. This station, her garage, her house. It was enough.

Usually this time of afternoon would bring people who wanted car washes. With them came the impromptu knitting circle that would form in the small seating area Fiona had created with two sofas and three wingback chairs. While Fiona and Stephen washed and detailed cars by hand, women chatted and knitted, making liberal use of the free stitch markers Fiona kept in a bowl on the low coffee-table. Just because she didn't knit didn't mean Fiona was clueless as to what industry drove the town. Cypress Hollow lived, breathed and ate knitting, and any place a knitter could sit and chat with another was a place that could turn a profit.

Not, however, on a grey, drippy day like this. No one needed a car wash, no one sat in the comfy circle of chairs. So Fiona fell backward into her favorite green seat and fished out her cell phone, which had somehow stayed miraculously dry in her front pocket.

She dialed. Waited. She wondered how he'd take the idea of the lighthouse being razed.

"Hey!" Tinker's voice boomed. "What's new with my favorite daughter?"

As if he had more than one daughter, as if anything ever changed in Cypress Hollow.

"Not much. How about you, Pops?"

Fiona's father, on the other hand, could always be relied upon to have a new story to tell, even if it had been less than a day since they'd talked.

"Well," he said. "You'll never guess how many we sold today."

"Where are you again?"

"New York City! I told you that!"

"It's hard to keep track of you sometimes. Is it cold?"

"The worst. Snow like you wouldn't believe. At night we have to run that little propane heater."

"Inside the truck?"

"It's safe! Trust me!"

Fiona rolled her eyes. Even if it wasn't safe, there was nothing she could do about it. She heard a rustling in the background and then a grinding noise. "Gloria's still working?"

"You wouldn't *believe* how many people want our pencils."

"Uh-huh." Fiona pulled out the small drawer of the coffee table and lined up the tape measures, which were marked *Fee's Fill.*

"Nabbed a huge sale today," said her father.

Fiona cradled the phone between her ear and shoulder, trying to keep it from slipping. Her head tilted, she said, "Oh, yeah?" She could just imagine him—he'd be standing outside in the cold in that old, black parka he'd worn since she was a child, the one with the holes at the wrist. He'd be perched on the back bumper of the pencil truck, his black cowboy hat, which matched her own, pulled down so that his ears, never his best feature, stuck out at an almost ninety-degree angle. His heavy, white eyebrows would move with each word and his white teeth would flash with each grin. God, she missed him sometimes, so much it was like an ache in her bones.

Tinker continued, "I said to myself, 'Self, who needs to erase things?' And there it was! The answer! Musicians!"

That wasn't what Fiona would have come up with. She shut the drawer softly and ran her fingers through the beaded stitch markers in the bowl.

"Think about it," he said. "What do they do?"

"Play music?"

"*Write* music. And the people who write those little notes down on staff paper—they need to be able to erase, right? So me and Gloria found the music school, you know, that big one they made that movie about. We set up the truck right in front." Tinker and Fiona's stepmother, Gloria, lived in the equivalent of a taco truck, only instead of carne asada, they sold sharpened pencils. *Artisan pencils*, Tinker said. *Each one sharpened by hand with love.* And it was true, Tinker loved everything about sharpening pencils. He actually had an honest-to-God mail-order website, and people ordered pre-sharpened pencils from him in bulk. He made money. It boggled Fiona's mind on a regular basis.

"So we set up, and they came pouring out between classes, and I'm telling you, daughter, the smell of freshly shaved wood blew right up their noses. I couldn't take the dollar bills fast enough. New York, right? I gotta hustle. It's cold, so they're moving on if my line doesn't roll. A guy selling roasted chestnuts wanted to beat me up—I was taking his customers. Gloria had to go right out there and give him a four-pack and show him how nice they write."

"A line for pencils," Fiona clarified.

"*Artisan* pencils."

"Of course. Good for you."

"And you? What are you doing today?"

Fiona leaned back and looked out the window at the gas pumps standing idle under the canopy. Rain dripped from the roof to the sidewalk. "I went to the city council meeting last night."

"The wild chickens still living in the rosebushes there?"

She'd seen them last night, three or four bedded down for the evening. "You know, you could come check on that yourself sometime. It's not like your house doesn't have wheels."

"Someday, daughter. Someday."

That's what he always said. Fiona tried to believe him today. For once.

"Hey, Dad. I'm going to work on getting the lighthouse taken down."

A silence met her words.

"And a public park put in its place." She waited to see if he'd say anything. When he didn't, she continued. "With paths. Maybe a little playground."

"Torn down, huh?" A pause. "Guess it's probably time."

Fiona gave a laugh that sounded empty. Should she mention...Oh hell, why not? "Mom would have liked that, huh?"

Another pause. Fiona heard him cover the receiver and mumble something to Gloria. Then he said, "You know, your mother never understood what it meant to me to be the lighthouse keeper those few years."

"I know, you've told me—"

"You were young. You don't—"

"I was a teenager. Of course I remember." That, and so much more.

"Why are you so stuck on that part anyway?"

Fiona couldn't remember anything else.

Tinker went on, "So many other wonderful memories there."

She had the urge to hang up. To just hit the red button on her phone. Before he tried recalling the good times and not being able to come up with any.

An old blue pickup with a white stripe pulled under the awning. A 1942 International Harvester, to be exact, a real beauty. Abe Atwell's truck.

"Like when we found the baby seal and brought it home. You remember that, Fee? How cute it was in its box?"

"It died the next morning."

"Oh."

Abe got out of his truck, stretching long and tall, like he always did. He stuck his card in the machine, put the nozzle in the tank, and leaned on the open door, eyes facing across the road to the water. He was one of the few customers who used the time to look at the waves, not his cell phone. It was one of his oh-so-many attractive features. It was almost as sexy as the way his dark hair curled at the nape of his neck. His hair was more out of place than normal—maybe from the rain. If so, Fiona *loved* rain.

"Well, don't forget the view of the fireworks on the fourth. From the top?"

Mom had been drunk three of the four years they watched the show from the top of the lighthouse, and Fiona had been so worried about her falling to her death on the rocks far below that she'd barely looked up at the overhead explosions.

"And the way the foghorn sounded, so close."

Well. That had been nice. She could still hear it at night, of course, but not as clearly as they had from that spiteful little piece of land.

Abe replaced the nozzle and punched the button for his receipt. Like always, he'd get back in the truck and drive away without even glancing at the shop. Not once had he ever come inside, not for a drink, not for one single Slim-Jim.

Except that this time he didn't get back in the truck.

Abe headed for the front door. He'd been caught in the rain at some point, and his jacket was dark across his wide, heavily muscled shoulders.

Holy hell.

"Dad."

"And the smell of seaweed? Such a great smell. Almost as good as pencils, am I right?"

"Dad, I have to go."

"Fee, honey, I'm sorry...I didn't mean to bring up bad—"

"No," she interrupted. "Customer! I have to go. Love you, Pops." She'd never hung up on him for a customer before. Usually she either left the phone on the countertop for a moment or, more often, she just handed the phone over and Tinker said hello to the customer and caught up with whoever was in the store.

Fiona caught a glance of herself in the convex security mirror over the door. Her hair was parted sloppily, which made sense since she'd barely run a comb through it this morning after her hasty—as always—shower. Where was her damn hat? Had she even put it on today? She couldn't remember. Glancing down, she counted three separate oil stains on her jeans. Her steel-toed boots looked as if they'd been run over, which made sense given the number of tires she'd scuffed them against. Her mother's voice rang clearly in her head. "If a woman's wearing lipstick, she can get away with *anything.*"

Fiona hadn't even put lip gloss on this morning.

God, if she stood here like this, staring like a guppy, he'd figure out about her crush for sure. She bent over to straighten the gum shelf, but her hand knocked a box of spearmint breath mints all over the floor.

"Let me help," said a voice above her.

Abe bent to help her pick up the errant boxes.
Only one word escaped her lips.

"Yawwmmp."

CHAPTER FOUR

I thought once that when I became a master knitter,
I'd quit being surprised by my stitches.
Now I know the surprise is the best part. – E. C.

The woman wasn't speaking English, as far as Abe could tell.

"'Scuse me?" he said.

"Flamminjol."

"Couldn't have said it better myself." Abe was still worried. Had she had a stroke? He examined her face. Neither side gave the droop he would expect of a stroke victim. She straightened, and all her limbs seemed to be working. For a second, his glance got hung up on her rack—nicer than he would have predicted. Maybe he should have been a little less antisocial all these years instead of buying his gas outside. But—he could admit it—when she'd bought the filling station and body-shop, making it over into this...whatever it was, with all the flowers and candles and crap, he'd been a little bent out of shape. He'd liked the old station, with Roy who was deaf as a post and didn't give a crap that the Twinkies on his shelf were seven years old and hard as rocks.

Roy hadn't said words that didn't make any sense, either.

The girl with the tangled hair said something like, "Phmlump," under her breath.

"I'm sorry, but could you repeat that, Felicity?" Didn't hurt to be polite.

Her eyes widened. "Did you just call me *Felicity*?"

"Crap. Fiona, I mean..."

She stared at him and then blew out a breath and spun on her heel, making her way behind the counter.

"I know your name," he said hurriedly.

"Now you're just covering your ass because you think I have a shotgun back here."

Abe's spine jolted. "Do you?"

"No. I've been robbed twice, and both times the robbers were very polite. I'd rather give my money to a dumb kid than shoot one." She narrowed her eyes again. "Though I don't know why I'm telling you that. I like people to think I'm armed."

"I won't tell anyone."

"Okay. Thank you." Her cheeks colored prettily and Abe wondered again why he'd been stubborn about not coming inside the store.

FIONA'S FLAME

"Look," he said, "I'm Abe Atwell."

Fiona of Fee's Fill laughed.

Jesus, the woman *laughed*. What the hell did she know about him that would make her do that?

"Is everything all right?" He didn't like this feeling, this not knowing which direction their exchange would take next.

"Fine," she giggled. "Fine. Yeah, I know who you are. I'm Fiona Lynde. Not Felicity." She stuck out her hand. "You can call me Wrench."

Her small hand was cold in his. "Do people really call you that?"

"No one. Not one single person. I've been trying to get it to catch on for years, but somehow it hasn't yet."

"You don't look like a Wrench."

"Yeah," she agreed with a sigh.

Still feeling off-kilter, Abe said, "So. I just came in to say hello."

Another giggle greeted this. "You *did*?"

He nodded. "And to invite you out for a whale-watching trip."

She stopped laughing. "Excuse me?"

Oh! Did she think...Hurriedly, he said, "Not like a date, not like that."

Fiona grabbed for a broom that stood behind the register and started jabbing at the floor with it. "Of *course*. I knew that."

"Just a trip out on my boat. I run tours, you know."

She met his eyes and something strange lurched under Abe's feet, as if she'd jabbed his boots with her broom. Which she hadn't.

"I know," she said.

"Thought maybe you'd want to watch the whales. Maybe talk about the lighthouse proposal. You know, since we both have ideas."

She tilted her head, and for the first time was still.

"Just to talk."

"About the lighthouse?"

"Yeah." He glanced down at his boots, noticing for the first time how dirty they were.

"Not to state the blindingly obvious, but we have *different* ideas," Fiona said.

"We do. Guess I just thought it might be worth speakin' about."

There was a pause.

"Okay," Fiona said.

"Yeah?" Relief coursed through him. "Okay, then. Great. That'll be great. I think you'll like it. We'll have a good time. Most of the tourists do. Not that you're a tourist." What, did he suddenly talk too much when he was nervous, also? "I'll go now, I guess. Before you shoot me or something."

She had a great dimple when she smiled.

As Abe left, he noticed he was smiling, too.

Fiona Lynde didn't look one little bit like Roy who used to own the filling station. Not one little bit. Abe was categorically opposed to unnecessary change, but this one might be okay. Might be just fine.

CHAPTER FIVE

Wool is our water. – E. C.

Whale-watching was such a tourist thing that Fiona had never considered doing it, not even once. For that reason, and the fact that she couldn't trust herself not to fall overboard while anywhere near Abe from sheer nerves alone. Plus, she just wasn't that great on boats. Once she'd spent four hours hurling over the wooden edge of a rowboat on a clear, flat day at the lake. That had been a pretty terrible first and last date with a doctor, who surprisingly turned out to be not so great with vomit.

But she was going on this trip today, seasickness be damned. Boy howdy, how embarrassing would getting sick be? And in front of Abe. But the last time she'd tried taking a seasickness pill, she'd had a reaction and practically passed out on her friend's dinghy, and Fiona didn't want to miss this trip. She'd only ever seen whale spouts from shore, the faraway plumes of water that signaled their migration. In Tillie's Diner, Fiona had often heard the tourists talking about the trips they'd just been on. "Oh, John, did you *see* it when it flipped?"

"Breached, Martha."

"Whatever. I thought we were going to *die*. It was *amazing*."

They always looked electrically excited, eyes still bright, their hair and jackets blown askew. Fiona wanted to be one of them.

She stood on the dock, reading Abe's sign over and over, trying to get up the nerve to move forward. Instead of boarding, she pulled her black cowboy hat lower and stuck her hands into her jean pockets. She should have worn gloves, probably. It was a pretty day, clear and sunny after the rain that squalled itself out last night. But it was *cold*. Usually the fog that socked in the cove warmed the air just inland, but with the day's clarity also came the chill. It had been freezing overnight, and when Fiona had pulled up her bay door at work this morning, she'd had to crack ice on the metal. She'd started the small space heaters and when Stephen arrived she'd instructed him to stay inside the store as much as possible. They had no body work scheduled, just two interior details which he could do between customers, so Fiona had been able to leave him in charge. He was a good kid. Fiona was glad every day she'd listened to her gut three years before when a skinny eighteen-year-old boy barely taller than her shoulders had turned up with a black eye, needing a job. "I can do anything with my hands," he'd said, and he'd said it exactly the same way Fiona always had. "And I'm trustworthy." Anyone who had to say that out loud hadn't been thought so at one point.

Fiona, using his deep-set dark eyes to judge by, had chosen to believe him. She'd given him the job—and the keys for the bank drop—on the first day. Those same dark eyes had telegraphed the gratitude he'd never found words for. He'd never needed to. She knew.

Stephen had crashed on the couch in the garage for the first six months, always telling her he'd just worked too late on his sculptures the night before and hadn't had time to go "home." He wore one shirt while the other one hung drying in the bathroom. He *was* incredible with his hands, an ironworker from a family of giant men who hadn't trusted the runt to work with them. The enormous items he made in the back— chickens with body armor and robots with microwaves for hands—sold so well on commission at the shop that they paid for his apartment now. He was saving for arts school. Fiona force-fed him tuna salad sandwiches and he always thanked her, even though he knew he didn't have to anymore. Stephen felt more like family than an employee. And it was nice that she didn't have to worry about the shop when she wasn't there.

Now, as Fiona stood on the dock reading Abe's sign one more time as though it might have changed, waves smashed underneath her. The dock itself didn't sway—the town had rebuilt it five years ago, so it was sturdier than the old pier Fiona had grown up fishing from—but each wave still thudded with a force that Fiona felt through her boots.

"You going on this trip, too?" The male voice behind her was cheerful.

Fiona turned, nodding.

The tourist was short and stout, firmly in the latter part of his middle-aged years. He wore nothing but a brilliant blue and red Hawaiian shirt, a pair of long shorts and flip-flops. His belly was round and his short white hair stuck straight out from his head. Inwardly, Fiona groaned. He'd be the talkative kind. She could tell by the way he was already bouncing on his toes. He'd also be the frozen kind in about one minute. Tourist popsicle.

"Us, too." He gestured at the woman and young man behind him. "We're going. Been waiting *years* for this. Junior here, he's got a thing about whales."

"Huh."

"Did you have to wait a long time for reservations? Man, we were on the wait list for ages. This is the best ride, if you read the Yelp reviews. The captain's supposed to be a hoot."

Abe? A hoot? With difficulty, Fiona kept her eyes from straying to the boat's deck. Abe was so sexy it should be illegal, to protect the innocent. Tall. Oh, so broad. He had sadness lurking in the depths of his clear blue eyes.

But a hoot? Abe Atwell didn't seem the comedic type.

"Bob," the man said, sticking his hand out. His handshake was surprisingly emphatic. "This is my wife, Robin. And that's the Beast." He gestured at the teenager.

"The Beast?" Fiona smiled in the boy's direction, but he didn't meet her gaze. Instead, he shuffled his feet in place, rocking slightly, keeping his eyes up and to the right.

"His name's Robert, but he answers to Junior, too. I call him the Beast because he's horrible. A worse son, a man never had. Plagues me half to death. I might just chuck him overboard, I'm thinking. Go home without him."

His words were harsh, but Bob's voice was warm and he chucked his son on the shoulder, earning a fierce smile that blazed across the boy's face.

"He's developmentally disabled," said the woman, slight and stoop-shouldered. There was no apology in her voice.

Bob said, "I like to say he's touched! It's a much more useful term, don't know why they won't let us say it anymore." He grinned at Fiona. "He's touched by angels, that's what I like to think. He sees and hears things that we don't, that's for sure, and what he sees seems pretty great."

Junior, who was as wide as his father but at least three inches taller, watched a seagull land on a light post overhead. As Fiona followed his gaze, she noticed for the first time how very white-blue a gull's wing was. She'd always thought of them as dirty white, but the bird practically reflected the sky.

"Look, there he is—the captain. I met him yesterday," Bob said proudly.

Fiona gripped the railing.

Abe Atwell threw a length of rope around a post and drew the boat up more snugly against the dock. Zeke Hawkins was on his heels, skidding a long metal ramp onto the pier.

A few more clusters of people joined the group waiting on the dock—most of them tourists carrying binoculars and cameras with telephoto lenses.

"Welcome aboard the *Rising Hope*," called Abe and unlocked the gate, swinging it open.

Was it Fiona's imagination or did his gaze linger a little longer on her than it did on the others?

No. She was seeing things now.

She would be *cool* today. Collected. Smart. Lightly humorous, but not obnoxiously so. Not like this was a date, duh. Abe Atwell, according to town gossip, hadn't really dated anyone since Rayna Viera jilted him at the altar eleven years ago. Everyone knew that Rayna had moved on and that Abe hadn't. It was part of town lore. While Abe waited at the top of the aisle, Rayna had already been on the back of hardware store owner

Tommy Viera's motorcycle, racing to Vegas for a quickie wedding.

"Okay, y'all. Listen up." Abe gave a short safety spiel. To Fiona's surprise, he was funny. "When you put your life vest on, don't forget to do up this clip on the side, see this right here?" He looked around the small group. "Pull it nice and tight. If you fall into the drink, you'll look thinner in the water that way. See, compression can be a good thing." He showed them where the life preservers were and how to hold on to the rail without falling over if the boat suddenly pitched.

Junior was the only one with a comment. "I don't want to wear this." He plucked at the webbing that went across his chest.

"You have to, honey," said Robin.

With a tug on the strap, Bob said to his son, "Hey, Beast, you fall in the water and you're done for. I can't swim and I didn't buy the rescue package from the man. Can't afford to get you back, so keep your vest on."

Junior continued clicking and unclicking the clasps.

"Come on, Junior. You can do it." His mother nervously patted the vest and pushed his hands down to his sides.

Abe stepped forward and said, "Hey, buddy, who's your favorite superhero?"

Junior's hands stilled and he said without hesitation, "Spiderman."

"Nice. I like him too. So your favorite colors are red and black, I bet."

Junior nodded hard.

"Beast!" boomed Bob. "He's got your number!"

"Okay, hang on." Abe lifted a seat and moved a life preserver, digging under it. "Here it is. Go ahead and take off that one you're wearing, okay?"

Robin unclipped Junior's vest and handed it to Zeke.

"Check this out." Abe held up a red one with black webbing. "This is the most special one I have, and it makes you into an honorary Spiderman while you're on board."

"Wow. Okay. *Okay.*" Junior reached for it and put it on without assistance.

"That doesn't mean you can climb anything, though," Abe said.

Fiona watched Robin's face relax.

Abe continued, "When Spiderman is on a boat, his web powers are deactivated because of all the water underneath. So you can't climb, but that's no biggee, right? You're still protecting us?"

Junior nodded again, that hard, certain nod.

"Excellent." Abe looked around. "Everyone ready to spot some whales?"

Fiona liked the sound of his voice.

Damn it, she liked it so much.

CHAPTER SIX

*Knit outside. Let people watch you being so
interesting and so clever. – E. C.*

T he water was smooth on their way out of the
bay, for which Fiona was grateful. She hadn't
been on many boats, but she'd been on enough
to know she hated the lurching of her stomach and the
sick hollow feeling at the base of her skull when the
waves were set too close together. The farther apart the
swells rolled in, the better she usually felt, and today the
boat moved leisurely through the water.

What was she actually doing out here, anyway? Abe
had lured her with the promise they'd talk about the
lighthouse—hell, he obviously didn't know she'd have
come on his boat if he'd asked her to swab the decks—

but he'd been busy ever since they pulled out of the dock.

Until now. "How you doing, Fiona?"

She turned her head and felt her stomach swim up to her gullet. "Fine." She swallowed hard. "Just fine."

"Zeke, let me take that for a minute. Fiona, come stand with me?"

Abe took the wheel and Fiona had to wonder if there was a sexier thing for a man still wearing clothes to do. His hands were huge, his fingers long and strong around the wood. He stood with his legs apart on the deck, the wheel looking like an extension of his body, as though he were a tree and it was a limb.

Fiona smiled and pushed her hat down more tightly onto her head.

"Scared it's going to fly away?"

"That's not what I'm scared of."

Abe gave her another of those looks. One hand on the wheel, he dug his other hand into his pocket and pulled out a strip of pills. "You're green. Take a Dramamine."

"I'll be fine."

He quirked an eyebrow at her. "I recognize that look. You wanna know where the barf bags are?"

No. She did *not*. "Oh, all right, give it to me." She swallowed the pill dry.

"That should kick in quickly. Just breathe deeply through your nose till then, okay?"

Abe didn't make speeches as they moved farther out, he was just doing his job, steering the boat. His legs seemed to absorb the motion so that he was standing perfectly still as the boat moved around him, letting the group *ooh* and *ahh* over the view of the land behind them.

"You used to live there, right?" He pointed at the lighthouse.

"How did you know that?" He'd barely known her name the other day.

"It looks good from out here," he said, not answering the question.

"Mmm," said Fiona.

"You don't agree?"

To her, it looked the same as it always had. A leaning, hazardous pile of wood that would eventually collapse, probably hurting someone on the way down. "It looks dangerous."

"Huh," said Abe, the wind whipping back his thick, coal-black hair. "Looks solid to me. Looks safe."

A man and woman carrying a young baby held the child up for photo after photo. They asked Fiona to take a picture of them, saying it was the baby's first boat ride. The way they stood, though, made Fiona wonder why they were together. They were careful about not touching one another while they practically fought to be the one to hold the child. Their eyes didn't meet, and they didn't speak to each other. They spoke, instead, through the baby. "Tell Daddy he needs to get out your hat." "Mommy should probably see if you need to be changed yet."

Miserable. Why did people stay in miserable relationships? Fiona was glad all over again that she'd never been involved with anyone long enough to sink that low. Of course, she'd never had a boyfriend for more than six months. But that wasn't exactly her fault—it was just something that happened with her. Boyfriends turned into friends. One morning she'd wake up next to a man and realize that she'd changed. And he hadn't. That was the point at which she usually told him that yes, she wanted to keep watching baseball with him (or rock climbing, or spelunking, or whatever else they'd gotten into together) but that they were better off as friends. She tried to *will* the change to happen before the man ever professed love, and normally it did. She'd been too late on one occasion and it had made her heart ache to watch Ian's face crumble as she told him that yes, she loved him, too, but not in that way.

The parents were now arguing desultorily through the baby about whether he was or wasn't feverish. Zeke and Abe were embroiled in discussing something with words she didn't understand like *horn cleat* and *eye splice.*

Fiona moved farther away, standing near the rail where Bob, Junior, and Robin had taken up their post. How Bob wasn't freezing his cojones off in those shorts, she had no clue. Fiona was cold even though she'd worn her down parka over a cream sweater. It was boxy and wide, completely out of fashion, but it was the warmest thing she owned. She'd found it at the thrift store in Half-Moon Bay, and Toots Harrison swore Eliza

Carpenter had knitted it. The first time Fiona had worn it into Tillie's, five women had formed a circle around her, all their hands out, touching and plucking at it as if it were made of something precious, spun gold or platinum instead of the cream wool it was. "A prototype," they'd said. "I remember this. She gave it to someone down the coast..." "Can you imagine?" "A thrift store?" "You lucky girl, you." Fiona had just liked the way the cables formed a tree on the back—it was subtle but gorgeous. Most importantly, it was warmer than any coat she owned. She tugged it lower, pulling it down to her hips.

Junior's eyes were glued to the water.

Bob nodded at Fiona. "He's not gonna look up, not if you offered him a million dollars. He's gonna be the first to spot a whale, you mark my words."

Robin said softly, "He knows all the whale names."

Junior said, "Orca, gray whale, blue whale, humpback, killer whale isn't a whale, it's a dolphin. *Look!*"

Abe was suddenly next to Fiona, Zeke back at the wheel.

"Thar she blows," he said in a low voice, just to her.

Would it *kill* the man not to be so sexy? All the time? Fiona took a deep breath and willed her stomach to stop heaving.

"What is it? What is it? What is it?" All of Junior's fingers were at his lips, and he bit the tips between words.

"It's a gray whale. I hear they're Spiderman's favorite whale."

Junior's eyes widened. *"They're my favorite, too."*

Abe nodded in what looked like satisfaction. "I thought maybe they were. What else can you tell me about them?"

Fiona had known that whales were big, but she hadn't been prepared for the show they put on. Abe had found a group that acted as though he'd paid them to be utterly amazing. They rose and fell and blew spouts of water in a strangely precise V-shape. They stayed near the boat, practically posing for photographs. Fiona found herself unexpectedly entranced. They were magical beings, prehistoric and wise.

Abe caught her eye. God, he had dreamy-sad eyes, so smoky they almost looked smudged with eyeliner. So clear, light blue, as blue as an early morning sky. "What do you think?"

She hugged her arms around herself in a sudden cold breeze. "We're so *small* next to them."

He smiled then, and Fiona was startled by how his eyes changed with that little movement. They warmed. "That's what I've always loved best about them. They put it into perspective. All of it."

Fiona felt the boat heave under her feet, a bigger motion than they'd been feeling up until now.

"Yeah," he acknowledged. "That's something."

"They're...underneath us? Did one just roll down there?"

"Yep."

A slow thrill of fear coursed through her. "Will they flip the boat?"

"Doesn't happen often." He was teasing her. Right? It made her even more nervous than she already was.

She glanced around the deck. "Well, I'm a good swimmer. I'm going after Junior if that happens."

"Good to know. That leaves less for me to do."

"Who will you go for first?" Fiona wanted, ridiculously, for him to say her name.

"Zeke." He pointed at his friend, now steering the boat. "He's massive, but a lot of that is fat. Don't tell him I said so. He'll float, even without a life vest. I'm letting him tow me in—the rest of you will have to fend for yourselves." Abe paused, looking toward the bow at the two small girls who were squealing as another whale breached less than thirty feet away. "I'd better go check on them."

He winked at Fiona as he went, and she shivered as though he'd reached out and touched her.

She moved down the rail to join Bob and his family. Junior's eyes were still wide, his gaze transfixed.

"He's loving this, huh?"

Bob's smile beamed brighter than the old lighthouse had ever been capable of. "I can't believe we've waited this long to get out here. But it's far, you know, and going places costs money. We've been a bit down on our luck lately, but with the economy turning around, I've been making more, and with that comes a whale trip!"

"What do you do?" Fiona imagined him as a high school gym teacher. Or a baker. A job that would allow him to tell bad jokes all day and make people laugh.

"Undertaker," he said.

Fiona coughed. "I...wasn't expecting that. And that's affected by the economy?"

He nodded affably. "Oh, yeah. Big time. When people are broke, they bury their loved ones in simple pine. Or they go for cremation and don't even have a service. But in good times, everyone wants to honor those who've passed with the big ticket items."

"I never would have thought..."

Bob looked cheerful. "No one does. It's just nice that business has picked up. How's it going, Beast?"

Junior glanced over his shoulder. "I've seen four gray whales. They said five. But it was four."

Robin, who'd moved toward the front of the boat, gestured for Bob to join her and look at something. Fiona stood next to Junior and watched the water. Fifty yards out, a broad, gray barnacled head broke the surface and blew a great gust of air.

"Amazing, isn't it?" Fiona wasn't sure if Junior would answer her. It was okay if he didn't. She was happy just to stand there and watch the giant creatures with him.

Junior said, "Just like Spiderman."

"What?"

"The Amazing Spiderman."

"Ah. Yes. You're right."

"I can't climb, though, not with this on." He pulled at the strap across his chest. "Usually Spiderman can climb. But not with this on."

Another whale's spout blew. The noise was comforting. Familiar, somehow.

"That's right. But you have his other powers, right?"

"He just climbs. And I can't shoot a web, I already tried."

"He saves people. Maybe if someone needs saving, you can help."

Junior's face brightened. "Yeah. And I can jump."

"You can! You can probably jump high!"

"Can I swim?"

Fiona wanted to say yes, but they were surrounded by water. "I don't think so. I think the vest doesn't give you that power unless you already have it."

"I can swim already."

"Then you can!" Did her voice sound as sleepy as she suddenly felt? Fiona wished she could lie down, just for a moment. Let the rocking of the boat move out of her bones, where it was still stirring up her stomach. The sleepiness felt good, though.

"I can jump and swim."

Fiona focused on Junior. "What?"

"I can jump *and* swim."

A nervous chill darted down Fiona's spine. "Well, only if..."

Junior moved faster than she would have thought possible. He climbed over the rail in less than the two seconds it took her to catch her breath. Before she knew it he was leaning forward, holding on to the metal with only one hand.

"Junior, *no*." Without thinking, Fiona reached forward to grasp the back of his vest.

Junior let go of the rail, and for a terrible moment the only thing keeping him on the boat was Fiona's grip—she was digging into the webbing as hard as she could. The rail cut into her stomach, and she felt a pull in her lower back—Junior was a large boy, and it was taking all her strength to keep him from falling.

"Dad!" screamed Junior.

"Abe!" yelled Fiona.

And then Abe was behind her, next to her, reaching past her to grab Junior's waist. "Okay, buddy. I've got you."

But Junior leaned farther out, reaching his hands out into the air. In a moment, they'd lose him.

Keeping one hand on Junior's life vest, Fiona threaded a leg over the railing.

"What are you *doing?*" said Abe. "Get back over here. That's not safe. *Fiona.*"

It wasn't safe, she knew that. Keeping one hand on the rail, Fiona pulled as hard as she could on the jacket webbing while Abe dragged him from the waist.

"Harder," Abe said. "Pull!"

Bob and Robin were behind Abe now. "Come on, buddy, come on back. Spiders don't swim, remember?"

Junior put one hand behind him and his father grabbed it. Turning slowly, Junior grasped the rail. Fiona kept her hand on the small of his back.

"Good, over the rail now." Abe hooked his arm through Junior's. "One leg up, that's good. That's great. Now swing your backside up, yep, just like that."

And Junior was safely back on board. He fell forward to his knees with a cry, jerking out of Fiona's grasp.

For a moment, she felt nothing but relief. Then she realized she wasn't focusing right. Something was wrong with her vision. The rail seemed to be getting farther away. Shit, shit, *shit*. She couldn't hold on, she couldn't grab—something was wrong with her. So exhausted.

"Fiona!" Abe's voice was sharp.

She shouldn't feel like this, this wasn't what relief felt like, it was...*Hold on, grasp*. So dizzy. Just a second more and she'd be back on board...*So exhausted*...

Her fingers slipped on the fog-damp rail and Fiona fell backward, all the way down into the frigid water.

CHAPTER SEVEN

Sometimes the knitting doesn't go so well.
I find a nice long nap often straightens that out.
If that fails, try another one. – E. C.

A be knew the coldness of the water she'd just plunged into, and his heart seized for a split second before kick-starting again.

"What do we do?" Bob, his arms still wrapped around his son, looked frantic.

Abe grabbed the life ring, made sure it was well attached to the stanchion, and threw it over.

Fiona had just surfaced. She sputtered and gasped, and then reached for that damn black cowboy hat which had popped to the top of the water with her. She shoved it onto her head and looked up at the boat with eyes that strangely weren't as shocked as they should have been.

The cold was the worst part, he knew. She had to grab the ring before she got too cold to do anything else. "Fiona! Grab the life preserver! *Now.*"

She made no move to reach for the floating ring. Instead, she closed her eyes as she treaded water.

"Fiona!" Abe couldn't go in after her—not unless things got much, much worse. To do so would put not only himself in danger—which would be fine—but it would endanger his passengers. Zeke was an okay sailor on open water, but he couldn't reliably guide the boat into the narrow passage that led back into the Cypress Hollow bay. And left alone in open water, neither Fiona nor he would make it for long.

His father's face flashed in front of his eyes.

"*Goddammit, Fiona, grab the ring.*"

In the water, Fiona coughed and jerked. She reached for the foam ring that was floating next to her head.

"She's got it," said Zeke from behind him.

"*Hold on,*" Abe roared. "Whatever you do, do *not* let go, do you understand me?"

A weak nod. She coughed again.

Gently, ever so gently, Abe pulled on the line. She needed to get close to the boat fast, but not so quickly she lost hold of the life preserver. Abe's heart was pumping so hard he could feel it throbbing in his ears.

Below him, Fiona bumped into the side of the boat. Her eyes were closed again. "Fiona! Grab the side ladder." This would be the hardest part. Her hands would be frozen, and it looked as if she were going into shock. Her face was as white as the foam at the top of a wave.

But she lifted a hand, slowly grasping the first rung.

"Good girl." Shit, he'd go overboard for her in a minute, damn the consequences. "Grab the next one. Use your feet."

She was moving as slowly as the tide. First one hand up, then the next.

"You're amazing. Keep that up, sugar. You can do it." Abe was over the side now, reaching down with one hand. Just two more rungs...

Just one more...

And then he had her. He grabbed her by the hand and pulled as hard as he could, knowing nothing could tear her from him now. With Zeke's help, they both came over the rail cap. She landed on her back, coughing and flopping like a fish.

"Blankets," gasped Abe. "Down in the main salon."

"On it," said Zeke, racing toward the stairs.

Bob and Robin still had their arms around Junior, apologizing profusely. "It's our fault, it was because of Junior—"

"It's no one's fault."

Two girls who'd boarded with their mother were staring, clutching at each other's arms as if they were at risk of falling overboard themselves.

Abe half-crawled toward Fiona, twisting his body so that he was practically on top of her. He touched her face, her eyes, her forehead. Her lips were pale blue, but she was breathing. "I know you're cold." Her skin was ice. "We're going to warm you up. Can you hear me?"

No response. Her eyes stayed shut. Jesus, did she have a medical condition of some sort? She'd crawled up that ladder herself, so she should be able to respond to him. "Fiona?" He slapped her cheek lightly, watched as her chest rose and fell. He needed to get her out of those thick, drenched clothes as soon as possible.

Zeke returned with the blankets. "Here you go, I brought them all. Can I help? Can I do something?"

"Turn the boat around, and yell for me when we're near the channel."

Looking relieved at being asked to do something, Zeke hurried away saying, "It's all right, folks. It's all gonna be okay. Just a little added excitement for no extra cost. Now, let's see if we can find another couple of whales or dolphins or something to cruise by on our way back in..."

Abe leaned forward, pressing both his hands against Fiona's cold cheeks. Her lashes were so damn long. Jesus, he wanted them to flutter. "Open your eyes, sweetheart. Come on."

Fiona's lips twitched, and then her lashes lifted. She met his gaze, looking at him as if she'd never seen him before.

The relief was so great that without thinking he pressed a kiss to her forehead, leaving his lips on her skin for two, maybe three seconds. As if it could warm her. Pulling back, he said, "Fuck, Fiona. You scared the hell out of me."

Fiona blinked and looked as surprised by the kiss as he felt.

Shaking his head to snap himself out of it, Abe said, "Can you stand? If I can get you below, I can get you out of those clothes."

She giggled, almost drunkenly. Maybe she'd hit her head on the way down. He didn't see any blood...

Her gaze wandered from his face to a point over his left shoulder. "I can do it out here, sh'no problem."

"No, let's just..."

Still lying on her back, she was already pulling at her coat. When it was off, she tugged at the bottom of her cabled sweater.

"Okay, why don't we go inside? Downstairs, where it'll be warmer."

"What?" Her voice was louder now. "Do you think I'm *shy* or something? Because I'm not. I don't mind what people think of me." Without hesitation, she pulled her sweater up and over her head. Underneath it was nothing but a black sports bra. "I mean, I *do* mind. I *totally* mind. But I *pretend*."

"Here, wrap this around yourself." Abe held out a blanket, willing himself to look away from where her nipples had budded in the cold under the black lycra.

"Just a *second*." Fiona yanked at the buttons of her jeans.

"No, no, no." Abe hooked his arms under hers from behind and lifted her till she was standing. "Downstairs. You aren't taking off your jeans up here." She was enough of a spectacle already. To starboard, a whale breached, but the passengers didn't even spare it a glance—they were too busy watching Fiona.

"Fine, fine," she grumbled, stumbling in front of him.

"Use the handrail," he cautioned. Damn it, he should have gone down in front of her, to catch her in case she fell.

"I'm not *five*. I know how to *walk*." With those words, Fiona fell down the last two steps, landing on her knees.

Abe leaped forward and over her. "Are you all right?"

She looked up at him with a giggle. "That was fun. Let's do it again." She rolled onto her back and her hands went to her fly again.

Christ. Well, she did have to get out of those sopping clothes and at least down here no one was watching but him. He grabbed at her dripping hat, ignoring her weak protest.

"Pants off," she muttered. "Pants..." She pulled her jeans down over her hips, shucking her sodden black boots off at the same time. She wriggled sideways, and then said, "Off! We have *success.*"

Her panties were a red slip of lace. The astonishment of finding this out struck Abe stupidly mute for a moment. He'd have laid good money on the bottoms being as utilitarian as her bra. But no.

The other thing that made him feel as though a crab's claw was stuck in his throat was her tattoo.

Right at her hipbone, where her panties curved in and she curved out, she had an intricate snowflake, about two inches across. Icy lace, draped over her skin. It was about the last image he would have expected to find on her. A wrench, sure. A sports car like that green Alfa Romeo she drove. A cowboy hat, yeah. But a delicate blue snowflake?

He tried to clear his throat and coughed instead. "Blanket," he managed. "Sit up here, on the couch. Come on." If she stood, he could get a dry blanket around her, or if she sat on the couch, he could at least drape a couple over her.

"Where's my hat?"

"I put it on the couch. It's wet. Let's move you now."

"I like it *here*." She spread her arms over her head and looked up at him.

Christ on a fishhook, Fiona was practically naked in the main salon of his boat.

"Fine," he mumbled. "I'm just going to put these over you, okay?"

"Good," she said, pulling the wool on top of her. "This is nice." Her eyes closed again. "So nice. Can I have a pillow?"

He took one off the couch and put it under her head. She rolled to her side, sticking her bare foot out. Abe took another blanket and wrapped it around her legs. "You can't be comfortable here, Fiona."

Sleepily, she said, "So comfortable."

Abe rocked back on his heels. What the hell was she on? The fall into the ocean should have woken her up. Should have made her shake all over. Instead, she was acting like she'd had three shots of Jack on an empty stomach. "Did you take something?"

"Mmmm."

Pills, maybe? Was she a closet drinker? He felt a strange, intense disappointment at the thought. "What was it? Tell me, Fiona."

"Just what you…"

"What?" He leaned closer. She smelled of wet wool and salt and something sweeter, a spicy floral scent.

"That pill you gave me." She opened those big hazel eyes one more time and looked straight at him. Her gaze felt like a touch. "You have *no* idea what a huge crush I have on you, do you?"

He laughed in surprise. That sure wasn't what he'd been expecting. "Oh, yeah?"

"Yeah. Not love or anything." Her words weren't slurred, but they were slow, and exceedingly deliberate, as if she was thinking about each syllable before she made the sound. "I don't *think* it's love, anyway. How would I know? But I know it's lust." Fiona touched her bottom lip and pulled it down in what she might have thought was a sexual way but which actually read more like a drooly, teething puppy. Sure was cute, though.

"Lust, huh?"

"*Hoo* boy," she said, touching her cheek with her wet finger. "I'm just sayingif you were to take off your pants right now? I'd be in them like *this*." She attempted a snap, which came up more as a hand-flap.

He gave a bark of laughter. "You're just saying that because my pants are warm and you're still cold."

"You'd warm me up." Her eyelids dropped seductively. And then they dropped farther, until they closed entirely. She pushed her cheek into the pillow and then gave a small snore.

"Wow," he said. She was utterly surprising. Entirely. He hadn't seen that one coming. And damn, she had a smokin' hot little body underneath those clothes. A body he hadn't thought to look at with wishful X-ray vision earlier.

He was feeling something else about her, too. It took him a moment of staring at those long dark eyelashes to figure out exactly what it was.

Curiosity.

Abe hadn't felt that particular emotion in so long he almost hadn't recognized it. But there it was.

And it felt...good.

CHAPTER EIGHT

Knitting is really just warm wrapping paper
for people we love. – E. C.

Abe and Zeke managed to get Fiona off the fishing boat and onto Abe's houseboat with minimal fuss. She'd stood and walked, the blanket still wrapped tightly around her, but she'd babbled as she went, not making much sense. Something about the lighthouse and pencils? He'd made a quick call to Dr. Naomi Fontaine, who'd told him that it sounded like she was having an abnormally strong reaction to the motion sickness pill, and to bring her in to the office if she had any other symptoms. "Don't worry, though, if she's just sleepy. Keep her warm and let her sleep."

"What about hypothermia?"

"Just look out for any skin color change. If she's too pale or blue or starts shaking hard, call an ambulance. But she sounds okay. Keep an eye on her."

Three and a half nerve-wracking hours later, Fiona groaned.

Abe dropped his book to the floor. "You all right?"

A small sharp scream was his answer. "What the hell?" Fiona lifted the blankets and looked under them. "What the bloody *hell*?" She scrambled to a sitting position, dragging the blanket with her.

"You passed out."

"*Why?*"

"The Dramamine, we think."

She groaned again and rubbed her face. "Am I still on the boat?"

"A different one. I figured my houseboat would be better—at least you could be in bed. Ignore the mess." Abe laid his big green robe over the blankets and said, "The head—the bathroom—is that wooden sliding door there."

Fiona raised her eyebrows.

"I already dried your clothes. They're in there, too."

She peeked under the blankets again. "Turn around. Please."

He did, not bothering to point out that she'd already walked down two docks in nothing but a blanket and her panties.

Behind him, she scuttled into the bathroom, clicking the lock behind her.

While she was changing, he tried to make a little more order of the mess. He'd started while she was sleeping, but he'd wanted to be quiet, so hadn't been able to do much. It was just so *cluttered* in here. He liked it this way—all his things close around him—but he knew it wasn't what most people would think of as tidy. His few dishes were washed, but seldom put away. His antique fishing floats sat next to the ships-in-a-bottle his father had loved making. As a kid, Abe had sat next to his father for hundreds of hours as his dad used long tweezers to manipulate tiny pieces of balsa wood inside different bottles. His father had cursed as often as he sighed in satisfaction, and the sound of it, a sailor's streak of blue words, most of which Abe didn't even understand until he was of double-digit age, was comforting.

Now he couldn't get rid of a single ship in a single bottle.

Abe still used his father's favorite mug—an ancient, heavy pottery piece crafted to look like a sea monster with long green locks, grasping hands, and bugged-out eyes—to make the same hot chocolate. Made from hot water and white packages, with a dash of cinnamon, it stood up to any grandmother's homemade chicken noodle soup for pure comfort. The handle of the mug was chipped, and Abe knew if he ever dropped it, even if it smashed into tiny bits, he'd take however long it took to glue it back together. Things were precious. Things were memories. You kept things to help you remember where you came from.

Believing this didn't stop him from looking around the cabin and being aware that cozy wasn't really the word any outsider would apply to the space. Cramped, maybe. Disorganized, certainly. It felt homey to him, but did he look like a hoarder to an outsider? It had been a while since he'd had a woman in his space.

The bathroom door clattered. Shit. He hadn't told her the secret of not closing it all the way. She'd never get out.

"Abe?" Her voice was tentative, and the door rattled again.

"Hold the latch and lift the whole door upward a little. I'd do it from here but there's no handle on this side."

Another few tries, and the door flew sideways, rolling into its storage pocket. His father had crafted the door, and like many things his father made, the idea was more durable than the execution.

"Hi," she said softly.

"Hi," he said back, surprised by how his voice croaked.

She looked...amazing. How was that possible? She'd just fought off hypothermia—remembering which, he moved the spare chair closer to the small space heater— and her long brown hair was a crazy tangle. She wore no makeup that he could discern, and her face was still as white as a brand new, unscuffed buoy.

And she was gorgeous. He felt something clash inside him, something that sounded like spoons hitting the floor.

This was unexpected.

"Sit," he stammered. "Get as close as you can to the heat."

In confusion, he turned to the stove, lighting the flame to heat the metal pot. Then he glanced at her again. "Hot chocolate okay? It's all I've got."

"Fine. Great. Thanks." She wrapped her arms around her torso and leaned forward toward the warmth.

An awkward silence filled the small space. Abe was intensely aware of every sound he made as he moved about the galley. She sniffed, and he offered her a handkerchief, his best red checkered one.

"Thanks," she said again, and blew her nose. "I'll wash it for you."

"Whatever." It came out as rude when he hadn't meant it to. "It's supposed to be used."

"I like handkerchiefs. I don't think anyone has ever loaned me one before."

"Well, you've been hanging out with the wrong guys."

She simply nodded, pushing her hair over her shoulder. She held her hands toward the heater.

Did she remember what she'd said to him?

Fiona made a small sound like a hiccup. "I fell in the ocean?"

The water was almost hot enough. If he stared at it hard enough, maybe it would boil faster. "You did."

RACHAEL HERRON

"That kid, is he okay?"

"Junior's fine. He was pretty damn excited about his adventure."

Another noise. Oh, God, was she crying? He'd need more than a handkerchief to deal with that.

Then she did it again. It wasn't a sob. It was a laugh. Fiona was *laughing*.

"I fell overboard! The first time I get on a boat in *years*, and I fall overboard! That pill! I knew about it and still took it. I'm a moron!" She giggled, resting her elbows on her knees.

"You could have died."

"But I didn't!" She laughed harder. "My mother always said I was such a klutz I could fall off a two-lane highway, and lord knows I trip over the concrete pad of the pumps on a weekly basis even though it's eight inches high. But this! It's a whole new level of klutz!"

It wasn't funny. Not to him. It couldn't be funny to him, not after what he'd watched the ocean take from him.

But damn it, as she lost herself in the giggle fit, he started to feel the corners of his mouth twitch. Okay, it wasn't funny, but *she* was. The way she was flopped forward, laughing with her whole body...it was sexy and funny and it made him want to laugh, too.

He focused on the hot chocolate instead. When she took a breath, suggesting the laughter had almost played out, he said, "There's some cinnamon on top. You want marshmallows? Or something harder? A slug of brandy in it?"

She looked up at him and smiled. A man would do a lot for a smile like that. "All of it?"

"Yeah. Sure."

Their drinks doctored and laced, he sat on the couch next to her chair. "Bottoms up. Warm you from the inside out. You know. Liquor...and it's warm..." He was babbling again.

Fiona took a sip and blinked hard.

"Too strong?"

She shook her head. "Just right. It's the cure for what ails me. Eh. I guess that would be too much to hope for. I don't think there's a cure for terminal stupidity."

"Going out over the rail wasn't very smart."

"I know. I didn't think." She blew on the top of her chocolate. "I've gotten into a few pickles from not thinking, actually."

"Like what?" The drink was sweet and strong. A little like the woman sitting in front of him.

She took a sip. A tiny bit of chocolate clung to her upper lip. "Once I went backpacking by myself. Which would have been fine, except I forgot to tell anyone where I was going. And I ended up getting lost for two days."

"Holy crap."

Fiona shrugged. "When the search helicopter flew over, I signaled with the cup of my thermos, flashing sunlight off it. A good MacGyver moment. I got a wilderness patch from the search and rescue team." She brightened at the thought.

"What else?"

"Oh, there are too many to mention. Let's just say I tend to leap before I look."

"It was brave of you to help Junior get back on the boat. And it was good of you."

Fiona frowned, as if she didn't know how to process his words. She took a quick sip of her hot chocolate and sputtered as it went down the wrong way.

Abe leaned back, the old brown fuzz of his father's sofa scratching the back of his neck, as it always did. What was this new power she had over him? To make him feel tongue-tied every time her eyes met his? It was ridiculous.

"Are you seeing anyone?" His voice didn't even sound like his own.

Fiona jumped. "What?"

"Boyfriend? I don't think you're married, but I don't always get the gossip in town as fast as anyone else. Fact is, I hardly get any, since I refuse to listen to most of it."

She blinked. Her lashes were separated into clumps from her swim, as long as if she were wearing fake ones. Her eyes, he noticed, were deeply green, flecked with light brown, exactly the color of the algae in the tidal pools below the lighthouse. Not that she'd appreciate the analogy, most likely.

"Well, most of the town gossip is crap."

Having no idea how to answer, Abe just waited.

"No," she said. "I'm definitely not seeing anyone."

"Ah," said Abe. He took another sip of his hot chocolate. Maybe it was the brandy that had given him the courage to ask that insane question. It was waiting for the follow-up question, obviously. *Will you go out with me?*

Instead he said, "So, you've really had a crush on me for years?"

Fiona couldn't have looked more surprised. Her eyebrows disappeared under her bangs and her mouth formed a small O. "Shmitterzop," she said. Or it was something like that.

He smiled. "You wanna get a bite sometime? Maybe Friday?"

"Me?" she squeaked.

Abe didn't have any spare words left. He nodded.

She looked deeply into her cup as though the answer were hidden there. Abe's stomach jumped, and he rested his hand against the wall closest to him. Through the wood, he could feel the splashing below him, the slight sway of the tide's dance. The houseboat creaked as it rubbed against its mooring. There was a thump from the deck above and then he heard Digit's nails clicking as the old cat came downstairs.

Fiona opened her mouth to answer and then looked at the animal. "Is that the cat you found in a mailbox?" she asked.

"How do you know where I found him?" Incredulous, Abe wondered if gossip in Cypress Hollow was so prevalent that it even included pet stories.

"He's old now."

"Old. And just as crotchety." She was avoiding the fact that he'd just asked her out.

She stuck out her fingers so Digit could sniff them. "Curious," she said.

The cat and him both.

"Careful. He's terrible." Abe loved the old scruff, but Digit was an asshole. "If he starts to bite or swipes at you, move fast. Don't let him get you." Once Digit's claws were in something—anything—he didn't let go till blood was pouring out of his target.

"He's just an old softie," Fiona said, her voice low.

And sure enough, Digit was pushing against her hand, getting her to do exactly the right kind of chin rub. "He doesn't like many people," Abe said. Or any people, really. Not even him half the time.

Finally Fiona said, "You really want to go on another...not-date, like you said?"

It was a strange question, oddly worded. "No. A real date."

"To talk more about the lighthouse?"

He shrugged. "If that's what you want to call it." Suddenly, he didn't want to call it that at all.

"What would we do?"

"You pick," he said expansively. Didn't matter to him.

Her eyes lit, a brighter green. "Really? You like it there, too?"

"What?"

"U-Pick? Oh, you meant I should *pick*."

"I'm so confused." It dawned on him. "Are you talking about the scrap metal yard?"

She laughed. "That's not really a thing people do together, is it? I love it there...I just thought for a second...sorry."

"I'd love to go there." He was astonished to discover how true it was. He'd go to a quilt show with her. A banana museum. A retrospective of kitchen countertops.

Fiona suddenly looked like a kid opening birthday gifts—excited and flushed. "I'll plan it all. The...date. I love planning."

"Okay." He'd let her steer his boat into the channel if she asked, damn the wreck that would follow. Where was this *coming* from?

Fiona nodded and fished out a marshmallow with her finger, sucking the foam off. Abe tried not to stare as he drank the last bit of his hot chocolate. It tasted sweeter than anything he'd ever had.

CHAPTER NINE

Never be afraid to ask another knitter for help. She asked someone else the same question once. – E. C.

The next morning, Fiona dragged herself through a shower and downed a cup of cold coffee left over from the day before. She'd slept through the alarm clock again. Even with two clocks set, Fiona could sleep through both the buzzing and the music. Once she'd been given one of those alarms that you throw against the wall to shut off, and she'd thrown it right through the bedroom window. And she'd managed to drift back to sleep even after registering that the tinkling noise that followed was falling glass shards.

Finally dressed, Fiona tromped through the small garden to the shop. When she unlocked the door, Daisy rolled in, Tabitha running past her to the back of the shop.

"You're early," grumbled Fiona.

"You're opening late. Give me my breakfast, quick." Daisy glared at Fiona, but Fiona didn't buy it for a second.

Daisy started over. "Okay. May I please have whatever health food you're pressing on us this morning?"

"Pineapple bran muffin with a side of fruit," said Fiona, pulling them from where she'd packaged them up last night when she got home.

Daisy pouted prettily. Once Fiona had heard someone describe Daisy as a Disney princess on wheels, and she had to admit, while she'd never tell Daisy about the comment, it was an apt description. She had a head of amazing Dolly Parton blonde curls and huge blue eyes. She sewed herself whimsical dresses, and allowed Tabby to wear whatever she liked, which meant that sometimes both of them went out wearing gauzy wings and frilly tutus.

"He asked me out."

"*He did?*" Daisy rolled her chair so close to Fiona that she had to step backward. "What did you say?"

Embarrassment filled her. Again. Fiona flopped sideways onto the couch and looked out the window where two cars she didn't recognize were filling their tanks. "I said yes. And then I asked if I could plan the date."

Daisy blinked. Her lashes were long, soot-black, and curled. "Why?"

"I don't know." It had been important to her, for some reason, at the time. "I just thought I should."

"What are you going to do?"

Fiona straightened, willing her spine to be made of steel alloy, not mercury. "U-Pick Metal Scrap."

Daisy's voice was a breath. "You wouldn't."

Fiona nodded hard. "Oh, yes. I would."

"Do you know what you look like when you get back from ripping cars apart? It's like you've dived into the first burned out, smashed car you see in there and rolled around, smearing yourself all over the greasy front seats. You remember when I couldn't get that piece of—what was it, a broken coat hanger or something—out of your hair? And it was full of that muddy *oil*? That short haircut I had to give you did *not* suit you, by the way."

"I'd had to shimmy under the Rolls Royce to get the metal finding I needed for that contracted pair of earrings, remember? The one for that rich Santa Barbara witch who only wanted Rolls parts and then refused to pay after I mailed them to her? I had to grind my head in the dirt for like an hour under there."

"Would that woman have known the difference between parts from a Rolls and a Nova? And now you're going to take Abe Atwell with you to search for tiny pieces of metal. You're going to what? Give him a pair of pliers and meet up with him when he's pulled off enough parts to fill your bucket? Or should we not talk about your bucket yet?"

"Oh, my God, stop it. Eat your bran muffin. Tabby?" Fiona called into the back of the store.

"*Je nettoie la salle de bains!*" a small voice yelled back.

"You don't have to clean the bathroom, kiddo!" Daisy shook her head. "She's obsessed with Windex right now. She's cleaned every mirror in the salon like three times a day this week."

Fiona said, "Isn't that a little OCD?"

"Nah," said Daisy, looking with suspicion at the muffin. "She's fine. She gets it from her dad. I've never met a clean freak like Nate. Highlight of the divorce was kicking him out and leaving the dishes in the sink for three days straight. *Why* do I have to eat this?"

"Here's one for Tabby, too. Promise me no McDonald's this morning."

Daisy groaned. "But we pass that one on the highway on the way to school..."

"Promise me."

"McMuffin?"

"I need my girls to be healthy." Fiona bent down for the kiss Tabby flung against her cheek, and walked with them out to the van. She ruffled Tabitha's fluffy blonde curls. They were exactly the curls that Fiona had dreamed of as a child—perfect storybook locks. Fiona pushed her long, ordinary, mouse-brown hair behind her ear.

"Which is why you make me stop by here every morning. To torment me with whole grains?"

"Yep." Fiona knew that while Daisy protested, she loved the attention. She worked so hard to take care of herself and her daughter, putting in extra hours at the hair salon she owned while making sure Tabby had everything she needed. Single motherhood was hard enough. The legs she'd lost the use of in a car accident in her teens didn't slow Daisy down, but Fiona knew the disability made everything exponentially more difficult.

Tabitha, an expert at seven, helped her mother navigate into the front seat and then folded up the wheelchair, placing it on the rack behind the driver's seat where Daisy could get it out alone later. "Nous allons à l'école, Tante Fee."

"You're going to an elephant?" Fiona leaned in the van window. "When is she going to start speaking English again? My French is not so good. Maybe she could switch to Spanish? I'm better at that."

"You never know. She'll be on to something else in three months. You know that's how she is. Hey, let's talk Cowboy Ball real quick."

"I don't speak that language, either."

Danny Tweipo honked as he pulled away from the pump. Fiona waved and smiled. "Saved by the horn."

Daisy took the key out of the ignition. "I'm not leaving until you tell me you're going to it with me."

"This is not news to you. I don't do dances, lady."

"What if Abe is there?"

Fiona felt an uncomfortable tension in her chest. Could she be having a heart attack? Was that what it meant when your heart did that little flippy thing, speeding up, skipping, and then slowing down again? She caught a glimpse of herself in the dark glass of the window behind Daisy's head.

Shit.

She looked as tired as she felt, and almost as frantic. Her eyes were wide, her face pale. Seriously, would it *kill* her to buy a lipstick? Maybe she'd run over to Zonker's later and pick one up. Pharmacies had makeup, right?

"I told him something I shouldn't have."

"Fiona." Daisy's eyes went wide. "What did you say to him?"

"I was on a mind-altering substance."

"This story can only end badly."

"I told him about my crush."

Daisy laughed and gestured for her to go on with a jingle of her keys. In the backseat, Tabby was chanting, "*J'aime, tu aimes, il aime...*"

"It's not funny. I might have told him I wanted to get in his pants. To be in them, actually. With him. At the same time."

Daisy said, "Wow. Just...wow. That is *awesome*. What did he say?"

"I passed out before I could hear his answer."

"Even better," said Daisy. "You've been in love with him for how long now?"

Forever. Since the day of the kitten. She'd still been in college, commuting on the days she wasn't helping Roy out at the station, long before she saved enough to buy the place.

That day, Fiona had been tucked up in her favorite chair in the Cypress Hollow library, studying for an econ final. The chair was in a tiny annex, hidden behind a curtain, and she'd only found it because she'd once spied Phyllis Lynch sneaking out of it carrying an empty yogurt container. The librarian had smiled at her and nodded for her to go ahead. "It's the best spot in the house."

And it was. The wingbacked chair with its lumpy seat faced the street and was advantageously located behind a large fern on the other side of the window. Fiona knew from checking that no one could see in, but the seated person could peek out between the fronds—a perfect place for spying on the world outside.

That day, she'd been idly doodling with her highlighter more than she'd been studying, staring sideways out the window. Abe Atwell walked by. She knew him by sight—he'd been a few years ahead of her in school, but she'd never really noticed him. People felt sorry for him because his father had died in a boating accident when he was in high school.

Abe stopped suddenly in front of the mailbox on the sidewalk, staring at it as though it had jumped out and poked him, tilting his head to the side once, and then again. Why hadn't she ever noticed how chiseled his jaw was?

Abe opened the mail slot and peered in. He took a step away from it, and then back toward it. He looked around as though to check if someone were spying on him. Fiona instinctively held her breath. Could he see her? Did he feel her noticing that he had the sexiest butt she'd ever seen? His rear was packaged up tight in his Wranglers as if he were just another Cypress Hollow cowboy instead of the sailor she knew he was.

But instead of looking harder through the fern at her, Abe went back to staring at the mailbox. He moved to the back of it and appeared to be trying to open it. He put his ear against the side and then looked in through the slot again.

By now Fiona was overcome with curiosity. What could he hear in a mailbox? She leaned forward, almost not caring if he caught her staring.

He took out his cell and made a call. Fiona couldn't quite make out the words, but through the glass she could hear the tenor of the conversation, and it sounded important. Urgent. She thought about going outside to try to help, but if he couldn't get the mailbox open, who was she to try? Plus, by now she'd noticed how thick and ropy his forearms were, right there where his elbow bent...She should probably just stay in place and keep watching.

Not more than two minutes after he made the phone call, a police cruiser pulled up. Had he heard a bomb ticking? Officer John Moss got out, tucking in his blue shirt. He wiped at the perpetual sheen on his forehead and listened as Abe talked animatedly to him, before doing the same thing Abe had done, pressing his ear against the mailbox. He said something into his radio and then they both took up a waiting stance, arms folded, eyes on the road. Abe looked west, Officer Marsh looked east. Only one of them looked amazing from the back, though, and it wasn't the cop. Fiona didn't mind if whatever they were waiting for took all day as long as Abe kept his back turned like that.

Cindi Smythe in her animal control van arrived at the same time Marshall Gedding careened up in his postal truck, both of them jostling for the same parking spot. Fiona watched with fascination as Cindi got out a stick with an adjustable wire loop on the end. It was an animal of some kind, then, not a bomb.

Marshall opened the back of the mailbox with a key, Cindi pressed in tight on one side of him, Abe on the other. All three leaned forward, and Abe came up with a kitten.

Even from her spot in the library, Fiona could tell the cat was too young to be without its mother. It was dingy and gray, a tiny tabby. Abe cradled it in one hand against his flannel-shirted chest.

When Cindi reached to take the kitten from him, he turned away, shaking his head, cupping his other hand around the animal.

Fiona lost her heart at that moment. *Bam.* It jumped out of her body and into the already full hands of Abe Atwell. When she heard later that he'd adopted the little cat and had taken it to live with him on his boat, the deal was done. Irrevocably, her crush had developed and grown, bursting instantly into full-bloom. And with it came the jitters, the nerves, and the complete assuredness that he had no idea who she was.

Now, years later, her palms still resting on the sill of Daisy's open van window, Fiona blinked. "What?"

"I asked you how long you'd been in love with him."

"It's just a stupid *crush*. I'm thirty-three. I should know better." Suddenly, she didn't want to talk about it anymore. It was too much, standing there under Daisy's unwavering gaze.

"You have to tell me what you're going to do on the date. Besides taking off his pants, obviously."

"No."

"Okay. You'll be taking off *your* pants?"

"No."

Daisy tilted her head to the side. "No pants-wearing at all? Open the door pantless?"

Fiona laughed. "Stop."

"Why? Pants are funny. And no pants is the platonic idea of pants being funny. Just the word is great. *Pants.*"

Fiona crouched and touched the bottom lip of the door frame. "Do you know this is loose?"

"Don't change the subject on me." Daisy craned her neck out the window to look at it. "But yeah. It's been flapping."

"Come in this afternoon when you finish work. I'll fix it."

"Fine." Daisy started the engine. "We're going to be late."

"Bye."

"Cowboy Ball! No pants!" was Daisy's parting cry.

Pants. The imagined vision of Abe, pantless, filled Fiona's mind for one incredible second until she pushed it away. She went to refill the paper towels at the tanks.

Daisy was right about one thing. *Pants* was a very good word.

CHAPTER TEN

I heard a woman say she was too old to knit. That made me sad. Then I gave her cashmere and a pair of large needles, and she's been much better ever since.— E. C.

M om?" Abe set the cardboard box down on the lumpy green settee that had always perched in the front room of his mother's house. He went through to the kitchen. "Where are you?"

She wasn't in the room she'd presided over for more than forty years, the room where Abe always said that time had stopped. Over the window hung a piece of a fishing net Conway Atwell had tied so long ago that a breath would probably untangle it. His father's German beer stein stood on the stove. An old broken oar leaned against the coatrack—his mother, Hope, used it to chase the raccoons away from the trash on nights when they made too much noise outside. The kitchen still smelled of the cinnamon Abe's father had added every evening to his cup of hot chocolate. Abe had once caught his mother rubbing a bit of cinnamon into her wrist. "What are you doing?" he'd asked. "Making myself smell good for your father," she'd said. Conway had been dead for seven years by then.

His mother wasn't delusional—she knew her husband was dead. Hope Atwell, though, would never stop wishing for a miracle. And Abe loved that about her. It frustrated the hell out of him, of course. When a woman half-hoped to see a dead man come walking in the door every time it opened, that same woman would be to prone to forget how important it was to a son to occasionally be greeted without disappointment.

But Abe had nothing to say about that. Nothing at all. Where was she?

Hope wasn't in her bedroom or the bathroom. She wasn't anywhere in the house. The garden? She knew gardening made her rheumatism worse, but she was a stubborn old woman. Abe was like his father in many ways—his patience with difficult catches, the ability to tie a thousand different knots—but his mulish stubbornness came directly from the woman who had insisted on finishing the sweater she'd been seaming while her water broke. She'd gotten to the hospital minutes before Abe came pushing his way into the world, the darning needle still clutched between her fingers when the nurses handed her Abe, squalling like a wet cat.

"Mom?" Abe called again, pushing through the screen door. Outside, the fountain that he'd made for her burbled just like it was supposed to, and a sparrow chirped just once, in promise of the spring that would hopefully come soon.

Otherwise, it was completely silent.

Fear rose inside of him, dark and ugly. He called more urgently, "*Mom.*"

"Up here," came a voice from above.

Relief. Not today, then. It would come someday, though, and then what would he do? Abe could picture how it would be one of these days, when he'd arrive to check on her only to find her fallen somewhere in the house, hurt, unconscious. Or worse.

But not today, thank God.

"What the *hell* are you doing up there? I thought you were going to stop scaring me out of years of my life."

Her face peered over the edge of the roof. "Cleaning the gutters." Her short gray hair, never under control at the best of times, was sticking straight out and was full of leaves and cobwebs. She was wearing a cream Aran with a large darned patch at the stomach.

"Are you freaking kidding me?"

"You didn't do a very good job last time you were up here."

"Where's the ladder?"

She pointed to the side of the house and disappeared again.

Abe sprinted to where the rickety ladder perched precariously against the chimney. He climbed as fast as he could, pulling his way up the old, splintered eaves.

His mother stood on the far edge of the roof, jabbing a broom into a gutter that didn't look at all clogged.

"Would you quit that?" Abe stepped over the ridge and started down toward her.

"I'm fine." She didn't turn around. "I've never fallen off this roof before, and I don't plan on starting now."

"If you make one more move, I'm going to push you off and blame your fool-headedness. I'll tell the fire department I found you in the jasmine."

That made her laugh, at least. Next to the sound of waves splashing against the side of his houseboat during a rainstorm, it was his favorite sound in the world. "No one would believe you. They'd accuse you of my murder. A perfectly lovely old lady, cut down in her prime."

"Show me the old lady on this roof," Abe said lightly.

His mother kissed his cheek. "Careful," she said. "If I fall I'm taking you with me."

"You'd better."

Abe kept his arm around her waist until she was seated on the edge of the roof—when had she gotten so thin?—and then went down the ladder before her so he could catch her if she fell. "One step at a time. No, slower than that."

"If I go any slower I'll stop moving," she said crisply. "I'm not an invalid, Abe."

He nodded, but as he walked with her into the kitchen, he noticed that her head wobbled the slightest bit now as she walked. It bobbed, as though her neck wasn't strong enough to connect to her body anymore. She sat at the kitchen table at his insistence, while he fixed her a cup of tea and set out a plate of MarieLu biscuits.

"Eat, all right, Ma?"

"Only because you're a nag," she said, and took a small sip and held a cookie in her hand as if weighing it.

"It was foolish to go up there. You know that."

"God loves children, fools and drunks. Will you go up and finish?"

Abe sighed and ate a cookie in one bite. When he'd finished chewing, he said, "You know I cleaned the gutters two months ago, before the rains started."

"Well," she said, sitting straighter, looking more like herself. "I'm sure you did your best. Your father, though, never let a gutter leak."

Of course he hadn't. "Fine. I'll finish it now. Please, for the love of God, don't get out any power equipment while I'm up there, okay?"

"Well," she said, hiding her smile behind her mug of tea. "Here I was planning to grab the chain saw and take out that old sycamore in the front."

"Dad planted that."

"I was teasing," she said gently. "I love that tree."

Up on the roof, Abe used the same broom she'd brought up with her—how had she managed that?—and poked at the leaves. She'd been wrong, the buildup wasn't bad. It was normal. In November he'd replaced a couple of gutters that had come apart at the seams, and they were still holding firm.

Below him, Evelyn Archer walked her three tiny, yappy dogs past the house. She glanced up, and Abe waved.

"Are you a burglar?" she called, clutching the dogs' leashes as though they were knives.

"Cat burglar," he said. "Don't mind me."

He thought she would laugh, but she didn't—she hurried away, squinting at the phone in her hand.

Were they all like this in the neighborhood now? As Abe cleared a section of gutter by hand, he realized he hadn't spent any real time at the house for years. He drove up from the marina, brought his mother's groceries and cleared out as soon as she gave him that look, the one that said it was okay for him to go. He hadn't talked to any of her close neighbors in ages, and now that he thought about it, he couldn't even remember if he'd seen Mr. Hill in the last twelve months. What if the old painter had passed away? Would his mother have even told him?

Abe threw more leaves to the ground below and stood, leaning on the broom for a second as he took in the view. The air was still so cool this afternoon that he could see his breath, and he thought again how foolhardy it had been for his mother to be up here. What if she'd fallen and had to lie in the backyard, alone, in the cold? If she hadn't broken her neck, she could have suffered hypothermia if no one noticed she was missing before nightfall—it had gone to freezing point every night this week.

And Abe didn't check on her every day. Most days, sure, but not every single one. He felt shame flood him in a cold wave. What kind of a son was he? What would his father have said? That was going to change, starting now.

He looked over the Harrison's roofline and down to the corner of Main Street and Encinal Avenue. Steam billowed up from Tillie's roof, and he saw Whitney's pink frosting-mobile take the turn at the gazebo. From here he couldn't see the marina, but if he strained he could just hear the seals barking on the pier.

This roof should feel like home. The house below his feet was the place he was raised. Too bad he only felt comfortable when water was underneath him. His mother would have liked it if he'd moved in across the street, instead of onto the houseboat she hated, if he'd gotten married instead of remaining stubbornly single. Well, he'd tried the getting married thing. It would have helped if Rayna had showed up, instead of breaking his heart in front of the whole town.

No other girl had seemed worth pursuing since. Worth changing his routine for. Worth changing *himself* for. Because he knew one thing: all women wanted their men to change. Probably for the better, sure. But not when it came to him. He was fine the way he was.

But Fiona...She seemed different. She wasn't the kind of girl he usually noticed. He was a red-blooded American male, after all. If a pretty tourist driving down the coast threw herself at him at the Rite Spot, he usually didn't complain too much while making his way to her hotel room.

Fiona, on the other hand. He hadn't ever really *noticed* her before. She was a woman, sure. Two arms, two legs. Nice enough face. Rather...forgettable. He knew Fiona was friends with the woman who owned the place where he got his hair cut. Daisy Lane. Fiona had a good laugh—he'd noticed that over the years. She did always seem to be laughing. She drove a kick-ass Alfa Romeo Gran Turismo Veloce. It was bright emerald green, sweet little thing. She ran Fee's Fill. When Roy had owned the place, Abe'd had to walk inside the station to pay and put up with whatever the locals were going on about inside. Now, he just slid his card, grateful he didn't have to push past the knitting klatch that was usually taking up space inside on those couches Fiona had put in. Hell, she'd practically made the old gas station into—what did you call them?—a place where girls got manicures. She was smart, he knew that. She'd probably tripled her income, just getting those women to come in and sit and spend money on snacks while their cars got spit-shine detailed. And opening the body shop? When he'd heard the news from Zeke, Abe had been mildly impressed that a woman would go that road alone. She'd made a name for herself, and now, instead of driving to Half-Moon Bay, locals took their dings and dents to her. He'd seen what she'd done to Zeke's Capri. She was good, he'd give her that. But besides looking at the many cosmetic imperfections on the body of his beloved old International and deciding they didn't matter, he hadn't given her profession another thought.

Now he wondered. She was small-boned. Practically delicate. How did she get the torque to force big pieces of sheet metal to do her bidding? That kid Stephen Lu she had working for her wasn't much bigger. How did she cut and lift and fix?

And why the hell couldn't he stop thinking about her? He'd asked her out on a *date*, for Chrissakes, and he couldn't remember the last time he'd done that. Or the last time he'd had to do that, thanks to tourists who got off on hitting on harbormasters.

A gust of cold wind blew under Abe's jacket, and he was reminded that he had one more section of the roof to get to. As he moved to the far north line, he felt a shingle below his foot give spongily.

"*Shit*."

His shoe plunged through the wood, and he stumbled. His legs twisted, his right foot still stuck under the broken shingles, and he landed on his knees, then his hands, sprawling his way toward the edge. For one terrifying second, Abe was sure he was going to be the one broken into pieces in the backyard, that his mother would find him in the morning, his face covered in frost, bleeding out from a compound fracture.

But his stuck boot caught him. Damn, that would hurt tomorrow. As he twisted his way out, he could feel the swelling start. His heart thumped uncomfortably, and he hoped that his mother hadn't heard the ruckus.

Below, a siren whooped. He stood, gingerly, and peered over the edge. Officer Moss had pulled up to the house, and without getting out of his patrol car, rolled down his window and waved.

"Got a call about a burglar," he yelled.

"Evelyn Archer needs glasses, John. You know that," said Abe.

"That's what I thought." John lifted his hand in salute, and cruised slowly away.

Sure. The cops checked on *him* when he was on the roof. Where were they when his mother was up here?

In the kitchen, his mother was knitting.

"You're done?" she asked. "Did you get it all?"

"Yeah." Abe pulled out a bag of frozen peas and sat, propping his foot on the opposite chair.

"That *was* you I heard. You fell."

"That roof has had it. I've been telling you for three years, we need a new one."

"Your father put that roof on. It's perfectly good."

That was their whole problem, Abe realized. Neither of them wanted to change a thing, even when it was called for. "My foot went *through* it. Your bedroom is gonna leak like a crab pot if I don't fix it fast." Abe looked around the kitchen, taking in the pale yellow walls that used to be bright, the browned ceiling over the old stove, the sagging cabinet door below the sink. The photograph on the wall of Conway on his boat, his hand on Abe's shoulder. Two years before he died. "This place is falling apart."

With her free needle, his mother rapped the table. "I'll thank you kindly to butt out. My house. My rules."

Abe held his tongue, but barely. He needed to start fixing things. "That's some yarn," he said.

His mother used to be a master-knitter. She'd designed Arans that she could have sold for hundreds of dollars but chose to give to people she loved. Now she looked like a child, struggling with the oversized needles.

"Abigail brought it to me. I asked for something fun."

"Oh." Bright red ribbon, it was some kind of crazy novelty yarn. She was using needles thicker than her pinkies, and she still had trouble gripping them. The stitches she made were painfully slow.

"So," she said, struggling to keep the last stitch on the huge needle long enough to knit it off. "Sunday?"

"Yeah," he said. "Of course."

She shook her head. "Every year I worry you'll forget."

Forget his father's deathiversary? As if he could. "The city's taking over the lighthouse," he said. "I mean, the feds are giving it to them, and then the council is going to let it go to some developer. Or tear it down." He adjusted the peas on his ankle. No way was he going to the doctor. He'd ice it all night if he had to.

"No." Hope's hands stopped moving, and Abe instantly regretted telling her. But she had to know at some point.

"It's practically a done deal."

"Stop it, then."

"With all my vast political clout?" His light tone wasn't convincing and he knew it. "They want me to present my preservation idea. I've got to figure out how to do that."

"They'll make it into something else." The needles had fallen into her lap and her face looked frightened. "A store, or a coffee shop."

He closed his eyes briefly. "I've heard talk about a hotel, actually. And an amusement park, but I don't think either of those would get by city council." He paused and leaned forward to lift her needles carefully, taking care not to drop a stitch. He placed them on the table. "One woman wants to tear the whole thing down and put in a public park. I could see people liking that."

"*Abe*. Think about your father. We can't let it go, not the lighthouse. Think of him."

"Yeah, Ma." He took another cookie that he knew he wouldn't be able to eat. "That's all I ever do."

CHAPTER ELEVEN

I dreamed I lived in a yarn store. Then I woke up and realized it was true. – E. C.

Fiona's mother had bought *Breakfast at Tiffany's* as soon as it came out on Betamax, again on VHS. Most of the time Fiona was growing up, the movie had been playing in the background. If it wasn't, then the Mancini album was on the stereo. The look on Audrey Hepburn's face when she entered the jewelry store on 5th Avenue—that look of peaceful joy... Fiona knew—she could feel it—that her own face went the exact same way when she finished the half-hour's drive down the long, winding highway, through broccoli fields surrounded by sand dunes and dirt roads, and she finally thumped over the one-way metal spikes at the entrance to U-Pick.

RACHAEL HERRON

Thank God the front leather bucket seats of her Alfa
Romeo GT were wide enough that Abe wasn't within
easy touching distance. If she'd had to brush his arm in
order to shift gears...well, it would have been a long ride
to be attempting to breathe like a normal person.

Fiona was bringing him to her safe place. The place
she sunk into herself and wandered, quietly, sometimes
for hours. It had started out as an unreasonable
challenge in her mind—she could take him to U-Pick
and he'd no doubt be disappointing, and she'd quickly
get over her crush.

But he hadn't uttered a word of complaint since she'd
picked him up as agreed in front of Tillie's. He'd thrown
a tool belt onto the floor of her backseat.

"You brought tools?"

"I figured you'd have yours."

Of course she did. Her tool belt was in the trunk.

Damn. Him tossing that heavy belt into her car was
maybe the hottest thing she'd ever seen.

Abe had been content to just sit next to her and
watch the countryside unrolling outside his window.
"Nice day," he'd said once, and she'd agreed, still feeling
tongue-tied, loath to spit out a nonsense word just
because she was nervous.

It was one of the first mild days, the promise of
spring floating through the sweetly tinged air, the
jasmine growing on farm fences just starting to bloom.
"Gorgeous," he'd said as they passed a windmill standing
proudly in front of a vineyard, the vines black and

barren, wild yellow mustard just beginning to bloom at the top edges.

And he'd sounded like he meant it.

At the gate Dorito, the owner—perpetually clad in extra-short jean shorts and t-shirts decorated with tractor logos—unlocked the gate for them. Dorito knew every single car that got hauled in. In the late afternoon, once the daily scrap-haulers had left, he wandered the site and ran his hands across the bumpers of the old Datsun Zs whose engines had rusted right through, his big, friendly pit bull Nails trotting at his side. He made itemized lists of everything that might be salvageable from the Hondas that had been stolen in Pacifica, joy-ridden down the coast, and burned in Santa Cruz. He loved nothing more than old VW buses whose seats could be yanked out and sold.

Now, as Dorito came toward them scratching his head with satisfaction as though he'd just woken up, Fiona glanced at Abe. He had a small smile on his face. A nice smile. He looked happy.

"Greetings and salutations!" Dorito doffed his rusty-orange baseball cap. "It has been altogether too long since our last communion. What brings you to these humble parts?"

Fiona grinned. Dorito spent a lot of time alone in the booth, waiting for drop-offs, reading old Dover reprints of Shakespeare plays. He often said that whatever a man couldn't find in the Bard wasn't worth the time spent searching, and Fiona chose to trust him on that point.

"Just looking today," she said.

Abe leaned closer to her so he could peer out her rolled-down window. "Howdy."

"This is Abe Atwell, the Cypress Hollow harbormaster."

"You run that craft with the blue bow, is that not correct, good sir?"

At that point, Fiona knew Abe could do one of two things. He could mockingly match Dorito's tone with an Olde English rejoinder, or he could laugh and not know what to say. When she'd first met Dorito, she'd done the latter.

Abe, however, simply answered with, "I do. You should come aboard some time, and we'll go whale-watching. Or fishing. At your pleasure."

Dorito looked delighted, a grin splitting his weather-beaten face like a knife split old leather. "I'd like that very much, though a landlubber I be on most days the sun chooses to rise."

"You'd be very welcome. I can always use a capable pair of hands when it comes to dealing with tourists. Fiona here, she was better than most the other day. She threw herself off the side of the boat after a kid who almost went diving for pearls."

"Indeed," said Dorito, with an admiring gaze, "I cannot say I'm surprised by that confession."

Fiona put the Alfa Romeo in gear. "Okay, we'll park up by Nails's kennel, okay? I want to look at the Mustangs. Maybe revisit that Benz."

"You will be pleased by our recent procurement of a small fleet of older Hondas. West of the Fiats."

She nodded. The antennae of Hondas were pliable, easy to use for her favorite wide-hoop earrings.

The scrapyard was surprisingly organized for what it was. Cars were arranged meticulously by first make, then model, then year. Wide rows led to narrower ones, and when Fiona was inside the very depths of the yard, she sometimes looked up at the cars stacked around her and felt as though she were in *Star Wars*, the compacter about to crush her at any moment. Instead of being a scary thought, it was exhilarating. How fast could she climb? Would she get over the metal, scaling it like a rock-climber took a steep cliff face? Or would she remain at the bottom, being crushed from the feet up by the metal that already seemed like it made up her blood and bones?

"You love being here," Abe said as they turned down one of the narrower alleys. The cars were stacked low here, one and two deep. Still easy to find fenders that could be stripped, beaten and shined into perfect submission. Or better, metal that she could snip, cut, and make beautiful.

Fiona nodded, not looking over her shoulder. "This way. You've really never been here?"

"I'm more likely to go to the boating scrapyard in Santa Cruz."

Fiona felt a prickle of excitement. "Oooh. I wonder what I'd find *there*?"

Abe laughed, a deep rumble. "What are we looking for today?"

"We'll know it when we see it."

"How?"

She grinned and ignored him. Here. It was here somewhere.

"Not far now."

Years ago, Dorito had made a steep ramp out of some two-by-fours, and in one harrowing attempt had pulled his favorite, dead, '64 Mustang up to the top of a ten-foot platform using a winch and a rickety old side lift crane. Now the gorgeous blue beast was the marker of where the yard suddenly changed. In front of the 'Stang, closest to the entrance, Dorito piled the more boring cars. Hondas, Nissans, Toyotas. Out there it was easier for the junkyard scrappers to get what they needed quickly. Back here, on the other side of the Mustang, Dorito carefully placed the classic cars.

"This is where the good stuff is."

They peered up at a '69 Chevelle resting precariously against a '65 Chevy C10. Next to it one of Fiona's favorites, a purple '39 Nash Lafayette, rested in peace. No tires, no windows, just that gorgeous luxury body rusting where it stood.

Abe tilted his head to see more. "Does he ever sell these whole?"

"Nope." Fiona ran her hand over the rough oxidized hood of the Nash. "He parts them out, as needed. Only to people he deems worthy. He says he does more good in the world that way."

Abe shot a crooked smile at her, and Fiona's palms went damp. He said, "Obviously, you're one of those."

"Not sure why he likes me so much, but yeah, I am."

Abe nodded, and Fiona had to look away from him. He had *no* idea how much he smoldered, did he? Just standing there in those Wranglers, his broad muscles straining at the biceps of his coffee-colored t-shirt, she could barely make herself look at him. He was so good-looking it hurt. Like looking at the sun or something. Unlike the sun, though, her eyes were drawn back to him. Over and over.

Job. She had a job here. She cleared her throat. "So, I've been working with this '56 T-Bird. Up here, on the right."

Abe let out a long, low whistle when he saw it.

"Right?" Fiona said, sinking into a crouch and pawing through a zipped pocket on her tool belt. "Isn't she gorgeous?"

Abe didn't answer, just walked around the eggshell-colored body, touching first the driver's door handle, then the rounded window in the back. "Look at her lines. They don't build 'em like this anymore. This looks like a porthole, over here."

Exactly what she always said about that window. She took out her sheet-metal snips.

"What are you pulling?" He walked around and pushed the bumper with his boot.

She smiled. "The little things."

"I'll help. Tell me how."

An hour later, they had a reasonably nice pile of pieces that Fiona would keep. She'd used the cutting torch to take out pieces of the already rusted floor on the passenger's side. Never touched by sun, the metal was intact, still the most gorgeous, pale white—the exact shade of half-and-half. Fiona touched the metal reverently. Oh, the *fun* she'd have cutting this up. She'd put Abe on the job of removing the antenna and the narrow metal strips that held the rearview mirrors in place.

Abe dropped another small piece on their pile. "I give up."

"What?" Fiona rubbed her dirty hands on her jeans. They'd been clean when she picked him up, but they certainly weren't now. She felt in her hair for stray bits of car parts.

"You can't be parting this out for another Benz, unless you're building it in miniature. You do body work, right?"

Fiona nodded. "And details."

"You're not using this stuff in detailing unless you're shaving it up and making your own steel pads." He shook his head. "So what is this?"

First she shoved her hat down further on her head so that her eyes were hidden. Then she put her hand in her right front pocket. Should she? Yes. She'd debated wearing the earrings when she picked him up, but she hadn't felt daring enough. If she'd been wearing them then, it would have *really* looked like a date.

Which, of course, it was. She could feel it in the flutter in her stomach, in the way the nervousness only increased as the minutes went by.

So she slipped the first long earring in. Then the other. They felt good, the small weight of them swinging against her neck. She tilted her head slightly upward so she could meet his eyes.

"Beautiful," he said without hesitation.

"Rolls Royce," Fiona said, tilting her head so that the earrings danced.

CHAPTER TWELVE

Sometimes the prettiest things are things we'd never noticed before the right moment—long, pleasing lines of ribbing, or the sound a marker makes, slipping to its new home. – E. C.

Abe struggled to find his breath. He'd misplaced it somehow when she'd put those long silver earrings on, and he wasn't sure where to find it now. It was almost sunset, and they were losing the light. The woman in front of him—in her dirty jeans that showed off every curve of her body, that cute as hell pink-and-white plaid shirt, in that beat-up black cowboy hat that did absolutely nothing to hide those eyes, which were flashing deep hazel in the last rose light of the sky—was making him feel something he didn't know what to do with.

It was actually painful. She made him rock-hard, just standing there, one finger swinging her left earring.

"You okay?" Fiona frowned and took a step closer. "You look funny."

"Fine. You made those? From a car?"

She smiled again, and Abe shifted his weight to make himself more comfortable.

"It's a hobby." Her words came quickly. "You know, everyone in this town makes things, and just because I'm not the best with yarn doesn't mean I'm not creative. It's fun."

Abe nodded, stupidly.

"I mean, it keeps me busy." Fiona gave a short laugh and knelt to pack up her snips. Poking the smaller pieces of metal into an inner compartment in her tool belt, she sighed. Then she stood, picking up several of the bigger pieces.

Abe snapped to. "Give me those." He stepped forward and took a twelve-inch piece of scarred metal from her hand. Their fingers touched for a second too long, and Abe felt an electric pulse that had nothing to do with static. Shit, what was he? A horny teenager? *Pull it together, Atwell.*

"You think they're idiotic." She started to tug one off.

"No, no! They're...awesome." Inwardly, he groaned. He couldn't find a better word than that? Did he have to sound like a teenaged boy?

But it worked. She brightened like phosphorescence. "Really?"

He tucked the piece of metal under his arm and rocked back on his heels.

"Yeah," he said. And lord help him, he couldn't help it. He reached forward and touched the earring. Long, thin metal, cool to the touch. His fingers brushed the side of her neck. So warm and soft, the absolute polar opposite of the jewelry.

She didn't step toward him. But she didn't step back, either.

Abe felt elated, as if someone was giving him a gift he hadn't even known he wanted. What if he got a little old crush of his own? Right back at her? When was the last time he was really crushed out on someone? Was it Rayna? Could it really be that long ago?

Hell, this could be fun. "Let's get out of here. Does this date come with food?"

She blinked those big eyes—they were darker now—and pushed her crushed cowboy hat lower on her head. "You bet it does."

"Good. Lead the way."

When they got to her car, she astonished him by saying, "You want to drive?"

He stared at her. "You sure?" The car was her baby, she'd told him so on the drive over. The Alfa had been her first purchase as a grown-up, the first thing she bought when Fee's Fill finally went into the black.

"Why not?" She tossed him the keys over the hood of the car.

"I'll be careful," he said.

And she surprised the hell out of him again. "Screw careful," Fiona said. "She's meant to be driven. Open her up."

He followed her instructions to the letter, depressing the accelerator to its full limit out on the highway. As they twisted through the thick trees on the winding two-lane blacktop, he switched on the lights. "Yellow lamps."

"Stock."

"*Nice*," he said.

"Faster," she said, rolling the window down and putting her hand out to catch the wind. It was almost full dark now.

Abe cast a sideways look at her. God, she was hot like this, comfortable in her car, in her knowledge of what it could do, what he could do with it.

She caught his eye and then looked back out toward the sunset. "There's a curve up there, right where it meets Printz Road. You know it?"

He did. Years ago, he'd had a motorcycle and he'd laid it out there once, right on that bend. Broke his pinky finger and had been lucky he hadn't broken his neck.

Fiona said firmly, "I hit seventy-four on it once. See if you can beat that."

Abe hit seventy-five, and she whooped out the window into the growing darkness.

He couldn't have been much more turned on if she'd started taking off her clothes.

"You like hot dogs?" She still had her arm out the window.

"Does the Pope like his ring?"

Fiona said, "Never been Catholic, so I have no idea. But I'm going to guess he does."

Curling his fingers more loosely around the wheel, still learning the feel of the car, Abe said, "I love hot dogs. Ketchup, no mustard."

"Well, there's where you're wrong, but I'll let it slide this time. Do you like Dandy Dog?"

The fact that at no point in the evening did it sound like he'd need to use a cloth napkin just made everything even better. This was the best date he'd been on in years. By far. Maybe ever.

Entering the town proper, Abe took a right and then a left around the old movie theater. The street lights had come on, glowing warm in the light fog. "You mind if we go this way? My mom lives on this street, and I like to make sure the house hasn't burned down in between my visits."

Fiona stilled. Then she nodded. "No, I don't mind. She was my English teacher in seventh grade."

"Of course she was. She knows everyone," he said. "I hope she gave you an A."

His mother was sitting on the porch in the oversized swing, the large knitting needles resting motionless in her hands. She watched the car pull into the driveway and frowned when she recognized Abe in the driver's seat.

"Just take a minute." Abe got out of the car, suddenly conscious that he was bringing a woman to his mother's house. While on a date. He really should have thought about this before taking the turn onto her street.

"Hey, Mom. Just checking to see if you need anything."

Fiona stood next to him then, and Abe felt an irrational urge to take her hand. He didn't.

Hope didn't stand but she patted the swing next to her. "I'm fine. Don't need a thing." She smiled at Fiona. "Nice to see you, Fiona. Will you sit with me?"

"No, we're not staying," Abe hastened to say. "Just wanted to make sure you're okay."

"He thinks I'll drop dead every time he doesn't have me in his sight," Hope explained to Fiona, who nodded. "You should have told me you were coming." She pushed at her gray hair, combing it out of her eyes with her fingers. She was wearing the same old cream Aran she'd been wearing on Wednesday when she'd been on the roof.

"Student of yours, huh?" said Abe. "Like everyone else in this town?"

Both women nodded. Fiona looked at the ground. Hope, on the other hand, was staring at Fiona with what looked like open fascination.

"I didn't know *you* knew each other, though," said Hope.

"Yep," said Fiona lightly.

"The lighthouse!" said Hope in satisfaction. "*That's* it. You're the one with the tearing-it-down plan. So, you're working on a new plan together?"

"Mom—" Abe's voice was a warning.

But Fiona didn't need his protection. "It's something we're going to talk about later, for sure. What are you knitting?"

"This?" His mother looked down blankly at her lap. "It's nothing." She looked back up. "Did you make those earrings you're wearing?"

"I did. Do you have pierced ears?"

Hope's rheumatic fingers fluttered to her ears. "No. No, I never did that."

Fiona touched one of her own lobes. "I have some clip-on ones at the station. I'd love to give you a pair. Come by and pick some out, okay?"

Hope looked confused. "You want to give me...Do you knit? I don't remember."

"Sadly, no."

"But..."

There was a tension between the two women, something below their words Abe wasn't understanding. "Mom, I just wanted to—we're going to go, okay?"

"Okay," his mother said, picking her needles back up.

Abe realized at that moment that he'd wanted to show his mother off to Fiona. He'd wanted them—and he couldn't explain this to himself at all—to get along. To be friends. He'd wanted them to chat lightly about something while he listened.

He'd never wanted that before, not with any woman besides Rayna.

"Let's get those hot dogs."

Fiona said, "Bye, Mrs. Atwell."

Abe's mother just waved.

Well, hell. He'd figure out what that had been between the two women later. Right now, he wanted to make Fiona laugh again.

CHAPTER THIRTEEN

The sheep your wool came from was exposed to sun, rain, starlight, and moonglow. Do yourself the same favor. – E. C.

The food came quickly, filling a red paper bag. Fiona headed toward one of the picnic tables in the parking lot, but Abe waved the bag in front of her like he was bullfighting. "Where should we go?"

"Go?"

"Dandy Dogs taste better away from the site of their creation. Come on, let's go." He walked toward the car, but then passed it. Fiona trotted to catch up with him. He had such *long* legs.

"Where are we going?"

"If I told you, it wouldn't be a surprise."

"What do I get if I guess?" Was she actually getting better at flirting?

Ahead of her, without turning his head, he said, "Just follow me."

His deep voice sent a delicious tingle down her spine. For a blissful second, she let herself fantasize about the man in front of her, let herself wonder what it would be like to be touched by him. To be kissed by him. And then she tripped over a rock, stopping herself from falling at the very last minute.

There was really only one place they could have been headed, but Fiona ignored the signs as they walked. Headed south on foot, going this way, Abe could only be leading them to either the old dump or the lighthouse.

Fiona could safely assume the landfill wasn't his first choice, though they *had* just done the scrapyard.

The wind picked up. It always did here. The coastal breeze which normally caressed the rest of Cypress Hollow scoured the ground. Ice plant rusted on the dunes, turning the red-brown of blood in the cold air. Seagulls whined above, wheeling restlessly. If the birds headed north toward the marina, Fiona knew they would find plenty of scraps from the fishing boats. But here, there were usually only a few skinny gulls, relentlessly complaining. Fiona had always imagined they were the same three birds from her childhood, now older and even more unhappy.

"I can't believe you *lived* here. Isn't it great?" Abe stopped, his boots loud on the gravel. He looked up at the lighthouse with an expression of...was it longing? Happiness? Fiona crossed her arms over her chest and watched him. Just gazing up at the old pile of wood made Abe look like he'd had a delightful, unexpected thought.

"Sure," she said. Who was she to dampen his excitement? She hoped the damn thing wouldn't be standing much longer. And he liked the ancient wreck. What was it the mayor had said? Abe wanted to make it into a museum? God, the only thing worse than leaving the building standing would be honoring it, making it into even more than it was.

"Come on," he said, taking her hand in his. His skin was cool and his palms were calloused, as she would have predicted for a man in his line of work. What startled her was how well her hand fit in his.

It made her dizzy. Maybe next she'd accidentally fall off the side of the cliff, and he'd have to rescue her and then she could just go ahead and die of embarrassment. Get it over with.

"It's good we have the moon to guide us tonight," said Abe.

"If we didn't, there's no way in hell I'd walk out here," said Fiona.

"Scared?"

His hand tightened around hers, and for one second she considered putting on a higher-than-normal voice and flirtatiously saying, "Oh, yes, *ever* so frightened, Abe." She didn't think she could pull it off, though. Fiona might be scared of many things—too many—but she wasn't scared of the dark.

"No. I'm just sensible. It's a cliff. In the dark."

Abe nodded. "But no one's ever died. Any idiot who's gotten too close to the edge has just been banged up."

"They should at least put up a good permanent street light or two. If people are going to walk out here, they should make it safe." If they built a city park it would have good, environmentally responsible lights that would burn cleanly all night. They'd put up a rail at the edge so that kids could skate and rollerblade right to the edge, safely.

"Or people could use better common sense and stay away from where it crumbles."

"Remember when June Hampton fell? She didn't think she was close to the edge, but it was dark with fog and no moon."

Abe's thumb rubbed against the back of her hand. Fiona's heart rate spiked. Did he know he was doing that?

He spoke as though they weren't connected, as if he could still think straight. "June Hampton can polish off a forty-ounce faster than an eighteen-year-old doing a kegstand."

Fiona attempted to cover her laugh with a cough. "Maybe. But someone could seriously hurt themselves."

Now at the old bench, the one on the far side of the lighthouse, facing the ocean, Abe let go of her hand. Fiona curled her fingers into a fist, as though she could hold the feeling there a little longer.

He brushed off the seat with a napkin from the bag.

Fiona smiled. This wasn't so bad. This used to be her favorite place when they lived here. Even in storms she'd liked to sit out here, bundled in sweaters until her father pulled her in, soaking and shivering, when the lightning started to dance on the water's horizon.

Out here, Abe's face relaxed, as though getting this close to the water did something to him. Maybe being on the water for him was like being under a car for her. Fiona could see him breathing deeply, his ribcage expanding, his shoulders dropping. She took her own deep pull of salt-tinged air into her lungs.

This wasn't bad.

She hadn't done anything completely embarrassing. Yet.

And she'd just keep her back to the lighthouse.

"Sorry," he said with a chagrined look. "I think it'll take more than a napkin to get this seat actually clean."

"You might not have noticed I just shimmied out from under a classic Thunderbird. I'm not fussy." She sat. The ground beneath the bench had been eroded by years of people kicking their feet, and her black cowboy boots didn't touch the ground. "I've sat on worse. Yesterday, in fact."

They ate. Fiona felt Abe looking at her but she kept her gaze on the tallest rock poking out of the water. She couldn't quite make out all its lines in the dark, but the blackness where it rose from the water made it seem as though the ocean—just there—was deeper and matte, as though it had taken a breath and sucked in the light. The auto-strobe light flashed exactly as it had for years and years now from the next spit of land, illuminating the rock so brightly that it hurt her eyes for a split second before they were plunged into darkness again.

"Not even the light from the lighthouse comes on anymore," said Fiona.

Abe nodded. "I hate that. It's what I loved the most about it. What my father loved the most, too."

Fiona finished the last bite of her hot dog, making sure she didn't miss a speck of the mustard on her fingers. Whoops. Maybe you didn't lick your fingers clean on a date. It probably wasn't what the cool kids did. Was he judging her? She wriggled on the bench, feeling the weight of his gaze. What was he seeing? It was dark. Even if she'd dropped a glob of mustard on her shirt, he wouldn't be able to see it, so what was he staring at?

Self-consciously, she pushed her hair over her shoulder. "Why?" she said.

As though he'd forgotten that he'd spoken last, Abe said, "What? Oh, the light."

"Why did you love it? It was so...*nosy*. Poking its way into every house, every boat." The only place the light hadn't illuminated was the small house at the base of the light, where Fiona had lived for those few years.

"Exactly," he said. "In the dark, it was like a friend."

Not in Fiona's house. Her mother Bunny had hated the light from the very first day they moved in.

"It was like a nightlight," he continued, "except you could only see your way around the room in flashes. I used to navigate through the house like that while my parents slept. I used to play a game where I could only move when it was dark, and I had to make it certain distances before the light went on again. From the bed to the door jamb. From there to the piano. Getting from the piano to the kitchen was the hardest part because you had to cross through the living room, but I could just make it."

Fiona's legs swung over the sandy dirt below. "No siblings?" She knew he didn't have any. It felt like a lie to ask. She was aware of so many things about him, and he knew so little about her. It was cheating.

"I had a sister."

She stilled her leg, and tucked the hot dog wrapper carefully into a space between the slats to keep safe until she could throw it away. She took a moment to push it deep, so that the wind wouldn't steal it. "You did?"

"She died when she was six months old."

"Oh, no."

"Her name was Marina."

She wanted to touch him reassuringly, but how did one do that? She kept her hand still, instead. "How did she die?"

"No one ever knew. My mother went to get her up one morning, and she was dead. They called it SIDS, but we learned that year that SIDS just means the doctors have no fucking idea why the baby died."

"I didn't know." The words were so small, so ineffective.

"How could you?" Abe stretched his arms out in front of him, and then lowered them to rest on the bench behind them. It didn't seem as though he even knew he'd done it. He probably didn't notice that his arm was now touching her upper shoulders, resting against her with the slightest pressure, a warm comfort. "I was a kid. I barely knew what was going on."

"Your poor mother."

He nodded. "My poor parents. My dad took it hard, too. I know he loved me, but he'd been so excited about having a little girl." A long, lead-weighted pause fell between them.

Fiona didn't know what to say. She racked her brain for the right condolence and couldn't find it.

Abe said, "What about you? We don't know much about each other, for people living in the same town, huh?"

On winter days, you wear a denim jacket lined with sheepskin. There's a hole in the right elbow. In the summer you like blue t-shirts emblazoned with the Rite Spot, the ones Jonas gave away to everyone three years ago for free. Your truck makes a signature pop-brrrsh noise when it comes around the south curve right before the station. Your eyes get sadder as night approaches, like sleep is someplace you don't want to go.

"Only child," Fiona said.

"Ah. Spoiled?"

"No way. My mother was the spoiled one."

"Was?"

"She..." Fiona never knew how to say exactly what had happened. "She left. A long time ago."

"I'm sorry." Another flash of the auto-beam lit his face, and he *looked* sorry. As if he got it, somehow. He'd lost his father, of course, so maybe he did.

"Me, too."

A pause. From below came the mournful sound of a lone sea lion barking, echoing against the rocks and then out to sea.

"Marina, huh?" Fiona wanted to move closer to him. She didn't.

But she wanted to.

A low laugh. "Marina Anemone. My father was pretty adamant that my mother got to be in charge of everything child-related except our names."

"I get Marina. But Abe?"

"Uh-uh."

Fiona swung her legs up and twisted at the waist so she was half-facing him. When the beam hit the side of his face again, his clear blue eyes looked almost transparent. "Tell me."

"No way."

"Please? I hate not knowing a secret." Her voice *was* flirtatious now, she knew it, and she was almost embarrassed at herself. Daisy would be *thrilled* if she knew. The very thought alarmed her.

And it excited her, too.

Abe's mouth twisted. "God, I'm going to regret this, aren't I?" He paused. "Abalone."

Fiona's mouth dropped. "Abalone Atwell."

"He loved a good mollusk. I was lucky not to be named Limpet or Conch or something even worse. Stop laughing."

But she couldn't. *Abalone.* It was so not *him.* It was a pearlized name, the name of a polished ashtray lined up next to the Cypress Hollow sweatshirts the tchotchke shops sold to tourists along Main Street. "God, I'm sorry." She laughed again. "I'm so sorry. But...middle name?"

"Grunion."

Fiona lost it then. She couldn't help it.

Abe waited for Fiona's laughter to die down, leaning backward, a resigned look on his face. Finally, he said, "Yep. It always brings the house down."

On a giggle, she said it out loud, to test it. "Abalone Grunion Atwell." Oh, it was just too much.

"Used to be worse when I got carded. You wouldn't believe what a bartender can do with that name."

Fiona loved the way her cheeks hurt with the grin that was splitting her face. It felt good to be sitting here with him. Right now.

"So," Abe said, "in an obvious and desperate bid to change the subject, were you and your mother close? Before she left?"

The laugh died at the back of her throat. "Oh. No."

"Why not?"

And in a moment that swung quickly from levity to seriousness, a moment that actually felt comfortable,

Fiona was tempted, right then and there, to tell him about Bunny. And she *never* talked about Bunny. To anyone. Fiona tilted her head to clear her thoughts and shook out her fingers to stop them from twitching. She shouldn't trust this feeling. "I wish we had been." There. She could leave it at that.

Abe didn't push it.

And the fact that he didn't, that he took his arm back and stood easily, taking their trash and tossing it in the trashcan, made her comfortable in her skin again.

She was still on a date with Abe Atwell. A shiver danced down her spine, trailing silver sparks. Her eyes had finally adjusted to the dimness, or maybe the moon was reflecting better against the water, because she could see him now. She could see him clearly.

And that simple fact gave another delicious shiver that reached into her with a low throb.

Abe looked right at her, and stretched out his hand. "Wanna spelunk, Snowflake?"

CHAPTER FOURTEEN

Knitters get things done. – E. C.

Fiona's hand froze in his. Abe watched as she went from flirty—which was adorable—to stiff as a frozen cod.

"What?"

"Come on," he tugged her hand. "I know you've been down here. But how long has it been?"

"Did you just call me *Snowflake?*"

Abe tightened his grasp on her hand. She wasn't pulling it back but he sensed she might, any minute. "Maybe?"

"Because you saw the tattoo on my hip."

"Yep. Nice placement, by the way."

"Fizzshoop." A funny little stomp accompanied her bizarre word. "At—at! It's *at* my bikini line."

"But not under it! I didn't see anything illegal, I swear." Abe took a step closer. They were inches apart. He should stop talking about the tattoo, but damn it, now it was all he could think about. "It's perfect where it is. Like lace."

Fiona closed her eyes.

He gave her a moment, running his thumb softly against the back of her hand again. She shivered.

Then she smiled. "I'm just going to ignore that whole last exchange. Let's go to the caves."

Abe realized he liked it—maybe too much—when she blew that inner fuse and made up words. It was his new goal to make that happen more often.

Also, to see that tattoo again.

Fiona's hand in his was perfect. She was small, so of course her hand was, too, but it was strong. Her palms were so soft, but her fingertips were callused. And Jesus, that was sexy. A woman who used her hands to work. As they carefully went down the steps, Abe counseled himself to breathe. To get over these teenaged jitters that were running through him.

Taking her down the path was such a cliché he was almost ashamed of himself. What Cypress Hollow boy *didn't* try to get a girl down in the caves on Moonglass Beach? So many kisses had been stolen, so many trysts. More than one romance had been consummated down there, he knew, and more than one lovers' spat had been witnessed by the tides that chased the more timorous to higher ground. But he wasn't a kid. And Fiona wasn't anything he'd thought she was.

Honestly, he hadn't thought about her much. Ever, really. So everything was surprising.

Now he wanted to lead her down the steep steps, one at a time, holding tight to her hand so she didn't fall. He hadn't held a woman's hand here since the last time he led Rayna down here. Rayna had dumped him at twenty-five, so it had to be at least eleven years. Since then, if he'd held a woman's hand at all, it hadn't been for long—and never on the sand.

And now he was taking Fiona down to the caves to kiss her.

Hell, yes he was.

And nothing more. He didn't let his mind go past that moment. Fiona wasn't the kind of girl you took home just for a night. She was a Cypress Hollow girl, through and through. You didn't mess with a local, he'd learned that the hard way. Tourists were for bedding, for one-night-stands.

The thing was, Abe had no idea what he wanted Fiona to be, besides in his arms, the sooner the better.

At the bottom of the old concrete and iron steps, Fiona tumbled past him, loosing his hand as she scampered across the pebbled shore to the water's edge. She bent at the waist and picked up a stone. She looked over the shoulder of her pink-and-white plaid shirt. The moonlight was just bright enough now against the water that he could see her wide, joyous grin.

"I can skip a stone farther than you can."

"You sure about that? Challenge accepted." *No one* was better at skipping stones than he was. How many hours had he spent on the beach as his father fished from the tide pools? While his dad trolled for the elusive, monkey-faced eel, Abe would find the best, flattest, roundest stones and spend full afternoons adjusting his angle, his pitch, the tilt of his arm. Once he'd counted seventeen skips, which had to be a world record of some kind.

"Ladies first," he said, feeling through the rocks at his feet. He didn't even have to look to find the best stones. It was as though they jumped into his hand, ready to soar. Maybe he'd go easy on her. Throw a gimme or two before he sent his best sailing.

"Okay then. Read 'em and weep." Fiona brought her arm back, her wrist at—he had to admit—the perfect angle, and let fly.

Damned rock skipped so many times he couldn't even count. "Shit."

She shrugged. "It's a gift. What can I say?"

Twenty minutes and at least fifty stones later, he admitted it. He had to. "You're better than I am."

"Thanks," she said simply.

They both looked down in the bright white moonlight. They both reached for the same stone.

She was so close now that if he'd wanted to, he could wrap his arm around her waist and draw her close. He could put his lips against her laughing ones.

And then what? Jesus, then what? Abe was no rookie. Far from it. But being around Fiona made him feel like he'd never even set foot in the game.

"Race you to the cave." On a breathless laugh, Fiona wheeled and ran.

She had a head start, and she was *fast*. Faster than she should have been with legs half the length of his. But even though she had the element of surprise, Abe grabbed back his breath and lit out after her.

He wanted to catch her. He wanted to reel her in, and then...

As he chased her laughter through the moonlight, he realized he only had one thing in mind.

CHAPTER FIFTEEN

Once is not enough to knit a pattern that sings the whole way to completion. Once is too many times to knit a pattern that has no rhythm at all. - E. C.

Fiona, like every Cypress Hollow girl, knew the cave at Moonglass Beach like the back of her hand. Judd Parsons had been her first kiss—he'd led her into the beer bottle side of the cavern and then stuck his tongue in her mouth where he let it flop around like a dying fish. She'd sworn off kissing for almost a year after that first traumatic experience. But Chad March had warmed her up to the idea again, when he'd cornered her at a beer bust one warm September night.

Now, though...

She felt heat flush through her, heat that had nothing to do with the pounding of her feet or of her heart.

Fiona was terrified. Deliciously, awfully scared. At any moment, he'd catch her. Oh, *yes*.

As she raced into the cave, she knew from past experience that it would take more than a few seconds for her eyes to adjust to the tiny amount of moonlight that filtered in from the front opening and from the old blowhole above. But she still knew how the white limestone wall curved inside, and she remembered the tall second wall of stone that curved to the right. She threw herself, gasping, behind it, holding in her almost-hysterical laugh as best she could. She pressed her back against the cold wall and willed her heart to stop pounding—it throbbed in her ears so loudly she was sure he'd hear it.

Only a few seconds behind her, Abe raced into the cave. She heard the wet *scrunch* his feet made in the rocky sand. Fiona held her breath.

Please, please find me.

As if he were using sonar, he came directly around the rock. He couldn't see her yet—her own eyes had just adjusted enough to see that he was blinking hard. But he didn't hesitate.

Abe took the two steps needed to reach her.

Fiona could feel his heat, inches away. She stayed stiller than she ever had in her life.

Then he took the one extra step.

Fiona couldn't tell who kissed first, whose lips were more ready. All she knew was that his kiss was what she'd been waiting for, so much longer than just tonight.

Abe's mouth was hot. Needy. He kissed as if he had every right to kiss her like this, to make her knees go instantly shaky, to heat her skin even hotter. She felt a matching blaze hit her cheeks.

"Abalone," she murmured against his mouth.

Without stopping the kiss, keeping his lips on hers, using his tongue to lick her bottom lip and then softly bite it, he said, "Don't call me that."

She laughed low in her belly and leaned into him. There. She could feel how rock-hard he was. How ready. When the kiss had started it had felt as though he was leading it, but now that she wrapped her arms around his neck and trailed her mouth upward, feeling that wonderful sharp stubble scrape her lips, she knew she was the one leading now. Her left hand rested lightly on his chest, and she could feel the escalating rhythm of his heartbeat under her fingers. Still unsure where this courage was coming from but grateful for it, she tugged on his earlobe with her lips. Abe gasped and pulled her tighter against him, thrusting his hips so that his hardness was evident against her stomach.

"Jesus," she whispered into his ear. "What do we do now?"

Abe groaned and then took a full step backward. He kept his hands on her wrists so she couldn't move forward. "We slow it down."

He released her hands and she lurched forward ungracefully.

"I don't—"

Abe wiped his mouth with the back of his hand. Was he wiping the taste of her away? On purpose? Fiona ignored the tiny pang she felt. She was taking this all too personally. "I'm sorry," she said, confused. "I didn't mean to..."

"No," Abe said, shoving his hands into his pockets. "Nothing to be sorry for. I started that."

Then finish it. But she couldn't say it. She was the one with the crush, not him. Fiona took a deep breath and carefully skirted her way around him in the moonlight. Her eyes were so well adjusted now that she could see the bulge at the front of his pants, the bulge that echoed the hot slickness between her thighs. Good. He felt it, too. At least she knew that.

"It was because I said your real name, wasn't it?" She kept her voice light. A kiss like that was probably nothing to him. She could make it mean nothing to herself, too.

Given ten or twelve years.

"That's not it..."

But his voice trailed off, and he didn't finish the sentence.

Awesome.

She should have known. *You're not good enough. Never good enough.*

"Time to go." Fiona glanced at her naked wrist as though she was wearing a watch. "The Alfa turns into a pumpkin soon, and then we'll be stranded." She wanted to take back the words as soon as she said them. God forbid he think she was comparing herself to Cinderella.

"Fiona," Abe said, reaching for her hand. "Wait..."

"It's okay," she said, leading the way out of the cave. "I understand."

But she didn't.

At the top of the steep path, Fiona paused to let him catch up, trying not to think of how she must look, out of breath with the exertion and flushed. It wasn't like she *never* worked out. She went for a run at least once a month, whether she needed it or not.

Keep it light. Just get home.

Abe was next to her, still much too quiet.

Fiona gestured up toward the lighthouse. "Wanna just kick it down with me? Come on."

He didn't say anything, just stared at her with those crystalline eyes.

"It wouldn't take much," she said. "Just a few solid hits, probably. The city would pay *us*, if we saved them the cost." She needed to get his mind on anything but what had happened in the cave. Make him stop staring at her lips like that, like he was ravenous and she was sustenance. No gaze had ever felt so good, and it needed to stop if she couldn't satisfy his need. "We could make it into a pile of splinters and then have ourselves a big ole bonfire. Roast some marshmallows."

He looked as jarred as she'd meant him to. "It should stand."

Good. She wanted to get him riled. "It has to go."

"Fiona. It's our history as a city. It was your home, for cripes sake."

"It's a nightmare."

Frowning, he said, "We can talk about it another time. Tomorrow maybe."

"Now. This was the plan, right? For us to talk? I can't believe you actually want to preserve that old jalopy." Fiona turned her back and started walking away, toward the highway and her car, which was still parked at the hot dog stand. He'd either follow or he wouldn't. She wasn't sure which she wanted.

"I can't believe you *don't* want to save it."

Abe caught up to Fiona and walked shoulder-to-shoulder with her. They didn't say another word until they reached the car. She reached to unlock the door for him, relishing the fact that *she* was driving now, that she was in control of this at least. If not of her own damn emotions.

"I'm sorry," he said once they were both seated with the doors closed, the sound of the pounding waves dampened by the metal.

"Nothing to be sorry for." Please, please let him be quiet for the short drive back to Tillie's where he'd left his truck. She wanted to die of embarrassment. Yeah, he'd been obviously turned on, but that was only because she'd thrown herself at him. Like the fool she was. She should have known *better*. Abe Atwell wasn't interested in someone like her, and if he was, against his better judgment, of course that wouldn't—couldn't—last more than for a fling, which would just end up being embarrassing for everyone involved.

After a long, very awkward pause, after she'd taken the curve to Main Street perhaps just a little too fast, he said, "Maybe we can agree to disagree."

On the kiss? Fiona was horrified and jammed the stick into second, making the engine sound as upset as she felt. "It's fine. We can forget it ever happened."

Oh, God. It hurt.

CHAPTER SIXTEEN

Stick to using your best needles when you can.
What are you saving them for? – E. C.

N ot that," Abe said quietly. "I meant about the lighthouse."

If Fiona had put just one ounce more energy into the engine via her pedal foot, the car would have fishtailed into the parking spot with a satisfying scream. As it was, the engine roared as she gave it extra gas while moving it into neutral. "We don't need to agree on anything."

"Can't you see that Cypress Hollow *needs* the light?"

"It has a light. No one's wrecked on the shore in thirty years. The auto pulse works just fine, and every single sailor uses GPS devices now, anyway. A full third of the whole country's lighthouses have already been decommissioned, did you know that? More every year. They're obsolete." Why didn't he just get out of the car? Couldn't he see how humiliated she felt? She'd thrown herself at him and he'd done an amazing job of rejecting her. If only he'd finish the job. Oh, yeah—fishermen clubbed their poor injured fish over the head after they dragged them out of the water. Maybe that was next.

"My father loved the lighthouse," said Abe. "Once he almost died trying to get the boat in during a storm. I was three and my mother was pregnant with Marina. The old light hadn't been working for a few days."

Fiona suddenly remembered how stressed her father would get when he was waiting for a part to come in from the East Coast. He'd watch the weather, cursing if clouds grew.

"Then, at the moment he'd completely lost his bearings, it lit up. Flashed. Showed him where to go. We would have lost him that night if it hadn't come on."

Instead of drowning then, Abe's father had just drowned later. But she didn't say this out loud, of course.

"Bring it up at the meeting, then," she said lightly. "I'll see you there." Yeah, the next time Abe got gas, she'd look out the window of the station, just like she always did. It would be terrible now that she knew exactly what she was missing—those strong hands, those perfect lips that fit hers like they were made to do nothing but kiss her...

But he didn't get out of the car.

"I can't," Abe said. "I mean..." His voice was guttural. His fingers clenched in what looked like frustration.

Fiona said, "Sorry?"

"I can't bring it up at the meeting. I don't...I don't do well in front of people. Talking."

Fiona frowned. "You talk in front of your passengers all the time."

"That's different. That's what I do."

"You have stage fright?"

Abe shook his head. "Fear of public speaking." He said quickly, "It's very common, you know."

Fiona felt a headache start behind her eyes. She wanted so badly to be home, safe, alone. Politely as she could, she said, "I'm sorry about that. Maybe you can get coaching or something..."

"Or I can convince you to save the lighthouse."

"No." She felt a pit at the bottom of her stomach. That wasn't why he'd gone out with her in the first place, was it? Was she *that* big a fool?

"I don't know if I can explain it to you. But I have to try to make something of it. Build the museum my dad wanted. It was his biggest hope, what he was going to do when he'd finally saved enough to retire."

"Yeah," Fiona said, keeping her eyes straight out the front window, looking at a bent parking meter, willing him to get out of the car. "You should pick another place for your museum."

She opened the car door and stepped outside, sucking the damp night air into her lungs. Maybe he'd take the hint now that she was out of the car. *Jesus, Abe, get out.*

How had she thought for even a minute that she could be as attractive as Abe would want a woman to be? That she could imitate someone beautiful, classy, interesting and smart? Obviously, he'd kissed her down in the cave and found there that his plan to get her to change her mind on the lighthouse couldn't include seduction. She was no Cinderella. She was no Rayna, for God's sake.

Instead of turning into a beautiful princess, Abe's kiss had reminded them both she was still just a frog.

Abe finally exited the passenger side. His hands flat on the roof of her car, he said in a strained voice, "Fiona."

She wondered if he remembered that day at Tad's Ice Cream. What was it, twelve years ago? Twenty-one years old, Fiona had been eating a turtle sundae by herself in a front booth that looked out onto the street. She'd just dumped a guy who thought her boobs should be bigger (Gino had offered her money for a breast enhancement and had said he wouldn't have sex with her until she accepted—she'd cried for hours after she'd told him to get the hell out). Still hearing the echoes of his words, *You eat too much sugar. You need to grow your chest, not your hips,* Fiona took herself to get ice cream. She'd eat it in front of God and everyone. Screw Gino.

Because she'd had such a good view of the sidewalk, she'd seen Abe before he saw her. Damn, *that* was what a man should look like. Broad enough to lean on, strong enough to trust. And that's exactly what Rayna was doing.

They'd entered and ordered, and Rayna had looked around for a place to sit. Her eyes lit up when she saw Fiona sitting in a booth by herself. She'd pulled Abe behind her.

"Just you here?"

Fiona had nodded. She didn't want to share her booth with the most romantic couple in Cypress Hollow. Her embarrassing crush on Abe Atwell in those days had been much smaller, but it grew every time she saw him.

"Big booth," said Rayna with a smile. "You mind if we join you?"

What could she say? "Sure."

They'd slid in on one side, hip-to-hip. Abe hadn't looked at her, his eyes glued on Rayna. Fiona knew a girl that pretty could have anything she wanted, up to and including the cherry on top of their shared sundae (which was half the size of the one Fiona was polishing off by herself, she noticed).

The couple had spent more time kissing than eating ice cream, and Fiona had left the last quarter of her sundae regrettably untouched. "Okay, see you," she mumbled.

Rayna came up for air long enough to smile and say, "You have a little...on your shirt."

RACHAEL HERRON

Fiona looked down. It wasn't a little anything—it was a lot of chocolate, all down the front of her t-shirt, as though she were four years old.

Abe, though, hadn't glanced at her once.

Now, on the other side of her car, he was looking at her. For sure. But he was seeing her in terms of business. He'd gone out with her to talk about the lighthouse—to change her mind on it, to get her to speak for him.

It hurt. A lot. Her headache flared, throbbing with the rhythm of her heart.

"Okay, see you," she said, intentionally echoing her younger, more naïve self.

Abe stepped back slowly, letting his door shut. "Fiona. Wait."

Fiona got back inside the car and started it. He bent and said something at the window, his eyes looking dark and hurt, but she locked the doors.

And then she gunned the shit out of the engine, her wheels spitting rocks. She hadn't put all that time and money into this engine without knowing that she could hit sixty in six point three.

Six point four seconds later, she was going a mile a minute down the coast road, leaving the sexiest and most dangerous man in the world standing openmouthed in a gravel parking lot under a treacherous moon.

CHAPTER SEVENTEEN

Touch every ball of yarn in your house once a year.
Otherwise, they get restless and
will form small armies against you. – E. C.

Abe knew his mother had loved many things she couldn't now do: she had loved to spin yarn, and bead, and weave. But above all, she had loved to knit. When she'd lost that, the ability to use her hands for the fine knitting she loved—due to the arthritis that left her able only to manipulate the huge needles she hated—she'd lost one of the last remaining joys in her life.

So when she called Abe and said, "Meet me at Tillie's for breakfast," Abe jumped. Heck yeah, he'd take his mother out for scrambled eggs with melted cheddar cheese on top. Being at Tillie's would do her good.

It didn't hurt that he might see Fiona there.

He hadn't seen her since Friday, four days before. A storm had come in with a vengeance over the weekend, and he was kept busy all day Saturday making sure both boat and houseboat remained shipshape. When the worst of it hit on Sunday, he hadn't gone aboveboard all day. Just him, Digit, his mystery novels—and a creak on the deck every hour or two that made him wonder if it was her, come to kiss him again. If she'd come to look at him with those sea-green eyes. If she'd come to push him down on his bed, straddling him with those small, shockingly strong arms.

But no. Nothing. Besides waving out his kitchen window to Luther on the houseboat next door, he hadn't seen another soul in days.

His mother entered Tillie's, and from this distance— four booths and the coat rack—Abe could see the difference in her. The last time they'd met for breakfast, she'd been more upright. She hadn't grabbed the back of the stools to steady herself like she did now. Her back hadn't been that bent. Now she looked so *small*.

Abe stood and hurried to her, putting an arm under her elbow.

"What?" she grumbled. "You think I need help just to sit down?"

Even though he knew she was sturdy, Abe used both hands to steady her as she slipped sideways into the booth. "You okay, Mom?"

She gave him a sharp glance. "Don't treat me like a hothouse flower, Abe."

He leaned back into his own side of the booth. "I don't know what that means, besides that I probably shouldn't water you more than three times a day."

"I'm fine."

"I know." Damn it.

"Why do you have that look on your face, then? Oh, yes please, Shirley. Hot and black, thanks." Hope turned back to Abe, cup gripped between her hands as if she was trying to warm them. "There it is again. That look."

"I don't know what you're talking about, Ma. I only have the face I was born with, the one you gave me."

"That face that says you're worried I'm going to kick the bucket any minute."

"That's not what I'm thinking." But yeah, it was. One morning, he'd go over there and find her fallen in the bathroom in the night, slapped with a stroke, unable to call for help.

Dying alone. Just like Dad had in the ocean. Dying without anyone she loved near to help.

She smiled. "I'm like those alley cats I feed in the backyard. Tougher than I look." She stretched a hand out to touch his forearm. "I really am. You shouldn't worry so much." She took another sip of her coffee. "You remember when you were in grade school? You couldn't have been more than seven or eight, and you came home crying because your teacher told the class that everything dies."

Abe shuffled his boots uncomfortably. He hadn't thought of that traumatic moment in a long time. Sweetness, the class guinea pig, had turned up stiff and cold when the class got back in after a weekend. Over the crying of twenty-three seven-year-olds, Mrs. Blanship had said, "It's okay to cry when we feel sad. Everything dies eventually."

Everything. His father would die. His mother would die. *Abe* would die. It was an existential crisis of massive import, even though he was only seven. When he'd arrived home from school that afternoon, he'd clung, sobbing, to his mother's neck until she'd gotten out of him what was wrong. "Oh, honey," she'd said, kissing him hard on the side of his face. "We're not going anywhere. Daddy and I are healthy and strong, and we won't die until you're old yourself, until you won't mind us going."

She'd been wrong.

"And that's the *exact* look you had then. Would you please stop it?"

"I'm telling you, it's just my face."

"Where is she?"

Confused by the sudden lurch in the conversation, Abe said, "Who?"

"Little Fiona Lynde."

"She's not a kid anymore, Mom. And I have no idea."

"Doesn't she come in here in the mornings? Everyone else does..."

Fiona did come in here. He'd often seen her here Monday mornings with her friend Daisy. He'd just never *cared* so much before. "I don't know," he lied.

His mother sighed. "For once, I'd like you to give me a real answer."

"Fine. I think she does."

"That's why you can't take your eyes off the front door?"

"I'm not—"

She looked amused. "Okay, then. So you won't want to hear that she's on the sidewalk outside?"

Abe couldn't help the way his head swiveled, like it was on a bobble-head doll.

There she was. Fiona.

Goddamn, how had he never noticed her before? She wore a black t-shirt, short denim jacket, and blue jeans. Like she usually did. No big deal. But as she walked down the sidewalk and pulled open the front door, Abe wondered how he'd never noticed how *well* her clothes fit her. She was small, but curvy. Her breasts were high under that tee, and there—as she turned to open the front door—he got to see how well her ass fit into her pockets. How could a man help wanting to slip his hand into those pockets, to make her jeans just the smallest bit tighter...

"Oh, Abe."

"What?" he said defensively. "I need more coffee."

"Ask her over here," his mother said on a sigh.

"She doesn't want to come over here." Abe watched as she and Daisy moved through the room, greeting people with half-hugs and kisses. Daisy, with her long blonde curls and buoyant smile, would always get a bright reaction. Daisy was so fun, so gregarious and *happy*, that everyone lit up when they saw her.

What Abe had never seen before, though, was the way they reacted to Fiona. Elbert Romo took Fiona's hand and kissed the back of it chivalrously. Of course, that was just Elbert, but then Fiona greeted Deacon, the local ironworker's union president. Deacon smiled so big Abe thought it might hurt his jaw later. As Daisy rolled her chair and Fiona walked, people leaned in to them. Wanting to be near them. It wasn't just Daisy. They cared for Fiona, too.

He was an idiot for not seeing it before. And damn it, he wanted to be near her as bad as anyone else did. More.

"Go *on*," said his mother. "Have her sit with us."

"She won't want to, Mom." Fiona had acted so unhappy the other night, and he still hadn't figured out why. It had started when he slowed their kiss down...but that couldn't be it. Had he hurt her feelings or something? What had he said to make her get that overwhelmed look in her eyes?

But he raised a hand and waved anyway.

Daisy gave a small whoop and, not glancing back at Fiona, rolled toward him. "Just the guy I wanted to talk to. I heard my friend here jumped off your boat."

"Sit with us, won't you?" Hope asked. "You and Fiona."

"Happily." Daisy set her wheel lock. "Come on, Fee. Sit."

Fiona looked miserable. Had he done that to her?

"Hi," he said.

Fiona mumbled something and stared, apparently unable to decide which side to sit on.

It looked like he may have fucked everything up on Friday night. Maybe she'd figured out why he'd asked her out in the first place.

But she had no idea how much he'd loved being with her.

And *damn*, he wanted her to sit on his side of the booth.

CHAPTER EIGHTEEN

Knitters have a funny sense of humor. Check your bags when you get home to make sure they haven't snuck a little acrylic out their door and into yours, in the way people leave zucchini on doorsteps in summer. – E. C.

Fiona would kill Daisy. She would murder her slowly. Maybe with a spoon from this very diner. How could Daisy just roll over here after listening to Fiona spill her guts about that awful date the other night? What kind of a friend *did* that?

The kind of friend who was tugging on her front belt loop. "Sit there. Next to Abe. So I can see all of you."

Fiona would look ridiculous now if she took the coward's route and sat next to Hope. She'd look scared.

She wasn't scared.

She was just...dang, she didn't know what she was.

Fiona slid into the booth carefully. Slowly. She took great pains not to touch any part of Abe, though God knew she *wanted* to.

Hope said, "I hear you like my son."

Daisy let out a guffaw and reached into the bag attached to her left handle. "I have *got* to knit for this. And I'd kill for coffee. Where's Shirley?"

Fiona was hoping she hadn't quite understood what Hope was getting at. "Your son is quite nice." As if he were a cup of tea.

Hope's smile was kind, the way it had been when she'd explained the meaning of Steinbeck's "The Chrysanthemums" in seventh grade. "Well, dear, I heard you got drunk, professed your love for him, fell off his boat, and then passed out once you were hauled back on board."

"Holy *shit*," said Fiona.

"Mom!" Abe looked horrified.

Daisy leaned forward eagerly. "Where did you hear that?"

"From Gordon York, who talked to Sugar Watson, who knows Zeke Hawkins from the bait shop."

"I'm gonna kill him," said Abe. "He's fired."

"He's actually your employee?" asked Hope. "I thought you were just pals."

"Goddammit, I'll hire him just to fire his ass. He knows that's not what happened."

Hope faced Fiona squarely. The small old woman came off as both sweet and intimidating, just like she had so many years ago. She looked like she was after the truth, and would know if Fiona moved away from it even the smallest bit. Hope said, "So what actually happened?"

Abe said, "Mom—"

Fiona cut him off. "I'll tell you what happened." She couldn't look like more of an idiot, could she? If people believed what they were hearing, she was already well past idiot and into moron. "I took a Dramamine on the boat. I react to them way more than I knew."

Hope nodded, her gaze steady. "After how much alcohol?"

"None."

"Other medications?"

"None."

"I believe you. Go on."

"When I was helping a kid stay *on* the boat, I fell *off*. That's all."

"Did you make a pass at my son?"

"Is making a fool of yourself the same as making a pass?"

"Often," said Hope, who looked like she was trying to hide a smile.

"Then yes, I did."

"How?"

Fiona shoved her hands under her thighs and pretended she was in a dark, quiet room all by herself. Not sitting next to the man who heated her inner core to temperatures that thermometers couldn't read. While his *mother* grilled her. "I might have mentioned something about a crush." She closed her eyes and wished for invisibility.

"Past tense? Or present tense?"

"Mom," said Abe on a groan. "Don't do this."

"It's all right," said Fiona. And strangely, it was. The worst had happened. She'd been on a date with Abe, the single sexiest man alive. The man with the eyes that reminded her of the sky on a clear day. The man who had *kissed* her, for God's sake.

The man who hadn't thought her sexy enough to keep kissing. The man who'd tricked her into a date so he could change her mind on local politics.

So *that* was the worst part. His mother asking super-awkward questions—that was minor in comparison. "The crush is still present tense. I just plan on fixing that." Fiona could feel Abe's tension, as if she were plugged into the same socket he was. She continued, "It's no big deal. Honestly."

"And now you'll date."

"Jesus, Mom. You can't do this to someone. You can't just—"

Hope held up a hand. "And you'll fall in love."

Abe said to Fiona, "I didn't know she'd do this."

Fiona shook her head and addressed Hope. "With all due respect, ma'am, I doubt you're right about that." She was aware that Abe could barely stand to sit next to her, he was about to climb over the back of the seat at any second, just to get away from her.

"You'll have to learn to knit."

"What?"

"If any woman loves my son, she should know how to knit."

Abe put his head down on the table and rocked it back and forth.

"Eliza Carpenter tried to teach me once," said Fiona.

"Oh!" Hope's face betrayed surprise. "That's right. She did. I remember that."

Abe frowned at them. "What...?"

"I'm still not good with my hands when it comes to stuff like that."

Hope said, "That can change. I'll reteach you. Come to my house tomorrow afternoon."

"I have to work—"

"Get that boy who works for you to cover." Her voice brooked no opposition.

"Ma'am—"

"Stop calling me that, please. It's Hope. And tell me how your date went the other night."

Abe half-stood, one hand on the table, making a shooing motion at Fiona. "Mom. You're embarrassing all of us."

Hope ignored Abe and leaned farther forward over the table. "Did he talk to you about the lighthouse?"

"Here, Abe. I'll let you out." Fiona stood and leaned against Daisy's chair. Abe's hand pressed against her waist for balance as he scooted past her and Fiona took a moment to feel it. Even that slight touch, even the most casual...

"I'll pay for breakfast, Mom, but you can finish eating it on your own."

Hope *humphed*. "Ungrateful. See if I knit you a sweater this Christmas."

Pulling crumpled money out of his pocket and tossing it on the table, Abe said, "Did you forget you can't knit anything but gigantic scarves anymore?"

Fiona had been slipping back onto the booth's seat, but she froze. "Don't be rude to your mother."

"Me? She's the one putting us both on the spot!"

"She just cares about the lighthouse," said Fiona, noticing that Daisy was now knitting so fast her needles were a blur. They were drawing attention from all over the restaurant.

"Only because the building reminds her of my father. Just like everything else in this goddamn town." Abe clapped his hand on the back of the booth, sending a plastic *thud* through the vinyl.

"Please," said Hope, desperation in her voice. "The lighthouse is all I have left of my husband. Don't take that from me, Fiona."

Something short and taut snapped inside Fiona, but she stayed standing. "The lighthouse has nothing to do with your husband. And I have a bigger investment in it than either of you ever could."

The words drew Abe up short, and he turned. His eyes were the intense blue of sea glass still wet from the waves. "I understand that you've got emotion tied up in knocking that old thing down, but we do, too. It's worth talking about."

Fiona pulled back her shoulders. "Talk at city council."

Daisy's needles clicked faster as she watched. "Oooh."

He took a step toward her again, the one he'd taken away. Now he was so close. Too close. Fiona could smell that combination of sea-salt and sharp metal coming from him, and she cursed herself for noticing.

"You don't believe in change," she said. "But towns change. They get better, and someone has to make that happen. Don't you see that?"

"I believe in progress," said Abe. "Within reason."

"Do you? Do you think we should have built the city-funded park over on Biddle Road?"

Abe scowled. "That was and remains a terrible idea. They've been putting in the playground for what, seven months? And it's still not done? They should have left it as the oak grove it was."

"And the extension on the library?"

"That library was good enough for us when we were kids, wasn't it? My card still works. Books still stay dry and safe there. It's not like they had a real reason to expand."

Fiona glanced at Hope, whose face gave nothing away. "Room for more books isn't a good enough reason for you?"

"They already have enough room for books. They're adding a conference room and a bigger women's bathroom. We've already got enough meeting rooms in this town, and you're telling me there's some kind of line crisis at the girls' room? I'm not buying it."

Fiona was startled that he knew this. He *did* follow items in the paper, then. That was something. "You're stuck. You think Cypress Hollow should stay the way it's always been."

"Nothing stays the same. But some things are good and should be saved. Should be held on to. Saved."

"Fine," she said, stepping carefully around him. "Bring it to city council."

"If I do..." Abe made it sound like a threat.

Hope spoke to her one more time before she could respond to him. "Come see me tomorrow."

"I won't be able to learn to knit. I already know that." Hope obviously just wanted to talk to her more about the lighthouse. Why would she put herself through that?

"I knew your mother. Before she married your father. Before...Come tomorrow."

Hope was a clever woman.

Damn it.

Fiona looked down at Daisy. "Enjoying the show?"

Daisy dropped the knitting in her lap and clapped. "Do it all *again*."

"You're a terrible friend."

Abe was already striding away out of the diner, his gait sturdy, determined, as though he were walking the deck of his boat in a storm.

CHAPTER NINETEEN

Memories are half of what holds your knitting together.
The other half is tension. — E. C.

A second storm blew in from the south, battering the sides of boats and houseboats that had been spared by the last round. It matched Abe's mood—dark and thunderous.

He'd had to cancel his tours, and they'd been good ones, more than fifteen passengers on each roster. It would have been a sizeable chunk of change to be able to put into his pocket. Instead, he was stuck in the harbormaster's office at the marina, catching up on paperwork he'd been too busy lately to process.

Abe filed yet another barge application and sighed. Damned paperwork. But besides filing licenses and accepting dock fees, the harbormaster's gig was pretty cushy. He didn't have to pay rent for his houseboat mooring, and he could make his own schedule with the whale and fishing trips. Which was good, since he was going to need all the time he could find this week to come up with how to present his idea to city council. He'd already filed the paperwork with the state—the lighthouse could automatically be considered an historic site, because of its age. But because of its current state, it had to be brought up to code before it was protected— something that would take time and, more importantly, money.

He shook his head to clear the thought and stared at the license he was trying to file. Simple numerical order seemed to have fled his brain temporarily.

That kiss...

Just a kiss, right? Just a girl on a beach. There'd been lots of girls on beaches over the years.

But that one...

A soft knock came on the door of the portable trailer.

"It's unlocked!" he yelled, shoving the sheet of paper into the very back of the file folder. Close enough for government work, right?

"Hey there, Tiger."

Abe's head snapped up.

Rayna. She was the only woman to ever call him that, and he had to admit, he'd always loved it. Having *Tiger* breathed into your ear made a man feel like growling in just the right way.

Rayna knew it, too.

"You look good." It had to be said. She did. Her hair, that long, flowing mane, was shiny, like she'd just washed it with the shellac he used on his wooden decking. Her eyes were smoky with something dark that looked like it would come off on her pillow or whatever got too close. She looked like someone on TV, someone pretty and smart and kind. And she *was* all those things. His mother had always said Rayna was the nicest girl who looked like trouble.

"Thanks," she said simply, accepting the compliment as her due.

"This is a surprise," he said, gesturing to the only extra chair in the room, a folding metal one rusting at each foot.

Gracefully, she sat. "I know. I've been meaning to drop by. It was good to see you at the council meeting. I tried to get over to you, but it was so crowded in there..."

But you don't drop by, he thought. Rayna hadn't dropped in on him once, not ever. Not in the years that had passed since she'd broken his heart, run off with another man, settled down and had that man's babies. Not once. After a couple of years, he'd started being cordial to her in public. He waved back at her at the grocery store (ignoring the checkers' whispers), and he'd helped her drag her kayak out of the water one morning, but apart from neighborly encounters, they'd never really talked.

"How's Tommy?"

She smiled, a smile that could haunt a man's dreams. Ask him how he knew. "Busy with the hardware store.

You know how that goes, running your own business. He's always got something up his sleeve."

"And the kids?" He couldn't really care less, but it was what people said.

"They're great. Big now. Little Tom's almost seven, and Ruth's five, if you can believe that."

"Growing up fast." Words, they were just words, just something to fill the air while he waited to hear what she was really here for.

"They do," she said. "Like weeds."

He sat in the desk chair that always rattled and threatened to break underneath him, praying the imminent collapse didn't come today. That would be fun—hitting the dirt in front of the woman who'd thrown him into it once upon a time.

Folding his hands carefully on the desk, he waited.

"I heard you're gunning to save the lighthouse."

"I am."

"That doesn't seem very you," she said.

It shouldn't have, but her inference made him grumpy all over again. Why did people seem to think he couldn't take an interest in civic matters? "I don't appreciate that," he said, opening a cabinet drawer just so he could shove it closed again. "I happen to care more about this town than most people do. I don't want it to change into another Santa Barbara, or something worse."

"Oh, come on, there's little chance of *that* happening," she said. Her voice was teasing. It always had been. "You remember when I cut my hair?"

He stared at her. "You serious?" Like he could forget a fight of that magnitude. He remembered every disagreement they'd ever had. And that one had been a doozy.

"I asked if you'd mind."

"And I said yeah."

She smiled, that sweet crooked smile that used to affect him like a gut punch. Funny, it didn't seem to have the same force anymore. When had that changed?

"And I said screw you."

Abe inclined his head. "Something like that."

"Then I went and chopped off my hair."

"You looked like a boy," said Abe, knowing he shouldn't.

"Damn you, Atwell." But there was no heat in her words. "I looked cute as hell."

She had. With that close crop of shiny hair, she'd looked like a pixie or something. "I remember just being pissed that you didn't look..."

"Like myself."

Abe nodded. How the hell was he suddenly in the middle of a twelve-year-old fight?

"That's your problem right there, Tiger. You can't accept change."

"Why are we rehashing this again?"

"Because I'm worried about you. Worried the old place will get torn down, and you'll be left in the rubble. I'm just concerned. That you're doing this for the right reasons."

He ignored the image of Fiona that flashed into his mind, black cowboy hat smashed against her head, wide hazel eyes.

Rayna continued, "And not just because you're trying to prove a point."

The chair under him groaned as he leaned back, lacing his hands behind his head. "That's really why you're here?" It wasn't. There was something more here. Bigger.

"Yeah." She shrugged. "That's it."

"What's really going on, Rayna?"

She let her head fall backward, lifting her heavy hair over the top of the chair. She took a deep breath, and then she shrugged again. "I don't know."

"Trouble with Tommy?"

Her head snapped back and she stared at him. "Why do you say that?"

You drop by to visit a guy who hasn't existed for you in years. "Just throwing it out there."

She rubbed the skin under her eyes, pushing it upward. "How do people know they're supposed to be together?"

"You're asking *me* that?" He was the one who'd gotten it wrong, after all. "You got married. I've been able to stay firmly committed to my cat. That's about it."

"Have you even dated since we broke up?"

He couldn't help it—he laughed. "You think you turned me into a monk?"

"No...I—"

"I date." *I fuck* was what he meant, and he knew she heard it.

"I know, I didn't mean to imply...I just haven't seen you get serious with anyone. Since...you know. Me."

Abe didn't have to say it out loud. She'd broken his heart into tiny little wave-beaten sand-dollar shards. She knew it better than anyone else. But for once, it didn't hurt like it always had. For years, he'd felt that stab of regret whenever he saw her on the street, a child's hand held in hers, whenever he saw her take a corner in her sturdy, family-sized SUV.

Right now, though, he was picturing Fiona's eyes snapping brown-green at him. "I do okay."

"I know..."

Abe let the silence hang between them. It was hers to fill.

"Tommy...he's been seeing someone else."

"Shit." Abe hadn't seen that coming. "I'm sorry."

"Me, too. I think I might kill him."

"You want help?"

She smiled thinly. "I'll be able to manage it on my own, the way I've been feeling."

"Does he know you know?"

"No. I saw them." She laughed, but it turned into a dry, painful noise.

Abe leaned forward and took her hand. It might have been the first time he'd ever touched her without his heart racing. "You don't need to—"

"I want to. I saw him. I saw Tommy. My *husband*. I'd gone to Half-Moon Bay while the kids were in school. You know that sports shop there? I thought it would be fun if I got him a new tennis racket. He's been so into it lately, and it was his birthday the next week. I stopped at that coffee shop on the corner to get myself a mocha."

With whip, medium hot. He remembered.

"And there he was, in line in front of me. She had her hand tucked in his jacket *pocket*." Her voice broke again. "That's what got me. Her hand in his jacket meant...it meant she was comfortable enough with him to do that. That's not a first date move. That's a been-together-a-while move, you know?"

Abe hoped she didn't expect him to answer her question—he honestly couldn't remember any moves at all.

"I turned and walked out. I waited in my car, hoping he'd see it, recognize it. Freak out. Or maybe he'd just wave at me and then I'd recognize her as someone at the hardware store, and I'd know that I got it all wrong. But then I saw him driving her car, a little, stupid red Miata. He was driving her *car*." Rayna's voice was tired. "That was even worse than the hand in the pocket thing."

Now she was waiting for him to say something and God help him, Abe didn't know what the hell a guy should say in this circumstance. "Like I said, Rayna, I'm really sorry."

"Yeah. You did say that." Her words were dull, just like her eyes.

"I'm just not sure..."

She nodded. "You don't know what I want from you."

He had no freaking idea, actually.

"I don't know either," she said. "I just thought maybe it would make me feel better. Coming here and..."

The light went on, and Abe felt stupid that he hadn't understood it before. Rayna wanted him to still be aching. To still be broken-hearted. Did she expect him to hit on her? For him to be unable to resist? If anyone had asked him two weeks ago, he'd have predicted it would hurt like a barbed hook to the lip for Rayna to come confessing this kind of stuff to him. Instead, he just wanted to do two things: First, to punch Tommy Viera for being such a stupid asshole. And second, to track down Fiona and argue with her some more.

About anything, really.

"I'm going to go." Rayna stood and rubbed her hands against her dark blue dress. It had red stripes. A navy-like dress, a dress girls wore for sailors home on leave. Had she worn it on purpose?

"I'm sorry I bothered you while you're working."

Abe said, "I really wish I could help somehow."

She'd been moving fast toward the door but she stilled and looked at him, fixing him with those pretty chocolate eyes. Those eyes that had always been able to get him to do any damn thing she wanted. "You already have." In two steps, she was in front of him, lifting up on her toes to kiss his cheek. Her lips lingered maybe a second longer than they should have. She smelled the way she always had—the exotic, heady mix of flowers and vanilla that used to send him reeling.

It didn't make him feel that way anymore. In fact, he didn't want her kissing him at all, not even on the cheek.

Behind her, the door opened. Fiona tumbled in out of the rain. Water dripped off her hat, ran down her jacket, pooled around her cowboy boots.

"Oh!" she said.

"No," said Abe.

Rayna took a quick step backward, removing her hand from where she'd had it on Abe's shoulder. "Anyway. I'll see you later, okay?" She gave a warm smile to Fiona. "Bye, Fee. See you at the station." She moved easily around the other woman and was gone, opening her umbrella with one clean shake.

"I won't bother you," said Fiona, turning in place. "I didn't have—oh, crap."

Abe caught her by the elbow. "You're soaked."

She raised an eyebrow. "Master of the obvious."

Abe wanted to open the small window behind her to let the wet salt wind blow the stuffy perfumed air out of the room. But he didn't want to take his hand off her arm. He wanted to wrap her in his arms, but he was worried she'd bolt—she had that frantic look in her eyes, like a fish caught at the end of a line.

"What's up, Snowflake?" He meant it to come out softly. An endearment.

She frowned, though, as if she thought he was teasing her. "Forget it."

"No, what is it?" He moved to step in front of her. "I'm sorry. I was just kidding. Jesus, Fee." He shoved his hand through his hair. "I'm so glad you're here, I can't even tell you."

Fiona swiped at a rivulet that ran from her neck right into her cleavage. Rain dripped from her long metal earring to her shoulder.

He wanted to help her dry off.

"I'm sorry to interrupt. I'm on my way to your mother's house, and I just wanted to know..." She trailed off, looking at her wet hands stretched out in front of her. "I'm a grease monkey, aren't I? I should have at least showered. I can't ever get it from under my nails..."

As gently as he could, he said, "What did you want to know?"

"I wanted to know if there was a particular treat I could bring her, but I feel terrible—awkward. I'm so sorry, interrupting you and Rayna—"

"There's nothing going on."

"But—"

Abe touched her chin and tilted Fiona's head up. "I promise you, Snowflake. Nothing's going on with me and Rayna."

A tiny smile lit her face. "Oh." The smile got a fraction wider. "Anyway, I'll figure it out myself. I'll see you." And she was gone, a light click as the door closed behind her.

"Shit." Abe sunk back into his chair and rubbed his temples. He felt like he didn't know much right now, but

he knew this: Fiona was the cutest damn grease monkey
he'd ever seen.

CHAPTER TWENTY

Breath by breath. – E. C.

F iona sat in the kitchen where Abe had been raised. This was the home he'd shared with his parents, and for a while, with his baby sister. There weren't any photos up on the walls, Fiona noticed, or at least not in the normal places. From the kitchen she could see into the living room—there were only paintings of old boats on the walls. Nothing hung in the hallway at the entrance. In the kitchen there was just a calendar from the local SPCA. Fiona had the same one hanging on her wall at home.

No baby pictures of Abe or Marina, at which Fiona felt strangely disappointed as she clutched her teacup and waited for Hope to come back to the room. She'd said she'd be right back, but she'd been gone at least five minutes now. Long enough for Fiona to get truly nervous.

Of course Rayna had been at Abe's office. Why had Fiona even been surprised? Rayna and Abe had been an item for so long—how did you change that? Did a relationship like that really ever stop?

Even though he'd said it had?

"Here I am," said Hope, coming back into the kitchen with a large canvas bag in her hands. It was chock-full of gorgeously colored skeins of yarn. Hope tipped the bag, and yarn balls covered the top of the table, as many rolling and jumping to the floor as stayed on the tabletop.

"Oh, let me get those..."

"Leave them, dear. Unless you like the color."

"But the floor..."

"They're from sheep. This stuff has seen worse than my kitchen tiles. All wool can be washed."

Hope sat carefully, slowly, as though she might do it wrong if she weren't careful. She pushed back the gray hair that fluffed around her face. "Now," she said, "where should we start? What color are you drawn to?"

"I get to choose?" Fiona had overheard enough impromptu knitting lessons at the station that she knew most new knitters didn't get much of a choice. "Aren't I supposed to choose something smooth and light-colored? Gray, or white, or something boring?"

Hope shook her head. "Whatever you like best is the right color."

Oh, that wasn't hard, then. Fiona reached past a small heap of green balls to grasp the red one, the one flecked with yellow and orange.

"Good choice. Here, let me." Hope did something with the yarn, her fingers fumbling a bit. In less than two minutes, there were stitches lined up on a wooden needle. Hope leaned sideways. "I did the first two rows because they're the hardest to learn. Now I'll show you the basic move."

"Isn't that cheating?"

"Remember when Eliza taught you? Out on the bench at the lighthouse?"

They were going to talk about it, then. Damn it.

"Not really," said Fiona.

"Eliza Carpenter always said it wasn't fair to start a beginner out with a row that could make her fail. I'll teach you how to cast on later, when you're good at the basic knit stitch."

Well, *that* would probably be never. Fiona watched Hope's hands, her knuckles wide, the skin reddened. Her fingers moved slowly, as if they ached.

"Do your hands hurt?" Fiona couldn't help asking.

"Yes," said Hope quietly. "But it's all right."

"No, no." Fiona leaned forward and put her hand on top of Hope's cold fingers. "It's not. I don't need to learn this. I've gone my whole life in Cypress Hollow without learning."

"You *need* to learn." Hope's eyes met hers with startling intensity. Fiona could see where her son got that crystalline shade of blue. "I want to do this. Let me."

Fiona gave up. "Okay. Show me."

An hour later, Fiona had made a horrible-looking tiny cape. She held up her needles. "It would fit a mouse. One of the three blind ones, maybe."

"It's lovely." Hope smiled at her lap, where her hands awkwardly held her own enormous needles.

"It's not. It's awful." Could Fiona go soon? Would it be rude? The yarn didn't feel right in her fingers, and yet another stitch disappeared under her manipulation. "Shit." Fiona sucked in a breath. "Sorry."

"I was married to a sailor," was all Hope said.

How did you know my mother? Fiona let the words tumble around unsaid in her mouth for another minute. Maybe she could hold on to them for long enough to make them sound less desperate. If she spoke them now, Hope would hear the aching need in Fiona's voice, and that wouldn't do. Not at all.

"I don't even know what happened to that stitch," said Fiona in disgust. "I can't catch them like you do." She passed the knitting over to Hope again, who dug around inside the rat's nest she'd made and pulled the loop back up onto the needle. "Thank you."

"You're welcome." Hope picked up her own work. "Breath by breath. That's what Eliza would always say. You just do it breath by breath."

A clock on the wall, too fast by two hours, ticked loudly. A pipe creaked in another room.

Hope continued, "I think it applies to a lot of things, don't you?"

As another stitch committed yarn suicide, Fiona blew out her breath in frustration. She let the whole mess drop into her lap. "How did you know my mother?"

Hope smiled without looking up, as if she'd been expecting the question. "She was in my class."

Fiona struggled to do the math. Her mother had gotten pregnant very young, too young...

"Beatrice was in the first English class I ever taught. We were only about ten years apart, she and I."

Beatrice. No one ever called her mother that. She'd been Bunny to everyone. Fiona tilted her head. "I never knew that." Bunny, at thirteen—what a thought. "What was she like?"

"I taught her to knit."

"No way." The mother she'd known was only crafty about two things: her drawing, and disguising vodka in soda cans.

Hope laughed. "She did it for extra credit, which she desperately needed. She stayed after school every day for a week. I just wanted an excuse to be with her, to try to help." She blinked several times before going on. "I wasn't any good at my job yet, and she knew it as well as I did. We went some rounds in the classroom that I'm not proud of. And I could lie and tell you that the knitting straightened her out for a time, that it helped calm her down, but I think you'd guess that wasn't true. Knitting made her furious with frustration."

Fiona bit the inside of her mouth. Bunny had liked instant gratification in all things. Of course she'd hated knitting. A stitch sailed sideways. "*Damn* it."

Hope reached for Fiona's knitting again. She caught the errant stitch again and passed the work back. "I remember how your mother moved. Like there was something sparking under her skin, something that itched, as if she was allergic to air, or water."

That was exactly it. Bunny had never been still for a moment. "She couldn't even watch television. A sitcom was too long for her."

"Did you know your mother had been abused by a family member?"

Those words didn't make sense. "I don't know what you're talking about." Fiona's grandparents had both died before she was born—she'd never known any relatives on her mother's side.

"An uncle of hers. Your great-uncle. He molested her. For years."

The words were tiny detonations—awful explosions that took Fiona long seconds to work through. She sat straighter, as if that would help her understand. "Why are you telling me this?"

"It's good to know where you come from," Hope said and made another clumsy stitch with her swollen fingers.

"So I come from trash? You're trying to say I'm not good enough for your son?" Fear that felt like anger started to burn at the ends of Fiona's fingertips, and she watched the immobile yarn to see if it had started to smolder.

"No! Not at all." Hope looked as upset as Fiona felt, her face pale. She dropped her knitting and held the edge of the table. "I'm saying your mother didn't choose to be the way she was. She was hurt by someone. She never recovered."

Fiona hated that tears were filling her eyes. "Why didn't she tell me, then? She told me everything else. She talked non-stop. She never thought to mention she was *molested*?"

And did Bunny get to blame everything on that? Is that why she drank? Why she had left? No matter how horrible the fact that she had been abused was, it didn't excuse leaving your child behind. Or did it?

"Do you remember when I came to see you at the lighthouse? When Eliza Carpenter and I came?"

Fiona frowned. Of course she did. They'd separated them—Mrs. Atwell going with Fiona's father, Eliza Carpenter taking Fiona outside to the bench that overlooked the ocean. She'd tried to teach her to knit.

Her mother was already gone.

"You know what I'm talking about, don't you?"

"Bunny didn't do anything to me."

Hope's fingers stilled. "Do you believe that?"

"My father took care of me."

"Your father couldn't protect you from her. You couldn't hide the black eye. And it was my job as your teacher to protect you. I'd failed your mother—I didn't want to fail you, too."

That had been such an awful time. The police report, the interviews...The detective involved had told her that when her mother came back, she'd have to appear in court for sentencing.

She'd never come back, though. Her father knew where she was, Fiona knew he did. But she'd never asked him. And never would.

Fiona stood, the knitting falling to her feet and bouncing under the table. "This is..." She couldn't find the word she needed.

"I'm sorry," Hope said.

As Hope looked at her, her eyes also filled with tears, Fiona could tell she *was* sorry. And that just made it worse.

Breath by breath.

"Thank you for the knitting lesson." Manners. Her mother had always said that manners were important.

Then she fled.

CHAPTER TWENTY-ONE

Sometimes the sweater you think you'll never wear turns out to be the most flattering one you'll ever have. A best friend, like the best pattern, is not always recognized instantly. – E. C.

"Do something," said Fiona, settling herself in Daisy's chair at the salon.

"I can't believe you're letting me touch your hair." Daisy used the hand-pump Fiona had installed three years earlier, the one that raised and lowered the cutting chair, bringing Fiona down to Daisy's chair level.

"Let's not talk about it. Just do *something*."

"Oh, I will. Believe me. I can find the shape your hair wants to be..." Daisy lifted a lock and let it drop again. "...somewhere under this rat's nest." She lowered the chair so that it dropped into the recess Fiona had built when she installed the lift. Now Daisy was seated higher than Fiona.

"Just because I cut it myself doesn't mean I do a bad job of it. I like to change it around. Never the same thing twice."

"Darling, I cut my own, so I agree." Daisy smiled at herself in the mirror and tucked a long blonde curl behind her ear.

"You don't get Fabio to do it?"

Fabio was the hair stylist who rented space from Daisy. He was short, round, and bald. He couldn't have been further in looks from a romance-cover hero, and no one could remember where he'd gotten his nickname anymore.

Daisy whispered, "No. He's good. But come on." Daisy looked at herself in the mirror, again. "I'm vain enough to know what I want. But you, honey? Are you using the metal snips from the garage again?" She tugged a lock of Fiona's hair.

"Just once, and that's only because Stephen was using my good scissors for one of his projects..."

Daisy sighed heavily. "It's a good thing I could fit you in. It's a crazy day, what with the..." She paused, and Fiona closed her eyes, hoping she wouldn't guess the real reason she was there.

"Oh!" Daisy froze. "This is for the Cowboy Ball tomorrow night! *That's* why you're here."

"No."

"Oh, *yes* it is."

Fiona groaned. "I saw Mayor Finley at the station. She said it would be a good place to talk up the park proposal, maybe get some of the council members on my side early."

"No way. You're not going for politics. You're going for Abe."

"Didn't you witness our little spat at Tillie's? You really think I want to see him?"

Daisy lowered Fiona's chair another notch. "That was a spat? Because it sounded like foreplay to me."
Fiona bit her lip. There wasn't much to say to that, she supposed.

"Okay. A swan's haircut." Daisy sprayed water on the back of her head, sending a chill down Fiona's spine.

Fiona froze. "What?"

Daisy laughed. "I'm teasing. You know, duckling to swan? For the ball?"

"Hey, you know what, I should probably get back to the shop, Stephen had a thing..." Fiona reached behind her to undo the black cape Daisy had affixed around her neck.

Daisy looked horrified. "Oh, honey, I'm so sorry. I was only teasing."

Bunny sat on the back steps of the lighthouse, her cigarette a raw red glow against the night sky. The foghorn mourned half a mile away. The talent show was the next day, and Fiona danced down the steps to show off the green dress she'd borrowed from Traci to wear for their "On the Good Ship Lollipop" song. For once, she wasn't wearing an old thrifted t-shirt and too-big jeans. The ruffle of the dress flounced at her knee. The bodice, a collection of green ribbons, made her feel like a princess. Fiona felt thrillingly beautiful. Like her mother. "Mommy, look! Look at me!" *Bunny had taken a long drag of her cigarette and tilted her head to one side. Her cat eyes went to slits.*

"You're like the ugly duckling who just won't grow up."

Now, in Daisy's chair, Fiona struggled to breathe. It wasn't bad to be the ugly duckling. It just was what it was. Daisy was pretty. Tabitha, Daisy's daughter, was pretty. Rayna Viera was pretty. Some people started out that way. Others got that way later...if they were lucky.

Fiona looked in the mirror. Her hair was slicked back with water, and her face was pale. Her lips had lost their color, almost disappearing against her skin. Her eyes watered.

"This was a silly idea."

"No, no." Daisy touched her upper arm. "I'm sorry. You're gorgeous, my friend. I was only teasing you about your homemade haircut. I shouldn't have. I know better than that."

Gorgeous. That's what friends did for each other. They lied. Fiona leaned back in the chair and shut her eyes. No matter what, her hair could use a trim, and Daisy would undoubtedly do it better than she would herself in the too-dark bathroom at the shop.

"Give me a blue streak."

"What?"

You talk a blue streak but you manage not to say anything. Once Bunny had slapped her so hard for talking out of turn she'd had to stay home from school for a week because of the bruise on her cheek. "Bright blue."

Daisy nodded. "You got it. I'll go mix it up now."

An hour later, Fiona woke in the chair with a start. From behind her, Daisy laughed. "Good morning, Sleeping Beauty."

"Are we going to flip through all the Disney princesses today?"

Daisy whispered, "Look who's in Fabio's chair."

Fiona looked. "Oh, crap."

Two chairs down, Abe was sitting bolt-upright, the same kind of black cape around his neck. He looked as uncomfortable as she felt. His eyes were screwed shut as Fabio combed his hair straight.

"He looks about five years old, right? He comes in every six weeks, sits there for half-an-hour and then bolts out."

Fiona hoped desperately that the noise of the dryers covered their lowered voices. "Did you *plan* this?"

"How could I have done that? I didn't even know *you* were coming in this morning."

"But you knew he might show up," Fiona hissed.

"As much as I know that anyone in town might choose to drop in. I'm not psychic."

"Sorry." Fiona tried to tear her eyes from Abe, but for a long moment she couldn't look away. His legs were splayed in the chair, but there was tension in his face, a kind of tightness. What was he thinking about? Fiona's heart dropped. Had he seen her? Of course he had. She'd been asleep in Daisy's chair when he arrived. So not only had he seen her, but he'd seen her looking her absolute worst.

Awesome.

"Are you almost done?" Fiona pulled again at the neck of the cape.

Daisy hung up the blow dryer. "Totally done. And guess what?" She spun the chair so that instead of facing Abe, Fiona faced the mirror.

She barely recognized herself.

"*What...?*"

"Right? Who *is* that gorgeous woman?"

Fiona's dark hair hung in long, soft waves, the kind she could never seem to get by just towel-drying her hair. And just above her right eye started a long, brilliant blue streak that ran to the very tip of the thick strand. Her eyes, usually so muddy, were bright green next to the blue. She looked like someone else, someone edgy and punk, someone interesting. She looked...almost pretty.

Okay. Maybe actually pretty.

Fiona leaned forward and turned her head. "I don't know how you did that."

"It's a good cut. Thank the magic of my talented scissors." Daisy clicked them between her fingers. "And that blue is perfectly you. It's heavenly. No clue why I didn't think of that first."

Fiona glanced over her shoulder. Had Abe...

No. His eyes were still closed, but the tension in his shoulders showed that he was keeping them closed intentionally. No one could sit like that and actually be asleep.

Man, he was gorgeous, though. Fiona let her eyes rest on the long plane of his cheekbone. From here she couldn't quite see his eyelashes but she knew they were there, curling against his cheek, something that should have made him look less manly but instead just highlighted his masculinity, his harder edges.

And then, as if he felt her looking at him, his eyes opened. He looked directly at her, and he didn't look surprised.

Fiona gasped.

Abe's lips twisted into a smile that was for her. Only for her.

Daisy undid the cape and Fiona spun in her chair, digging her hand into her back pocket for her wallet. "How much?"

"As if I'd charge you."

"This is why I don't come to you. You have to let me pay." Fiona was saying the words by rote. She wasn't listening to herself or, for that matter, to Daisy. She could only pay attention to the way Abe's gaze felt on the back of her neck. She had chills. As if he'd reached out and touched her, run his finger along the length of the blue streak that now flashed at the side of her vision.

"No money. I have a dent in my van's side door, though..."

That got Fiona's attention. "You do? Why didn't you tell me?"

"Because you'd insist on fixing it without letting *me* pay."

Fiona smiled. "I hear you. Swap?"

Daisy shook the hand Fiona held out. "Swap."

Fiona leaned forward and whispered in Daisy's ear, "I'm going to run away now."

"You've been spotted, you know."

"That's the problem."

"At least say hello to him."

Fiona exhaled. "Do I have to?"

"No. But you might want to look in the mirror again before you make that decision. Because you look amazing."

She had a point. Fiona wasn't going to look this good again for a long time—there was no way she'd be able to make her hair do whatever it was Daisy had whispered it into doing.

The few steps it took to cross the salon felt like a mile. Abe didn't blink. He still had that smile, that inward one. Fiona imagined, just for a second, what he would do if she just straddled his lap. If she draped one leg over each of his, and wrapped her arms around his neck, lowering her head to kiss him. Hard.

Breathe.

"Hi," she said. Her voice was scratchy.

"Hi yourself," he rumbled.

"Okay. That's all I wanted to say."

"You going to the ball tomorrow night?"

Fiona nodded. "I guess I have to. That's what the mayor said, anyway."

"Yeah. She told me the same thing."

"Oh."

He cast a glance at Fabio, who was still dragging the comb through Abe's hair. "Can I have a minute?"

Fabio tucked the comb in his shirt front and said in an aggrieved voice, "It'll dry wrong, but I guess you don't care about that."

"Thanks." Abe waited until Fabio had gone to the sink before he continued. "Will you go with me?"

"Where?" Fiona had lost track of the conversation. Had the pretty she'd seen in Daisy's mirror worn off yet?

Abe smiled again and Fiona's stomach flipped. "To the ball. With me."

For one moment, Fiona felt like a princess. "Oh. Floop. Yesh."

"Yesh?"

Fiona blinked hard. "I mean yes. Of course. Yes." *Not too eager.* "Are you sure?" *Gah.* "I don't mean that. I mean, sure." She felt herself color. "I'm going to stop talking now."

"But I like seeing you confused like this." His eyes danced.

Fiona couldn't help grinning. "Okay. See you tomorrow, then."

"Pick you up at eight?"

"Good. Fine. Good. Um, fine."

"See you then." He looked amused, which was natural. She was acting like a freak. A complete idiot. Fiona turned, conscious that his eyes were still on her. As she left the shop, she waved at Daisy with one hand. With the other hand, she tapped out on her cell phone a desperate text. "Dress needed. ASAP. 911!"

Within seconds, Daisy's text came back. "Already got you covered."

CHAPTER TWENTY-TWO

Sometimes a woman likes her wool
with a little shine to it. – E. C.

The problems Abe had with the Cowboy Ball
were the same problems he'd always had with
the damn thing. Too many people. Too much
dancing. Too much idle chit-chat at the edges of the
room, gossip flying with the speed of a pissed-off harbor
seal. The ball was a tradition now, started dozens of
years ago by the cowboys who worked on the ranches at
the outskirts of town. They'd wanted their own party,
always held in a local barn, one where they didn't have to
get too gussied up. One where they could wear their best
western shirt and jeans and, after shining their boots,
could call it good.

In the forties and fifties, the ball had become Cypress Hollow's biggest dance, drawing all the belles of town out into the arms of handsome, hard-working cowboys. It had been the catalyst for many marriages and more than one divorce. But as the ranches merged and folded, the ball had become less and less important, until the tradition had almost died. A few years ago, Mayor Finley had decided it was too good a tradition to let go, and had proposed that the city boost it. She'd pushed press at the dance, to the point that national magazines had done pieces touting Cypress Hollow's Good Old Downhome Cowboy Ball.

So this dance, instead of being what he remembered—a dusty, sleepy gathering with a bluegrass band and a caller half-drunk on whiskey before the first dance—was a big damn *event.*

The barn used this year was on the MacArthur property. Cade MacArthur had rented a big wedding tent—not for the party, but to house his horses and sheep for a few nights. After mucking and scrubbing, his everyday barn was now clean-smelling and empty of everything but decorations and people ready to dance.

The city had paid for the decorations, and Abe had to admit, the barn did look great. The only source of lighting was myriad white, twinkling strings of lights. Strands were strung over every rafter, along each beam. Someone on the decorating committee had come up with the idea of sticking bare trees in wine barrels, lacing the lights through the skeletal branches. If Abe had been asked, he'd have guessed that was a bad idea, but he would have been wrong. It looked like a magical wooded forest in that damn barn, not that he was going to tell anyone about that thought.

Well, maybe he'd tell Fiona. If she asked.

She wasn't talking much, actually, which was making him nervous. Hell, he felt like a teenager, raging hormones and all. But even though he'd lost his breath at the sight of her in that blue dress, which practically sparkled like the night sky, he'd managed to say, "You look nice."

You look nice. That was the very outer edge of what he should have said. What he'd thought was, *How the hell do I keep from pulling that dress off your body right here in front of everyone?* Instead, he'd told her she looked nice.

She'd smiled, though, her hazel eyes that danced between brown and green, the exact way the ocean did after a storm kicked up the sand from the depths.

When they'd arrived at the dance, Fiona had looked nervous. She met his eyes, just for a second. "I've never been to one of these."

"You're kidding? You're from here. How did you get away with that?"

She held out her arms. "I'm wearing my normal cowboy boots! Do I look like the kind of girl that goes to a ball?"

He laughed. She looked down at the delicate dress and her black boots, which she'd obviously shined to a high gloss. "Oh," she said. "I guess I do."

"You do," he'd said. The blue of her dress was the exact blue of that damned streak in her hair, the streak that was driving him wild. He wanted to catch it between his fingers and tug it, pull on that lock until she brought her lips to his again, like she had in the caves.

But she was treating him like a friend. Sweet smiles when he managed to catch her eye, which wasn't often. How was he going to get through tonight? All Abe could think about was taking her out of this barn and back to her house, where he'd walk her through that little garden and right up to her door. And then he'd kiss the hell out of her.

He hadn't gone beyond that in his head. If he did, he'd get so hard he'd have to hide behind one of those lighted trees until he calmed down.

"Punch?" he said.

Fiona socked him in the arm and then laughed.

Surprised, he rubbed his bicep. "Hey. You're stronger than you think, you know."

She shook her head, and the blue streak fell over her eye. "Nah. I know how strong I am."

Tonight's earrings were from a Lexus, she'd told him. Cotter pins and something that looked like a piece off a broken mirror—they flashed and twisted in the dimness as she moved, reflecting the sparkling white lights back at him.

"What I meant was, would you like some punch?"

She grinned again. "Yes, please. And spike it." He left her standing there in the dimness, next to a bale of hay almost as big as she was, and he wondered if she were a figment of his imagination. Would she still be there when he got back? Could he be that lucky?

If he *could* get that lucky, what had he done to deserve it? And could he do it some more? To keep her close, a little while longer?

"Abe Atwell!" said Phil Jenkins, glittering in a sequin-covered western shirt. "Glad you're here, son. How's the prep going for the council meeting? I hear you're gonna try and talk us into saving the old lady of the shore."

Abe glanced over his shoulder at Fiona. "Prepping as hard as I can, sir."

CHAPTER TWENTY-THREE

There's nothing wrong with forgetting which way you were going when you put the knitting down. You'll learn to read where you are, and to know that the working yarn is attached to the right-hand needle. Until then, just knit on. — E. C.

R ayna Viera had to be the prettiest girl to ever live in Cypress Hollow, Fiona decided. Tonight she was wearing a yellow gingham dress with red crinolines that flashed as she danced with her husband, Tommy. No one else could get away with that, though several girls were trying. Whitney from the bakery came close, with her blue square dancing dress cut low and tight. Her husband Silas couldn't keep his eyes off her. And Trixie Fletcher looked like Cyd Charise, though her dance partner, Royal Berring, looked more like Fred Armisen than Fred Astaire.

But Whitney and Trixie both looked like they were wearing costumes, and Fiona understood exactly what that felt like. They'd dressed up for the Cowboy Ball in clothes they probably wouldn't wear to the grocery store.

But Rayna? She could prance out of here in that yellow gingham and carry it off while ordering salmon at Gertie's Fish Market, Fiona reckoned. Her hair—that gorgeous hair flowing like mahogany-colored silk—was styled exactly the way Daisy had styled Fiona's yesterday. The long, beautiful waves moved the way Rayna did: gracefully.

Fiona hadn't even tried to get her hair to go the way it had the day before. She might have been able to figure it out with some time and a curling iron, but it felt like...trying too hard. She'd refused Daisy's offer to stay and do it for her after she'd dropped off the loaner dress. Fiona had straight locks instead of waves, and she knew the back of it probably looked like a pile of scrap metal, since she'd merely brushed it. Her eyes felt heavy with the makeup she'd applied, and she wondered how long the mascara would stay on before it started running down her cheeks. What if she sweated? Would it come off faster?

Jeesh. Fiona liked—no, *loved*—making other things look good. Just not herself. It just wasn't worth the effort. Not even on a night like tonight.

She watched as Rayna approached Abe. She greeted him with a kiss, of course. Why wouldn't she? She probably even smelled better than Fiona did. Fiona had forgotten to put on the one brand of perfume she had, and instead had to hope that her deodorant was floral enough to smell good.

Fiona wasn't exactly jealous—that wasn't quite it.

Instead, she was disappointed that she didn't clean up as well herself. She was disappointed that this blue dress, so prettily tailored to look like it was from the forties, sweetheart neckline, narrow waist and all, didn't quite fit in the bust because she didn't have enough to fill it. If Rayna had put it on? Or Daisy, who owned it? Either of them would have filled it out to the point where they could stop a train.

Fiona wouldn't even stop a bicycle. People swooped by her on their way to the makeshift dance floor or to get another drink without even noticing her, blue streak in her hair or not.

She took a deep breath. She was used to being the grease monkey, the girl who wasn't seen as a girl.

But that didn't stop it from hurting anyway.

Next to the drinks station, Abe said something that made Rayna laugh and then, with a quick touch to the pretty girl's shoulder, he headed back to Fiona.

"You could have talked to her longer," said Fiona. "I wouldn't mind." She wouldn't have, either. It would have given her more of a chance to watch the way they communicated. The way Rayna flirted. So naturally. To women like her, flirting was like breathing. Did they come out of the womb like that? Winking at the doctor and giving perfect little coos to the nurses? Probably.

Fiona knew from her father that she'd come out screaming and, due to a nasty case of colic, hadn't stopped for the first six months.

"But I want to talk to you," said Abe.

"Why?"

Abe blinked.

"I don't mean to put you on the spot. But why do you want to talk to me?" Fiona was curious to know what he'd say.

"I think I'm supposed to talk you out of presenting your tear-down-my-lighthouse idea," he said. "But I haven't done a good job convincing you yet. I've got to work harder, I guess. I keep looking at you in that dress and forgetting to do it."

Fiona opened her mouth to answer, but Abe continued quickly, "Why do *you* want to talk to *me*?"

It was too late to pretend anything around him. Too late to lie about anything. "Because I've had a crush on you for years."

"But why? I don't think you ever told me."

Fiona felt a thump in her chest that she couldn't attribute to Peggy Murphy whacking away up there on her stand-up bass. "I don't really know."

"So from not knowing me at all, you start to like me."

"Yep." Fiona prayed for an earthquake. A tidal wave would do, too. Just something to stop this conversation, which had spun completely out of her control. "Want to dance?"

"In a minute. I just want to know one more thing...How am I measuring up?" Abe tugged on his ear and looked like he was totally serious. "You had a crush on a guy you didn't know, and I'm not sure I'm good enough to warrant it."

How was he measuring up? In that black shirt, which did nothing to hide the width of his chest, with that silly blue bolo, which just happened to match her dress exactly? With that smile, which could power a million of the little strands of lights hanging inside the barn? With that bright, unnerving spark his eyes flashed at her? "You're doing just fine," Fiona said.

Abe reached out and touched her cheek, surprising her. His touch was light. A caress.

It was exactly what she'd wanted all night.

"Okay," he said.

"Okay, what?" Fiona shifted from one foot to the other.

"Okay, let's dance."

The band was playing a lively two-step when they took the floor, but the song ended as soon as Fiona put her hand in Abe's. They laughed, Fiona feeling bubbles of nervousness play along her veins as though her blood was carbonated. They waited.

A waltz was next. Good. At least Fiona knew how to dance this one.

And so, it turned out, did Abe. He pulled her against him as they both took a breath. Abe whispered in her ear, "One, two, and *one*, two, three."

The way he led made her feel like she was flying. They didn't talk, neither of them counting steps after that initial pairing of limbs—they just whirled around the floor, staying to the inside of the swirling mass of bodies. The older dancers and the more unsure ones, the ones who were tromping on their partners' toes every few measures, stayed to the outside. But five or six couples, of which they were one, danced in the middle, gliding past each other, twirling and spinning, parting and coming back together.

Fiona trusted him completely. When Abe stepped back, pushing her into a spin, she kept the beat with her feet, and then at the end of the measure she was in his arms again, as if she'd never left.

She could have danced like that all night.

When the song ended, she automatically dipped into a curtsey, and he matched it with a bow. "Thank you, pretty lady," he said.

"You're welcome," Fiona stammered. Was that just something he would have said at the end of a dance with anyone, no matter what?

Rayna Viera glided up behind him and tapped him on the shoulder. "Dance, Abe? For old times' sakes? You don't mind, do you, Fiona? I know you have to dance with the one what brung ya, but Tommy's had one drink too many, and I'd love to two-step with this guy."

"Of course I don't mind." A polite and unavoidable lie.

They spun away. Rayna probably felt like she was flying, too.

"That was amazing," said a voice at her elbow.

"Daisy! There you are!"

Daisy, dolled up in a dress that was made of approximately three blue silk flounces, looked for all the world like she'd stepped out of the thirties. The bodice of the dress was perfect, and suited her figure wonderfully. Her blonde hair was in slick finger-waves and her makeup was applied so she looked big-eyed and pale, with perfect red lips.

"You look insanely awesome," said Fiona with wonder.

Daisy patted her curls with satisfaction. "I worked hard at it."

"Who are you going for tonight?"

"Why would you ask that?" Daisy countered, moving her chair coyly to the right and then the left.

"Because I know you."

Daisy leaned forward and tugged at Fiona's arm until she came down into a crouch. "You know that guy Zeke, the one who works for Abe sometimes?"

"Sure."

"I've decided I think he's cute."

"Careful. He seems like such a nice boy."

"And?" Daisy's thin eyebrows danced upward.

"You're a man-eater."

"I'm *not*."

"You are! Name me one guy you've dated for more than six months."

"I...well. Okay, you name *me* one, missy!"

"Touché," Fiona said, rocking back on her heels. "At least I keep all my exes as friends."

"That's because that's the way they all start out."

Fiona hit her own chest with the flat of her hand. "Here. Right here is where you wound me."

"Oh, stop." Daisy craned her neck to look around her. "See, there he is." Zeke was on the far side of the dancers, moving slowly and awkwardly around the floor with a woman old enough to be his mother.

There was no grace to his lumbering and even from a distance, Fiona could see the wincing of his partner every time he stepped on her toe.

"Hmmm," said Daisy. "You think he's always that clumsy?"

"Ex-linebacker on a dance floor? Yes. Probably."

"But that also means he's *fast*. And *accurate*."

"Sexy words, from you," teased Fiona.

Daisy laughed. "Words that get me hot. I love accuracy. If a guy talks about his budget on a date?" Daisy leaned farther forward. "I get wet."

Even incapacitated by giggles, Fiona still knew exactly where Abe and Rayna were on the floor. *Abe and Rayna.* Their names still went together. They did a move where Rayna spun away from him and then kept spinning until she reached out a hand and he caught it, wrapping her up in his arms. They'd obviously done that move a hundred times, and they looked more graceful than Fiona had ever felt in her life.

"You kind of look like her."

"What?" Fiona was startled. "Like who?"

Daisy rolled a few more centimeters forward. "Like Rayna. Yeah. I didn't see it until this new haircut."

"No way."

"I can see it."

"Just the hair then, and I couldn't get it to go the way you had it yesterday anyway."

"No, it's more than that. You have the same body style."

Fiona glanced down at the unfilled portion of her dress. "Are you kidding me? Do you *see* her boobs?"

"Besides that, you're the same frame. Same coloring."

"You're telling me I'm a washed-out version of Rayna Viera. Thanks." Maybe that was it exactly. Maybe *that* was why Abe was so interested in her suddenly—he'd seen a woman who reminded him of his fantasy.

"Of course not. You're more vibrant and gorgeous than she could ever be. She's got that married-with-three-kids look."

"Well, that looks good on her then. She looks amazing. What look do I have? The oil-under-my-fingernails look?"

"You have the I-could-give-you-a-reason-to-stay-up-all-night look."

"Huh." Fiona crossed her arms over her chest. Flat-chested women could do that, at least. "I don't think I give off that vibe."

"On a normal day you don't, agreed. But as soon as you see that man? You start to hum like a telephone line, girl. You're smoldering."

Fiona didn't believe Daisy, but it was still nice to hear. *Smoldering.* Rayna didn't smolder. Rayna was the All-American girl next door with big boobs. She was warm. Abe's face was happy right now, dancing with her.

But when Abe looked at Rayna, he didn't look...bothered. When Fiona and Abe had danced together, there'd been tension between them, a trembling tautness that collapsed and grew every time they touched. As she watched Rayna and Abe spin by, she saw comfort. Familiarity.

Well, everyone liked familiarity.

Did Abe like *that* in Fiona? With her hair blown out and makeup, Fiona felt like a copy of Rayna, with less color. Except that blue streak, which she was almost regretting now that all the old ranchers in the room were staring. She'd overheard one saying, "You think she did that to her hair on purpose?"

The future Fiona, the one she wasn't yet but *would* be, that Fiona was good at this flirting thing. That Fiona believed she was pretty even when she didn't feel like it. That Fiona didn't feel like a fake.

Fiona had never been scared of the future. She closed her eyes and concentrated. When she opened them, she would *be* the future Fiona.

That's what she told herself, anyway, but part of her was listening to the old version of herself. That version was way more convincing.

CHAPTER TWENTY-FOUR

A party can't start until the knitters arrive. — E. C.

Abe had never been in this position before. Having Rayna in his arms always felt good. The two of them fit. He wondered if it was possible that bodies could actually remember other bodies—if they danced so well because they'd done it so many times before. It had to be, even though it had been too many years to count since they'd worn a groove on an old wooden floor.

He'd been mad at her so long that it shocked him to find that dancing with her was fun.

It was sweet.

And it was in *no* way as sexy as Rayna apparently thought it was. The way she was sighing whenever he held her was making his ear itch. And she was pressing herself way too close to him, as if she was paint and he was the wall. Now, if Fiona had chosen to press herself that tightly to him, he couldn't have been held responsible for what she would feel pressing back. But with Rayna...it was just old times. And not necessarily times he cared to revisit.

At the end of the dance, he bowed. "Thanks, Rayna."

She nodded and kissed his cheek—damn, she was kissing his cheek a lot lately. "We always did have chemistry, Tiger."

Chemistry? Was that what this boredom was? He doubted it but smiled at her anyway, trying not to give away the fact that he was having a hard time not searching out Fiona, not letting himself stare at the woman with the electric blue hair and hazel eyes that sparked heat.

Fiona could melt an anchor with one of the looks she was shooting him. He was trying to go slow with her, trying not to scare her off. There was no way he'd tell her any time soon how much he was thinking about her, how freaking hot she looked standing there next to Daisy. No woman wanted to deal with that kind of intensity, did they? Not from a man they barely knew.

He couldn't explain where these feelings were coming from, anyway. Better to just keep them bottled up. He knew how to do that. Abe was an expert at that.

He left the dance floor before the next song started, leaving Rayna looking disappointed, but what was he supposed to do? Keep dancing with her? He didn't want to. Not when Fiona was right there, partnerless. He caught Fiona's eye and his heart did some weird, fish-flopping motion in his chest. He mimed lifting a drink to his mouth and then pointed to her with a questioning look. She smiled and nodded, pointing to Daisy and holding up two fingers.

The bar was being tended tonight by Jonas Harrison. An unofficial extension of the Rite Spot, there was a hand-lettered sign on the back wooden wall that said "The Almost Correct Spot." Bottles lined the shelves where tack usually hung.

"What can I get you, Abe?"

"Three spiked punches, thanks."

"Coming right up."

Tommy Viera pulled up the stool next to him. "I think you should buy me a shot, at least," he muttered toward Abe.

Rayna had left Abe at the altar for this man, yeah, breaking Abe's heart in the process, but Tommy appeared to be a good father to their kids, and he was a solid businessman. The hardware store had tripled its size in the time Tommy had owned it, and both his customers and employees were loyal.

It didn't stop Abe from thinking Tommy was a horse's ass. But he *had* danced with the man's wife. "I s'pose I could do that. What's your poison?"

"Rye."

"Jonas? Two shots of your cheapest rye."

When the shots were lined up in front of them, along with the three glasses of punch, Tommy said, "One of those for my wife?"

"Nope."

"Huh." He tossed his shot back without formality, and Abe followed suit. Well, if that was all he had to do to get off the hook, he should be glad. He wondered how many shots Tommy would have to buy Rayna to make up for cheating on her.

"I guess I'll see you." He didn't add what his head said. *Asshole.* Abe knew he should leave before he got riled up. He might be closer to being over Rayna than he had ever thought he could be, but that didn't mean he wanted Tommy to hurt her.

"Don't dance with my wife again," Tommy said conversationally, keeping his eyes forward.

"'Scuse me?" Abe kept his voice low.

"Don't put your hands on my wife again."

"As long as you keep your hands on her and on no one else, that shouldn't be a problem."

Tommy stood so fast he knocked over his barstool. "What the *hell* are you trying to say to me?"

Abe shrugged. "Rayna's not stupid, Tommy. Don't treat her like she is." He picked up the three glasses and started to turn with them. Now was the time he might get cold-cocked, just like that. He wouldn't be surprised if Tommy hit him. He didn't *want* him to, but neither did Abe want to take back his words. It would be a waste of good drinks, though, if he did get hit.

But Tommy just stood still, as though his boots had turned to concrete, looking for all the world as if he had taken a sucker punch. For one strange second, Abe felt sorry for him—that was real pain on the man's face. Then he remembered Tommy was the one who was cheating.

Abe gestured to the dance floor. "Looks like your wife needs a dance partner."

And Abe strode off, three pink drinks in his hands. The spiked punch was what was making them all act like they were high-schoolers. Whoever had said those were the best years of your life—that's who deserved to be smacked right in the kisser.

CHAPTER TWENTY-FIVE

Never be ashamed of what you've made. — E. C.

Fiona of the future was brazen.

Maybe that's what flirting was? Letting the sexual feelings—and boy, she had them—burble up to the surface, letting them spill over.

While she and Abe danced, she tried putting the thoughts she was having into her gaze—thoughts about him naked, above her, of him keeping her from breathing with the pressure of his kiss. She tried to make it a brazen look. A *sexual* look.

Abe said, "You okay? Looks like you have a headache."

Darn. "Fine," she said and let Abe twirl her under his arm again. She was obviously better at dancing than seduction.

It didn't stop her from thinking about it, though. The way his hands would feel against her skin, if he reached back and unzipped her dress...Abe brought her in close after another spin. She didn't even have to think about her feet. Fiona gasped as she felt him, as she realized that he was, perhaps, a little turned on, too. In that last full-body contact before he'd spun her out again, she'd felt his hardness under his jeans.

"Isn't it...*uncomfortable* to dance like that?" Fiona said without thinking.

Abe's blue eyes widened and he stopped dancing. He just stopped right there in the middle of the song, in the middle of the dance floor, so he could bend forward and laugh so loud other people lost their steps, too. He straightened, slapping his thigh with his hand. "God, girl! Yes! It is! So damn uncomfortable. I don't think a woman alive has ever asked a man that question, though."

Fiona shrugged. "I just wondered." If only he knew what else she was thinking...

Abe reached for her again, folding her hand into his, placing his other hand at her waist. "I'd apologize but I'm not actually sorry at all. A little embarrassed, sure. But not sorry." He drew her in close again, and Fiona wondered if he could hear her heart.

Abe's arms tightened around her. "You're blushing."

"Oh!" Fiona felt herself blush harder. "Just...hot in here, isn't it?"

"Some people still have their coats on. It's not warm."

"Huh. Maybe I should..."

"Let's get off the dance floor," said Abe, guiding her off the old wood planks.

"Can we go someplace quiet?" Nerves danced down Fiona's spine.

Abe looked at her carefully. "Sure." He pointed. "Over there. Away from the crowd."

He led Fiona to the back of the barn, past the bar and down a narrow hallway. Through the dimness—no sparkly lights back here—he led her to a hay bale set in a tiny, unused stall. They were only sharing the space with a wall-full of old tack and the smell of wool. "Here. Sit. Take a deep breath. No one can see us in here, so take your time cooling off."

No one can see us. Fiona giggled.

"What?" Abe asked.

"Nothing." She giggled harder. God, she was losing it. How do you pull it together when the object of your every lust is right in front of you? Fiona couldn't stop thinking about the bulge she'd felt on the dance floor.

And what she could do with it. How she could fix it.

"I'm a fixer," she said. "I like to make things better."

"What?"

She laughed again, this time harder. Abe, balancing on the balls of his feet, grinned as if he was ready to go along with the joke, but oh, God, what made it so damn funny was that it *wasn't* a joke, and Fiona realized that she wanted to sleep with this man like she wanted to draw breath. It was impossible to stop.

She stood. She moved fast. Maybe a little too fast—she'd knock him...

But he was moving as fast as she was. They slammed against each other and then Abe pressed her up against the wood, catching her arms just as she'd imagined, lifting them over her head, pinning them there against the wall with one hand. His mouth was heavy on hers, dragging his kiss over her lips, her cheeks, scraping his teeth along the curve of her neck, and then back to her gasping mouth. They went from zero to a hundred in the space of four seconds. Fiona couldn't breathe, couldn't see, could only feel—feel his tongue rasping against hers, feel his body, huge and hard, holding her up.

She worked one hand free and reached down, pressing her palm against the front of his jeans. There. There it was again. Abe groaned and loosed her other hand, propping himself up against the wooden wall. "You shouldn't do that," he warned against her mouth.

"Why?" she whispered, plucking at his belt.

"Shit, woman! Are you trying to kill me?"

"Yes," she said. "That's what I'm trying to do." She undid the first few buttons of his fly, just far enough that she could sneak her hand in. And yeah, he was exactly what she'd imagined.

Only bigger. And harder.

She gasped. "Holy..."

Abe bucked against her and then groaned, catching her by the back of the neck, drawing her up to him for another kiss. His mouth told her everything she wanted to hear—his lips were insistent. Demanding.

And Future-Fiona, brazen Fiona, could be the same way. "I want you," she said into his ear as he bit her neck softly.

This time it was Abe who gasped. "Snowflake, *damn.*"

She was still touching him, rubbing his cock, loving the terrified flip she felt in the pit of her stomach when she imagined him inside her. Fiona needed to fix this longing. Maybe if they fixed it really well, the need wouldn't come back. She'd finally get over this guy who had such a hold on her mind, and apparently her body.

"We can't do this." Abe pulled backward, lifting his mouth from hers. He pushed gently at her hand, giving a light moan as she released him. "Not that I don't want to. Because I do. Jesus, do I."

"Then why wait?" She could fix both their urges. Right here. Right now. Just because she'd never done anything like this before didn't mean she couldn't start.

Voices suddenly rang outside, and the rising sound of laughter. It came from nowhere, filling the old stall before Fiona could even rearrange her expression, before she could dry her lips from his kiss. The wooden door of the stall banged open and a light bulb hanging on a chain snapped on overhead.

Fiona blinked in the light.

Abe jumped away from her, buckling his belt.

Cade MacArthur finished his sentence, "...and this is the stall I'm going to put the new goats in, as soon as I..."

His voice trailed to a stop. Fiona couldn't tell who was giggling behind him, but she thought it might have been Cade's wife, Abigail.

Rayna, though, wasn't laughing. Fiona could see that—it would have been obvious from outer space. The look on Rayna's face wasn't disappointment or even anger. Instead, it was confusion.

That hurt.

Rayna didn't even see Fiona as someone who could seduce her ex. She was *confused* by it.

"Pardon the intrusion, you two," Cade managed. "Go right ahead and...*ahem*." He snapped the light back out, and under cover of darkness, the little crowd he was leading tumbled laughing down the barn's hallway.

"Oh, no," said Fiona. She sat down on the hay bale and smoothed her hair. "Damn it."

"Let's get out of here."

"What?"

"Let's go."

"You're embarrassed," Fiona said. He was *ashamed* he'd been caught with her. In front of Rayna. Goddammit.

"Hell, yes, I am. Aren't you? We just got caught having a literal roll in the hay."

"So?" Fiona was pushing. She couldn't help it. His reaction hurt. "We're both adults."

"I don't like people seeing what I don't want them to see," he growled.

"Wow. Must be nice to be able to control that."

Abe moved to the door of the stall. "I'm sorry. I wish that hadn't happened."

That hurt worst of all. He regretted the whole thing.

"Yeah, let's go." Fiona straightened her dress and flicked off an errant piece of alfalfa. Then she followed him out.

Being ashamed of herself was exhausting.

CHAPTER TWENTY-SIX

Hold the yarn lightly. It doesn't need you to tell you what it is already. — E. C.

The party was still in full swing when Abe reached the main floor of the barn again. Fiona passed by his elbow, and he could feel the heat of her as she moved in front of him. Her ass looked like heaven in that dress, and his eyes traced her strong calves to where they disappeared into her shiny black cowboy boots. She went right over to Daisy and smiled down at her, crouching so they could chat.

Abe could *not* read Fiona. And he desperately wanted to. He wanted to skip to the end, read her like one of his mysteries, unlock the puzzle so that he could just sit back and enjoy the book, knowing the author would end up solving all the problems for him. But life didn't work like that. And that sucked.

Looked like Paul Dunbar had tied a couple too many on—he was wearing a bra on his head and whooping about a hockey game he apparently had quite a lot of money on. His wife, who didn't come close to needing a bra that size, was leading him out by the elbow—and by the looks of it, if he didn't cooperate soon, she'd drag him out by his ear. Mayor Finley was dancing off to the side, watching her husband play a guest spot with the band. Everyone knew he was sick, but the Finleys didn't talk about it much. He'd not only made it to the party, but he'd made it up on stage with his fiddle, and the mayor looked like she was about to cry.

Zeke ran up to Abe, his long arms swinging at his sides. Sometimes Zeke reminded him of nothing more than an overly large child. "Hey."

"Hey." There was no *way* gossip about him and Fiona could have blazed past him in the hallway and beat him out here. Was there? He motioned for Zeke to follow him to the bar.

Once there, Zeke said mischievously, "So, Fiona?"

Of course. "You know what, I think she's embarrassed we got caught, so do me a favor and just squash whatever rumor you hear, okay? *Damn* this town sometimes." Abe drove the toe of his boot into the base of a wooden barstool.

Zeke nodded. "I have *no* idea what you're talking about. I got your back, though. But hey, I was just going to say, you know her friend Daisy?"

"Yeah. From the salon."

"She asked me out. I think. I mean, maybe. I'm not quite sure. I think she was asking me out."

Abe signaled to Jonas for another shot of rye, and the bartender pushed it down the bar to him. "You think?"

"She said she wants me to take her out for dinner."

"That's a date."

"But I'm all freaked out now."

"Why?"

Zeke stared at him as if it should be obvious. "Because I don't have room in my car for a wheelchair."

"Okay."

"How would that *work*?" Zeke looked frantic.

"Do you want to date her?"

"Have you *seen* her? Of course I do!"

"Then meet her at the restaurant."

"Huh?"

"She's got a car of her own, right?"

"Yeah, I guess."

"Then she meets you. It's not the law that you have to pick her up. I thought a college degree came with that football scholarship."

Zeke's face wreathed in a smile. "It also came with sixteen concussions over the course of four years. And that was before I turned pro."

"Let's blame it on that."

"So, where's Fiona now?"

"Not with me." That was the only thing Abe knew for sure. The rye burned going down, a clean fire.

"There they both are, look!" Zeke pointed and before Abe could signal him—hiss at him or kick him, something, anything—Zeke waved. "They want us to go over."

It was true, Daisy was smiling. Fiona, on the other hand, looked as if the only thing keeping her from running away as the men approached was Daisy's hand, which was clenched around Fiona's wrist.

"Ladies." Zeke bobbed up and down on his toes, looking like a kid again in his eagerness.

Daisy said, "Your haircut looks good, Abe."

"Fabio always does a good job." So this was how people made small talk. Words just slid out of your mouth while you thought about the one thing you shouldn't. At the moment, that one thing happened to be the shape of Fiona's mouth and how her bottom lip had tasted just like sugar.

That same mouth was twisted now. "I really should go," said Fiona. "I just remembered...a bumper...I promised I'd get it done..."

Abe imagined Fiona sliding under a car wearing that shimmery blue dress. How the *hell* was that image so sexy?

"Let's go, then," he said.

"Know what? I think I'll walk," Fiona said. "But thank you."

"Didn't you come with Abe?" Daisy frowned. "It's miles back into town."

"I feel like a walk." Fiona glanced down at her dress. "These boots are comfy."

"I brought you—I'd like to take you home." Abe was trying to be polite about it but he wasn't actually planning on arguing. He was taking her home. Period.

"Fine," said Fiona.

Daisy said, "What *happened* back there?"

Fiona said, "Nothing. Absolutely nothing."

Zeke said, "So...Daisy, about that dinner..."

Fiona gave a small, unhappy wave. "Night, darlin'," she said. "Don't eat this guy alive, okay?"

"Oh, all right," said Daisy, smiling winningly at Zeke.

Zeke said, "Oh!" again.

Abe followed Fiona out of the party. She left a small wake as she passed, people happy to see her, arms that touched, cheeks that were kissed. He took a larger step forward and put his hand on the small of her back. He was glad that she let him.

They exited the barn into the dark as a couple, waving together at the Wildwoods and the Brooks.

It felt bizarre. Jarring.

Perfect.

Like what he'd been waiting for without knowing it.

Now he just had to get her to talk to him again.

CHAPTER TWENTY-SEVEN

The holes in lace hide a multitude of sins. — E. C.

The drive back to town in Abe's International was quiet, aside from the roar of its V8. Fiona didn't mind—she was pretty damn sure if she opened her mouth one more time today she'd only end up saying something else she'd regret for a long time.

The best thing that could happen would be if Abe dropped her off, and from that moment on they pretended they didn't know each other. They could go back to the way they'd been before. He'd come and buy gas, and she wouldn't go out to help him. They'd see each other at city council meetings—*damn*. That was only two days away.

"You can just drop me in front of the filling station," she said. "I wasn't lying, I really do have a car to work on." Of course, Joan Quandt didn't expect her Lexus back for another three days, but it would be a nice surprise for her to get it back early.

"You can't crawl under a car wearing that." Abe reached out as if he was going to touch one of the beads on her shoulder strap but his hand stopped moving before he reached her.

Fiona looked down at herself. She hadn't considered that. "Well…" Also, it was none of his damn business.

"I'll walk you inside. Then you can decide what to do." She gave a short nod.

What did he *mean* by that? Then she could decide…what? Did he think she was going to sleep with him? Okay, even though she'd given him every impression that's what she wanted, up to and including telling him so… "I don't want—I mean, I'm not sure…"

Abe smiled. "I know. We had a moment. A crazy second. That's all." He got out of the truck.

Fiona opened her door and slipped down off the high seat, landing awkwardly on the gravel.

"Hey, I was going to do that for you."

"What? Open my car door?" Fiona laughed—she couldn't help it.

Abe looked abashed, his smile crooked. "Sorry. I guess you're probably better at opening car doors than I am."

"I get a lot of practice." Fiona paused as she replayed to herself how that could be taken. "Not like, on dates…I meant inside the shop. You know…"

Laughing, Abe took her by the hand. "Just walking you to your door. Come on."

They threaded their way through the overgrown garden between the shop and her small house. "Sorry. I keep meaning to get out here and prune some of this jungle back, but I haven't had time."

"It's nice," Abe said.

He was wrong. The way it was overgrown was actually embarrassing. She could make this yard look gorgeous if she just had a little more time. "No, I know exactly what I'm going to do. See the side wall there?"

Abe nodded.

The motion-sensor yard light flipped on, bathing them in its yellow glow. A moth threw its heavy body at the light almost immediately.

"I have an old, glass-paned door. I'm going to paint the wood black and the glass rainbow colors and then prop it against the wall." Fiona looked at the yellow flaking paint on the wall, noticing the spider webs. The whole place could use a new coat, yet another thing to add to her list. "Then I'm going to set low shelves in front of it, and let geraniums tumble down. I love geraniums."

She was babbling.

At the door, Fiona stopped, key in her hand. Would he kiss her again? Or should she attack him like she had in the barn? Why were these questions so *confusing*? She was a grown woman, for God's sake. Why was the man behind her—the quiet, stubborn man with the sun-creased lines at the corners of his eyes, with the gaze that seemed to see right inside her soul—why was that man making her into a woman who could hardly see straight, let alone make important decisions?

It just wasn't right. She was smart. She could do this. Sensibly.

Fiona turned around. Yep. There he was, just standing there, hands in his pockets, a small smile as he watched her fight her internal battle.

"Would you like to come in?"

"*Hell*, yeah," he said in that low rumble.

Easy as that. His voice felt like a caress and Fiona shivered inside.

But she still had something that needed doing. "Okay. Wait here."

"What—"

Fiona slid through the door and almost closed it behind her, saying through the crack, "Two minutes. I need just two minutes."

"Fiona—"

"Minute and a half."

Inside, she became a whirlwind. The heaps of clothes she'd taken out, tried on, and left on the couch near the full-length mirror were shoved into the hall closet. She kicked old issues of *Car and Driver* under the sofa. In the kitchen, the dirty dishes she'd left in the sink went unceremoniously under it, next to the recycling. On the bedroom floor was the other half of her closet, and it took two armfuls to chuck them back in. A huge push convinced the groaning closet door to close. She made the bed by pulling the quilt up and over the bunched sheets. Looked good from the outside. Fastest tidying job ever. It wasn't like he was going to come into the bedroom, after all.

Right?

Fiona didn't know the answer. She couldn't even tell if deep in her own heart, she *wanted* him to.

Okay, that was bull. She wanted him in her room.

She wanted him as close as another person could possibly get. And even thinking about it made her hands shake. He'd be able to tell, if he looked at her. In the mirror over her dresser, she saw the hectic flush on her cheeks. She pressed cool hands against them and paused.

One breath in. Next breath out. That was the way she was going to get through whatever happened next. What was that phrase Hope had told her? Breath by breath, Eliza Carpenter had said.

Abe must have thought she'd lost her marbles by now. She hurried through the house and flung open the door.

"Sorry," she said on what turned out to be a gasp.

Abe gave that sleepy smile again. His arms were crossed, and even in the dress shirt she could tell how heavily muscled his upper arms were. "No worries."

"So."

"You gonna let me in, Snowflake, or you just want me to kiss the hell out of you here?"

CHAPTER TWENTY-EIGHT

Be brave. Everything can be fixed, given a crochet hook and enough determination. – E. C.

Fiona opened her mouth but nothing came out. So instead, she stepped backward and motioned him in. Abe stepped forward with that long-legged stride. Fiona, still backing up, bumped into her couch. "So, this is the place..." Her voice trailed off. Abe wasn't looking around. He wasn't looking anywhere but at her.

And in a very specific sense, he was looking at her mouth.

He reached forward with one hand and grazed her bottom lip with his thumb. "You have any idea how much this has been distracting me lately?"

"What?"

"This." He swept his thumb across her mouth, so lightly it sent a tickle through her, raising goose bumps on her arms and legs.

"The shape of it. This mouth was made to be kissed, Fiona." He paused. "By me."

Oh. Holy cats. As Abe leaned forward, Fiona kept her eyes open. She wanted to see him—she wanted less speed, less intensity this time. Maybe if they took their time, she'd have a choice when it came to controlling the kiss. She hated being out of control, and God knew Abe had taken the reins in their previous two kisses.

His lips were firm. He used no tongue, but neither was the kiss chaste. No way. How could it be, when he was using his body like he was? One of his hands went to the small of her back, and he pulled her flush against him. He twisted the fingers of his other hand into her hair and pulled her head back lightly.

As Fiona's breath quickened, so did Abe's. He stroked her tongue with his own, earning them both a gasp. How could a man—just a guy, as far as Fiona could tell—taste so good? It wasn't of mints or toothpaste, it was more real than that. His upper lip tasted of salt. The tip of his tongue reminded her of rye whiskey—sharp and shocking. And deeper? When he pulled her—yes, just like that—hard up against him, when he claimed her mouth, he tasted darker. Richer. He tasted like chocolate without the sugar.

"Damn it," he muttered.

"Wha...?" Fiona took a step forward as he pulled away. Abe caught her with a hoarse laugh.

"Easy there."

"I believe we were establishing that." Her voice was light but she wondered if he was going to pull away like he had on the beach. This time she couldn't run—she was already home.

Abe's eyes darkened and he looked as if he might kiss her again, but he didn't. Instead, he took a deep breath and grinned at her. "I swore to myself that I wouldn't attack you if you let me in."

"Do you come armed?" she asked lightly. "Or just these guns?" She wrapped her fingers around his bicep, prepared to make another dumb joke, but as she felt the heavy, thick muscles leap and contract under her touch, she forgot what she was going to say. "Oh," was all she could mumble. Her heart lightened. He was here. That was enough for now.

Abe cleared his throat. "Show me the place." Shoving his fingers into his hair, he took a deep breath. Then he looked around, clearly seeing it for the first time. "My God, Fiona, this is wild."

Fiona warmed even more than she already was. "Thank you."

"Whoa." He ran a hand along the edge of the dining room table. It was made out of the hood of a car and had chrome edges. "What the hell? Did you make this?"

"Yeah," she said.

"'70s Benz?"

She nodded in happiness. "Don't you love the flatness of it?"

"It's unreal. When do you have the time?"

"I made most of this stuff before the shop was doing so well—I had time then. I kept it all out in the yard, and I'd run up to the store when someone ran over the bell line. When Stephen first came, he helped me. He's a much better art welder than I am now."

He ran his hand along the back of her low sofa. "The couches?"

"Corvair bench seats, circa 1968." She was so proud of those. She'd fixed the broken springs, added padding, and welded the leather seats to thick iron legs. Matching pillows made of roof liner. The sofas were solid. Once she'd had a dinner party and Tim Snopes had ended up drinking too much. His wife Tina left him behind and he slept on one all night. In the morning he tried to buy it from her. He'd stopped upping his offer when she turned down eight grand.

"And this?" Abe went into the red and black kitchen. "The island?"

"An old Formica tabletop put on top of a cabinet ripped from the Lawlor's kitchen when they did their rebuild."

He touched the top of the island, running his finger along the Formica. "It's funny. It looks just like the ones at..."

"At Tillie's. You remember when Old Bill put in the jukebox? About sixty years after everywhere else bought one?"

Abe nodded.

"He had to get rid of a table to make it fit, and I saw it in the back room through the kitchen curtain."

"He gave it to you?"

"You kidding me? Have you met the man? Never met a dime he couldn't polish. I had to bribe him as well as pay him."

"What did you bribe him with?"

Fiona shrugged. "Sex."

"Oh, good." Abe didn't bat an eye. "How was it?"

"Well. The countertop was a little cold and greasy..."

Abe closed his eyes. "Please stop."

"You think I paid too much?"

With a guffaw, Abe bent to look into her small, round fish bowl. "Fighting fish?"

"A betta, yeah." The bright green and purple fish was the only pet Fiona had ever had and she was periodically shocked at how much she loved the little creature.

"What's his name?"

"Tamale."

Abe raised an eyebrow.

Fiona said, "He's spicy and a little corny."

Abe sat in a dining room chair. "I'm not sure you should be allowed to name things."

"It's a perfect name for him." Fiona wanted to brag that the chair he was sitting in was from a '76 Firebird and that she'd broken her pinky finger (which had been *such* an annoyance for the next month) ripping it out of the vehicle at the U-Pick, but she didn't.

Abe touched her elbow and then took Fiona's hand, tugging her down onto his lap. His arms were strong around her. Secure. "I kind of just want you to tell me about the way you use a blowtorch. But if you did..."

"Then what?"

He kissed her then, hard and fast, and there in his kiss was what Fiona wanted to know, what she'd been wondering.

Abe wanted to stay. She could feel it. Hell, she could feel him now, underneath her thighs.

Fiona had to make a decision. And it would probably be better to make it sooner rather than later.

A reasonable person would rise and thank him for the date. Perhaps she'd say yes if he asked for another one. Good girls didn't sleep with guys on the—what was this? Their second outing?

But most girls didn't come pre-stocked with a crush the size of a 1972 Chrysler Town and Country station wagon. They didn't have to deal with a man who looked like the model other men wanted to be built on.

But she *liked* him, too. She couldn't help it.

Did he get this all the time? Should she at least *try* to play the game, even if she had no clue what the rules were?

"What is it?"

Fiona jumped, and Abe's hands, which had been on the sides of her face as he brought her down to kiss him, went to her hips. She felt him adjust under her and she squirmed to stand. "Am I hurting you?"

"No." He pulled her down again. "You're not. Now tell me what's going on in your head."

"What?" Fiona's fingers curled at his collar. The fabric was soft. Warm.

"You were with me, and then you weren't. Where'd you go?"

Fiona leaned her head back and looked at the ceiling. How long had those cobwebs been up there? Would he notice them?

Abe waited as if he had all the time in the world. As if her weight wasn't probably making his legs go to sleep.

"Is this weird?" she finally asked.

"Yes."

"What?"

"Hell, *yeah*, it's weird. I've only ever known you as the girl with the gas station. I never thought I'd be sitting in your kitchen, you making me all hot and bothered."

"Right?" Relief flooded her. "What did you think about me?"

"About you?"

Gently, Fiona touched the crease that formed between his eyes. "Did you think of me at all?"

He paused before answering, taking her hand in his own and helping her rub his forehead. "That feels good."

She leaned down and pressed a kiss against his temple, then moving her breath to his ear.

"Um, don't start that," he said, "or I can't be held responsible for my actions."

Impulsively, Fiona wriggled against him. She felt his thighs tighten and he shifted again.

"Lord have mercy, woman," he said. "Stay still and I'll answer you." His breathing was shallow, and Fiona felt a moment of exhilaration.

He took another breath and then said, "Don't be mad at me."

That didn't sound auspicious, but Fiona nodded.

"I...*didn't* think about you."

Fiona realized the fingers of the palm she had propped against the wall were pressed too tightly into the wood, so tightly she was getting a cramp in her wrist. "Oh."

"You were Fee's Fill."

"Yeah," Fiona said.

"You wore that black cowboy hat all the time."

Fiona brought her chin up, ignoring the fact that her feelings smarted. He hadn't noticed her. She'd been practically in love with the man, and he hadn't even known her name. "I didn't wear it tonight, did I?"

"No."

She pulled her hair back, wishing for a rubber band. "I love that hat."

"And now I know that. You're hot as hell in it."

She narrowed her eyes. "Don't push your luck, buddy."

"I mean it. You look like...you look like you're thinking a sexy secret when you wear it, all pulled down low over your eyes. Something you're not going to tell anyone else." He paused a moment. "I think you hide behind it, maybe."

He wasn't wrong, but she wasn't about to tell him that.

Abe went on. "And now I also know you're a beautiful, smart-as-hell, creative, talented artist who can do just about anything she wants with metal."

Only one word in the sentence stuck out. "Beautiful?" Her voice was small, and she was embarrassed. But she couldn't stop from repeating, "You think I'm beautiful?"

Abe smiled. His *eyes* smiled in a way that melted something cold, hidden deep inside Fiona. "Once—and only once, might I add—I wasn't paying attention on my dad's sailboat when he was coming about. The boom busted me in the gut. Felt like I couldn't breathe for a week. That's how I feel now. When I look at you."

Fiona started to speak, but then realized she didn't know what to say.

So she just said, "The bedroom's that way."

CHAPTER TWENTY-NINE

Sometimes it's good to know the specific names for the stitches we use. It's not necessary—you certainly don't need to know a name to make a connection with a stranger—but it helps. It's nice to know your ssk from your k2tog. – E. C.

Fiona was lighter than a parachute dry fly. He could have carried her all night, and when they got to her bed, the only thing that made it okay for him to let her go was the bed itself.

"What the hell...?" Abe reached out and touched the grille—the grille!—of the bed frame. "What *is* this?"

Fiona bit her bottom lip. "It's a 1969 GMC C1500 station wagon. Or it used to be."

The footboard of the huge bed was as shiny as the day it had come off the line. The bed's sides were hubcaps held together with what might have been tension struts. And what should have looked like a child's car bed looked more like something that would be installed at a museum. "It's fucking amazing."

Fiona's face broke into a pleased grin. "You like it? No one's really seen it." She caught herself and said, "Well, not many...I mean...Oh, God. I don't know what I mean."

Was that shyness on her face? Was she nervous? "I'm not sure there's much you can't do."

She held out her hands and looked at them critically. "My fingers are strong. I'm good with metal." Her smile slid sideways. "It's all the other stuff I'm not always that good at."

He knelt on the edge of the bed, still admiring the way the chrome gleamed in the low light of her bedside lamp. It would be too much if he told her what he was noticing, that the sparkle of the metal actually matched that same shine in her eyes. So instead of embarrassing himself with that, he kissed her.

As his mouth covered hers, he felt heat slam the pit of his stomach, a twisting, falling feeling that made him dizzy, the way he felt when an unexpected wave dropped his boat into a trough. She kissed him back like she was on fire and he was the only thing that could cool her—or maybe it was the other way round, fuck, he had no idea about anything anymore. Whatever it was made him lose track of where he was, where she began, and he only knew that damn it to hell, he wanted this woman more than he could remember ever wanting anyone before.

He was fast, moving his hands to his belt buckle, but she was faster. She unzipped his fly for him and helped him shove down his jeans.

Fiona said, "*Damn*, Abe."

And he had to admit, her admiring voice felt almost as good as her hands did, touching him, caressing him in a way that was bound to drive him crazy way too fast.

"Slow down there, Snowflake." He stilled her hand. "Let's even the odds here, what do you say?"

Fiona looked up at him, a triumphant gleam in her eye. She released him with what seemed like reluctance. "Yeah? How would you suggest we do that?" She grasped the grille at the foot of the bed and Abe thought his heart might stop. Kicking off first one, then the other cowboy boot, she straightened and turned slowly, displaying her back and the zipper that dipped low below her shoulder blades. "Help a girl out, Sailor?"

Her words were bold, but Abe heard a vulnerability beneath them. Slow. He'd move slowly with her. He had all the time in the world for Fiona.

Abe swept her hair off her neck and pressed his lips to the bare skin at the top of her spine. Then he tugged the zipper, slowly—so slowly—running it down to the small of her back.

Something in his chest stuttered and then almost stopped when he saw the clasp of her black bra. How did something that lacy do any job at all?

Fiona hunched her shoulders slightly, as if she knew what he was thinking. "I like pretty things..."

"It's astounding. *You're* astounding." He leaned to kiss the side of her neck, and then, moving as gently as he could, he slipped the right shoulder of her dress off, then the left. The dress slithered to the ground. "You know how your bed frame shows off your bed?"

Fiona nodded, her lower lip between her teeth.

He turned her, keeping his touch soft, so that she faced him, standing in front of him in nothing but two pieces of dark lace. "This," he touched the top of her bra and skimmed a finger along the top of her panties, "this is a frame, too."

"But...my bed needs a frame to stand up..." she said uncertainly and Abe caught immediately what he'd said wrong.

"No, no. Not like that. You don't *need* this, are you kidding me? Let me show you."

"What are you..."

Abe slipped one strap off her shoulder and then the other. Then he ran his fingers along her shoulder blades, loving the way her skin felt as goose bumps rose, following his touch. She shivered as his arms went around her. With one hand he unsnapped her bra, and with the other, he tugged off the black lace, tossing it onto the floor.

"Hey," she said weakly. "That's eighty bucks."

He rocked back on his heels. "Seriously?"

"I may wear boy clothes on the outside," she said, "but I like pretty underthings." She said it as though she had to justify it.

"That is," Abe said, "the hottest thing I've ever heard."

She lit up again, her face brightening. God, he loved doing that to her.

"It is?"

"Yeah," he said, bringing his lips to her neck again. He couldn't stop touching her there, the skin underneath her jaw so soft he could barely feel it. She smelled of jasmine, the wild, open sweetness he associated with night. "It is."

Still gently, so as not to spook her, he led her to the bed. Never breaking the kiss, he leaned her backward, then slid off her panties. Even though she was kissing him, meeting his touch with her own, she was still holding something back. He took her nipple in his mouth and sucked until the peak of it was hard. Then he released it and blew, the shock of the cold air stiffening it even more. Almost as stiff as he himself was. Jesus, he wanted her.

But he wouldn't rush her. She reminded him of a little sailboat he used to have—no matter which direction he'd wanted her to turn, he had to make sure he wasn't too rough or she'd spook.

Cupping her other breast in his hand, he slid up her body until he was lying alongside her. He willed himself to breathe deeply. *Pace yourself.* There was no hurry. They had all night. Might as well face the fact that he was thinking about tomorrow night, too.

"Tell me what you want."

Fiona didn't hesitate. "I want you."

Did she have *any* idea how hot she was? Those words forming in her mouth like that?

"I want you, too," he said, and he couldn't help the growl that formed in the back of his throat as he nipped the side of her jaw with his teeth. "I also want to know that you're totally here. With me."

Fiona moved onto her side so that they were facing each other. "I've wanted you forever."

And I've wanted you for days.

It was different, this need. He knew that. And he hoped that it could be enough for her, for tonight.

She took a condom from a drawer next to the bed. He put it on, never breaking eye contact with her, her hands helping him roll it on. Abe kissed her again, and before he could decide what she might like best, what he should do to please her exactly the right way, she put her hands on his chest and pushed him onto his back.

"Whoa, there."

"Let me be in charge." She straddled him, agonizingly slowly.

Well, hell. If that's what she really wanted..."You can do whatever you want, honey, as long as you don't stop what you're—" He broke off as she put him inside her. "But go as slow as you need..."

Fiona didn't heed him. In one smooth, fast stroke, she slid down his cock, taking him completely inside. He heard a silent roar in his head, and the fever that blazed awake in him, low inside, was matched by the fire in her eyes. Without saying a word, she lifted herself, slowly, so slowly, slower, and then slid down him again. She tilted her head back, finally breaking their eye contact, as if she had to focus on something deep inside.

She was the most beautiful thing he'd ever seen. Her breasts, high and small, nipples tightly budded and dark against her skin. Her stomach, flat, with that snowflake, blue and lacy, just above her hipbone. Now that she tipped her head away from him, her hair fell so far back that he felt it brush his knees—he'd never known such a light touch could make him feel like his world was about to tear apart.

"Holy mother of—" He couldn't finish whatever it was he might have been saying. Fiona was speeding up now, raising herself and pushing back down onto him in a perfect rhythm. His hips matched her thrusts, and when he put his hands at her waist, fingertips at the small of her back, thumb pressing in just below her hipbone, she tipped forward again, landing with her palms pressed against his chest, mouth on his, never stopping that perfect, perfect rocking. He was so close now. He shouldn't be—God knew he should take more time with her, so much more time—make her come first, make her come hard, but he couldn't stop, not when she moved like that...

Fiona put her lips to his ear and whispered, "Abe, Abe, Abe," in time with the motion of her hips.

He lifted one hand to the back of her head, threaded his fingers through her hair and said, "Jesus, Rayna."

Fiona stopped moving. Completely.

CHAPTER THIRTY

Of course, no matter what you call it, a left-leaning decrease will always be a left-leaning decrease. – E. C.

I t took all Fiona's will to stop moving when every single fiber of every muscle was screaming at her to keep riding, keep rocking, with Abe sunk so deep inside her she didn't know where she ended and he began.

But she stopped. She held herself so still that she felt the molecules inside her cells freeze. Slowly, carefully, she pushed her arms straight, lifting herself off, rolling to the side and then all the way over, so her back was to him on the bed. The air felt like ice on her overheated skin.

"Fiona."

If she ignored him hard enough, maybe she wouldn't have to tell him to go away, maybe he'd just figure it out like a rational adult, and she could just lie here and die of embarrassment by herself.

"Fiona, I'm so fucking sorry." Was his voice shaking?

Of course it was. He'd been so close. She'd felt the heat rising through him. Another twenty seconds...and she would have regretted it even more than she already did.

He put his hand on her shoulder but she shrugged it off violently. "Don't *touch* me."

"I don't know what happened. It just slipped out. Rayna and I haven't been together in...so long."

Fiona kept her back to him, kept her mouth shut. What could she say?

Abe rolled to his side of the bed, and Fiona felt the mattress bounce as he stood. She heard him walk around the bed, and then watched through slitted eyes as he knelt in front of her. He was still naked, and she wished he didn't look so fucking *good*, still so hard and so ready.

"Snowflake..." He reached out as if to touch her hair and then pulled back as she glared. "Fiona. Please listen to me."

Fiona reached behind her and pulled the blanket up. She shivered. "Can you please put your clothes on?"

"Fiona..."

"Just put your damn clothes on before you say another word? Can you do that, please?" It was imperative, somehow, that he be dressed. That she not even have the option of reaching out to him, of touching his skin again.

Abe stood and pulled on his jeans, then his shirt, which he left unbuttoned.

"I wish I could take it back," he said, kneeling at the side of the bed again.

"I wish you could, too." He'd felt amazing inside her. She'd felt...Fiona had felt so *pretty* when he'd looked at her that way.

"It's just that...with your long hair and those big eyes..."

Fiona stared at him with horror and then sat bolt upright, dragging the blanket with her. "Are you saying what I think you are?"

"No, not—"

"You're saying I look like her? So, what? It's *my* fault you called me the wrong name?"

"You don't look like her."

"I *know* that," snapped Fiona.

"You look nothing like her. She's just Rayna. You're Snowflake—"

"Don't *call* me that."

"You're incredible."

"Go. Get out," she said through clenched teeth.

"Fiona, you're beautiful. So fucking hot that I couldn't handle it. My brain melted down somehow. Reverted."

"Clearly."

"I'm sorry. I can't begin to apologize in the right way."

Fiona looked at him. He looked miserable.

Good.

"Go," she said. It felt like the only word Fiona had left. Under it, the pain sat, hot and leaden—molten iron she wouldn't be able to twist into anything else.

CHAPTER THIRTY-ONE

Some people are lucky enough to have their mothers be their first knitting teachers. – E. C.

Fiona barely slept. After Abe left, she'd stripped the bed and remade it, but the air had still smelled of him somehow, like salt and wood. Leaving both windows open made her shiver while she lay under the covers, but at least the foggy damp finally cleared the room.

In the early dark hours, after nightmares in which she climbed a huge tree root to get to the top of a mountain only to discover she was too scared to climb back down, she woke and showered. She got out the toolbox she kept in the house, laid the kiln brick on her kitchen counter, and fired up the small blowtorch. Earrings. Intricate ones. Long, silver dangles with angles and arcs that curved around themselves—she made the tangled tree root of her dreams and then used the pliers to bend them. To master them.

As dawn broke, without asking herself why, she went through her closet and found her good jeans, the black ones she kept for special occasions. She'd bought them because Daisy said they made her butt look curvy. Then, instead of an old black t-shirt, she pulled on the red v-neck that she only wore out to breakfast with friends.

In the bathroom, she looked in the mirror. Her eyes were as puffy as if she'd cried herself to sleep—she *hadn't*—and her cheeks were pale. She didn't allow herself to look at the stubble burn Abe had left on her lower jaw. Instead, she scrabbled in the drawer next to the sink. It was full of sticks, tubes, and lotions, things she didn't often use but liked, more than anyone knew. She didn't wear makeup to the shop, but sometimes, at home, alone in the evenings, she liked trying different techniques using tutorials she found online.

Fiona surprised herself with how steady her hand was as she drew the thick cat-eye line on her upper lid. She took the time to curl her eyelashes and then stroked each one thickly with mascara. Dark lip liner, then, followed by a deep gloss.

She took out the box of hair chalks she'd bought the year before. Some of the chalks were more used than others—the pinks and greens, for sure. Fiona separated out a long hank of hair, wetted it, and picked the purple chalk. Purple today, right next to the bright blue streak

Daisy had given her. She grated it along the lock, stubbornly pleased by the bright color. Setting it with the hair dryer, she watched as her cheeks took color back from the heat.

Abe didn't matter.

What he said didn't matter.

She didn't *want* to be Rayna.

Fiona took out the curling iron from under the sink and brushed off the dust. Just because she didn't use it often didn't mean she didn't *know* how to use it. She did her hair in long, loose waves, smoothing it over her shoulder. It was almost as good as something Daisy would have done to her.

She looked in the mirror and a different Fiona met her gaze.

Good. Yet another new one.

It was busy at the shop, and Fiona fixed a running lamp, replaced a step bumper, and calmed a nervous Toots Harrison when she thought her tire felt loose. "It looks lower. Doesn't it look like it's losing air? An inch of air? On the right side?"

"It looks fine," said Fiona, steering her to the couch and pressing a cup of tea into her hands. "Do you have your knitting with you?"

"Can you check it? What if it just falls right off while I'm driving and my car drives over it? Would it be like tripping over your shoelace? If a car lost its tire?"

"It probably won't fall off, but I promise I'll check."

Toots got out her knitting, a teeny red sock. "Do you have a level? Can you check it with a level?"

"I promise I'll use my level."

The tire was deemed fine. Fiona worked her way through two more mini-emergencies, drinking more coffee than she knew was a good idea. The harder she worked, the less time she would have to think about Abe.

She just wished that was actually true.

In the afternoon, Daisy and Tabitha stopped by. Daisy wheeled in, a small white bag on her lap. Tabitha kissed Fiona's cheek with a smack and ran to the couch, where she buried herself in *The Haunted Showboat*.

"She won't put it down. It's all Nancy Drew, all the time. She's read everything the library has and now she wants me to buy the rest." Daisy opened the paper bag. "Do you have any idea how many books that beeyotch Carolyne Keene wrote? She's trying to break me. Besides, she's seven. Should I even be letting her read them?"

"What," Fiona said, "you're scared of all the sex and violence in them? You don't want her to start saying 'Shucks'?"

"She should be reading *Clifford the Dog* books."

"She also shouldn't be obsessed by French and by the pheromones of moths."

Daisy shrugged. "True that. Here. You have to eat half this bear claw."

"If I put that much sugar in my body, the top of my head will come off. You have any idea how much caffeine

I've had today?" Fiona reached behind the counter. "No, *you* have this bran muffin. It's good. Applesauce is the secret. That's what Whitney said. Here, one for Tabby, too."

Fiona handed over the muffins and then rubbed her eyes, stifling a yawn.

"Late night, huh?" Daisy looked smug. "The way Abe looked at you at the dance last night…Y'all made up? I'm assuming that's why you're all dolled up today?"

Fiona scowled. "What? I am not."

"Really? Because you look like you're going out on a date, not about to pull apart a grimy whatever it is your inner grease monkey has to pull apart next."

Fiona reached for Daisy's bear claw and tugged off a piece. "Gah. This is all sugar."

Daisy's eyes danced. "That's why it's so *good*."

"It's going to kill you."

Daisy sighed but tucked the paper bag into her back pouch. "Fine, Mom. I'll just eat it when you're not looking. Don't you know that sugar and white flour is the American way? Are you a Communist or something?" She laced her fingers in her lap. "So. What time did he leave?"

"Who?"

Daisy didn't bother to answer, raising her eyebrows expressively.

"He just dropped me off."

Daisy blew out an exasperated breath. "What? You did not avail yourself of the opportunity to jump those fine bones of his? What is *wrong* with you?"

Fiona opened her mouth to tell the truth, but then the front door dinged. Lucy Harrison, owner of the local bookstore, came in. "Oh, good." She passed Fiona a twenty. "Can I have that on three?"

"Of course."

"And you're exactly who I was looking for," Lucy said to Daisy. "We got a new magazine in at the store, *Nancy Drew and You.*"

"Moooooooom," yelled Tabitha from the couch.

Daisy rolled her eyes. "We'll run by there next. Thanks for the heads up."

"You bet." Already one foot out the door, Lucy turned to look at Fiona. She tilted her head. "You look good, Fee."

"Thanks." Fiona rubbed at a spot on the counter where half a price sticker still clung.

"Different somehow."

"She's just showing off the pretty," said Daisy, satisfaction in her voice.

Fiona didn't look up, but she felt herself blush. "Why can't I just wear a little makeup every once in a while without everyone freaking out about it?"

"Because you never do it," said Daisy.

"Do too." Fiona knew she sounded childish but couldn't help it.

Lucy's eyes narrowed as she stared, concentrating. "No, it's something else. You look like someone..."

Daisy brightened. "Maybe like her mother? I always say she looks a little like Bunny—"

"Stop," said Fiona.

"No, someone else." Lucy snapped, the sound crisp and loud, making Tabby jump on the couch. "Rayna Viera. That's who it is. You look like her. If I didn't remember when she moved here with her parents from Oregon, I'd swear you two were related."

"Well, we're not," Fiona said flatly. She scratched at the sticker on the counter so hard her nail bent backward.

Daisy rolled forward, staring. "You're right! With your hair curled like that? And your eyes all made up? I don't think you look so much like her as much as you just look as glamorous as she always does."

"Right!" said Lucy with a laugh. "If she weren't so nice I'd have to hate her. Always so perfectly put together. So there you go, Fiona. You should feel good about yourself."

Fiona couldn't even answer. And worse, she couldn't stop the tears that rose to her eyes. Horrified, she covered her mouth with one hand and ran to the back bathroom.

The overhead crystal chandelier she'd found at a garage sale cast too low a glow to clearly see herself well in the mirror, but she knew one thing. She didn't look like Rayna. Maybe there *was* something about her, though, something that made...people...think it.

Unwilling to wait for the hot water to warm up the pipes, Fiona scrubbed her face with icy water. Boraxo, the powdered soap she used to get grease out from under her fingernails, scraped at her skin. She rubbed it mercilessly along her lips, dragging the soap over her eyes and mascaraed lashes until her eyes stung and burned. After she'd dried her face with shop towels, she raked her hair back into a messy ponytail, securing it with a rubber band she found next to the air freshener. She wished she hadn't put the extra purple stripe into her hair—it was still visible at her hairline, next to the electric blue. A *fun* touch. Something for sure that Rayna would do, and she would look adorable and hip and cute.

Screw that. Fiona was a mechanic. That was all. A goddamn body mechanic.

When she went back out, Lucy was gone.

"She asked me to apologize for her, but she had to get back to the bookstore," said Daisy. "She feels really badly about upsetting you."

"She didn't mean to."

"Why did you mind so much?" Daisy gestured at Fiona's face. "Why did that make you scrub all that pretty off?"

"If pretty can be scratched off, it's not really pretty, is it?"

Daisy leaned forward, placing her elbows on her knees. "Honey, what's really going on? You know you're pretty as a picture. Is this about Abe or something? Or the fact that he was into Rayna back in the day?"

Fiona just shook her head.

Daisy looked at her watch. "I *hate* that we have to go, but Fabio had to be out by five. I want to talk more about this."

Fiona forced herself to smile. "I'm fine."

"I don't believe you." Daisy turned her head. "Come on, Tabby."

The little girl raced to them. "*Allez-vous me donner un tour?*" Tabitha held her backpack in one hand, the Nancy Drew held tightly in her other.

"You know you're getting too big for this, right?"

Tabitha ignored her mother's protestations and thumped herself into Daisy's lap. "Go fast."

"You got it, kiddo."

Fiona felt her fingers unflex from the fist they'd been curled in. "You're a good mother."

Daisy took her hands off the push rings. "And now a compliment? What is *with* you? Are you dying?"

Fiona shook her head. "*Je t'aime.*"

Daisy smiled. "You, too."

As Daisy sped toward the van, Fiona could hear Tabby's voice singing "*Je t'aime, je t'aime, je t'aime,*" over and over again.

CHAPTER THIRTY-TWO

If you're not as lucky as others, the ones with mothers, come sit by me. We can listen with empathetic joy—no jealousy, never jealousy, that's the surest way to lose your favorite cable needle—as our friends talk about sweaters their mothers and grandmothers made. Then you and I will sit next to each other, pleased with the families we've chosen for ourselves. – E. C.

That night, Saturday, Fiona made herself a huge pile of spinach, cooked in garlic and oil. She thought about having something else, steak or chicken, but the idea of going to the store was exhausting. Spinach from the winter garden was good enough.

She sat outside, balancing the plate on her lap. She could hear Stephen whacking metal against metal in the garage—he'd been working on a robot-insect series that was her favorite of his creations so far. She'd already written to two trade magazines about him, and next week a reporter was coming to interview him, something that made him nervous every time she teased him about it. A good nervous. She'd bring him the extra spinach when she was done and make sure he ate it. Sometimes she swore that he went whole days eating nothing more than the Snickers bars he insisted on paying for.

Above Fiona's head, something that looked like a satellite moved slowly across the night sky. Its light was clear and cold. Next to it, the other stars looked static.

Stuck.

In her pocket, her cell rang. Probably Daisy, going to grill her more about what happened last night. She didn't check the ID. "I don't want to talk about it, I really don't."

A pause. Then Abe's voice filled the line as warmly as if he were sitting next to her. "Okay. We'll talk about something else."

Scared she might drop her plate, Fiona moved it off her lap and to the small iron table next to her. "What do you want?"

"To say I'm sorry."

"You said that." *It wasn't enough.*

"To be honest, I'm at my mom's house."

The sudden subject change confused her. "So?"

"She wants to see you tomorrow."

"So you're calling because your mother wants a date."

"Basically."

"Well, put *her* on then," said Fiona firmly.

There was a slight scuffling noise and then a small voice came through. "Fiona?"

"Hi, Hope."

"How's the knitting going?"

Fiona tucked her legs under her on the iron garden chair. No matter what, she didn't feel as if she could be ready for whatever this phone call was about. "Excuse me?"

"The knitting. Have you done any more?"

"No. I can't." It didn't even hurt very much to admit. "It's just not my thing. My fingers don't work that way."

"I have an idea about that. Can you come with us tomorrow night?"

"Where?" Fiona folded her legs underneath her and drew her sweater tighter.

"To the lighthouse."

Her gut said *no.* Her mouth said, "Why?"

"I want to show you a knitting thing. And tomorrow is a special day for us. We'd be combining trips, which, for an old lady, is a nice thing to do."

It felt like a trap.

"Hope..."

"I'm going to give the phone back to my son. It would be nice to see you, Fiona."

Another fumbling noise. Fiona touched her lips and then, softly, the place where her jaw was lightly whisker burned. She wondered what Abe was wearing, and then she cursed herself for wondering.

"It's not a trick," he said.

"Sure feels like one."

There was a pause. Fiona didn't jump to fill it.

Finally, he said, "It's the anniversary of my father's death. We always do a little memorial. This year my mother is completely fixated on you coming. She says she had a..." Abe sighed. "She says she had a dream about it."

Fiona let out an exasperated breath. "It's not fair. To use your mother like that, when you're the one who screwed up."

Quietly, Abe said, "If you let me, I'd try like hell to make that up to you."

Fiona imagined it—Abe over her, braced on his huge arms, ready to penetrate her, a look of confusion on his face as he tried to remember her name.

No way. Too painful.

But his mother...Fiona felt badly about the way she'd left Hope's house on Wednesday—Hope had only been trying to help her deal with her feelings about her mother leaving. Of course, lobbing a family bomb like a story of an uncle abusing her mother wasn't the best way to have a person stay for tea and a knitting lesson. But Hope had been trying, and she'd been kind. Fiona had run instead of listening to more, and she regretted that now.

"I'll meet you there—"

"Thank you—"

"But it's for her, not for you."

"I'll take it."

Fiona clicked off after he gave her the time to meet them.

Then she sat in the dark. It was getting colder, quickly. The clarity of the sky was good for star-gazing but the cold was starting to win against the wool of the old sweater. If she went inside, though, she'd just go to bed, and it was still too early for that. She didn't want to lie in her bedroom, thinking of the way his skin had felt against hers.

Her phone was still in her hand. She hit the first speed-dial.

Her father's voice was sleepy. "Honey? You okay?"

"I'm fine. Just checking in." Her voice surprised her, breaking as though she might cry. Desperate to not have him hear that, she said, "Sorry, eating spicy food. How are you and Gloria? I'm sorry I'm calling so late. It must be almost midnight there or something."

"Nah, we're on the west coast now."

Fiona sat up straight, a shaft of happiness piercing her heart. "You are?"

"Sorry, Fee. Shouldn't have gotten your hopes up like that. We're way up on the border. Went to Vancouver where we had a little trouble..."

"What?"

"Turns out that pencils are like bananas."

"You've lost me."

"In gross quantities, they read a little...radioactive, maybe."

"You're saying you were thrown in the slammer for importing nukes?" Fiona wrapped her free arm around her waist and hugged herself.

"Only for a couple of days while they got their experts to go through the van."

Fiona's head spun. "Days? And you didn't think to call me?"

"Didn't want to worry you, did we? We knew we'd get out, and we did! And now we have a dinner story that'll keep us in free hot dogs for *years*. And Gloria made a friend!"

"Oh, good! Your wife was adopted by an inmate? What was she in for?"

"Got caught for some white collar something. Maybe extortion."

"Dad! Are you lying to me?"

"Okay, maybe it was embezzling. That's not the important part of the story. The big part, and the absolute best part of being in jail, was learning about the one kind of convention that is going to fund our retirement."

Fiona stretched her head back and looked up at the stars. One twinkled, disappeared, and then came back. She blinked her eyes clear. "I thought you were already retired."

"It's fun to retire. I plan to do it as much as possible. And get this. You ready, daughter?"

"Ready." A shooting star streaked the night above— flaring out before Fiona could really focus on it.

"Crossword puzzles."

"Huh?"

"Those people have conventions, did you know that? They're *crazy*."

Fiona searched for more falling stars. If she saw two more, she could make a wish. "I didn't know that."

"There's a convention in Seattle on the weekend. Imagine, just take a minute to imagine, how many pencils *those* people go through."

"Don't the experts work in pen?"

"Myth. Pencils are the only way to go. Pens are used by the wannabes trying to show off."

Fiona scooted down in her chair so the back of it supported her neck. The sky was quiet. "Sounds like you have your plan."

"We're gonna sell hundreds. Maybe thousands. You should see the pencil bouquets Gloria's come up with."

Another star blazed across the sky, going the same direction the other had. Fiona held her breath and listened as her father told her what they'd last done to the pencil van—*big pads of paper, set up on easels, everyone gets to try! Getting a feel for the different grits, you know? So exciting!*—and tried not to ask what she most wanted to. Maybe if she saw one more star...

Her father droned on, and Fiona remembered what she both loved and hated most about her father. When not interrupted, the man just kept going. About anything. He wouldn't notice if a whole room full of people had wandered away. Hell, he wouldn't notice if they all started talking about something else entirely. He'd just keep going, his voice sonorous, even in pitch and rhythm. He used to talk like that over dinner after Bunny left, and sometimes Fiona would put her head right down on the kitchen table and go to sleep. He would only notice when she snored—otherwise, he just thought she was listening with her eyes closed. It should have been nothing but annoying, this narcissistic tic of his, but somehow it was endearing. It was him.

Fiona let him go until she felt her foot jerk, a precursor to actual sleep. She opened her eyes again, and gave a full-body shiver. A third shooting star lit up the western sky.

She interrupted something about where the convention was located in terms of other pencil suppliers. "Why haven't you ever told me where Mom is?"

There was a pause and she could imagine him frowning, unable to comprehend that his train of words had been lifted off the track. "What?"

"I know you know where she is."

"You've never asked."

"I don't want to know the answer."

Her father coughed. "I don't understand. Are you asking me where she is now?"

"No," Fiona said. "I'm not the one who left. She knows where I am." That was the whole point, really. Her mother could have found her at any time over the years. She'd just never come looking. When her mother had quit being a mother, she'd done it thoroughly. Surgically. "Never mind. I guess I still don't want to talk about it. Why don't you give that convention a miss and just come down and see me?"

"What?" Her father made it sound like she'd started speaking Macedonian.

"Instead of going to that convention. Come see me."

Another long bit of quiet. She could almost see him making hand-flapping motions at Gloria, could almost see her confusion. "But the convention lasts a week."

"Come see me and then go back up to it," she said. Goddammit, she shouldn't have to beg. He hadn't been for a visit in more than four years. Not since an old inventor friend of his had died and he'd come home for the funeral. So that didn't even really count.

"Honey, that's a great idea. We'll talk about it."

Yep, that was the line he used. Once again—as always—she came last. She knew he didn't approve of her working in the body shop, not really. While she was growing up he'd wanted her to use her hands, yes, but he'd gotten it into his mind early that she was an artist, the kind of artist he'd always wanted to be, doing the kind of art he hadn't dared pursue.

"Hey, Daddy, you remember when you thought I should be a painter? How old was I then? Ten?"

Fiona could hear the smile in his voice as he said, "You had a talent. A real talent. Don't know where you got it, unless it was something that Bunny passed on without ever showing an aptitude for."

Did all of her talents have to be attributable to one of her parents? What about the talents she'd cultivated on her own? With plain old determination and hard work? "Well, she did paint that snowflake on the wall of the lighthouse." The one she'd based her tattoo on. And in a small metal box hidden carefully out of sight under her bed was a collection of small sketches her mother had made. Most were of trees and flowers, but two of the sketches were of a little girl. Fiona had always liked to think it was her. Even though it probably wasn't.

"That snowflake was pretty, but it was a fluke."

"Why do you have to say that? Why do you always talk like that about her?" Why was Fiona *defending* her mother?

"She wasn't creative, Fiona. You know that. She probably copied it from a book."

Wouldn't that be something, if Fiona had marked her body permanently with an image copied from *Ladies Home Journal*?

"You know what's funny?" she said.

"What?"

"I *am* a painter."

"You've been painting, daughter?"

"I paint pretty much every day."

"Fee, I can't wait to see your work." The delight in her father's voice was painful to hear.

"You should come down. I'll show you one of my most recent cars. I did an argyle paint job last month on a SmartCar. It looks amazing. It took almost a week, and the owner is so proud of it she refuses to drive more than forty, worried a bug might smash too hard on the paint." Maybe the more words she threw at him, the longer it would take him to say what he was going to say.

"Honey, I thought you meant real painting."

Another star fell. A bonus star. Fiona didn't even bother wishing on it. "Good luck with the puzzlers, Pops."

CHAPTER THIRTY-THREE

Don't let anyone tell you there are any rules. (Even me. Don't let me tell you this rule is a rule.) You know how to make clothing with sticks and string. Make your own rules, and break them when it makes the most sense to. — E. C.

"Will she come?" asked Hope.

"She'll come," said Abe.

He wasn't sure if he actually believed it, or if he was just telling himself what he wanted to hear. Holy crap, in the throes of passion, when he was almost at his peak, with Fiona in his arms, in the bed where he wanted to stay for something like forever, he'd called her the wrong *name*.

And then his mother asked her for a favor.

There was a *very* fucking good chance that she wouldn't come to the lighthouse.

It didn't stop him hoping she would.

He'd arrived first, in his truck. He could have walked from the marina, but he wanted the knowledge that if he had to flee fast, he could, tires burning rubber in the small lighthouse parking lot.

His mother, as always, walked down from the house, refusing his offer of a ride, just as she did every year. It had been a tradition for her and Conway to walk to the lighthouse every Sunday night. From the time they were first married, they hadn't missed a week, not even on rainy Sundays. They'd bring a bottle of wine and a box of something sweet, cookies or chocolate. Hope would knit, and Conway would pour their wine. They'd watch the sunset.

Abe knew that they'd also been fond of the cave below, at the base of Moonglass beach. He didn't ask questions about that, not wanting to find out if his suspicions that he'd been conceived there were founded in truth.

When Hope met him in the parking lot, she kissed his cheek and then walked to the edge of the cliff, as she always did. She did this alone. Abe watched. He understood. There was still communion here. He could *feel* Conway this late afternoon. Here, he always could. He knew his mother felt the same way. In the old red plaid jacket she always wore, her gray hair flying wildly in all directions, she tossed pebbles over, lobbing them softly.

He'd asked her once about this practice.

"They're just rocks," she'd said.

"Why do you throw them?" From this distance, it looked as if she were throwing stones *at* the ocean.

"I always brought him home a rock from my walks. Now I just save the best ones up until this time of year and give them to him all at once."

Abe remembered that—if he ran to her as a child, after falling or crashing his bike, there would always be something hard in her pocket. Sometimes she'd give him one to hold, to take to school. "To remind you that I'm with you," she'd say.

Rock as comfort. Well, it was as unexpected as water for comfort, he supposed, and that's where he found his.

If he found any at all, that was. Every year, he hated this deathiversary more.

"You okay?"

Abe spun. He'd been watching his mother so closely he hadn't even heard Fiona approach.

She said, "You look funny."

He tried to smile. "That's my face."

She took a step backward, rubbing the tip of her nose. "It's going to be a cold night."

He nodded. Small talk it was, then. He didn't care. Just as long as he could keep looking at her. "You look great." She did. She looked like *her*. Black t-shirt, those broken-in jeans with the perma-grease trail at the cuffs, her hair an amazing tangle on her shoulders that had obviously fallen from where she'd stuck it under that old black cowboy hat. When she looked up at him, there was a challenge in her makeup-free eyes. It wasn't hard to read.

She wasn't Rayna.

Thank God for that.

Fiona stepped around him, looking at his mother down the path. "Is she throwing rocks?"

"She does that."

His mother turned and made her way back to them. "You came," she said to Fiona.

"I did. I'm not sure why."

Hope glanced up at Abe and then at Fiona. "I know why," she said simply. "Come. Sit over here with me." She made her careful way to the one spot of bermuda grass that grew stubbornly at the base of the lighthouse.

Abe helped Hope shake out the wool blanket—always the same blue one, the one his father had given his mother for their fifth anniversary. Was that normal? For a man to know what anniversary presents had been given on what date to his mother? Or was that the legacy of a lost father, a lost love?

Hope had brought the basket, too. Of course.

"I've never picnicked in the cold like this," said Fiona, drawing her thick sweater more tightly around herself.

"It's not so much a picnic..." started Abe.

"It's a memorial we have every year," finished Hope. "There's a Jewish term for it—*yahrzeit*. It's a good word." She drew out a bottle of bourbon and held it up. "I hope you're done with whatever you were supposed to be doing today."

Fiona didn't even look surprised, to her credit. "All done. Stephen was happy to take over."

"Good boy. First," said Hope, sitting back on her heels, "we tell a memory we have of Conway, and then take a drink. Now. How do you get this off?"

Abe reached to take the bottle from her, but his mother kept it close.

"I don't drink any other time in my life. Let me do this part, too," she said.

Fiona leaned close to him as Hope struggled to get the wax off the top of the bourbon bottle. "You're playing a drinking game?"

"Yeah."

"At five in the afternoon."

"Gotta get it done by dark."

"Hmmm."

Abe looked at her. He was ready for anything he might read on her face. She was probably still pissed as hell at him, and there was no reason she shouldn't feel as if they'd roped her into a private family tradition, because they had. It had been inappropriate of his mother to ask her to come, and it would be understandable if she wanted to get away as soon as possible.

But instead—astonishingly—she smiled at him. As if she meant it. "Makes sense," was all she said.

Hope had managed to get the top off the bottle. "I'll go first." She glanced up at the sky. "When Conway was tired, he yawned almost constantly until he fell asleep. I mean, he never took a break. I could see all the way down past his tonsils and just as soon as one yawn was done, he'd start another one, making that huge YAAARRRRRGH noise the whole time. Used to wake you up as a baby, Abe. Drove me crazy. And nothing could make me sleepier faster than that sound."

Abe hadn't remembered that in years. It had been like the sound of the ocean when he was a child, as predictable and soothing as a lullaby.

Hope took a large swig and handed Abe the bottle.

He hadn't planned this year. He'd been too busy thinking about the girl sitting next to him, and that was the truth. And it didn't help that she was right here, so close that his whole left side itched—ached—to press into her, to share his heat with her, to make her not need the extra blanket that Hope had put around her shoulders.

"Dad said I didn't deserve a good woman."

Hope opened her mouth, and then closed it. This was part of their unspoken contract every year. Each of them could remember anything, and the other couldn't make corrections. Later, afterward, Hope could tell him he was full of cowpie and that his memory was faulty and his father had spent way more than ten dollars on that crappy bike with the broken frame for his Christmas present but out here, bottle in hand, memory was gospel.

Why did it feel so right that Fiona was here? When she'd never been with their family before, certainly not when it was whole?

"The year he said that—repeatedly, might I add—was the year that I never came out of my room except for school, dinner, and when he made me work the boat on the weekends. One day, he said that I didn't deserve to have a woman in my life. That confused me, you know, because I was thirteen. The only thing I thought about girls was that they were pretty and scary, and none of them would ever measure up to my own mother in terms of cooking macaroni and cheese." He saw his mother smile and glance down at her lap. "I back-talked him on the boat when we were docking, saying something smart-assed, I'm sure, even though I have no clue now what it was, and he looked straight at me and said, "Son, act like that and you won't ever deserve a good woman." It felt like the worst thing he could say to me, as if he'd said I'd never be a real man. I remember panicking and thinking I wouldn't know what to do with a woman, but at that moment, all I wanted to be was someone he could be proud of."

Abe took a long swig of bourbon, the straight heat of it first burning his lips, then heating his body. Kind of exactly the way Fiona did, coincidentally.

He reached to hand the bottle back to his mother, embarrassed again that Fiona was having to sit through this. Luckily they didn't usually share more than a couple of memories. His mother didn't like to have too much alcohol on the one night she drank—even though this whole thing was her idea—and Abe would never tie one on in front of her.

But Fiona reached forward to grasp the bottle. "Do you mind? I have a memory to share."

CHAPTER THIRTY-FOUR

Forgiveness is like knitting backwards—a little tricky to learn and very uncomfortable at first—but when you need to know how, it's best to have already had practice. – E. C.

Abe let her have the bottle but said, "You don't have to say..."

"Let her," said Hope, as if she'd known Fiona would speak.

Fiona nodded at his mother. "Thanks." She took a deep breath and didn't look at Abe. "Once I ran away from home. I was about eight, and I knew I didn't have much going for me. I didn't have looks, and I didn't have talent."

Abe sat forward. What was she talking about?

"But I knew I had one thing. I had brains. My mom didn't like all the library books I brought home but they were free. She couldn't stop me from reading. And that's how I learned that kids could get out. *The Boxcar Children. My Side of the Mountain.* And *From the Mixed-Up Files of Mrs. Basil E. Frankweiler.* I had a spiral notebook that my father got me at the dime store, and I made a list of everything I'd need for a month away from home. I figured in a month, I could find a different..." Fiona's voice dropped away for a second, and Abe didn't know if it was because of the wind or the subject matter.

But it was against the rules to ask. He pictured her, a child, living on this very land where they were sitting. Sleeping in the lighthouse, inside the building she hated. He had to find out why she hated it. Maybe she was about to tell him.

In a moment, Fiona went on. "I figured it wouldn't take a whole month to find another mother. I stole one of my dad's old rucksacks he got at the Army Supply store, and filled it, over the course of a couple of weeks, with food I could hide away. Potatoes, even though I didn't know how I would cook them. Crackers from my soup. Two apples because they always last longer than anyone thinks they will. I had rope in case I needed to climb anything, and I had three dollars in dimes and nickels that I'd found in the parking lot behind the laundromat. I wanted to take my favorite doll, Joanne, but she wouldn't fit. Neither would Margot, the cat that lived behind the woodpile that used to be over there." Fiona pointed to the east of the lighthouse to where a small, dirty shed stood. "God knows I tried one Tuesday afternoon and she sliced me up so badly that I had to take care of all my scratches and couldn't leave till that Friday." She looked at the bottle in her hand. "This is turning out to be a long story."

"Have a shot, dear," said Hope in a quiet voice.

Fiona stared at the bottle and then tipped it up. After swallowing, she carefully placed the bourbon on the blanket in front of her. "So that Friday afternoon, I ran away. I knew that if I were to walk, I wouldn't make it far without being found by my father. If I hitchhiked, a murderer would kill me by nightfall. There wasn't much I was good at, but I'd been fascinated by boating books for a while. I knew that it was good if a deckhand was small so they could crawl into tiny spaces. I was small, I had that going for me. And for some reason, I thought sailors were so transient they might not recognize me, even though they berthed permanently at the Cypress Hollow marina. I took my bag, kissed Margot the cat goodbye, and marched down to the boats. When I got there, I put on a British accent."

Hope smiled and covered her mouth.

"I know. I figured if I seemed local then someone would try to figure out where I should be. But if I were a tourist, no one would care. I honestly don't know where I got that idea. I wanted to pretend to be from Italy or Germany, but I knew I shouldn't try to fake an actual language in case someone really spoke it, so I tried to be as British as I could." She paused, pulling down her hat so that her eyes were shaded from the sun dropping into the ocean. "I thought I could stow away. If I was caught, I'd speak with the accent and say I'd lost my passport. I made up a set of parents in London, and I thought that the worst-case scenario would be getting put on a plane headed to the British Isles." Fiona pointed to the bottle sticking out of the basket. "May I have some of that water?"

Hope nodded and passed it to her.

"Sorry," said Fiona. "I'm almost done. I'd just forgotten this. Haven't thought about it in years." She unscrewed the cap, drank, and put the cap back on as slowly as possible. Abe wanted to take it out of her hands and tighten it for her, and then hold those hands till they stopped shaking.

"Are you too cold?" he asked, breaking the rule. "You can wear my jacket."

She shook her head and still didn't meet his eyes. "I'm fine. Where was I? Oh, yeah. Headed to the marina as an eight-year-old crazy person. I got there, and my backpack already felt too heavy. I tried to get on board a yacht with a tall guy asleep on a front chair. I thought he was from out of town, and I'd just wait to see where he went, but then his gate was locked, and when I tried to force it, his dog woke up and barked his dang head off. I was terrified and ran down the first pier that had an open gate. The gangplank was down on a fishing boat."

"The *Second Hope*," said Abe's mother.

Fiona nodded. "I hid in the bathroom. I thought I'd wait till night fell and then sleep under the table, and then go out in the morning with the fisherman, whoever he was. I'd show myself then and I'd talk him—I wasn't sure how—into continuing to sail. I'd help him catch enough fish and rainwater, and we'd make it all the way to Fiji, or at least to the Channel Islands, and then he could leave me somewhere and I'd be Karana from *Island of the Blue Dolphins*. When I was old, twenty or so, I'd come back to the mainland and show my parents I could do fine on my own." Fiona rubbed her forehead. "I didn't actually want to leave my dad, so I was crying when I locked the bathroom door. Then I felt the boat move, and someone came aboard. I didn't realize it then, but he'd seen me break in. He knocked politely at the door and asked how he could help."

Abe could just see it. Some men might have stormed or yelled or called the cops. Conway, though, would have dealt with her the way he did everything—with great thought and careful handling.

"I told him I was from London and that I liked riding in black and white taxis. He told me he liked fish and chips. I asked him to take me to an island. He said he couldn't. That's when I started crying. Instead of freaking out, he asked me if I knew how to steer a boat. I said I did, and I'm sure he knew I was lying, but he took us out anyway. It was about this time of night actually." Fiona took off her hat and ran a hand through her hair. "Sunset. Cold. Like this. You see that boat out there?"

A sailboat was about four hundred yards out, moving across a long, yellowed ray of sunlight. "We were about that far out when he showed me how to turn the boat. I did what he said, and even though I had no idea what he was doing, he made me feel smart. He pointed up at the lighthouse. My house. He said, 'No matter what, you'll always know where home is.' We sailed another hour or so, then he took us in, and we docked in the dark. He told me I was a big help and he shook my hand."

Abe leaned forward and jammed his hands together. It was so damn hard not to touch her.

"And that was the wild thing. I went home. I wasn't sad I'd been foiled. I just felt relief he hadn't told on me. I unpacked my rucksack and my mom, who was having a good night, made mashed potatoes, which were my favorite."

Abe's glance tangled with hers in the golden sun's rays. She continued, "Your father treated me like I mattered. And I was only eight." She grabbed for the bottle and took a quick, short sip.

Fiona handed the bourbon to him, and their fingers brushed. He pulled his hand back, but she reached forward, lacing her fingers with his for just a second. When she let go, Abe's hand felt colder than ever.

Hope took the bottle from him and said, "When we fought, he always made sure he told me that he loved me. During a fight, no matter how stupid, I was always convinced we were over. That he'd leave me. He knew that, so in the middle of any raging we were doing, he'd look dead at me and tell me I was still the only woman for him. Then the fight would go on, just like he hadn't said anything." She paused. "That was wonderful. Your turn, son."

Abe crossed his legs awkwardly, conscious of Fiona's eyes on him. "I had a memory I was going to tell, about him at the fish market in Monterey, when he carried a drunk guy for more than a mile, but I just remembered something else." It came back to him in a rush, and he couldn't believe he'd forgotten it. He hadn't thought he'd forgotten anything about that night. "The storm was coming in." He didn't have to say which storm. "I was scared and I was trying really hard not to show it, since Dad was never scared of a damn thing. I asked him where we'd end up if we couldn't get through the channel into the harbor. He told me a story of a stowaway who wanted to go to Fiji. She was a little girl, but had worked out the way the currents flowed, and she'd tried to get him to drift away with her. First, he told me that no matter what, the worst was that we'd end up in Fiji where we'd fish for a few days before heading home to Mom. Second, he said that the reason he hadn't gone with that little girl to Fiji was that he couldn't leave me. Or Mom. That no matter what, he'd never leave us." Abe took a long pull from the bottle. "Hoo, damn. Don't let me have any more of that. Not if I'm going to drive back to the marina."

In other families, this was where Hope would lean over and hug him. Maybe cry a little. Tell him he'd been a good kid and that his father had always loved him. But this was *his* family, and they didn't work like that. Never had. Abe hoped that Fiona wouldn't mind or think they were broken.

Even though they were, in their own, Atwell way.

Hope gave no sign that she'd heard his story. She reached in her bag and pulled out what looked like a roll of wire. "This is my idea," she said to Fiona. She took out a pair of needles and looped the silver wire over the tip. She made a few laborious moves and then handed the whole metallic nest to Fiona.

Fiona took it, looking confused. "What am I doing with this?"

"Knit."

Fiona held the mass closer to her eyes. "Not to state the obvious, but this is metal."

"Silver plated copper wire, to be exact. Just do the moves I taught you last week. Same ones," said Abe's mother.

Abe watched as Fiona moved the needle, holding the wire like his mother usually held yarn. It took a moment, and then it clicked. He could actually see Fiona figure out what to do, what came next.

"If I turn the work here, can I add a stitch on either side on the next row?"

Hope nodded. "You've got it. I knew you would." Hope stood and briskly brushed off the front of her pants. "Will the lighthouse come down, then?"

Fiona looked as surprised as Abe felt and the wire stopped moving. "Yes. Everyone I've spoken to about my proposal for the park seems to be behind it. So far."

"So my son hasn't managed to change your mind."

She shook her head. "No."

"My husband loved this building."

"I know."

Hope shrugged. "Tearing down the lighthouse won't fix anything. I think you probably know that, too. But I'm glad you knew my husband. I'm glad he got you home safely." She looked at Abe, that look she'd been giving him since he came home alone that night. "He was good at getting people home safely." She tucked the bottle of bourbon into her picnic basket and tugged the blanket out from under them as they scrambled to their feet.

Then Hope walked away.

Fiona's eyes were wide. "Just like that? She's leaving? That's what you do?"

"What do you mean?"

"You tell heartbreaking stories and then just split? Alone?"

"She stayed longer than she usually does. Normally I just say something like I remember that Dad's favorite color was the shade of wet kelp, and she makes me drink a couple of shots and then she walks home."

"Tradition, huh?"

"All we have left."

Abe followed Fiona's lead and faced the water. The clouds were high. It was going to be a crazy-ass rainbow sunset.

Fiona dropped the wire knitting to the blanket.

Then, suddenly, she hugged him.

It was just a hug. Like any other he might get at Tillie's in the morning. But shit, damn and hellfire, it felt better than a kiss would have at that moment. Her arms were tight and her cheek was soft against his. The brush of her hair on his neck warmed him more than a bonfire.

After a long moment, she pulled away. "I'm glad I chose your dad's boat."

"Why were you running away?"

"My mother."

"She was bad enough to chase you that far?"

"Definitely. And more." Fiona looked around, turning her head to the sun. A reddish haze lit the side of her face. "You wanna see something? Can we leave our stuff here?"

"Of course."

She took his hand. "This way."

As he walked beside her, Abe knew that he wasn't forgiven. But her hand was in his like it belonged there, and that felt almost—*almost*—as good.

CHAPTER THIRTY-FIVE

Knit new memories. — E. C.

Fiona knew it was important that he see this. Before anything else could happen between them, he needed to be inside where she came from.

"Be careful," she said unnecessarily. It was a difficult walk, up the shallow broken steps, and then over the fallen boards. For years, the main door of the lighthouse had been boarded up, but the boards had been partially ripped off, and the building was now open to the wind and water. There were multiple signs posted, reading everything from *Hazardous* to *Keep Out* and *Trespassers Will Be Prosecuted*, but kids had been sneaking in ever since the lighthouse was decommissioned and left abandoned. Fiona knew exactly which boards to push aside to make her way in. Abe followed behind her.

"I don't think I've ever been in here," he said.

"Really?" She stopped so short that Abe bumped into her.

"Sorry," he said.

"Don't be. It's just that I think you're the only person who *hasn't* been in here. You didn't bring girls in here?"

"Nope."

"Why not?"

He shrugged, and his face darkened. Fiona realized that this place, in his mind, belonged to the father he'd loved. It wasn't a place to try to round second base with girls.

"Anyway," she hurried to say. "Over here."

"Right with you."

She took out her cell phone. "Flashlight app."

"I use it on the boat all the time."

"We live in the future," said Fiona. "This way."

They made their way into the lower body of the lighthouse itself. A few years back, an older woman with Alzheimer's had gotten stuck at the top, and the city had taken out the steps entirely. No one had climbed to the upper deck since, and Fiona was glad. There was nothing up there but wind and a bleak view that stretched out forever and never changed.

Fiona could admit that there were a few—very few—good memories still trapped up there behind the broken panes of glass. Her father pointing toward Hawaii, telling her that maybe tomorrow it would be clear enough to see a girl in a hula skirt. The *thump-click* noise the light had made as it swiveled in its perpetual arc. And up at the top used to be the only place Fiona could truly get away from her mother. Bunny had been afraid— terrified—of heights. Fiona now wondered if somehow, subconsciously, that's exactly why her father had taken the job.

"Through here." Fiona pushed at the door that led to the old keeper's house, attached to the side of the lighthouse. It felt locked, but it had always felt that way. That had been Dad's trick. *Use your shoulder!* She bumped it harder, and the door screeched open. Dust flew. In the surprisingly strong light of her cell phone, she could see the old green couch was sunken, destroyed. Something—a teenager or an animal with sharp claws— had sliced it open at some point over the years, and the room was decorated with piles of dirty stuffing. "It's horrible in here."

Behind her, Abe caught her elbow. "Hey."

She spun. "What?"

"What is this? What's going on?"

"I want to show you where I came from."

Abe didn't release her elbow, and Fiona realized she didn't want him to.

"Why?"

Oh. She didn't have an answer to that. She leaned her head forward, without thinking, and pressed it against his chest.

"Hey," he said, lifting her chin. "I don't care where you came from. Whether you sprung out of a pumpkin or fell off the back of a motorcycle, I don't care. Walking through an abandoned house won't make a spit of difference to me."

His words sounded good, and Fiona wanted to grab at them, to collect them and keep them for later. "But..."

"Look at this." He gestured with the beam of his own phone. "This place has nothing to do with you."

Fiona shook her head. "It does. It has to. Come this way." She would be stubborn about this. She led them through to a tiny bedroom. "This was my parents' room."

"Ah," said Abe thoughtfully. Then he peered forward through the darkness, shining his light on the back wall. "That's...Whoa."

It used to be bright white on a cerulean background. It was the one thing Fiona remembered her mother being excited about in this house. Bunny had drawn the enormous, intricate snowflake on the white wall in pencil, and then she'd painted the wall blue around the pencil marks, leaving the snowflake gleaming brightly through. It had been so beautiful Fiona sometimes thought it looked like it was actually falling.

Someday it'll snow here, her mother would say. *And then you'll see what you're missing. Snow covers everything up. It makes everything beautiful, even the ugly things. This is to remind me. Someday, it'll snow and you'll see.*

Now the wall was grungy. Large pieces of the old paint had rolled off. But the snowflake was still distinguishable, dirty gray against the dingy blue.

It was still beautiful to her. Fiona sighed. "Someday I'll see real snow."

"It's your tattoo," said Abe, still gazing at the wall.

"I got it so I would remember."

He turned slowly and lowered the light. He was so broad that he blocked Fiona's view of the wall, and for that she was grateful.

"What are you trying to remember, Fiona?"

She took a deep breath and grounded her feet on the dirty floorboards. "That you can't just paint something and make it pretty. That it's still exactly the same broken, useless thing underneath."

Abe's eyes softened. "You know you're breaking my heart, Snowflake."

Fiona couldn't respond. If she did, she would probably gulp or say a fake word.

He went on, "Sometimes when a person paints over something, they're fixing it. Seems to me like that's what you do at your shop."

Fiona knew he didn't get it. Bless him for trying. She turned. "So this is it. Just a little one-bedroom house."

"Ah," he said again. A pause. "Where did you sleep?"

"On that disgusting old couch out there. It wasn't as bad then, obviously."

"Huh." He frowned. "How long did you live here?"

"Till the lighthouse closed. It was a fluke for my dad—we'd been driving down the coast while he looked for work, and the old civilian keeper had just died. Dad basically lied his way into the job, saying that he was from a long line of lighthouse keepers, and that a great-uncle of his had actually built this one."

"Sounds like a flawed plan."

"He was good at it, actually." Fiona remembered how much time he'd spent at the top. Without her, without her mother. "Somehow Dad always thought it was best to leave us alone. *The womens*, he called us. He'd come down the stairs and find us sitting in the living room, me doing homework, her drunk and watching TV, and he'd say, 'How's my womens?' Before she left, obviously."

"That must have been hard." Abe's voice was quiet, and he didn't touch her. Thank God. If he'd reached out to her, there was a good chance the quaking in her chest would turn into tears, and that would be totally unacceptable.

"Her leaving was hard, yeah." Fiona couldn't quite finish the thought. She breathed in—underneath the moldy stench of salt-rotted walls and weeping sixty-year-old flooring, she could still smell her mother's perfume, a cloying gardenia-based scent that had always made her dizzy. "What was harder was how long she stayed."

"I'm sorry you had to go through that." Still that low, quiet voice.

Relief tasted sweet on her tongue. "Thank you," Fiona said, meaning it. "So...is it okay?"

"What?"

"That we have such different visions of this place? That I want it torn down..."

He nodded. "And I want it preserved? Yeah, it's okay. We can agree to disagree." He tugged on her hand. "I just want to be here with you. Is that okay?"

Fiona nodded. It was more than okay.

"Now how about we get out of here?"

She felt relief. "We can go out the side door from the kitchen. It locks from the inside. Not that it matters, I guess." She looked at the high, broken window. The silver moon was visible in the now-darkened sky. "Would you mind...giving me just a minute, though? It's been a long time."

Instead of answering, Abe stepped forward. Briefly, he wrapped her in his arms. He pressed his lips to the top of her head and kept them there for a long, long moment. Fiona breathed him in, stopping herself short of actually rubbing her cheek against the fabric of his shirt. "I'll be just outside," he said. "Holler if you need me."

He left her in the room alone, with the echoes of the past.

Put on some lipstick.

I'm only eleven, Mama. I don't need lipstick!

You're so pale. You look like an albino eel. How are you going to get a boyfriend?

I don't want one.

You're too thin, too. Eat another sandwich, and while you're in the kitchen, fix your father one, too.

But...last week you said I was fat.

Good thing you listened to me. Are those pimples on your chin?

I don't...have to show you.

You have to show your mother every part of yourself. That's the rule, that's what mothers get. Every little, ugly part. Someday, if you work hard enough, you'll be pretty, like me. Look at me.

I don't want to.

Come here. Get closer. You see this crow's foot?

No.

You're not looking. You see it right here? Here?

Yes.

How dare *you? That's not even a real wrinkle, just a tiny laugh line. Can you really see it? Is it awful?*

You're beautiful, Mama.

You're just saying that, just saying that because you want to be like me, but listen, little girl, you keep up what you're doing, running around outside in the sun, you'll be damaged by the time you're twenty. No one will want you. No one will even like you. Just keep that up.

The ghostly voices that she *knew* weren't real weren't going to stop. Not until this all crumbled into the pile of rubble it already was in her heart.

Fiona put her hand into her front pocket so that her fingers were right over her tattoo. Sometimes, like now, it still burned from the inside out.

CHAPTER THIRTY-SIX

Knit as if it will save you. Because sometimes, it does. — E. C.

Something was going on in that falling-down house, and Abe didn't like it. He hated the way he'd left Fiona in there, her posture bowed as though huge hands were pushing down on her shoulders. No one should look that sad thinking about their childhood. Even though it hurt like shit thinking about the way his parents mourned when they lost baby Marina, even though thinking of his father's death sliced wounds that would never heal, Abe loved looking back. He loved thinking of the way his father had slid under the bath water, blowing bubbles like a spouting whale, and how when his dad made chili he dunked the whole batch of cornbread into it, breaking it all up with a spoon so the chili was more like a Sloppy Joe. When Abe looked back, he remembered happiness. Laughter. He remembered the way his mother grabbed his father by the front of his fishing jacket, kissing him loudly full on the mouth before he left for the morning, the smell of his oatmeal and coffee still lingering in the air. The way his mother complained when he came home, fish guts smashed down the front of his work jeans. She'd make him change on the back porch, and throw his clothes right into her washer. Dad hollered and streaked naked through the house, and Abe rolled on the living room floor, laughing hysterically.

Whatever Fiona was remembering in there, it wasn't that kind of childhood. It wasn't any kind of childhood at all. He stood up from the log he'd been sitting on, intending to march back through the kitchen to that tiny, horrible bedroom where he'd left her, but at that moment, Fiona ran out as if something were pursuing her.

He caught her, and it struck him at that moment that he *wanted* to be the one to catch her. Not just right now. Tomorrow, too. And the next day. "Are you all right?" Stupid question. "Of course you're not."

She clung to him like a mollusk. Her hands yanked at his shirt. He lifted her off the ground and kissed her. She kissed him back as if he were the surface and she'd been held under too long. As if she'd been drowning.

"Come home with me, Fiona." He took a deep breath. "Say yes."

Fiona didn't say anything. She looked at him, though, and Abe felt her measuring him in that gaze. He held her eyes as steadily as he could. He wanted to be good enough for her. He wanted it so badly it hurt. More than he wanted to make love to her, more than he wanted to watch her come, more than he wanted to be the one she kissed in the middle of the night—he wanted to be good enough. He wanted to be great. He could change. For her. "Please say yes."

"Yes."

He drove as fast as he could to the marina, partially because he was worried she'd change her mind but mostly because minutes she wasn't in his arms were minutes wasted. Fiona talked the whole way there, and neither of them listened. Abe knew, beyond the shadow of a doubt, that if he'd asked, "What did you just say?" she wouldn't have been able to remember that she'd remarked on the paint job of an old Camaro parked on West Lincoln. She wasn't listening to her own words, and neither was he.

But their bodies were listening to each other. He could have said to the eighth of an inch how far her arm was from his. When she twisted her body to face him, as she said something about the way the tide was probably rising—either that or falling—he felt her breath touch his cheek.

Both of them were nervous as anemones when he pulled into his parking space at the dock. She was out, and pulling at the dock's gate before he could even get around the front end of the truck.

"Hoo, I'm thirsty," she said. Her seaweed-colored eyes sparkled at his in the moonlight, and he felt a surge of happiness that threatened to take his head off.

Fiona went on, "Aren't you thirsty? Sheesh, it's like I've never had water or something. I could just kill for a glass of water. Maybe even with bubbles. Do you have fizzy water? What am I asking? You don't have fizzy water. What guy just has fizzy water—"

"I have lime mineral water."

The answer surprised her, obviously. Again, he didn't think she'd even been listening to herself.

Then they were in front of the door. Her eyes were wide.

"It's unlocked," Abe said.

"You leave it unlocked?"

"You never know when a gorgeous mechanic might stop by and need some mineral water."

She blushed. Holy hell, he loved it when she did that.

Fiona went through into the kitchen. She stopped short and said, "I'm not actually thirsty anymore."

"Good," said Abe, and he carefully lifted off her hat. Under it, her hair was mashed so cute she'd never believe it if he told her. She looked like she'd been on the deck of a boat in high winds for hours. Hot.

Abe lifted her into his arms.

It wasn't far to his bed, but Fiona giggled the whole way there. "Put me down," she said. "I'm too heavy for you."

"You're just right," Abe said, cutting off her laugh. He set her on the bed so that she was sitting up, and he leaned forward so he could be extra clear about what he wanted to say next. "You're exactly right, Snowflake. Perfectly, exactly right."

Then he kissed her.

He kissed her the way he'd been wanting to since he'd screwed it all up the other night.

He kissed her like a man kisses the woman he loves.

The thought almost stopped him, almost rocked him back on his heels. He sucked air back into his lungs and broke the kiss, lifting her t-shirt over her head. Her eager hands did the same for him. Then she reached for his belt, then the buttons at his fly. She'd shucked him naked before he even knew what was going on.

"Hey, hey, slow your roll, woman," Abe said, moving his hands to her waist. "I have needs, too."

Her laugh was intoxicating, filling his blood with heat until he wasn't sure he'd be able to stand.

But he did stand, tall and naked in front of her. She stopped laughing, but a smile still played across her lips as she scooted forward to touch him, keeping her arms demurely crossed over her chest.

"No, no..." Abe undid her red lace bra. "Lord, your underwear drives me crazy, woman."

Fiona brought her hips to the edge of the bed and said, "Right now, this is making me crazy."

She took him in her mouth and he gasped in a shock of surprise. She teased, first just the tip of his cock, then she ran her tongue along the length of his shaft. The way her mouth moved in combination with her fingers..."Jesus," Abe groaned, resting his hands on the back of her head. "You're perfect."

She made a pleased sound in the back of her throat and took him deeper, her mouth hot, tight—the sweetest place he'd ever been.

But he couldn't take much more, and this wasn't the way he'd wanted to have her.

"Fiona."

She didn't stop, just looked up at him, her eyes wide and still amused.

"Fiona, for the love of God," he choked. "Stop." Cupping his hands around her ears, he used all his willpower to stop her, almost unable to make himself do so.

Her mouth slid off his cock with a slick *pop*. Abe swayed. It felt like a swell had just rolled under the houseboat, but the hanging lamp didn't move. It was just him.

"You," he managed to say. "Shit, Snowflake..." Bending at the waist, he pushed her backward onto the bed so that he was on top of her. He tucked a long blue strand of hair behind her ear. "We should talk."

Fiona's eyes widened and she pushed herself backward and away from him an inch.

"Seriously? About what?"

"No, nothing bad. We're just moving so fast. Foreplay is good. I say sexy words, you say them back. Doesn't mean I don't get to keep taking your clothes off." He unzipped her jeans as slowly as he could. "Because you have *way* too many clothes on."

"S'true," Fiona said breathlessly. "I might need your help with that."

"I'm your man," said Abe. The words felt big. True.

He slipped her jeans from her narrow hips; she lay in front of him wearing only a tiny piece of red lace. "Damn," he said.

"What?" She started to sit up, tried to cross her arms over stomach and breasts.

"No, darlin'. I want to leave you like this. Dressed like this."

"I'm *not* dressed."

He plucked at the thin red fabric with his first finger. "Some would say you were dressed just right. I think it's your color."

Fiona laughed again. Then she caught her breath as his finger explored its way underneath the lace.

"Then again," he continued, "I like this color of pink."

"It's red."

"No, right here." Abe slid the panties down her legs. "God, Fiona. Look at you."

Again, she made that half-effort to rise, and he kissed her down again. She murmured, "What?" against his mouth. "What is it? What's wrong?"

"Nothing's wrong. Everything's just so right. Like here." He moved his finger into her slickness while he lowered his head to take her nipple into his mouth. Moving his tongue lazily in circles, he touched her deeper, where she was so hot she almost burned him. "And here."

Fiona wasn't laughing anymore, that was for sure. Good. He wanted her like this, out of breath, super-heated, wanting more. Her hips started to move against his hand.

"Lots of time, Snowflake." He slid his finger in, slowly, so slowly, and then left it inside her. "Don't move."

She made a displeased noise.

"So. Let's talk. Wanna get to know each other?" As he rolled to face her, keeping his finger very still, he knew the smile on his face was cheekier than hell.

Fiona, though, played along. "Oh, good. I'd love to find out what your favorite color is. Right here. With your *hand* inside me."

He shook his head firmly. "That, my girl, is only one finger."

Fiona caught her lower lip between her teeth. "Oh, yeah."

"Oh, yeah." Jesus Christ, he could do this all night. "And my favorite color is the color of wet seaweed. Tell me about you."

"I like yellow. I run Fee's Fill. I'd shake your hand but it appears to be busy."

Abe leaned forward and nuzzled her neck. He was rewarded with a gasp. "Tell me something I don't know about you."

She moved farther away from him without moving a muscle, aside from dropping her lashes. "You start."

"Okay. What kinds of things do you want to know?"

She lifted her eyes, and he read the challenge there. "Secret things."

"Like when I broke my own truck's window practicing with my slingshot and blamed it on a seagull dropping a clamshell?"

"How old were you?"

"Four months younger than I am now."

She laughed. "I think the insurance company will forgive you."

"Forgive me? That window cost six hundred bucks to fix. They're not going to find out." He moved his finger almost imperceptibly, and Fiona's eyes fluttered. "And besides, we should only tell each other the *really* terrible things."

Her eyes, those beautiful hazel eyes with their sparks of brown flame, snapped open again. "Why?"

"Because everyone else knows the good stuff."

"Yeah."

"Let's be different for each other." Abe was so pulled to this idea—to this *woman*— that he *needed* this. To be themselves—their true selves—in front of each other.

"I think you're supposed to learn the bad stuff as you go."

Abe shook his head. "That's where it turns into a trick. Bait and switch."

Her cheeks were deliciously pink as she tried to ignore that his finger was inside her, still but persistently present. "Is that even a fishing phrase? Do you bait a line and then switch it for something else?"

"Yes and no. I don't care about fishing right now. This game is different. If we fall in love with each other because we think the other person is perfect, we can only go downhill. So, tell me something terrible. Tell me the worst thing. That way I'll know it first and it won't matter. As much."

Fiona's eyes were so wide there were perfect rings of white around that hazel gold. "L-love?" she stuttered.

"If. That's all." He kissed her lips softly. "No fear now. Just if."

"I don't fall in love," she said.

"Me, neither." Keeping his hand still, he kissed her again. He could do this forever. "So we're safe. Now tell me the worst part. I'm not going anywhere."

CHAPTER THIRTY-SEVEN

Be fearless. Not all of life is safe; not all of it can be undone.
Enjoy the stitches dancing on your needles even if they do the
wrong steps. Even the undoing of them is pleasurable,
if seated next to the right person. – E. C.

Fiona's heart was racing so fast she was sure the bed should be thudding underneath her. If he was serious...Oh, God, if he meant what he'd just said...

Love?

If he hated her afterward, and he probably would, it would be so far beyond awful that awful wouldn't even be in the same time zone. The last thing she thought she could handle was his disapproval.

Why, then, was she going to do this?

For one reason and one alone: Since the first moment he'd touched her, inside and out, he'd been gentle. He was running kisses down the side of her face right now—a touch that both heated and soothed her at the same time. He was *listening*.

She took a deep breath. "I gave a kitten up to the shelter when it wouldn't stop peeing on my clothes."

Abe shook his head. "Extenuating circumstances. Another one."

She wiggled her hips backward. "I can't be serious when I can feel—you—inside me."

Without protest, he slid his finger out of her and moved so that his wide hand rested on her belly. She wouldn't have thought she would like that—too much concentration on where she was soft and slightly rounded, convex. But Abe smiled and brushed her skin softly. His eyes were encouraging.

"I took on too much debt when I bought the filling station and almost lost my house a few years ago. I'm back on track, but it wasn't easy."

"That's just a hardship tale followed by a success story." His eyes crinkled at the corners. "That's like saying in an interview that your worst trait is your obsessive attention to detail. I'm not buying what you're selling, Lynde. Give me the real dirt."

His muscled body was so *heated* next to hers. Fiona felt a heady rush in knowing that if she flipped her leg over him, she could take this whole thing over. She could get what she wanted at any second. She could *make* him have sex with her and not tell him a thing.

And yet, Fiona stayed still. She wanted to give him what he asked for.

She tilted her head onto the bed, so that her cheek was against his chest. She didn't want to look at him when she said it.

"I was the reason my mother left us."

Abe's free arm tightened around her, and he pressed a longer, harder kiss to her temple. "Tell me."

Fiona felt the ridiculous tears spring to her eyes, pushing behind her lids.

"It's okay." His low voice rumbled, shaking her smaller body. It felt good. Maybe...maybe it felt right. "Whisper it to me if it feels better that way."

"Can't we just have sex?" Last-ditch effort.

"There's time for all that, believe me. So much time. Tell me, darlin'."

So she did. In a whisper, Fiona said, "My mother...As soon as I was born, my father was crazy about me. He knew, and I knew, that his love for me didn't take any amount of his love away from my mother—in fact, for a while, it probably only increased it. I remember Dad being totally wild about her. Over the years, it changed. She just...Nothing was good enough for her. Not our house. Not his job. Not the way we talked or looked or dressed. Not the car he drove, not the food he cooked at night. When we drove through Cypress Hollow, when he found out the lighthouse needed a keeper, she dismissed the idea. Even when he passed the civilian exam, she told him he couldn't take the job, that she wouldn't live in a house as old and decrepit as that one was. That it was too tall and too isolated. In the one act of defiance I ever saw him insist on, he took the job as the last Cypress Hollow lighthouse keeper. He knew it was slated to be decommissioned, but while they built and tested the auto-strobe light they still needed someone there."

Fiona rubbed her hands against her face. "So it was us. On that rocky ground, just outside of town. Remember Cypress Hollow then? It was smaller. My mom barely bothered to send me to school. Only the threat that she'd have to home-school me made her let me walk the mile and a half to Ocean View Elementary every day." Fiona didn't dare look at him. "In the rain. In the wind and frost. All my mother wanted in life was to be in a snowstorm, but God knows, if it had happened on a school day, she would have made me walk then, too."

Fiona paused to breathe. She'd almost forgotten to. She balled her hands into fists and rolled onto her side, drawing her arms around her knees. Abe rolled onto his side, too, facing her, creating an enormous C that she fit into. Perfectly.

"Do you remember the snow that fell in 1983?" he asked, his arm draped gently over her shoulder, their noses almost touching.

Fiona shook her head. "We weren't here yet. And I was only two."

Abe gave a low laugh. "My mother woke me up early that morning and wrapped me in one of my dad's fishing jackets. It hung to the ground on me. She said it was snowing, and I was so excited. I actually got dizzy, I remember, the way I ran around and around in my room, tripping over the hem of that coat, while I waited for them to get their cold-weather clothes on. I bounced from window to window. It was all *white* outside. Like a bucket of paint had just dropped from nowhere."

Fiona pushed her fists into his chest, letting his big hand wrap around both of them. As he spoke, she could feel the reverberations of his words in his chest.

"We went outside, and the big thing I remember is how disappointed I was."

"Why?"

"It was, honestly, cold. Not very fun to touch. And then there was the whole not-very-much-of-it problem. When I walked out the door, I'd been determined to make Frosty the Snowman, but I couldn't even get enough snow packed together to make a snowball, let alone a man with a carrot nose."

Fiona smiled. She liked thinking of small Abe. "Did you at least see it falling?"

He shook his head. "I missed that, too."

"I've never seen it fall, either."

"Oh, I've seen snow fall," he clarified. "But never on land. Only when I've been out to sea."

Fiona tucked her legs more tightly, still facing him, resting her bent knees on the tops of his thighs. It felt as if she were climbing him sideways. It felt wonderful. "What's that like?"

"It's like a magic trick. These little bits of snow—they really come down in those formations you cut out when you were a child—or here," he touched her hip. "They really look like that. But when you're on the boat, and they're falling, they're instantly gone. You see one land perfectly on your dark jacket, it's there for a split second and then it melts down into the wool. So it's just you on the boat, with this falling...art, and then it stops and you wonder if you dreamed it all."

Fiona straightened her body, straightening him out at the same time, so that she could press herself against his length. She needed to kiss him.

And Abe kissed her back. He was saying more now, with the kiss. She heard more, in the way his mouth moved against hers, in the way his breathing caught in his chest.

"Mmmm," he finally said. "Okay, more. Tell me more. Finish the story."

Abe held her tight as they lay, still both on their sides. He rested one leg over her, and Fiona was grateful for its weight. It would help hold her down.

"I was..."

"You were telling me about your mother and how she made you walk to school, even in snow. Or would have."

"It was three miles, round-trip. She wouldn't let me catch the bus, said I was too chubby and needed the exercise, even though when I look at my school pictures now I think I just looked like a normal kid." When Fiona had pulled out the photos, she'd been surprised at how sad her eyes had looked back then. "So every day I walked past the bus stop on Highway One. I'd ignore the kids who teased me. The same kids would blow past me on the bus, throwing spit wads out the windows, beating me to school by twenty minutes every day. One morning in seventh grade, I asked my mother to drive me. It was pouring. She said no and I pushed it. I said she was a bad mother. I was twelve, you know? I was just starting to feel like a pre-teen."

He nodded.

"She smacked me one." Funny, her voice sounded normal saying the words. "Right across my face. What I remember most about that moment was how loud it was. You expect the pain, I think, but not the noise of it."

"I've been in a fight or two."

"Did it hurt? When you got hit?"

"Like a motherfucker. Had she done that before?"

Fiona shook her head. "No. Or, maybe once. Maybe twice. I actually don't remember. I just remember this time." She covered her eyes with her hand as if she could hide—knowing she couldn't. "So I just heard this explosion in my head and I jumped at her like I was on springs. I hit her back across the face, as hard as I could."

Abe gently moved her hand from her eyes. "Really? Little ole you?"

Fiona dipped her head. "I don't know where it came from. I don't think I'd ever even backtalked her before. So both of us are just standing there, bleeding at the exact same place—I guess we both share thin skin at the eyebrow. We're staring at each other, and I say, 'You're fired.' "

A small smile from Abe. "Good for you."

"Well, she didn't like it. She hit me one more time on the other side of my face, and I was too shocked to move. She said..." Here Fiona paused. This was the part she usually tried not to remember. "She said, 'You can't fire me. *I fucking quit.*' " Fiona cleared her throat. Saying the words now, it felt like the blows were landing all over again. "I walked to school. In English class, your mom pulled me out and made me skip fourth period. She took me to the office nurse, and then after a bunch of paperwork had been filled out, Eliza Carpenter picked us both up."

"Mom and Eliza, yeah," said Abe. "I knew they did a lot of advocating for kids, but...I never knew who the kids were."

"*Good.*" The vehemence in her voice surprised her. "They took me home and talked to Dad in the kitchen with the door closed. I couldn't hear what they said, and God knows I tried my hardest. When they came out, Dad put his arm around me and said Mom was gone. I didn't really figure out what he meant until a week later when she still hadn't come back. She was just gone. And she never came back. Still hasn't."

"Where is she now?"

"Dunno." The word was casual. Fiona felt anything but. "I think my dad does, but I don't want to know the answer most days."

"You were how old again? If you were in my mom's class, you must have been..."

"Almost thirteen."

"I was sixteen then."

There was more to that simple statement, to the look in Abe's eye, than just an age calculation. Fiona, still lying on her side, twisted forward so that she was sitting, pulling the sheet with her, seated in the circle his body made. She put her hand on his pectoral muscle and felt it jump with tension. "What is it?"

"That's the year I lost my dad. We both lost a parent that year."

Now that he said it Fiona did, in fact, vaguely remember that. Of course, it had been huge news, something that had affected her own father. As keeper of the light, he took ocean safety more seriously than anyone else, and he'd been friends with Conway Atwell. Abe, however, had been in high school then. Fiona remembered seeing him for what felt like the first time right around that time. A school friend had whispered to her in front of Tillie's, "That's Mrs. Atwell's son. His father drowned."

At that moment, hunched into a jean jacket, a dark scowl on his face as he skateboarded past, Abe had looked as miserable as she felt. *That's what it looks like when you're missing a parent.* It had been the moment the seed of her crush had been planted, blooming with the kitten incident. Then she'd made sure she'd never spoken more than a passing civility to him until recently. She wished she'd been in a position to ask him this question long, long ago. "What happened?"

Abe exhaled heavily and rolled onto his back. He looked up at the ceiling, his eyes dull.

Fiona said, "Is it your worst thing?"

Instead of answering her, he said, "Why don't you fall in love, Snowflake?"

She hesitated. Then she whispered, "Not good enough."

"None of them were?"

"Me. I never was." The real surprise was that the simple truth didn't hurt as much as she thought it would, out in the open air.

"My story's worse than yours," said Abe.

"Try me, Sailor."

CHAPTER THIRTY-EIGHT

Say what you mean to say, and stick to your word. Try not to say ribbing when you mean moss stitch. Apologize when necessary and always, always carry a safety pin. – E. C.

His story was *so* much worse.

It was so bad, he'd never actually told anyone the full truth.

Ever.

Not his mother, not the cops, not the paramedics who'd whisked him to the hospital, not the Coast Guard patrolman. Not even the chaplain who had come to see him late that night. Abe could remember almost everything that guy had been wearing. No clerical collar for him, the chaplain had been wearing a Rip Curl sweatshirt and jeans with a hole at the knee. He'd looked younger than Abe's dad. There was no way he knew a thing about God. Abe had stared at the wall—cream and blank—until the chaplain had given up and walked out, his keys jingling cheerfully as he went. Abe had just rolled over in the hospital bed, not caring that he accidentally ripped out an IV line as he did so. It hurt, but it didn't matter.

Now, with Fiona's skin pressed against his, Abe said, "Tell me what you already know about it."

Fiona's voice was small, but she didn't sound scared. Just careful, as if she were weighing her words before she said them. "There was a storm that night. You two were out fishing, coming back late. The boat capsized, and you swam in to get help."

When she said it, it just sounded sad. Tragedy.

"Facts are right, mostly," he said. Outside the houseboat, a motorboat with a misfiring engine— probably Louie's—chugged by. A low wake rocked through. "Storm came up fast. I was the one who thought we could get farther out to open sea, and took us too far before we turned back. The grunion were running, and my dad laughed. He liked seeing me get excited about fishing. *Fish-and-chip off the old block*, he'd say. So we were out too far when the swells started. That would have been fine, but I did a stupid thing and I tacked south when we were too close to the rocks. I was just trying to get us in too fast, and I ignored Dad when he said so. I believed I was a man, and I think Dad was choosing to let me learn the hard way. He was probably going to take over any minute. He'd slap me on the head and bark orders at me, and we'd get in safe like we always did. But a big wave hit us starboard, and she took on water. Of course, it wasn't the first time that had ever happened to us, and we could have recovered from it. But Dad, who never lost his footing, slipped and hit his head on the rail as he went down. He was out for about a minute, and the whole while I was trying to wake him up and stop the bleeding...there was just so much *blood*, everywhere. I fell in it on the deck. When I did that, I lost control of what I should have been doing with the sails. Dad always said no matter what, you keep an eye on your masts."

"But your dad had—" Her hand was warm on his arm.

Abe shrugged off her touch. "Even if your dad hits the deck and you think for one terrible second that he's dead, you don't take your eye off the sails. You just don't. Three more sets of waves pummeled us, and we capsized. My whole life sailing, my dad's whole career at sea, and that had never happened. We'd trained for it, yeah, but when you're being choked with seawater and trying to keep your fingers dug into your father's life jacket, you can't think of anything past getting air into your lungs."

Abe fought the urge to get up. To pace. To get the hell out of this room. To get outside where he could breathe. He shimmied up the sheets and pried open the little window over the bed. He heard Digit land on the porch outside, making that mumbling-meow noise that said he'd probably caught a wharf rat.

Abe breathed.

Fiona pulled away from him, as if she knew he was feeling submerged. As soon as she did, he wanted her back. Close. Abe wrapped his fingers around her calf and she put her arm back on his shoulder.

"The ocean—it was like it was possessed that night. I knew it in every mood. I'd seen it in what I'd thought were its most challenging storms. And this one—was different. It tugged the boat out from under us, I swear it did. It sucked it down, and it tried to take us with it. I managed to hook my leg into a stack of two life preservers. They broke my kneecap as we fell off the boat, right before it went down. I had Dad, though, holding him in both my arms. The preservers kept me afloat enough to keep his head up. He woke when we hit the water, and shit, when he really figured out what was going on, he was *pissed.*" The memory was enough to make Abe's chest tight. "He tried not to show it, though. That was maybe the worst part." He paused, but only for a second. He could do this. He could tell her.

"He was just so *encouraging,* damn it. *You can do it,* he said. *That's my boy. Get us in,* he said. *Kick hard.* Hell, I could hardly move my left leg and it was taking all my strength to kick with my right to keep us afloat. We were going hypothermic, and we both knew it. We were less than a thousand yards off shore. I could smell it. Smell the land. I could see the lighthouse's beam."

For the first time, Abe wondered where Fiona had been when they were in the water. Fiona's father had still been the keeper then. Had she been in the attached house? It had always looked so bright and cheery, there below the lighthouse. The front porch light beamed, a tiny miniature light below the great one swiping its way along the coast.

"He told me to stay with him. That someone would be looking for us, and the ocean was too strong for me alone. But I wanted to swim for it. Toward the light. So he tried to swim with me. For me. But something...something had happened when he hit his head. He didn't quite know how to move his arms together, at the same time. He was slurring. I don't know, maybe he'd had a stroke, maybe that's why he fell on deck. His words were tangled up, like fish in a net. Maybe he never would have made it anyway. *Shore swim*, he started saying. *Light shore. Swim. Hope swim. Swim hope.* I didn't know if he was hoping I'd swim or if he was saying the name of the boat. Or my mother. He started to cry." Abe choked. This was worse, so much worse than he'd thought it would be. "He was clear about one thing, though. *Don't leave me.* He begged me not to leave him."

Abe felt Fiona shift next to him. He didn't lower his eyes from the paint on the ceiling, but he felt her slide along him, fitting herself into the space next to him. He ignored the fact that his vision was going blurry. He hadn't thought about that moment in...years. He was so *good* at it. Keeping it down, buried. Because there was no world in which it could possibly be okay that your father was dead, drowned, gone, taken by the ocean because you fucked up so big it was broken, everything was broken forever.

"I left him."

"You had to," said Fiona softly, her head now tucked against his shoulder.

"That's the thing. I didn't have to do anything. But I told him I was going to get help. When he finally understood me, he said, his words still garbled, to swim for the lighthouse. That the lighthouse had gotten him through every storm before, and it would save us. I left him. I went toward it, even though I knew maybe he was right. Maybe they were already looking for us."

"You'd have found that out when you swam in. Were they?"

God. "No. We hadn't been out long enough to be missed."

"So you were right. No one was looking. You had to get help for him."

Something flared in him, small and ugly. Fiona didn't get to *defend* the worst decision he'd ever made. She wasn't allowed to. No one was. "I swam away from him. I chose to leave. I knew he probably wouldn't be able to hold on to the preservers long enough for me to get help, for the Coast Guard to launch a boat or a helicopter. I knew I was leaving him to die." Abe paused, making sure she heard him. He gave it time to sink in.

"When I finally got in, I could barely talk. They had to heat me up slow so I didn't go into shock. The whole time, I was thinking about him, getting colder and colder out there, until he wasn't cold anymore." Jesus Christ, why was Fiona still here? If he'd been alone right now, he would have put his head down and howled.

But instead, he kept talking. "Everyone else told me I was a hero. My mother hung on my neck until I thought she was going to suffocate me. They said it was a miracle. No one—*no one*—seemed to notice I'd done the worst thing a man could ever do. I'd left a man, my *father*, to die alone. I should have stayed with him. We both would have died, but he wouldn't have been alone. I've never told anyone, not until now. I've never told anyone that I knew he was already hurt." Abe repeated the worst part, "I knew when I swam away from him I was abandoning him. Leaving him to die."

He didn't look at Fiona. Goddammit, if she wasn't here, Abe might just have cried the way he had that night in the hospital, hours after the nurses with tragic eyes had tucked the sheets around him, hours after his mother had been sedated. He'd cried so hard that night he wondered if anyone in the whole world had any tears left—he'd used them all. It had reminded him of the way the boat had been taken down—a sinkhole of pain, a hellish whirlpool he'd always, always be trapped in, always be plunging down, down, down, spiraling—doomed to keep bawling like some inept Greek hero cursed to repeat his mistakes forever.

That was why he didn't ever let himself cry.

Angrily, he cleared his throat.

"It wasn't your fault," said Fiona.

She sounded so sure. Damn her. "You don't know anything about it." Just like the chaplain that night. Just like the town, at the funeral. Just like anyone he'd ever met.

He sneaked a look sideways at her. He'd scored the blow he'd meant to—her eyes looked shocked. And hurt.

But she said, "No. I don't."

Her agreement surprised him. He'd expected her to insist that having chased her mother away—still alive—that she knew something about his pain.

"It's just," she went on, "I wish I could help some way. I can't imagine going through that alone."

"I was okay," he lied, still unsure why he felt like he needed to push her away when all he wanted to do was roll over and bury his face in her soft hair. "I started dating Rayna right after that, in my senior year. She helped. Hot little body like that, she was made to distract red-blooded, teenaged males."

Direct hit. Exactly what he'd been aiming for. Fiona's face blanched but she didn't even blink.

"Woop," she said, swinging away from him leaving the sheet behind her, putting her feet on the floor. "I have to go to the bathroom."

Naked, Fiona walked away from Abe's bed as if she had no self-consciousness, though he knew she did. Her neck was held straight. Her posture was rigid. Her buttocks, perfectly shaped, swayed as she swung open the tiny door that led to the toilet. From the side, Abe caught a glance at her small breasts, her nipples soft and delicate, as she closed the door behind her. He heard running water and a soft sound like maybe she was blowing her nose.

He was *such* a dick.

CHAPTER THIRTY-NINE

Always be brave. — E. C.

Fiona took her time in the postage-stamp-sized bathroom. She washed her hands, then washed them again. His soap smelled like green grass. Looking into the miniature medicine cabinet, she found hydrogen peroxide, a stack of Band-Aids, one razor, and one can of shaving cream. A blue stick of deodorant was balanced on the edge of the sink.

A clean washcloth. A black towel. That was it. That's all he had.

It didn't matter that he'd brought up Rayna deliberately to throw her off. It didn't matter that he wasn't brave enough to actually push Fiona away, so he used words to do it.

Neither of those things changed the fact that he'd told her something he'd never told anyone else. That had been real. That had been brave.

Fiona stood up taller, pushing her breasts forward, sucking in her stomach. Hair—check. It was a pretty color, with a redness that sometimes shone in sunlight. She'd painted a Mercury Comet exactly this color once, and the owner had said it reminded him of a bay pony he'd had when he was young.

Her eyes, she decided, weren't half bad. Right now they were more brown than green, but the brown was pretty, like the dark moss that grew at the base of the redwoods in the hills. She realized she liked how the color could change in a moment with her mood. That wasn't something everyone had. What color were they when Abe kissed her? Did they go lighter or darker? If they looked like they did right now, he might think they were pretty. Quite pretty.

Fiona turned sideways and then back, giving herself a frank appraisal. Okay, she didn't have Rayna's lush curves or her ridiculously long legs. But Fiona's breasts were high and pert. And if she took this moment to admit it to herself, she'd always kind of liked the way her belly was shaped. It wasn't flat, but it wasn't too big, either. Just right, really.

Sure, any red-blooded teenaged male would want to sleep with a teenaged Rayna. She'd been something from the likes of television and movies back then. There had been no one prettier, no one more self-assured. No one was even as nice.

Fiona felt a wave of kindness directed at Rayna as she leaned in again toward the mirror. Maybe this was what being thirty-three meant. Letting go of the things that didn't matter. That had never mattered. Embracing the things that were—she looked down again at her body— really, truly okay. That were good. Just the way they were.

Fiona opened the door of the bathroom, the handle turning smoothly for once.

Abe didn't look at her. He was still lying on the bed, face-up, staring up at the low ceiling.

"Hey," she said. She wanted to jump in the bed and pull the sheets over herself. She also wanted to throw her clothes on as fast as possible, jam her hat onto her head, and light out.

But she held her ground. Where she was. In the middle of the room. She would make him look at her. "Abe."

He shut his eyes.

"*Atwell.*"

Abe turned on his side and looked at her through hooded eyes. "You leavin', Snowflake?"

She raised an eyebrow. "Do I look like I'm dressed to leave?"

He twisted his mouth as if he were trying to push back a smile. "Uh-uh."

This took bravery.

Courage.

Fiona had both running through her veins. Maybe it was just being near him. Maybe it was something more. She didn't really care.

She crawled up, still naked, onto the bed. Abe hadn't taken his eyes off her, and they were getting that storm-tossed look again. *She* was making that happen.

"What if I told you I wanted you?" Yep, that was her voice. Unwavering.

"How?"

"How—" Okay, maybe her voice wavered a tiny bit.

Abe sat up higher on his elbow and stared. "How do you want me?"

"You're enjoying this."

The smile broke over his face then, and he reached for her, pulling her toward him. "How could I not? You're incredible. Gorgeous. You're perfect. And I'm a fucking *tool*."

"You were an ass, yeah." Fiona loved how he wrapped his arms around her, bringing her along him as if they'd done this a million times before.

"I didn't mean to be. It was just..." His voice trailed off, and he pressed his lips against the top of her shoulder. He gave her a gentle bite, grating her skin with his teeth. Finally he said, "You make me say things I don't normally say. You make me *feel*. Period."

"And you don't like it."

Abe twisted, rolling Fiona all the way under him. She gasped as she felt how hard he was. How ready.

"Scares the shit out of me," he said. "Most of the time I don't like it at all." His breathing was faster, and so was hers. All he had to do was open her legs, and he could be inside her—she was so wet he'd encounter absolutely no resistance.

But he didn't. He held himself above her. "And then other times," he continued, "I love it."

He said the word *love* slowly, as if he was tasting it. Testing it.

Fiona wound her arms around his neck and pulled him down to her, relishing the feeling of power that still rushed through her veins. The kiss was intense—hot, wet, and so fast from the very moment their lips met, as if they were on a deadline, and they had to *hurry, hurry, more, more, now.*

It was then Fiona knew. When they weren't talking, when he was trailing his tongue down her ribcage, she knew. This wasn't a crush. Not anymore.

She loved this man. This stubborn, cranky, stuck-in-the-past sailor who might never change. She loved him.

The thought was astonishing. And there was no way in hell she was going to tell him.

Instead, she stopped his mouth. Kicking with her legs, pulling on the sheets, she wrestled her way down so that their faces were close again, so that their bodies were flush.

"I had a plan, woman," Abe said. He cleared his throat. "I was headed somewhere." His eyes looked happy.

Fiona kissed him again. Kissed him with the knowledge that she loved him. With the knowledge that it changed nothing. That she wanted nothing more than just this moment. She, who always had a plan, who always knew what was coming next, knew nothing about tomorrow. She knew no moment in the future. And the man next to her only knew the past.

But she understood the feel of his lips on hers, his hands skimming her cheekbones, his tongue a gentle rasp.

This was all she needed. All she would ever need. Fiona memorized every second, burning it into her brain so she could replay it on cold nights when she'd be alone, when she'd need it.

CHAPTER FORTY

Love like you knit, like you were born to do it.
Because you were. – E. C.

Abe couldn't stop kissing her. And when he did, when he finally got around to moving down her body, finding the other places that made her give those growly purrs, she swam through the sheets so that they were kissing again.

He could kiss her for the next hundred years or so. That would probably be just about right.

But dammit, he had a mission. He'd almost driven her away. She'd almost left, he knew that. And who knew when he'd get her back? If he'd ever get her back. It seemed kind of doubtful, honestly. What with the way he was and always had been. Probably always would be.

So he needed to blow her damn mind.

Abe bit her bottom lip lightly and said, "Lie still."

"Oh? Bossy?" Her voice was amused.

"Always." He nipped at the skin on her neck—so soft, how could she *be* this silky?—and worked his way down to the top of her breast. Simple kisses. He tasted her, loving the combination of salt and sweet he found on her skin. Cupping one breast with his hand, he traced his tongue around the other one, getting nearer to her nipple but never touching. Just breathing, warmly. Then a quick puff of air that made her nipple tighten.

She gasped as the air hit her.

"Oh, do you want me to stop?" he said with a half-smile. "Is this too much for you? Maybe we should just lie here and talk some more."

"*No*," she grated. "Please don't. Don't stop."

"Okay, then." He tugged on her nipple with his teeth, gently enough to not hurt her, but hard enough to make her give that noise in the back of her throat again.

Jesus, he'd never been so hard in his whole damn life.

He slid a hand down her body, over her belly, to where the soft hair curled. She was—God—even wetter now than she'd been before when he'd touched her. Abe pushed a finger into her slickness and moved down her body, slowly, so slowly, until his mouth found the right spot.

Above him, Fiona said something that he didn't understand. It didn't sound like *stop*, though. Kind of the opposite.

So he moved his hand inside her and speeded up his tongue until she was panting above him like she'd been running for hours.

"I thought you were an old-fashioned kind of...guy." She gasped each word.

He nodded against her, taking her in. Lifting his head, he said, "Hey, I watch the pay channels."

Her breath got faster, and she got tighter inside until he could barely move his fingers, and then she made a sound that almost made him lose it, just hearing her.

"That's it, love. That's my girl." He watched her come, delighting in her, wanting more, wanting everything.

Love.

Once the word slipped out, he knew it wasn't wrong.

But it was going to fuck up his life.

Well, then. Bring it on. He wanted to say it again, but he didn't want to send her running away again. He couldn't take that. Not tonight.

Fiona's breath still fast, she dug the tips of her fingers into his shoulder blades and dragged him up her body. Without pausing to ask, she tipped her hips, opened her legs wider, and guided him to where she was slipperiest. A few precious seconds wasted fumbling with the condom, and then, her own juices still on his lips, she drew him into a kiss as she led him into her.

For a moment, Abe couldn't see. He couldn't think. The whole world had just blown apart, simply because of the way she was moving underneath him. When he could draw air into his lungs again, he started to move with her. She groaned, and he drove himself faster. Deeper. Her fingers curled into the muscles at the small of his back and she tugged him into her, deeper with every move.

Abe couldn't keep his eyes off hers. Fiona's gaze said so much, he wanted to hear her mouth say words that he was dying to feel against his lips—but in this moment, as they moved together, faster and faster, he let himself drown in her eyes.

Sometimes, maybe, drowning wasn't that bad.

Fiona moved her hands to the back of his head, drawing him down into a kiss so deep he felt dizziness swim through his blood. "I want to..." she started.

"Anything," he promised her, meaning it.

With a simple and sudden twist, she rolled him over onto his back, straddling him without losing contact with him, even for a moment. Even their strokes remained steady, as if it were a dance, as if he'd just turned her under his arm in a waltz.

Fiona looked at him. Her hands splayed on his chest, she tilted her head and looked at him so gently, so...lovingly...that he stayed with her, moving with her, matching her slower rhythm. There was no denying that she felt amazing. *They* felt amazing.

Speed came next. Abe watched her move on top of him, lifting one hand to brush her hair off her face and over her shoulder, her hips lifting, dropping, lifting, and then *pressing* down, so fast, then faster, and faster...

He felt her tighten, and her eyes dropped to his again. She caught her lower lip between her teeth and seemed to be trying to stifle a scream, so Abe drove his hips into her deeper, one hand capturing her buttock and pulling her hard. Harder. Her lip loosed, she cried out, spasming around him. Abe felt himself meet her, the heat of him releasing with a shudder, an ache he didn't know he'd held let go. Lost.

She tumbled, bringing her cheek down to the top of his chest, turning so that her ear was over his heart.

"So fast," she said.

Abe didn't know what she meant. The sex? How she—or he—came?

Or what he was feeling? Because damn, that was fast. Way too fucking fast.

And yet his arms went around her, and he kissed the crooked part in her hair. "Fast. But just right." He held her tighter, reveling in the way she pressed herself harder against him. "Just right."

CHAPTER FORTY-ONE

When presented with an instruction you don't understand, hold your ground. You are the boss of those needles you clench in your fists so tightly. – E. C.

Fiona woke to a splashing noise, stuck in a dream in which she was tangled—trapped—in a fishing net. The splashing grew louder, bigger and wider. It was below her, all around her. Her inner ear told her she was moving, just a little bit. Was she on a water bed? Fiona tested the motion in one leg carefully.

The bed remained still, blessedly so.

But the body next to her didn't.

Abe blew out a deep breath and slung his leg over hers. "Hiya," he mumbled in her ear.

Shit. She was tangled in *him*.

Abe was pressed against her, his arm over her stomach, her hair under his head on their shared pillow. He was huge, a warm, solid presence, hard in the places she was soft. His forearm under the tips of her fingers felt more muscled than the strongest ones in her calves. The man was made of muscle. An image from the night before, of her grasping the top of his shoulders, digging her fingers in between the ropes of hard tissue she found there, made her stomach twist in a not-unpleasant way.

God. How was this *fair*? What was a girl supposed to do, in bed with the guy she'd had a crush on for approximately eleven thousand years?

Get out as fast as humanly possible, probably. So she could plan the next day, without him. Before he confused her any further.

"So," she said, sitting up, trying desperately not to care that the sheet stayed underneath him, and that Abe was staring unabashedly at her breasts. "I've got to go see about a fish."

"Huh," Abe drawled. "So do I."

Fiona glanced down at him sharply and then dove off the side of the bed, coming up in her t-shirt. "Not the same at all. I'm going to feed mine."

"Mine are going to feed me."

She stood, pulling on her jeans as fast as possible. Her panties were nowhere to be seen, and while she tried not to care, those had been *expensive*. She got down on her knees and peered under the bed, which was surprisingly clean for a bachelor pad. More magazines than dust-bunnies.

"Looking for my porn?"

"The good stuff?" She slid out a glossy brochure. *Deep Sea Fishing in Alaska.* "Hot," she said. Good, if she could just keep up the banter, maybe she'd be able to find her panties and push them in her pocket, and get back to the shop before she was late to open. "What time is it?"

"Early as hell." Abe rolled onto his back and rubbed his eyes with the heels of his hands.

Fiona couldn't help herself—she stared. The way his torso was so wide at his nipple line, the way it narrowed in ridges, covered with a fine, dark hair that got darker the farther south it went...now she knew exactly what was beneath that thin sheet. And what was under there was growing.

A low laugh. "I wake up quickly. Even without coffee."

"I can see that." Tempting as it was—and dang, what she wouldn't do to get under those covers with him again and *stay* there—she wouldn't. Couldn't. She had to leave while she still had two brain cells to rub together.

"Enough." Fiona clapped her hands. "I've lost my underwear. Help me find it."

"Is there a reward?"

Fiona merely arched an eyebrow at him. "Help. Now."

Abe stuck his foot farther under the sheets. "This it?" Reaching under, he pulled out her scrap of red lace. "Can I keep it?"

She snatched it out of his hands. "No. These are my favorites."

"I'll say."

She sucked in her lips so her grin didn't give her away.

"What are you wearing tonight?" he asked, stretching his arms over his head.

Fiona—again—tore her eyes off him and shrugged into her jacket. "What?"

"Will you wear those again tonight?"

"I am so not rewearing underwear."

"I mean, something like them."

"At the council meeting?"

He gave her a huge grin.

"No," she said.

"Okay, what will you wear?"

She said, "I was thinking about my gray wool suit."

"Sounds hot. And I don't mean sexy."

"It's a *nice* suit. Don't mock me." Fiona pulled on one shoe. She knew she could be doing this faster, moving more expeditiously. She probably could have been out the door five minutes ago. Why wasn't she, then?

"Under it. What will you wear under it?"

Fiona shrugged. "The regular stuff."

"Like what?"

"Big white cotton gramma underpants."

He rolled onto his stomach and stared at her. Fiona felt the flame lick her again, low in her core.

"Tell me more," he said.

Fiona drew out her words, lowering her voice to a husky rasp. "Broken elastic, stretched *out*. A little too big. Saggy in the bottom area."

"More. What about on top?"

"Mmmm." Fiona licked her lips provocatively and spoke as slowly as she could, elongating every syllable. "Sports bra. Oh, yeah. Gray. The kind that makes a girl flat on top, wide in back."

"You know what?"

What if he actually really hated sports bras? "What?"

"You would be *so* fucking hot in that get-up."

She bit the inside of her cheek. "Really?" Immediately, she wished she hadn't asked.

He reached out his hand to her, confidently, as if he knew she'd take it.

She did.

"Really. You could wear those big flat leather sandals with built-in arch support and you'd still be the prettiest girl in nine counties."

"Just nine?" Fiona was joking, but the answer felt more important than she wanted it to.

"My buddy is married to Miss Universe 2012, and he lives about ten counties to the east, in Nevada. I'm not going to run you against her on a stage, but if I was the one doing the judging, you'd win that too."

This was getting ridiculous. "Cut it out," said Fiona. She finished pulling on her cowboy boots. She found her hat where it had been smushed by his cat, who had apparently been sitting on it all night. "Lord," she said, smacking it flat-palmed. Digit moved to settle on a low bookshelf in the sun.

"He sheds when he's nervous."

"Why would he be nervous?"

"There's air in the room. That's enough to spook that damn cat."

Abe's voice was gruff. He reached out a long arm to cuff Digit on the head, and the cat responded with a wild purr, rubbing himself along Abe's hands. "He's awful," said Abe. Digit growled like a dog and jumped onto the bed. Then he fell over on his side, drooling and purring at the same time.

"I think your cat is rabid."

Abe nodded. "That would explain a lot."

"So..." Fiona started, shifting to her other leg. *Wanna do this again?* It wasn't exactly the tone she was going for. "So. You're coming to the council meeting tonight?" Of course he was. She was saying it more to prepare herself than for any other reason.

Abe shrugged and leaned back on his pillow. Digit followed, batting Abe's hands with his huge paws. "Only if you give me a show."

"Excuse me?"

"If you wink at me from the stage, it means you're not wearing underwear."

God, he was cute. And there was no way in hell she was showing up for a city council meeting going commando. She'd probably trip and fall, ripping whatever she was wearing, and the whole town would see her bare ass—or worse—on display. "No. There will be no wink."

"What's the point, then?" he asked with a lazy grin. Fiona wanted to get back into bed and trace where that smile started and ended. First with her fingers. Then with her tongue.

She found her earrings on his nightstand. She didn't even remember taking them off last night.

The smile faded on Abe's face. "So you're still going through with it?"

"What?"

"Your argument for pulling down the lighthouse."

Surprised, she said, "Of course."

"After all we talked about, and what it means to me, you still feel the same way?" Digit growled a warning, and then struck at Abe's hand. He drew it back with a curse.

Fiona felt a little like lashing out at him herself. "Maybe you've forgotten what I told you about why I hate the place. Plus, we didn't even talk about the fact that it's completely unsafe. Someone's going to get hurt."

"You can't just..." Abe pushed the covers roughly aside, and lurched for his boxers, pulling them on so fast Fiona didn't even have time to ogle. Not that she wanted to, not at this exact moment. Not when she was suddenly this irritated.

She pushed her second earring through, yanking it too hard. A piece of metal broke off into her hand. She shoved it in her pocket. "I thought you knew this wasn't up for discussion. That we would agree to disagree."

"You know I'll argue against you."

Of course he would. Why had she thought he wouldn't? Somehow she'd thought by telling him the story of her mother last night, he'd understand her idea of making that plot of coastal land useful and attractive and safe—that there could be no better plan for the place.

"I've been working on my pitch for two weeks," she said, as if that would help. "How's yours going?"

"Don't worry. I'll write it today."

Fiona gave a disbelieving half-laugh. "You have to go fishing. You have a trip planned."

"I'm the boss. I'll cancel." As Abe pulled on his jeans, Fiona told herself to keep her damn eyes off his thigh muscles.

"It's a conflict of interest. The town's harbormaster can't discuss land deeded to the town."

Abe paused in pulling a white t-shirt out of a drawer tucked under the window. "Now you're just making shit up."

Fine. He had her on that one. "You're not prepared."

"Who else is speaking? Elbert Romo?"

She gave a brief nod.

Abe gave a thumbs up. "I helped him get home a couple of weeks ago after too many at the Rite Spot."

"So he drinks a little."

"I helped him to bed. You know he sleeps in a sleeping bag on the floor?"

"That's awful."

"No, it's because he's too lazy to wash the sheets."

"He still has to wash the sleeping bag..."

Abe shook his head slowly.

"Oh," she said.

"Explains those overalls he always wears, huh?"

They were getting off track. "You'd have to debate *me.*"

He raised one eyebrow. "I'm doing okay right now. I think I did okay last night, too."

Fiona saw a tiny flicker of amusement behind his eyes, and it made her stomach twist with anger. "Don't do this."

He didn't back down an inch. He didn't even blink. "Snowflake, no one's told me what to do for years. I don't expect that to change."

Fiona said, "*Felchitch.*" It was a combination of every swear word she knew, and it felt as ineffective as it sounded.

Turning sharply, she went into the living room, remembering to duck her head at the last moment before she opened the door. She'd already slammed it behind her—giving the screen door an extra kick for emphasis—before she realized that she'd left her hat behind. Shit, shit, *shit.*

She turned and barged inside without knocking. Abe stood on the other side of the door, her cowboy hat dangling from his finger. "It's sweet of you to leave this for me, but I have a hat of my own to throw into the ring tonight. Thanks."

Could the man have a cockier, more amused look on his face? Fiona snatched up her hat and turned again, just in time for Digit to dart under her feet as he raced out the open door. Fiona's arms windmilled but she kept her balance. Barely.

As she walked up the dock, she heard a laugh. His? Or a seal out in the bay, its bark echoing off the rocks?

Fine. If he was laughing, that was just fine. If he wanted to debate her proposal tonight?

She'd be the one laughing when he humiliated himself in front of the town.

Unless he wiped the floor with her and looked hot doing it.

Goddammit.

CHAPTER FORTY-TWO

You'll know a knitter by the way she treats wool—
casually, fondly, roughly, trustingly, lovingly. – E. C.

In city hall, with bodies packed all around her on creaky folding chairs, Fiona held her breath as she read the council's printed agenda. There was her name, and Elbert Romo's. But the page didn't mention Abe. Maybe this morning had just been a bad dream.

But that would mean last night wasn't real, either.

Fiona took out the roll of wire and her knitting needles. She was making something—she didn't know quite what, but it would be some kind of jewelry. Probably. Either that or just a hot mess, which would go nicely with her mood.

"You're knitting metal?" Daisy said incredulously. "Wait. You're *knitting*, period. When did this happen and why didn't you tell me?"

"Because I was too busy telling you about last night."

Daisy shook her head and took out her own knitting from the bag that hung on the handle of her chair. "I'm not sure what's more important, actually. Men come and go, but knitting is forever."

Fiona tried to push down her nerves and do a decrease at the same time. "Let me guess. Eliza Carpenter."

"Oh, no! Eliza believed in love more than anyone else. I said that," Daisy said with a grin. "I'm very wise, you know."

"Hey, speaking of men, how's Zeke?"

At least Daisy had the grace to look abashed. She said, "He's good. Cute. Fun."

"I spill my guts to you and that's all I get?"

Daisy looked down at her knitting. "He's pretty charming. For a football player."

Fiona pictured Abe's clear, blue eyes and stubborn jawline. He couldn't really be called charming. And God how she loved that.

Damn it to *hell*.

"So tell me," she said.

Daisy shrugged, and then leaned sideways in her wheelchair. She said out of the corner of her mouth, "We did it."

"W-ha-t?"

"Dude," Daisy said agreeably.

"And?"

"I'm here to tell you he's that wide everywhere."

Fiona laughed. "Good for you. Where was Tabby?"

"I had the sitter till ten. I made sure he pulled up to the house by nine-thirty."

"You did it in the van? In thirty minutes?" Was that a blush Fiona saw on Daisy's face?

"If you see the van a rockin', don't come a knockin'. Right? Anyway, where's Abe?" said Daisy, craning her neck.

"Who, dear?" Toots Harrison made her way carefully into a free seat. She was wearing a cranberry-colored sweater that looked like it was made up of murdered Muppets, and she had two circular knitting needles draped around her neck. Either she'd forgotten they were there or she was modeling a new kind of dangerous necklace.

"Abe Atwell."

Toots nodded knowledgeably. "Oh, our handsome harbormaster. I saw him in the back parking lot."

Daisy said, "Did he look nervous?"

"Don't ask," muttered Fiona.

Toots's eyebrows flew up under her tightly curled bangs. "Abe Atwell? Nervous?"

"Yeah."

"Well, why should he be?" Toots waggled her fingers at a clutch of knitters sitting several rows behind them. "I'll be back, lovies."

"See?" said Daisy triumphantly. "Told you. He was messing with you. He won't debate your proposal." Daisy sighed as she took lip gloss out of her purse. "It's almost too bad. I would have liked to have watched those fireworks. Maybe Elbert will take off his clothes again."

Mayor Finley, dressed in a yellow cardigan and slacks that looked like they'd been dipped in mustard, stepped to the microphone and tapped it briefly. "We'll start in just a few moments, folks, but a quick addition to the agenda—Abe Atwell isn't listed but he has a proposal, so we welcome his comments tonight."

Chatter buzzed, and Fiona felt a tap on her shoulder. Toots Harrison leaned ponderously over a metal folding chair. "How did you know, dear?"

Fiona said, "Lucky guess."

"Well," Toots blinked widely, "I'm a happily married woman, you know that. But I don't mind sharing that I won't object to that man taking the stage for a while. Our harbormaster is quite a catch, I'd say. Get it?" She winked at Fiona and went back to gossiping with the knitters.

"You'll kick his ass," said Daisy cheerfully.

Fiona stretched out her legs and slid down far enough in her seat that she could hook the back of her neck over the top of the chair. "I think I'm going to throw up."

"Ooof. Don't do that." Daisy looked over her shoulder. "He's here. With Zeke."

Fiona prevented herself—barely—from turning her head. "How does he look?"

Daisy said, "While you look great, of course, he might win for cleans-up-the-best. Or maybe you can have a dance off. Oh! Can we do that?"

"We're not the Jets and the Sharks. This is not the West Side."

"Right. This is Cypress Hollow. So, the crocheters and the knitters?"

Fiona put her finger to her lips. "I don't even really knit and I *know* you'll get in trouble for that."

"Okay. Auto buyers, foreign versus domestic."

"As long as I can be domestic. Fair labor. Mostly."

Daisy took another look. "He looks great."

Fiona put the wire on her lap and balled her hands into fists as she tried to tamp down the nerves that sang along her spine. "You going to like his proposal better, too?"

"Of course not. But you gotta admit, he looks good in a suit."

Fiona spun around so quickly she almost launched herself out of the chair. Crap. *Double* crap.

Damn it, how *did* Abe clean up that well? Yesterday she'd seen him in jeans and a flannel shirt, his watch cap pulled low on his brow. Last night and this morning, she'd seen him in nothing but stubble. It turned out he looked even more dangerous wearing pinstripes.

"Careful," Daisy cautioned in a lower voice. "Don't let him see you with that look on your face."

Fiona frowned to rid herself of it. "That obvious?"

"More. You've always panted when he was in the room, but you've never looked like *that*. Your skin is glowing like that steel does when Stephen's attaching something to a robot."

"Shit."

"Zeke doesn't look bad, either, huh?" Daisy's look was clearly appraising. Zeke wasn't as dressed up as Abe, but he was in a nice, light blue, button-down shirt and gray pants. "He looks like a strong barrel, doesn't he? Like you could just push him over Niagara and he'd pop up at the bottom, no harm done." She stopped for a minute. "Not that barrels are necessarily my thing. Unless there's wine in them."

Fiona could feel Abe's eyes on the back of her neck. Right at her nape. Where he'd pressed his lips last night. Where later on, he'd gathered her hair into a ponytail, tugging her head back, kissing her with desire. With flat-out *need*. Fiona pulled at the collar of her suit. It was too hot in here. She should have known better than to wear this outfit. It didn't breathe.

Neither did she, apparently.

CHAPTER FORTY-THREE

It's easier to see through lace than cables, but cables are harder to rip accidentally when you climb over barbed wire fences. Ask me how I know.– E. C.

T he council chambers were packed as full as a crab pot and twice as wriggly. Voices, high-pitched and excited, were making Abe's skin itch. Clashing perfumes assailed his nose, making him sneeze violently three times in a row. Mrs. Luby scowled at him and muttered something about rampant influenza. Another woman he didn't know stepped on his toe and didn't even apologize. Rayna Viera waved at him from across the room, and he just nodded.

"Fiona pretty pissed at you?" Zeke said.

"I reckon," said Abe. "I guess sleeping with a woman and then going against her in a city council meeting isn't the best way to get another date." Stupid qualms. They were everywhere. He was tripping over them at this point, scuffing through them in his boots.

Zeke gave a low whistle. "You got cojones, for sure."

He had something, all right. He was so rolled up in Fiona he could barely walk straight. But damn her, he'd really thought they'd made a complete, total connection. Body, soul, *and* mind. He'd thought she'd heard him when he talked about his father, about what the lighthouse meant. He had really thought she'd understood.

Elbert Romo stepped through the crowd and reached forward to shake Abe's hand. "So. I hear you've worked up a proposal-thingie, too." Elbert, no cap over his gray buzz cut, was wearing the same dark, creased overalls he'd worn at the ball. His dress overalls, obviously.

"Yes, sir."

"Well, that'll give 'em something to talk about."

"Sir?"

Elbert tucked his thumbs behind his straps. "Ain't you and Fiona making time?"

Abe should have known Elbert would be at the center of the rumor mill.

"If you don't mind my saying so, I think it's a little odd that you're bringing that up."

Elbert held his hands up as if Abe had stuck a gun in his ribs. "Whoa there, son! This ain't the stage. Save your fighting words for bein' up at the podium." He lowered his arms and rubbed his hands together. "Hoo. This is gonna be good. Where is that Fiona-girl? I hope she's wearin' something low-cut."

Abe couldn't help it—his shoulders went backward and he took an involuntary step forward. "Excuse me?"

Elbert bent at the waist in a howl of laughter. "*Damn*, this is gonna be fun. That was too easy. Keep your guard up!" He threw two mock punches in the air. "This is war!" Giggling, he scuttled sideways into the crowd.

"Dammit," said Abe. "He got me."

"You sure you want to do this?"

"Yes." *No*.

Zeke rocked back and forth on his heels. "But you like her."

Abe wanted to snarl at Zeke. It was more than simple *like*. He...

Shit. He satisfied himself with saying, "Shut up."

"So, why are you doing this?"

Abe kept his lips firmly shut. He'd learned his lesson. He was going to take his time and not say anything tonight that he didn't mean.

"For your dad, right?"

Adjusting his tie, feeling something that twitched suspiciously like nerves, Abe said, "No."

Zeke scrunched his eyes. "Your pop loved the lighthouse, et cetera, right?"

Abe shook his head. "It's for her." He pointed through the crowd to where his mother was sitting, small and stoop-shouldered, hunching over her knitting, her face so pale it matched her gray hair.

She was alone, and it was his fault.

And *that* was why he wasn't going to let his eyes stray back to Fiona, not even when they were up on the stage. He shouldn't have asked her to meet him at the lighthouse. He definitely shouldn't have invited her to his houseboat. To his bed. He had nothing to offer her. If they went on, if they went forward with what felt like the best thing that ever happened in his life, he'd only end up taking something away from her. Leaving her behind. Or she'd take a page from her mother's book and run away, ditching him like Rayna had. Nothing good ever stayed.

There wasn't anything left to do but fight for the one thing there was left that mattered.

CHAPTER FORTY-FOUR

Keep your knitting close in case of emergency. – E. C.

Mayor Finley stood tall at the microphone. The Pledge was done, and Fiona felt the crowd settling in for a show.

This was going to be bad, she could feel it. Why the hell had it been *Abe* who felt so compelled to fight her for this? Why couldn't it have been Herbert Stork or Theo McCormick? Men she could argue against and not want to throw herself at. Fiona felt a trail of sadness at the thought, followed immediately by anger, tiny pinpricks of it at the tips of her fingers. Maybe this was where magic came from—from women being so angry that they held up their hands to shoot fire out of their fingers.

Fiona took a deep breath and then another one.

Daisy touched her forearm and said quietly, "Don't hyperventilate. Think yoga."

"I hate yoga."

The mayor invited Fiona, Elbert, and Abe up to the three chairs placed on the stage. Fiona hoped desperately that she'd be put on the end with Elbert Romo as a buffer in between herself and Abe, but instead Mayor Finley put her in the smack-damn middle, with Elbert to her right and Abe to her left. Abe was seated so close to her she could smell his cologne, some amazing combination of fresh-cut pine and old cedar.

It made her stomach flip.

Mayor Finley said, "One of the things we love about Cypress Hollow is the dedication we have to tradition, while still remaining open to change. The Coast Guard has turned the lighthouse over to our local government. After we've heard your proposals, our council members will retire to privately decide which route to follow. Keep the conversation friendly in tone, please. Fiona Lynde, ladies first, of course."

The applause felt a bit too premature.

Fiona approached the podium and grasped the sides of it tightly. She leaned toward the microphone and smiled at the council members seated in the front row. "Hi there." Feedback squealed through the room, and people covered their ears. Betty and Alex's new son burst into frantic squalls at the rear of the hall.

Marshall Gedding scrambled up the side steps and adjusted something in the monitor at Fiona's feet. "Sorry," he whispered.

Having now moved beyond scared to downright terrified, Fiona said again, "Hi?"

It was still alarming, the way she could hear herself as her voice bounced off the back wall and into her ears, but she would just have to deal with it. She glanced down at her cards, shuffling them nervously.

Just start. She could do this.

"You all know me as the girl with the gas station. *Fee's Fill.* I wash cars. I do body repairs. I'm more often behind a blowtorch than I am behind a computer of any kind. The only paper I'm used to pushing is my Milky Way wrapper into the trash." This got a light chuckle, and Fiona felt her heart lift an inch or two.

"I believe in this town. I've lived here most of my life, and honestly, that's been by choice. None of my family is left here. It's just me. And that's okay, because Cypress Hollow *is* my family. I talk to almost every single one of you at least once a week. Except for Ted Sandyson and Maisie Dawson, both of whom converted to biodiesel and now run on the oil from Tillie's fryers. Maisie, where are you?"

A curly-haired large woman in a bright green top waved at her.

"I was behind you at the light the other day, and I have one complaint: the smell of fries coming out your tail pipe made me stop to get a chocolate double malt milkshake, so I'm not sure if I'm pleased or annoyed by your environmental choice. Oh, and you have a rust spot in your bumper, lower left side. So you should call me for an appointment."

More polite laughter. There was something lacking in the sound, though. The crowd wasn't with her yet. They didn't approve of her, not the way she needed them to. Fiona felt the spaces between her fingers get wet again, and she shuffled the notecards. It took her a second to find her place, and the rustling noises in the room didn't help—she heard a man honk his nose and the crying baby, who'd been taken outside, was carried back in, still snuffling. People shifted their feet, and she saw Lucy whispering behind her hand to Trixie. It was enough to throw Fiona off. She suddenly felt very small. And exposed.

"The future," she said uncertainly, reading from her notes. She gave up on the cards and leaned on the podium. "We haven't tried the future yet in Cypress Hollow. The only place with public Wi-Fi is Tad's Ice Cream, and that's only because Tatum Abercrombie who lives upstairs has forgotten to put a password on his residential account. We've barely accepted that years now begin with the number two. Some would say we need the lighthouse to be a museum, but a museum would just mire the town deeper in the past. The lighthouse is unsafe," Fiona went on, gaining strength. "We all remember when Owen Bancroft's mother made it to the top in that storm. We could have lost both her and Lucy that night." Lucy had stopped whispering and was nodding along now. Good. "Some say a complete earthquake retrofit would solve the problem, but we all know that one big shaker would topple it right over. We can make sure it doesn't hurt anyone." She really did believe that. "If we tear it down and make it into a public park with full handicapped accessibility, we'd be giving the town a gift that would give back for decades to come."

Fiona moved to the whiteboard, trailing the protesting microphone which gave another pained squeal. She ignored as best she could the feeling of Abe's eyes on her back. "Here's what I've worked out it would cost." She drew figures on the board, explaining as she went. She *knew* she was right about this. Fiona hadn't just spent weeks doing this research—she'd spent years. Ever since she and her father had moved out of the lighthouse, carrying carefully packed boxes of her mother's clothes, clothes her mother would never come back to pick up, Fiona had been researching how to make the lighthouse disappear. The time was right, and all of Cypress Hollow would benefit.

Then she explained, with more charts, how all the work could be funded by grants, grants that she would help apply for.

From the audience, she heard a single noise.

Old Bill, his head tipped forward on his chest, shook with the size of his gigantic snore.

The snore was followed by titters.

Good lord. She'd put him to *sleep.*

Flustered, Fiona said, "Progress is something we need in this town. Together, we can make something beautiful out of something ugly. Thanks for listening."

It was a wimpy way to end. That wasn't how she'd meant to sound, not at all. She hated the fiery blush that took over her face.

The mayor stood again. "Thank you, Fiona. Next, we'll hear from the thankfully fully clothed Elbert Romo."

CHAPTER FORTY-FIVE

Keep the needles moving. One stitch at a time. – E. C.

Polite applause floated through the room. Fiona sat down in her chair, facing the audience. She clapped and then, embarrassed, smashed her hands together behind her, praying that her smile didn't look ridiculous.

Elbert pulled the mike down toward him. "This thing work?" Satisfied that it wouldn't feed back like it had with Fiona, he launched into his speech without so much as a breath. "Urban sprawl. That's what Fiona wants for our little town. This little lady wants us to be just like San Francisco or Reno or something, with their *parks*. Parks that tourists will talk about and come to and then buy her gasoline. Think about it. Big towns come with lots of problems, and yes, we're talking about the hippies with their *chickens*." He spat out the word as if it tasted bad in his mouth.

Fiona coughed. In the crowd she saw Daisy trying desperately not to laugh, her sides shaking.

"With their hybrid vehicles and their shoes with the toes built right in. We want those all over our town? Smoking their crack and bringing in their guns to sit in our new-fangled park? My proposal is to make the lighthouse into a guard booth. Everyone drivin' by gets checked and gets a name sticker that they wear when they're in any part of Cypress Hollow. That way, if the guy's name is Howard, and he drops a gum wrapper, we can all yell, '*Hey, Howard, pick that up!*' at him. I ain't got no fancy drawings or numbers. Also, thanks for lettin' us go nekkid at Pirate's Cove. My behind has a wicked tan and I got a girlfriend named Hazel now. That's all." He tugged on his cap and stepped back.

Fiona didn't let herself grin. She couldn't, wouldn't.

A confused-looking Mayor Finley said, "Well. Thank you for that, Elbert."

Elbert shook his hands over his head and shouted, "Anytime!"

The mayor nodded. "Abe Atwell? Your turn."

Abe stepped forward and took hold of the podium in much the same way Fiona had found herself doing, as though it would prop him up. He was as uncomfortable as she was up there. The thought helped.

Too loudly, he boomed, "My name is Abe Atwell." He stopped and adjusted the microphone, fiddling with it, moving it up and down. Marshall leaped up on the stage again, but Abe waved him away. "I got it, I got it. Anyway. Yeah. I'm here for one reason: to save the lighthouse."

There was a light smattering of applause. Fiona tried to see who exactly was clapping, but it was scattered enough she couldn't tell. Damn it all, it should have been illegal for a man to wear a suit that made his shoulders look that good.

Abe spoke into the microphone quietly now, as if he'd figured out what it wanted to hear. "I was raised here, too. And I like the way we turned out. We're still a small farming town. We got ranches and the ranchers to run 'em. We got fishers and a place for our boats that I happen to be particularly fond of."

Was he purposely pouring on that extra-country flavor? Making his voice all syrupy? He was irresistible in that mode. And it was starting to tick Fiona off.

"Cypress Hollow is the kind of place that makes all Americans proud. It's the kind of place where the 4th of July parade gets more press than anything else in town all year. Our Christmas display at the marina got written up in that fancy Californian magazine last year." He paused, and leaned forward, propping one arm congenially on the podium. "That's the way we want it, isn't it? To be known for our small-town charm? What's prettier than a lighthouse, folks? What's more picturesque—an old building standing tall and proud on the coastline, a symbol of strength and safety, or a couple of swing sets?"

Fiona actively hated that she was facing the entire room. She could see how everyone was drawn right in to what he was saying, smiling and nodding already.

"Fiona's all about progress, right? Thinks that movin' forward is the only way to go. But the fact of it is that we all come from somewhere—we all have a past, and we can't just forget about that." He glanced over his shoulder at her briefly, but he didn't meet her eyes.

He looked like someone else. Someone she didn't know. Definitely not someone she'd shuddered next to, nails dug into his skin, when he made her come for the fourth time in a row.

"We *have* progress in this town. We have the stoplight and now we all know what it's like to wait in traffic, something we never had before. The new post office, think about that for a minute." Abe paused and raised his palms expressively. "Remember when we used to hang out in the post office? We all went there at ten because that's when the mail was out. It was our community center. The bulletin board showed everything from lost and found animals to what the American Legion was serving on Friday. Evelyn and Winnie knew everyone and everything. Now we got that new place where they're behind glass. Did you know that glass is bullet-proof? That's the way the USPS builds now. And to me, there shouldn't be anything like that between neighbors in a town like this."

Abe did that comfortable lean on the podium again, as if he had all the time in the world. Every eye was on him. People sat up straight, and Fiona saw nods throughout the crowd. Someone yelled, "Hey, our streets!"

He said, "Exactly. Another example, thanks for that, Tad. County Roads comes in to paint a bike lane, sure, and that's great, but what about our streets? In the name of progress, they repave every road, and we all know that Jim Biddle's company got that contract because he's in bed with CalTrans. Using his crappy method, he's done nothing but rebump every road. The potholes get bigger every time it rains. The bike race that used to come through here is going the long way around this year, because they can't take the risk of riding on our chewed-up roads. That's where progress gets you. The old roads were good, just needed a fixin'."

Fiona leaned forward, sitting on her hands to prevent clenching them into fists.

"Now, Fiona Lynde, she knows about fixing. That's her job. Covering things up. Some of that comes natural to her, sure. And some of that comes from the fact that she lived in the lighthouse when she was a kid. Maybe she didn't have the happiest home life when she was there—"

Fiona couldn't help exclaiming, "Abe! You can't—"

He shook his head and still didn't meet her eyes. "Just common knowledge, darlin'. I'm not telling them anything they don't already know. Just reminding them that you have a big stake in this—a bigger need than most of us to see the lighthouse crumble. And I don't doubt that it was a hard row what with your mother leaving back then..."

Ice covered her heart so that she could almost hear it crack. She stood, terrified of what he might say next, what cold pain his words might bring. "I lost my mother the same year you lost your father." She made sure her voice was loud enough to carry without the help of the microphone.

He stood straighter. "That's the truth. That's another piece of common knowledge, too. Everyone knows my stake in the lighthouse. It's what saved my life that night, swimming toward it."

"But it didn't save your father."

"No." His voice was gruff.

"Because you left him. A lighthouse couldn't save him."

"Couldn't save your mother either."

"Maybe it could have, but you *left* him. Even though he begged you not to."

Her words were a detonation. Fiona saw his face fall, his expression crumble.

She'd just told his worst secret. To the world. She didn't even know how those words had come out of her mouth. If someone had offered her a million dollars to say them on stage, she would have turned the money down. But with him standing in front of her with those eyes that had looked through her soul last night and now didn't appear to half-way recognize her, the way he threw her mother into the argument...she couldn't let him. She just *couldn't.*

Fiona sat, her body crashing into the chair, her heart thumping wildly, her breathing shallow. She found Daisy in the crowd, but her friend wouldn't meet her eyes.

No one would.

But he'd brought her mother up *first.*

Jesus. This was bad.

CHAPTER FORTY-SIX

When it comes to wool, sometimes you have to
take what you can get. – E. C.

Abe released the sides of the podium, leaning close to the microphone again. He felt a rush of heat behind his eyes, and a sudden headache bloomed. He felt nothing but white-hot anger.

He'd trusted her.

"Well," he started, trailing off because he didn't know what to do with his fury.

Sure, she'd trusted him, too. But everyone knew Fiona's mother had left. He hadn't—would never—tell the secrets that he knew, that she'd shared—that her mother had hit her, that Fiona had fired her from her job as mother and that Bunny had listened to her daughter, quitting the family forever.

No one in the room had moved since her outburst. No one whispered. Even the creaking of the chairs stopped. The room was waiting for him.

"Didn't see that coming," he said. "My worst night, divulged to you all in the name of progress. That kind of..." The anger heated him so much he almost expected his feet to start smoldering. "I'm not sure how that kind of information is supposed to talk a community into tearing down a historic landmark. It's true, though. What she said is true." His voice faltered and he hated himself profoundly, more than he ever had before. Eight rows into the crowd, his mother's eyes were swimming with tears. "Mom, I didn't tell you that part...I never wanted you to know..."

Hope just tipped her head to the side and gave him a watery smile.

Now his mother knew. What he'd done. How he'd abandoned—knowingly—the only man that mattered to her and ruined her life.

"Fuck it," Abe said, shoving the microphone away from him. He looked at the council members in the front row. "Fuck the lighthouse. Do whatever you want with it. You will, anyway. Maybe she's right, maybe it doesn't deserve to be saved. We're just going to lose everything anyway, that's all I know. We always do."

Without glancing at Fiona, he leaped off the stage and walked down the aisle. He stopped next to his mother, ignoring the pain in his chest. It was only his heart again, and broken hearts didn't mean anything.

"Can I please walk you home, Mom?"

Hope stood, slowly, so slowly. When she was finally standing straight, she pulled his head down and kissed his cheek. In that kiss was all the forgiveness he'd ever wanted—all the forgiveness he'd assumed he'd never get. His hands shook, and he felt sweat break out at his hairline.

As they walked out, his mother kept her hand on his forearm. As he pushed open the door for her, she said, "I'm proud of you."

Tears filled his eyes now, but he kept his gaze straight ahead.

She continued, "I've always been proud of you."

Outside, the night was cold, colder than it had been for weeks. The air smelled of wood smoke and garlic from the pizza shop. His mother shivered. Abe took off his coat to wrap it over her shoulders, almost doubling it around her.

"You can't be proud of me. Not now."

Hope stopped and turned to face him. "You came home to me. You did what you had to in order to come home to me."

"He didn't want me to leave him, Mom. I didn't bring him home. That almost killed you."

"What would have killed me is if neither of you had come home."

He said the words then, the words he'd heard in his mind, over and over. "I ruined everything."

Hope laughed then, surprising the hell out of him. "Darling boy. *You* are my life. Don't you know that?"

Behind them, the door of city hall flew open and Fiona's voice rang out. "Abe!"

"Come on," he said, leading his mother forward, not looking back. He couldn't handle an apology from Fiona. Or worse, a justification. He wouldn't—ever—take that from her.

It was just as well he'd learned a long time ago that happiness never stayed.

Otherwise, right now, he didn't think he'd be able to live through this pain.

CHAPTER FORTY-SEVEN

Your knitting knows when your heart doesn't care enough and you'll feel the piece slipping from your fingers as it pulls itself toward the unfinished pile. Better just to listen to your heart from the very beginning. – E. C.

At the shop the next morning, Fiona found Stephen cleaning out the tool closet without being asked, hanging up everything in their correct spots.

"You hear about the meeting last night?" asked Fiona.

"Nope," he said, not looking curious about anything except where the bumping hammer should go. "I was here, working on a new piece."

Fiona peeked into the side yard where what looked like half an enormous robotic-looking foot was resting on a small, steel bird. "It's looking good."

"Thanks," he said, grinning that white, wide grin of his. "Already sold it, too, to some guy in Oakland. Couldn't do it without you."

He was probably the only person in Cypress Hollow who still liked her today. Fiona hugged him tight, and he grunted in surprise, but hugged her back. "I made some black beans this morning. Couldn't sleep. Go get some from the house for your lunch, okay? Then take the rest of the day off. With pay."

Obviously startled, he agreed, hurrying through the bay to the back door. "Dude, I'm going kayaking!"

Fiona sighed and watched from the couch as two more people, Steve Robishill and Marty Smith, paid at the pumps for gas.

No one ever paid at the pump. Abe was one of the only ones who did.

Today everyone had.

Dark clouds rolled in over the ocean. It was going to storm again, Fiona could feel it in the back of her eyes— the air pressure was pushing on her sinuses as though she had a cold. Or maybe that was from the crying last night.

Daisy hadn't even come by this morning and, besides what Fiona had done to Abe, that was the worst part. Fiona literally couldn't remember the last time her day didn't include arguing with Daisy over eating something healthy, and hearing Tabby laugh.

She'd done just about the worst thing she could imagine doing last night. She felt nauseated all over again when she remembered how stricken Abe's face had been.

Right when she'd fallen in love.

In love. Wasn't that when bluebirds were supposed to wind ribbons in her hair and flowers burst into bloom as she wandered by, dreaming of him?

Yeah, that's when she'd chosen to eviscerate him in public, in front of everyone they knew. While they argued about something that, in the long run, didn't even matter that much. What did she care about the lighthouse, that heap of wooden trash? They could save it, hoist it up three stories higher, paint it bright red and remake it into city hall—she didn't care.

And she wished she could tell him that.

She worked half-heartedly on the knitted earrings she was making. She'd finished one in the middle of the night, before she started cooking. Maybe she'd never sleep again. Maybe that's what was going to come out of this broken heart. Lots more free time.

The bell over the door jingled.

Rayna Viera.

Well, she certainly deserved it.

Rayna wore a red, button-down shirt that fitted her just right, showing off her impressive curves, and a black short skirt that skimmed the top of her perfect knees. She smiled, her lips pinkly glossed. "I've heard you can fix the hell out of a broken mirror."

"Well," said Fiona, standing and placing the knitting on the counter, "that's definitely the nicest thing I've heard all day."

Rayna touched the top of the stack of newspapers. The lead headline of *The Independent* was "Council Saves Lighthouse in Landslide Vote." No one had dared come inside the shop to buy one from her today. But Fiona bet that Tillie's was sold out.

"Quite a show last night," said Rayna. Her eyes were kind. Soft.

"It was," said Fiona. She was surprised to hear her voice quaver. She wanted to say, *I'm so embarrassed. I want to cry every minute. I lost the man you gave up so long ago. I lost the only man that mattered.*

Instead, she said, "What happened to your car?"

"Oh, it was so silly. I was backing up in that stupid post office parking lot—" She broke off as they both realized she was referencing the new post office, the one Abe had talked about the night before. "Well, you know how it's laid out. I hit that dumb mailbox. Just tapped it. Didn't dent *it* at all, I think it's made of kryptonite or something. But it took my passenger mirror right off." Rayna looked down at her shoes. "Tommy said he would fix it for me, but I want to handle this myself."

"Let's go take a look."

This was something Fiona could do. And God knew, she wasn't going to have anything else to work on today. She told Rayna to wait inside, that she'd be done in no time. She had the part in stock and it would feel good to *do* something.

Thirty minutes later, the new mirror installed, Rayna paid with cash. She touched the knitted metal still lying on the counter. "This is pretty. What is it?"

Fiona pulled the mess toward her. "Oh, it's nothing."

"An earring? Oh, is it a snowflake?"

"You can see that?"

"Of course. It's so pretty. What pattern is it?"

Fiona blushed. It felt good to be praised. "My own, actually. I'm just playing around."

"Well, keep it up. It's gorgeous." Rayna ran the tip of her finger over the auto part jewelry hanging inside its case on the counter. "You're so talented. I envy you."

"What?" It was so ridiculous Fiona almost laughed. "You envy *me*?"

Rayna smiled at her like they were real friends. "You're single. So pretty. You have your own business, and while I'd never give up even a second with my kids, sometimes I envy what *time* you must have. For everything. For making this gorgeous stuff—I mean, *look* at this necklace!" She paused, and her voice was sadder when she resumed. "You're your own person."

"Sometimes I don't like that person very much, though," Fiona admitted, surprising herself. "Aren't you your own person?"

Rayna raised a shoulder and dropped it prettily. "I have no fucking idea who I am."

It was funny, hearing the swear word drop from her lips. Fiona found herself liking Rayna suddenly. Trusting her. "You're Rayna Viera. Your kids are as gorgeous as you are. Your husband is tall and handsome and owns the hardware store, providing employment to himself and others. I've heard you make the best lasagna in town. Your hair is perfect, your nails are perfect, even your shoes are perfect. Look at them! Not even scuffed." She pointed down at Rayna's patent black pumps. "Everyone wants to be you."

"Well, everyone isn't that smart, then. I'm a mother to two kids. I'm a wife to Tommy. I'm a soccer mom, for Christ's sake. I get a new Lexus every year. But my husband is having an affair, both my kids have ADHD, and I hit that mailbox on purpose."

Fiona laughed out loud. "Are you serious?"

"Yes."

"But your life is perfect."

"Nope." Rayna smiled.

"Man, I like you more now."

Rayna's smile faded. "I get it."

Crap. "That came out wrong. Like everything else lately. I'm sorry."

Rayna said, "I kind of thought you had the perfect life. And last night, I figured out I was wrong."

"Oh, yeah. You were so wrong." She pulled out two paper cups. "Coffee?"

Rayna nodded. "Absolutely."

Fiona poured and watched as Rayna added way too much sugar. "That's not good for you, you know. If you cut back slowly, you won't notice that it's not as sweet. You'll feel better in the long run."

Rayna said, "You really do try to fix everything, don't you?"

Fiona said simply, "It's what I do."

"Honesty?" Rayna made a between-us motion with her hand.

"Yes." She didn't know why she was agreeing. She didn't know this woman, not really, and certainly hadn't ever considered her a friend. But today was different. Fiona was different.

"Can you fix me?" Rayna's eyes were filled with simple longing. "I want my husband to love me again. For me, not for who he thinks I am. I would also like to stab the bitch he's screwing, but I'm worried I'll go to jail."

"There is that to worry about." Did Fiona's own eyes look as sad when she thought about Abe? Probably. "I think I'm not as good at fixing things as I thought I was."

"That whole letting-the-past-go thing?"

Fiona sipped her coffee. Hers could actually do with a little sugar. Maybe. "No, I'm good at that."

"Are you?"

Of course she was. "Yes."

Rayna narrowed her eyes at her. "Real honesty, right?"

Such honesty. It felt good. "Yes."

"When I left Abe at the altar? It was the worst time in my life. I was in love with Tommy, one hundred and twenty percent. I knew it was the right thing to do, letting Abe go, although I did it the wrong way, obviously. But I let that go. He has, too. Everyone moves into the future—"

"I know all this."

Rayna held up a hand. "Hear me out. Just for a second. You had a bad time in the lighthouse. Don't you think it's time to let that go? We all have messed-up backstories. Even the people who look like they don't."

"I have *so* let that all go." Fiona added a packet of sugar and stirred briefly before sipping. Holy crap, coffee was better this way.

"Have you?"

"Why do you think I want the lighthouse to come down?"

"If you'd moved past it, honey, you wouldn't care."

"What?" Fiona heard the words. She just didn't understand them.

Rayna leaned forward, cupping her coffee with both hands. "If you had let your mom go, really let her go, you wouldn't give two figs about what happens to the lighthouse."

Damn.

"Why did you have to say that?" Fiona smiled, but knew it was wavery, at best. "Crap."

Rayna touched her wrist, lightly. "Seems like moving forward, *really* moving forward might be good for you right now."

"Hey," she said, and then lost her bravery.

"What?" asked Rayna.

"How do you—" No, she couldn't say it.

"Get over Abe Atwell?"

Fiona pointed a you-got-it finger at Rayna.

Rayna shrugged. "Find another man. That's what I did."

"Nah," said Fiona. "I'm not sure I'm up for that."

"Well, then, you're screwed."

Yeah. She'd figured that.

Rayna smiled at her then, and Fiona realized she had a new friend. It was stupid, she could have had Rayna as a friend years ago, she was sure of it. But she'd been so busy being mad at her, angry that she'd hurt Abe way back when. Jealous that Rayna'd had the ability to do so. She'd held on to the past.

She, who was so good at moving forward.

Maybe that was just a cover for being terrible at it.

Daisy chose that minute to roll in the front door. "Well, fine. I see I've been replaced. Show up late just *once...*"

Rayna and Daisy both laughed.

So did Fiona.

And the sound of their laughter, combined, sounded a little like hope.

CHAPTER FORTY-EIGHT

Most of the time your knitting doesn't need to be watched.
Your fingers are clever enough to move the stitches by touch,
isn't that wonderful? Every once in a while, though, you should
pay close attention to what your hands are telling you. – E. C.

It wasn't raining yet, but the cold front was pressing down, exacerbating the headache Abe'd already had when he'd left this morning. Even in two sweaters and his coat, he was still cold on deck. The haul hadn't been worth it. Fifteen black and yellow rock cod and a kelp greenling which would make good eating later, that was it. Luckily he'd had no tourists slated to come along today. His mood wouldn't have done well with couples from Massachusetts excited about spotting a whale. Not that he'd seen one today. Nothing was going right today.

Kind of like yesterday.

This fury—when would it go away?

Abe had seen her face—he knew she'd regretted saying it the moment it had happened. And really, was it that big a deal?

So people knew he'd abandoned his dying father. Coldly. Callously.

Hell, *yes*, it was a big deal. The anger rose again and he swore as a splinter from the wheel dug into the palm of his hand. He'd sanded the shit out of this wheel—there should be no splinters, and the fact that there were made him even angrier.

Abe reached into the first aid box housed to his right and ripped the top off an aspirin bottle, swallowing two dry for his headache. Then he headed for the channel, the engine chugging below him.

His eyes fell on the lighthouse, small and gray against the slate sky. It was tiny from here.

Abe got out the binoculars and looked at the place. He couldn't help it. Abe always fought with himself for doing this—he shouldn't *need* to look at it every time he went past, but he did it anyway. Kind of like driving past his mom's house whether or not he had time to stop. Just checking in.

There was a person at the foot of the lighthouse today, near the bench he'd shared with Fiona. His stupid, traitorous heart ached. Idiot heart.

He couldn't tell who the person was, not from this distance, though he could tell the person was female. Something about the color of the coat, about the way the person was standing, made him wonder if it could be her.

Fiona.

Nah.

He shook his head and lowered the binoculars. He wouldn't think about it. It didn't matter who was up there. Didn't matter a bit that the woman was wearing a dark-colored cowboy hat. Plenty of cowgirls in town.

The boat stubbornly fought the gathering swells, moving closer to land.

"Don't do it, you pathetic loser," he muttered to himself. No. He wouldn't grab the high-powered Nikon 12x50 binoculars, the ones he watched the stars with. No way.

And then, of course, he did.

At that magnification, he could absolutely make out who it was. And it sure as hell was her.

With these binoculars, he could see the grease spot on the back of her jeans. When she turned in profile, he could see the tears on her cheeks.

She was holding a small metal box in one hand, and what looked like a lighter in the other.

The clouds were growing more ominous overhead, but Fiona was grateful the weather matched her mood. It would keep the tourists away. When she'd driven into the small parking lot, an old motorhome had been driving away. The young guy at the wheel had given her a snazzy salute, and Fiona guessed that later he'd use an app on his phone to process his lo-res ultra-grainy Instagram images of the decrepit building, posting them with words like "Super creepy old lighthouse somewhere on the coast. Great beer twenty miles south." Every time she searched for the Cypress Hollow lighthouse online, images like this came up.

Even she had to admit the building was gorgeous on a dark afternoon. It rose black against the pale gray sky behind it, jutting proudly up, light glinting from the shards of glass left at the top in the lantern room. From here, she couldn't see the rusted holes in the metal, the water and bird damage on the ledges, the broken boards and caution tape flapping at the bottom. She just saw its silhouette, still proud and fine.

Fiona walked to the bench at the edge of the cliff, the bench she'd shared with Abe. She would *not* think of him, though, not right now. This had been her own bench long before she'd been here on that date. She wouldn't think of the way she'd discovered, below in the caves, how his mouth felt on hers, wouldn't remember the way he heated her blood and made her head spin with delight at the same time.

Fiona was here to think about her mother. To let her go.

Rayna had been so right it hurt.

Contrary to what she'd always believed, Fiona had been nothing but a perfect failure in moving forward. She, who thought she had nothing holding her back from a bright future, had let the pain of her mother's leaving hold her bound, and she hadn't even known it. She'd tattooed her very body with the pain of that memory. She'd kept the metal box with her mother's sketches hidden under her bed. Fiona had thought, mistakenly, that keeping the box out of sight meant that she was over her mother's abandonment. Instead, she'd been keeping it close, keeping it safe.

All these years.

Her mother wasn't coming home. Ever.

From her pocket, she took out a bright red lighter she'd lifted from the counter at the station. She'd throw it out after this, wouldn't sell it on to someone else. Not after it had been used for something like this.

Taking the lid off the tin, she held up the first sketch. It was of a monkey puzzle tree—the one that used to be at the curve of the road just a couple of hundred yards away. It had blown down a few years before in a storm. The sketch was rough, the pencil lines faded now. Bunny had taken a book out from the library, Fiona remembered, and had studied how to draw the bones of the tree first, and then build around the shape. To Fiona's untrained eye, her mother hadn't been bad. The tree was recognizable, the horizontal jutting branches at a sharp angle to the trunk, the slight rise and curve of the road still the same as it was now.

Fiona flicked the lighter and held it under a corner of the brittle paper. It caught instantly, and zipped red and black up to her fingertips faster than she thought it would. She dropped it, and it harmlessly flared itself out at her feet on the gravel.

The ache cut less deep already.

The second one was a drawing of the very spot Fiona stood on. The lighthouse, the bench (still new then, unsplintered and smooth), the horizon far at the top edge of the paper. Two seagulls dove toward the bottom of the page.

It also burned cleanly and quickly. So did the others.

She saved two for last. Both sketches of a little girl, Fiona had never been sure if they were actually her or not. One danced near a snowman in front of a small cottage in the woods, someplace Fiona had never been. Bunny could have *imagined* her there, though, right? The hair was the right length, and she'd had those exact Mary Janes. But what little girl didn't?

The second was more likely Fiona, if either of them were. The girl, closer in this sketch, leaned her head against a car that resembled the old Pinto her father had driven. Her eyes were closed, and though she smiled, it was a sad, tired-looking image, and Fiona had always hated looking at it.

Having saved it for last, she ran the lighter along the bottom of the paper and said, "Goodbye, Mom."

As if the wind had heard her, a cold wind kicked up, carrying half the page, still blazing, to the foot of the lighthouse. Fiona sucked in her breath, but it was fine. Of course. A tiny ember like that couldn't catch the old wood.

But holy hell in a handbasket, it could catch the long-dead weeds at the base of the building. One flame licked upward. Then another.

"No. No. *No.*" Fiona ran at the weeds. She tried stomping the small fire out with her boots, but every time she stepped the fire moved sideways, and the wind whipped the flame through piles of dried leaves and detritus that swirled and blazed.

The edge of the windowsill caught first—a burning, twirling ember landing on a pile of clumped bird feathers. Fiona could actually hear them crackle as they ignited. She beat at it with her jacket, but it was too fast for her, the wood too old.

The whole damn wooden lighthouse was tinder, and she'd provided the match.

The heat of the spreading flame drove her backward, and she stared up at the building. Goddamn.

What if she didn't call 911?

The thought only rested in her mind for a second, long enough to regret having wasted any time. The pause, though, that her fingers felt as they reached for her phone...Fiona *wanted* it to burn.

And for that she felt nothing but true, deep grief.

The dispatcher told her they were sending the engines her way, and then asked if anyone was inside the building.

Fiona's heart broke. "Not anymore."

And then she ran for the door of the keeper's house.

Abe didn't understand how it caught so fast.

From midship, Abe watched the lighthouse spark and then go up like a Roman candle. One minute it was fine, and Fiona was in front of it. The next, he couldn't see her against the glare of the blaze.

The worst of it was his helplessness. Still scudding into the channel, Abe couldn't abandon ship—he'd made the swim to the rocky shore in high seas once, and he didn't know if he could do it again. He called 911, but couldn't get through, the lines probably jacked from everyone else calling. With his binoculars, he saw passing cars and RVs stop on the highway to watch the fire, carelessly blocking the fire engines that roared up.

He watched as the fire fighters aimed hoses on the blaze, watched as the water steamed up in white billows of evaporation against the heat. The top of the lighthouse had already caved in with a rumble he could hear even this far away.

But her.

He hadn't seen Fiona again. She should be running around—she should be up there on the road, watching with the tourists—she should be leaning in shock against the battalion chief's truck.

Desperately, he called 911 again.

The dispatcher's quick words tumbled over each other. "911, are you reporting the fire on Highway One?"

"I'm watching it. There's a woman. There should be a woman," he gasped.

"What?" Radio traffic squelched in the background.

"Tell them to check the lighthouse keeper's house. For Fiona Lynde."

"Are you saying someone might be trapped?"

"That's exactly what I'm saying," he roared. If Fiona had gone in, to get something out...It didn't matter that she'd started the fire, it just mattered that she was safe.

Through the binoculars, he watched as men who'd been putting up a ladder suddenly ran toward the keeper's house, the side of which was already blazing.

Barely breathing, Abe slowed the boat so he wouldn't go into the channel and lose sight of what was most important. He kept the binoculars steady, absorbing the motion of the boat with his legs.

Two firefighters carried someone out, rushing her away from the fire and over to the ambulance. They laid her on a stretcher, strapping an oxygen mask to her face.

When they took off the person's cowboy hat, long brown hair spilled out.

Abe pushed the throttle control to full power, taking the south curve into the channel way too fast. He didn't give a shit. There was only one place he needed to be, and it wasn't on the damn water.

CHAPTER FORTY-NINE

Working together can be hard, but if everyone knits a square, the blanket will be big enough to warm everyone.— E. C.

When Fiona woke up for the first time, she wondered why her father was smiling so hard it looked like he was crying. She tried to say something but couldn't even make a whisper. Tinker wiped his eyes and told her to go back to sleep and, pulled under again by medication and pain, she did.

The second time she woke, it was dark in the room. Monitors beeped officially behind her head, and from the hallway she heard a woman's brisk voice giving orders, "Get the mop behind the file cabinet. It rolls."

Abe—her darling Abe—sat three feet away from her. His chin rested against his chest, and his eyes were closed. In the dim light, she could see the shadow of stubble on his exhausted-looking face.

What the hell had she done?

Her chest ached almost unbearably. Then she fell asleep again.

Over the course of the next three days, before her father was allowed to take her home, Fiona learned that she'd received several, small, second-degree burns on the backs of both legs. The burns could have been tremendously worse, and she'd been lucky to escape with her life. She'd collapsed of heated-gas smoke inhalation, which worried the doctors until she presented no signs of lung infection. IV fluids, antibiotics, and pain medication had assured she would be fine.

But Fiona knew she'd never be fine. Not now.

She hadn't seen Abe since the night of the fire when she'd seen him at her bedside. She'd had no visitors but her father and Daisy, who'd brought her a new dark red geranium, "To plant in your garden later," but she hadn't brought Tabby, she didn't stay long, and she hadn't been able to meet Fiona's eyes. Fiona had been too scared to ask the questions that burned worse than the blistered, weeping skin on her legs.

She *was* lucky, she knew. Doctor Fontaine and the nurses kept telling her that. She could have been hurt so much more badly. She kept her eyes on Tamale. Her father had brought her fish to her, insisting that no one else should feed him but her. "He misses you," he said.

Tinker took her home on the fourth day, loading her into her own car, since, as he said, "Gloria's got the home fires burning in the pencil truck at your place. I mean, not *burning*. I mean...ah, crap, you know what I mean."

Fiona didn't care what he meant. It was just good to be in her little Alfa, the smell of the leather familiar and warm, neither antiseptic nor medicinal. Her father drove slowly, as if he might hurt her by going more than fifteen miles per hour, but Fiona's lungs and legs felt better. It was her heart that hurt the most, and there was nothing they could do about fixing it at the hospital. She held Tamale's bowl tightly so that no water spilled.

At home, Gloria climbed down slowly out of the pencil truck and gave her a careful, soft kiss. "I've got your bed all made up, fresh sheets. Tomato soup on the stove. Hold on to my arm." She was clothed, as she usually was, in long, flowing fabrics, a scarf over a caftan over a long tunic. Her long unbound hair was obviously freshly done, and shone deep purple in the weak sunlight.

"I'm okay," said Fiona. And she was. Physically. The pain had gotten to the point at which it was manageable with ibuprofen.

Stephen launched himself through the garden as they walked through from the back door of the shop. He reported quickly, "All's well, boss. I got three details today, but I'll have time to finish them before four o'clock. You haven't missed anything."

Fiona smiled and felt her mood lift for a brief second. "I'm so lucky I didn't have to worry about this place, not for a single minute. Thank you so much."

She could actually see his chest inflate with pride. Good. He deserved to feel that way.

Inside the house, Gloria insisted that she go lie down in bed. "I'll make tea. And then I'll get you a crossword puzzle and a pencil or two. We have *so many* crossword puzzles now, you just wouldn't believe. We're total addicts now."

Fiona conceded to the tea and to working out half a puzzle with Gloria. Gloria, though, left the room in a muddle after asking, "What's six letters for an extinguished match, ends with F? That can't be right. Oh, *dear.* Oh, *no.* I'll be right back."

"Tell her it's fine," Fiona said to her father with a sigh when he came in to tell her that Gloria had flustered her way across the garden to see if Stephen needed anything. "Everyone thinks I did it on purpose, don't they?" she finally asked. She kept her eyes carefully on the view outside her window. The only thing in bloom was a pink geranium that Daisy had given her two years before—it loved where Fiona had planted it and was now more than waist-high.

"No, honey, don't you worry about that." Her father, his heavy white eyebrows working as he stared at the crossword, spoke in a gruff, reassuring voice. It wasn't his fault that she didn't, couldn't, believe him.

"Why haven't the cops been in to talk to me?"

Her father humphed.

"You wouldn't *let* them," she guessed.

"No need. You didn't do anything wrong. But yeah." He erased a letter carefully. "They say they need to ask you some routine questions. I said maybe tomorrow. Maybe not."

"I didn't mean to do it." It was the first time she'd said the words that had been echoing in her head. "I was burning some sketches of Mom's."

At this, her father looked startled. "You *did* start the fire?"

"It was my fault." Fiona felt tears collect in her aching chest and pushed them back down. "It was totally my fault. The paper caught the grass, and then...then it was just gone. Too fast. So fast. I called 911, and they came...it was too late. But I didn't mean to do it."

"I know you didn't, sweetheart."

"They don't know, though, do they? Everyone else."

His white mustache wobbled.

"No one but Daisy has sent flowers. No texts or emails on my phone that aren't business-related." Nothing from Abe. "None of the nurses let me have the local paper. And I didn't see my own copy on the table with my mail, which means you've probably hidden it."

Tinker examined the pencil's eraser as if his next words might be printed there. "Why were you inside the house, Fee?"

Fiona pressed a hand against her chest where her breath went tight.

Her father leaned forward. "Never mind. Don't answer. You don't have to tell me. The cops are going to ask, but we can—"

She held up a hand. She *wanted* to tell him. "I had a stupid idea of ripping down the snowflake. She painted it on top of the old wallpaper, you remember, so I hoped I could get it. I couldn't lose it. I thought even if I couldn't get it out in one piece, I could take a quick photo of it." Her voice trembled, giving her away. "I didn't get a single photo. I went down so fast, I didn't know smoke could take a person out that quick..."

Fiona paused. Tinker seemed to be struggling to say something, but in the end he only managed, "Daughter..."

It was now or never. The words clung to her lips and then fell. Fiona said what she'd wanted to ask him since her mother had left, so long ago. "Where is she, Daddy? I want to ask her something."

"Fee—"

"I want to know why she never came back. I've waited all this time. It wasn't until the lighthouse was burning that I realized I needed to know."

"Honey, she's dead."

Everything stilled.

Her father's words had been quiet, but they were muffled *booms* in her head, like faraway fireworks.

Dead.

"When?"

Her father leaned forward, tugging off his cowboy hat—the match to hers—and dropped it on the floor. He plunged his fingers into his hair, raking it back. "Since four months after she left."

"Daddy." It wasn't a question—it was a plea, ripped from her.

"I screwed up. I screwed up so badly. I've never messed anything up bigger in my whole life."

"You didn't *tell* me?" Fiona choked. "How? How did she die?"

"Overdose."

"On what?" She didn't have to spare her father, not at this moment.

"Pills and alcohol."

"Did she mean to?"

Tinker desperately smoothed his mustache. "They didn't know. There was no note. I think she did, but we'll never know."

"Where?"

"In a hotel room."

"*Where?*"

"An hour north of here."

An hour. Just an hour. Four months gone, and she'd only managed to run less than a hundred miles? "Was she with anyone?"

"A man found her. A friend."

"Daddy." She couldn't reach out to him. Not yet. Instead, she dug her fingers into the blanket Gloria had pulled up around her earlier.

"I have nothing to blame it on, but I think that fact was maybe why I got it so wrong. I'd been so *mad* at her, for leaving us, for leaving *you* like that, but when I found out about him, I...I can't explain what I went through. And then, a month or two after that, I couldn't explain my silence. I knew, even then, that it might be unforgivable—as unforgivable as her leaving was, maybe. I worried that you were so hurt it would only damage you more if I told you she was dead. That maybe, since I was in so much pain, it would save you some if you just moved on. Learned to live without her, maybe stopped hoping she'd come back."

"But that was the problem," said Fiona, her voice thin. "I waited for her to come home. I wouldn't have waited if I'd known the truth."

He put his hand out. "I'm sorry. Daughter, I can't tell you how sorry I am."

Fiona had a choice. She could roll over. Ignore his hand. Face the wall and sob, the way she wanted to.

Or she could reach out to him.

His eyes, the same color as hers, looked as full of pain as her heart did. They were both scarred from love, from loss.

She took his hand. Of course.

Breath by breath.

CHAPTER FIFTY

You are so clever. Just look at you, what you're doing there. I think you're amazing. And you knit, too? Perfection. – E. C.

W as he imagining it, or did a hush fall over the Tillie's crowd when Abe walked in? It was almost palpable. No one actually stopped talking, but their voices lowered. Their words slowed as they stared and then regrouped, the conversations rising again, but thinner.

A minor hesitation was a major sign in a place like this. Abe held his chin high. He wasn't the topic of conversation, after all. She was.

He nodded to Old Bill who was seated on his stool, fingers resting on the cash register. "Morning."

"It is," said Old Bill. "Sit anywhere."

As if Abe didn't know how Tillie's worked.

Shirley poured his coffee and took his order. Her smile was curious but she didn't ask anything.

That kind of circumspection wouldn't last another minute in here, he bet.

And he was right. Toots Harrison, wearing a fuzzy, black sweater with an embroidered orange lion roaring on the front, sat right across from him without asking.

"How is she?"

"Good morning, Toots."

Toots's rapidly moving hands, never dropping a stitch of her sock, brushed aside his words. "She up and about yet?"

"I ordered the bacon. You like the bacon here?" He leaned back in the booth. A spring jabbed him in the ass, but he didn't move.

"I saw in the paper that the cops ruled it accidental after talking to her. Come on, Abe." She poked him— literally poked the back of his hand—with a knitting needle. "Tell me. What really happened?"

"How's Lucy doing these days?"

Toots broke into a smile. "Happy as a clam. She and Owen just adopted a baby girl, did you know that? I always said she missed the boat with you, but then Owen came along."

"Good man." Abe and Lucy had gone on one uncomfortable date in their early twenties after their mothers set them up. What relationship could survive that kind of start? "Better catch than I am."

From over his shoulder, he heard a lilt he knew. "That's not fair. You're still the biggest catch in town."

Toots's eyes widened, obviously already picturing the gossip-miles she'd get from this. "Rayna, sit! Sit with us!"

Rayna gave a wide smile, that sweet grin she'd always had. She could make anything easy. "Oh, Toots, would you mind lending him to me? Just for a minute."

Toots's face fell, but she tucked her knitting into her purse. "Oh, all right. I'll be at the counter if you need me."

Like a hole in the head, Abe thought but waved as graciously as he could as she slid out of the booth with some effort.

Rayna, as she slid in, was the polar opposite of Toots. Perfectly put together, as always. Not a hair out of place. She wore all that shiny eye shadow—always had—and it looked great, widening and deepening her already startlingly pretty eyes. She smelled amazing—sweet and happy. Abe just wished she'd believed him even once when he'd told her she didn't need any of the trappings, that she never had.

"Hey, Tiger."

There it was, that ease. It felt good to be near her. "Hey, you."

"How are you holding up?"

"You really want to know?"

"Yeah. I'm worried about you, honey."

And her face looked like she meant it. No ulterior motive. Nothing but a friend checking in with a friend.

And hell, she knew him better than most ever had in this town.

He felt sudden relief. "I'm a wreck, actually."

"Have you seen her?"

"Not since the first night in the hospital."

"Are you kidding me?" Rayna shook her head politely as Shirley pointed the coffee pot at her. "Why not?"

Abe tilted his head. "Not sure if you heard that whole debacle at city council?"

"I was there. She spoke out of turn."

"You think? And the second the council voted to save the lighthouse, she *burned it down.*"

"You were also a jerk up there, about her mom."

"I know." He felt terrible about what he'd said, but what she'd said was so much worse.

"Did she mean to burn the place down?"

That was the bitch about this whole thing. Abe poked at the eggs Shirley had just dropped off.

He just didn't know.

CHAPTER FIFTY-ONE

Knit through everything. – E. C.

I can't do it," gasped Fiona, her hand on the open front door of the station, unable to move forward.

Behind her, at the register, Stephen said, "You can. Go."

Daisy, in front of her, rolled away impatiently. "You're coming."

"I can't. Everyone will be there." Tillie's was, for Fiona, like going to church. It was her community.

The community that might run her out of town on a rail.

"It'll be fine," Daisy tossed over her shoulder.

It was true, thought Fiona, as she caught up to Daisy, that in the week she'd been back at the shop, it had been better. The officer in the arson division (of course her case was assigned to John Moss, because he'd recently been put in charge of all property crime) had questioned her. He had accepted her explanation that it was accidental and the fire investigator's findings had lined up with it. There was a question whether the feds might come after her for negligence, and she'd lost a full night of sleep worrying how she'd save the gas station if that happened, but then Moss got back to her saying that the Coast Guard didn't seem too upset that they'd lost a building they'd already written off. He thought she was probably off the hook.

Funny, that she felt so far from it.

Trixie Fletcher, of *The Independent,* who had run (another) front page story about the lighthouse disaster, had interviewed both Fiona and Officer Moss after Fiona made her statement. Trixie, though they weren't close, had always been cordial to her, and Fiona could tell she was relieved to be able to report that it was an accident. Fiona even thought Trixie might actually believe her. She wondered what percentage of Cypress Hollow did. There couldn't be anything more suspicious than the woman who lobbies for a building's destruction, who, after being both foiled and publicly humiliating herself, burning down the same building "accidentally."

But one by one, her customers stopped paying at the pumps outside. One by one, they came in. One by one, they smiled too broadly at her, looking everywhere but at her eyes. She felt as if her face had been scarred by the fire and they were trying to be polite by not letting their gaze rest too long on her.

And then, one by one, they started really looking at her. Joking with her again. The first time Cora Sylvan came in to drop off her jam for sale, she'd had almost a brittle sound to her voice, as if she didn't trust herself to say the right thing. But the second time she'd come in, for a car wash, her voice had returned to normal, and she had given Fiona a real hug.

Fiona knew she'd scared them all. They'd been terrified that one of their own would let them down so hard. Which was, in fact, the reason it was impossible to forgive herself.

"Come on, silly," Daisy said. "Don't be *peur*, as Tabby would say."

"You both speak more French than I do, and I took four years in high school and college," said Fiona. The feeling of walking down the sidewalk on Main Street, the ocean to her right, dark green and white-capped to the horizon, the sun still low in the sky over Tad's Ice Cream, the hills rising green behind the street, her best friend at her side, speaking gently, teasingly, with her, was almost more than she could bear.

Where was Abe right now? On a boat trip? In the marina's office, pushing a pencil with his rope-callused hands?

"A few more steps and then you get bacon," encouraged Daisy. "You brought your knitting, right? If you're nervous, there's nothing better."

"Than knitting? Doing something in public I suck at in front of people I'm not sure don't want to string me up? I'll do a lot for bacon, but I might draw the line there."

"Knitting metal," corrected Daisy. "There's a difference. It's what your hands already know."

Fiona stopped listening to her. They were now in front of the plate glass window. Inside, she could see Toots Harrison laughing with Buzz Archer. Anna and Jake Keller shared pancakes with Milo at another booth.

And there, at the third booth from the end, was Abe.

Sitting with Rayna.

Their bodies were leaning in toward each other, their heads tilted downward. Rayna was speaking very seriously, her face intent. Abe's gaze was direct. Focused. There was no one else in the room for either one.

Daisy was already at the open double doors. "Ready?"

Fiona pressed her lips together. She felt a surge of adrenaline in her knees as if she'd caught herself from almost falling. She shook her head just once.

"I believe in you." Daisy's words rang wide through the street.

A tiny earthquake occurred, not under Fiona's feet, but within her body. She noticed for the very first time that Daisy's voice reminded her of her mother's. Melodic. Beautifully pitched.

The only difference was that Daisy loved her. A mother—a *good* mother—loved her.

Her father loved her. Gloria did, too.

People in this town loved her.

And maybe bigger than realizing that, full force, was the epiphany that followed just as quickly and earth-shakingly—that she loved them back.

Fiona Lynde, in all her imperfection, loved back whole-heartedly. The way she'd always wondered if she'd be able to. She treated Stephen Lu like a son because she felt maternal toward the man who'd come to her as a boy. She force-fed Daisy and Tabby healthy food because she wanted to take care of them, for them to be healthy, so they would always be near her.

She had a family. She had mothers, a multitude of them.

She was loved. She had already succeeded.

So what if she'd done everything a woman could do to lose forever the man she loved?

Maybe someday her heart would recover, although Fiona doubted it. And it didn't matter anyway—not in the grand scheme of things. It would have been nice to have realized she was completely, hopelessly, totally in love with Abe Atwell before she exposed his greatest secret and burned down the object he loved the most, but since she hadn't, there was only one thing she could do now.

She touched Daisy lightly on the shoulder as she passed her.

"Do it, girl," she heard Daisy whisper. "You got this."

At Abe and Rayna's table, she stopped.

Rayna's eyes got wide. Her mouth dropped open. "Fiona!"

Over the sudden hush in the diner, over the clinks of cutlery and the laughter of the oblivious ranchers in the side room, she could only hear him. She could hear his breathing, caught in his chest, could hear his heart, racing almost as fast as her own.

"I'm sorry," she said.

Abe stared. The lines at the corners of his eyes were crinkled deeper, as if he'd had little sleep last night.

"I'm just so sorry. For all of it," Fiona said. She knew everyone in the room was listening, rapt. Shirley wasn't even pretending to move, her now-empty coffee pot still hovering over Abigail MacArthur's full cup. Toots's needles in the next booth didn't even twitch. "I've never said anything I regret more than what I said on that stage about you and your father. I was reacting to what you said about my mother, which you shouldn't have said, by the way." There, she'd gotten that out. That wasn't her point, though. "The fact is, you took care of your family that night when you swam home. You told me you abandoned your father, but that's just what you *think*. What I know is that your father was hurt, saying things that didn't make sense, and you tried your damndest to help him. When you couldn't, you saved yourself, because he wanted you to, and in doing so you saved your mother a lifetime of living without either of the men she loved."

She went on, taking a deep breath in order to keep her heart beating, so she could keep going, keep speaking to the man who stared at her like she was an apparition. "You swam toward the lighthouse your father loved. The lighthouse you loved. That night, you swam toward *me*, Abe. You just didn't know it.

"And then I burned it down. There's no way I can explain that away, and I'm sure you've read the papers, so I won't try. But all I can say is this, with no expectation of any kind, I'm so terribly, awfully sorry. I lost my mother, and I loved her. I never got to say goodbye. I know you loved your father, and the lighthouse, and you didn't get to say goodbye to them, either."

Fiona touched the Formica table that matched the island she'd built in her kitchen. Maybe it could keep her standing for the next, and last, thing she had to say.

"I love you. And...goodbye."

Then she spun on the heel of her cowboy boot and ran out of Tillie's, ran for the filling station as fast as she'd ever run before, ignoring the burning in her weakened lungs and the pain in her broken heart.

CHAPTER FIFTY-TWO

The grace of knitting is its forgiveness.
The grace of your soul is the same. – E. C.

A be wondered if he looked as stunned as he felt. Like a fish still on the hook, whomped onto the deck, right before it quit breathing forever.

Rayna brushed her hair off her shoulders and turned in her seat, raising her eyebrows at the crowd of people staring. She waited—pointedly—until everyone had gone back to a semblance of normal conversation. Then she leaned forward. "You *see*?"

"What?" Abe had absolutely no idea what to do with anything Fiona had just said. "What do I see?"

"She didn't mean to."

He thought back, his mind racing. "Did she actually say that?"

439

"What does your heart say?"

He closed his eyes briefly. Opened them and took a sip of his coffee. How could he trust his heart? How could anyone do such a foolish thing?

Rayna leaned back, keeping her arms outstretched, palms flat against the tabletop. "Did you know Eliza Carpenter?"

"Through my mother, yeah. I know who she was. I know Cade MacArthur, of course."

"So you know Cade was the great-nephew she basically adopted. But did you know she and Joshua couldn't have children?"

Abe shook his head. This was knitter gossip his mother would have at her fingertips, not him.

"She asked me once, before she moved, to drive her to see the elephant seals. On our way, she told me the story. They'd tried, for a long time, obviously unsuccessfully. They'd had a happy life. They were more in love on the day Joshua died than when they'd married. But once, many years before he died, a woman told Eliza she thought Joshua might be cheating on her. Sugar Watson had seen him in the living room of Margee Tindall's place every Tuesday night for a month. Eliza knew that those were the nights he'd said he was working with the pastor, building new pews."

Abe frowned, failing to see what this had to do with him and Fiona.

"Eliza didn't believe the woman. Even though evidence pointed to the contrary, she believed in Joshua."

"Did she ask him about it?"

"She didn't have to."

"Rayna." He picked up a piece of bacon and pointed it at her. "What's your point?"

She snatched the bacon out of his hand and took a bite. Around her mouthful, she said, "*That's* my point. She didn't doubt Joshua."

"But what if he *had* been screwing around? You can't trust anyone absolutely."

"You think that because you lost faith in yourself. You lost faith in me." Rayna looked down at the rest of the bacon. "And while women are throwing apologies at you, I don't believe I ever officially said that I was sorry. I am, you know. Not that I didn't marry you, because we weren't right for each other. But I'm so sorry I hurt you."

"Holy shit," said Abe. "I don't even..."

Rayna sat up straighter and polished off the bacon. "Anyway. She trusted Joshua completely. Eliza listened, then she shooed Sugar away. Two months later, Joshua brought her the stained glass panel Margee had been teaching him to make—an image of Eliza's favorite sheep, grazing on the hill behind their house. And Eliza wasn't surprised. That's the thing. It came up in the car, because I didn't know then whether I should trust Tommy or not. She told me her story. She knew she never had to doubt Joshua, because she just listened to her heart. I remember being so angry with her for a few weeks, because if I were to follow her advice, I would have left Tommy back then, years ago. I knew he was probably cheating on me then. Or about to."

"Leave him," said Abe. "Rayna. You have to."

She smiled. "I will. I am. I'll probably need your help. But we're not talking about me right now. You know whether she meant to hurt you with anything she did."

Slowly, Abe shook his head. "She didn't."

"Of course not. Anyone could look at her and tell that." Rayna gripped his hand and squeezed. "You just had to figure that out yourself. Now, what are you going to do?"

Abe moved his plate out of the way and briefly rested his forehead on the table.

What was he going to do?

When he lifted his head, he looked right at Rayna. "I'm going to get her what she wants. I've got to go." He threw money on the table and dropped a kiss on Rayna's upturned cheek. "Thanks, Ray. For everything."

Phone in hand at the marina office, Abe knew exactly who to call. Officer Moss owed him a favor from a year back when he'd run his wife's boat aground in the estuary. Abe had hauled him out and blamed a fast-running tide when it was really Moss's not watching where he was going that got him in the pickle.

Moss gave him the number he needed for the state of California, a friend who owed *him* a favor.

After three more phone calls, all chockfull of testosterone-driven who-do-you-know posturing, Abe learned what he'd set to find out. But it was the wrong damn answer.

Fiona's mother was dead. Years and years before, she'd died, the very same year she'd left. A bad year for Cypress Hollow kids to lose parents, apparently.

Dammit. What did he do now?

How did a man show the woman he loved that he believed in her? You sure as hell didn't take her that kind of bad news.

But now he'd have to tell her, because he couldn't not.

He needed to bring her something else, too.

Something good.

CHAPTER FIFTY-THREE

Love through everything. – E. C.

No," said Gloria kindly, as she took the plate out of Fiona's hands. "We can't. It's the principle."

"You can't sleep in a house? Period? Or just my house?"

Gloria shook her head and her long silver earrings, the very first pair of snowflake earrings Fiona had finished, glittered above her gauzy green scarf. "We promised each other."

Tinker, sharpening a pencil with a knife—to keep his hand in—nodded. "While we have a house on wheels, we sleep with each other, in our own bed."

"You have a tin can on wheels. What happens when you fight?"

Fiona almost expected them to say something annoying like *We never fight*, but her father said, "It's awful."

Gloria nodded. "Terrible. You should hear us rage."

They *did* fight? For all the unhappiness of her parents' marriage, Fiona had never heard them fight. The anger and tension was always just there, under the surface of every word, like heat rising from sun-baked asphalt.

"She screams like a witch on a bad acid trip." Tinker gave Gloria an affectionate pat on the rump.

"He forgets English! He uses made-up words!"

Fiona started. Was that where she got it from?

Gloria went on, "We fight until we're done fighting. No one in the bed till it's over."

Tinker dried the plate Gloria handed him. They were still treating her as if she was breakable. She was, just not in the way they thought. "What if your fight lasts three days?"

Tinker shook his head. "I can't do more than two days without sleep. So we patch things up quick."

Gloria patted her own cheek with a wet hand. "Darlin', I need my beauty sleep. I make him tell me I'm right."

"Even if she's not."

"Works for me." Gloria shrugged and handed him another glass. "Go lie down in the living room, honey."

Tinker said, "Okay."

"Not *you*. Your daughter. You stay and help me finish these dishes."

"Right," he said. "Right."

"I'm really okay, you two."

Gloria gave Fiona a gentle push. "Take your knitting. I'll bring you a glass of wine. Make me happy. Go lie down and watch the window. They said it might snow."

Fiona snorted. Snow. "That doesn't happen here."

Tinker dropped a fork into the drawer with a thunk. "Did in 1983!"

"So I've heard."

"Go," said Gloria.

Fiona went. It *was* a cold night, colder than it had been all week. The fire crackled in the fireplace, and she pulled a blanket over herself on the couch. She flipped on the outside lights so she could see into the garden and picked up her needles. Strangely enough, since knitting the wire snowflake earrings for Gloria, she'd understood how to knit with fiber. Her fingers had just gotten it, finally. Now she was working on a pair of lacy snowflake earrings made out of fine gauge white merino. She figured she could sell them next to the harder, sparklier, metal jewelry at the station.

Fiona's fingers stilled, and she looked outside. What did Abe's cat Digit do on a night like this? Did Abe have a fireplace on his houseboat? Or a stove? She couldn't remember. Maybe they curled up together, two grumpy males, stuck together out of habit and stubborn affection.

The thought physically ached, low in her chest.

She hadn't expected him to call. Not after what had happened this morning, not after what she'd said. She hadn't expected forgiveness.

Still, facing the fact that she'd never see hide nor hair of the man again—unless he was pumping his gas, facing the water—hurt more than breathing the heated gas in the keeper's house had.

Maybe she'd get a cat. Would it eat Tamale? Because that would be unacceptable, but it would be nice to have another warm-blooded creature in the house.

Something drifted by the window, catching her eye. Something white and small.

A powder of some kind?

More of it floated down, spinning in front of the geraniums and jasmine, falling gently to the ground.

"Snow!"

Fiona jumped up and pressed her hands to the windows. Snow, snow, *snow*! Right outside. Floating. Falling.

Snow being *snow* right outside her house.

"Gloria! Dad! Snow! It's snowing!"

They didn't come rushing in. They must not have heard her. Fiona let herself enjoy watching the glorious stuff drifting down for a moment. She'd go outside into it, yes. Of course. But for this moment, she let herself just watch.

Her mother would have loved this.

That didn't mean she couldn't love it, too.

A raucous, welcome joy in her heart, Fiona pulled on her thrift-store sweater, pushed her hat onto her head, and went into the yard.

Out here, though, it looked different.

The snow drifted down, but really only over the window. And when she tracked the drifting to where it started, it seemed to be coming from...well, it didn't make sense. It was flying *up* from behind a tall oleander and then falling again in front of the house.

And there was a noise, a low rumble, like a gigantic fan.

Fake.

It was fake snow.

What the *hell*?

"Hello?" Fiona followed the path of whatever it was that was falling—it *felt* cold—to behind the oleander.

Abe stood behind the large hedge, with what appeared to be a snow machine next to him. The white fluff was being pumped up and over.

Fiona couldn't decide whether to laugh or cry. "You brought me snow?"

He took one step toward her.

With all her heart, Fiona wanted to rush toward him. But not yet. "Why?"

"I wanted to bring you the one thing you wanted. But I couldn't do that."

Him, she wanted him. He couldn't give her that. This was his way of telling her?

"So I decided to bring you what your mother would have wanted."

"My mother is dead," Fiona blurted.

Abe's mouth opened and closed. Then he said, incredibly, "I know."

"You *know*?"

He pushed his fingers through his night-black hair. "After we talked this morning..."

They hadn't talked. Fiona knew she had just talked *at* him.

"After we talked, I tried to find her."

It was more than she'd done in all the years Bunny had been gone.

"I got the answer from a coroner's assistant, a little ways up north. I'm so sorry, love."

The word fell from his lips naturally, and again Fiona wanted nothing more than to be in his arms.

But not yet. Not yet.

"Dad told me. He *just* told me. I haven't figured out what to do with knowing yet."

"Let me help." His words fell like the snow, softly, beautifully.

"You brought me snow."

"I would bring you the moon if you asked."

"I'm so sorry." She couldn't say it enough. Ever.

"Don't." He held up a hand. "I wasn't there for you."

"What are you talking about? I sabotaged you at city hall."

"I don't care about the lighthouse. It never mattered," Abe said, his voice low. Strong. "I thought it did, but it didn't. What mattered was being on the boat, looking up at the lighthouse and seeing you there."

"What?"

"I saw everything. I saw you burn the papers, I saw the grass catch."

"You..."

"I saw you hesitate, Fiona."

"*Abe.*" She'd been wrong before. *This* might be the worst thing ever. "I didn't—"

"I know. That's what I'm saying. I know you didn't do it on purpose, and I know you didn't let it burn on purpose. Anyone would have paused, to watch, to see what happened next. You hesitated for less than a second. Less than a breath. I saw you call 911. Then I saw you run inside the house."

"The snowflake..." Fiona looked up at the snowflakes falling around her. There were more now.

"I figured. And where I was, I could do nothing—*nothing*—to help. The only thing I could do was get safely in to shore. Get to you. To know you were going to be okay. To pray to any God that would listen that you would be."

She smiled. "I am."

"It was the same that night, when I swam away from Dad. The only thing I could do was get safely in to shore."

She reached out, needing to feel his skin. He grasped her hand.

"I know," she said.

The snow fell faster, thicker now.

Abe took another step forward. Fiona closed the gap. His arms went around her, and she felt his heat through her sweater. Her hat fell to the ground, and she didn't care.

"I love you, Snowflake."

"Shoozwhump." She cleared her throat and tried again. "Someday you should totally call me Wrench."

His laugh rumbled in her ear. "I love you, Wrench."

"That's better, Abalone. And goddammit, I love you too," she said.

He kissed her then. A long, slow kiss that went on forever and barely felt as if it had started when he pulled back.

"Holy crap." Abe looked upward.

"*Lots* of snow," Fiona said in delight. "I can't believe what you did."

"Me neither. Not my snow."

"What?"

He roared with laughter. "It's not my snow. This is the real deal, love."

"Oh, that. I know *that*," Fiona said, drawing her mouth back to his. Her lips on his, she said again, "I know."

EPILOGUE

MEETING MINUTES
City Council Session

City Hall Complex,
Cypress Hollow, CA

Wednesday, June 10th, 7pm

PUBLIC COMMENT

Members of the public may speak to agendized items; up to three minutes per speaker, to be determined by the presiding officer. If you wish to address the Council on any issue that is on this agenda, please complete a speaker request card located on the table at the entrance to the Council Chambers, and deliver it to the City Clerk prior to discussion of the item. You are not required to give your name on the speaker card in order to speak to the Council, but it is very helpful and the City Clerk is a *very* busy woman who doesn't appreciate her time being wasted.

CALL TO ORDER

The City Council convened in a Regular Meeting. The City Clerk Hazel Montrose took the Roll Call as follows:

Present: 7—Mayor Finley, Councilmembers Smith, Capps, Harrington, Smith (L.), Walker, Fitzsimmons.

Absent: 1—Councilmember Keller (J.)

City Clerk Hazel Montrose announced that Councilmember Jake Keller is out of town fighting a wildfire in Ukiah. Evelyn Archer led a motion to send him good thoughts. Motion passed, though Mayor Finley said she shouldn't have brought it up before the Pledge of Allegiance.

The (carefully nondenominational so as not to tick off Sam Waters again) invocation was led by Pastor Trimble. Mayor Finley led the Pledge of Allegiance to the Flag of the United States of America.

Approval of May Minutes

Councilmember Harrington moved to approve the minutes of the May meeting. Harrington's motion passed 6-1. Councilmember Walker moved that they be filed as a waste of time since he's still apparently mad at Harrington not paying him rent on the Strawberries For Sale sign in his broccoli field. Walker's motion failed 1-6.

ACTION ITEMS

ZONING CASE #Z42: Cindi Smythe of Animal Control moved to look into leasing the old Valle property for a spay/neuter clinic. Buddy Hansen seconded. Tim Snopes wondered if this would be against the natural order, stating that cat and dogs "like to get it on and why would we stop them?" Retired veterinarian Jim Younger stated Tim Snopes should get his rat terrier Randy fixed before it knocks up the rest of the female canine population, passing on its stubby legs and crossed eyes. Veterinarian Mac Wildwood offered his services free of charge for any potential spay/neuter clinic. Tim Snopes removed himself from the meeting after stating he would meet his wife Tina Snopes at the Rite Spot after everyone else came to their senses. Motion passed unanimously in favor of exploring leasing options.

CONSENT AGENDA ITEMS

Pirate's Cove

Mayor Finley called upon Elbert Romo to speak.

Elbert Romo addressed the City Council in opposition to the new staircase being built at Pirate's Cove. Mayor Finley pointed out that Mr. Romo had missed the council meeting in April when everything was hammered out and that if he was so hopping mad about it he should have found time in his calendar to attend. Mr. Romo stated that as Head Pirate, he should have been alerted as soon as the proposal was drafted. Mayor Finley expressed surprise that Head Pirate was an actual position. Mr. Romo countered, saying it was indeed a position of *quite* some merit. Mr. Romo then called the Mayor a "horse's patootie" and said that if she wanted open access to every "Damn" tourist that drove through town, then the resulting anarchy would be upon her own head. He then departed, slamming the door behind him. The City Clerk is pleased to report that all present remained clothed throughout this exchange.

Lighthouse Memorial Park

Theo McCormick offered a motion that the art installation to be erected where the old lighthouse stood be his newly completed work, "Radio Tubes Through the Ages." Mr. McCormick's motion was rejected.

Fiona Lynde then offered a motion that Stephen Lu, of Fiona's Fill, be contracted to build a scale replica of the lighthouse in memoriam of those lost at sea. The City Clerk is pleased as punch to say that all present were in favor of this motion, and it passed unanimously.

Taking of Minutes

Mayor Finley motioned that the City Clerk be obliged to keep her own opinion out of the Meeting Minutes since "the meeting minutes are, after all, turned over to Trixie at *The Independent* for everyone in town to read and it's kind of embarrassing when you do that, Hazel." Motion failed, 6-1. The City Clerk was pleased.

Proposal

Abe Atwell motioned that he be allowed to take the podium. Mayor Finley allowed the request.

What follows is transcribed from the City Clerk's voice recorder (which, it should be noted, should be replaced and soon, since it doesn't connect to her new MacBook).

Atwell: You all know me, but for the record, I'm Harbormaster Atwell. Most of you know I hate talking in front of people. The last time I did this, it didn't go very well.

Pause for laughter.

Atwell: And the last time I stood up here, I was fighting for something that didn't matter. I put a whole bunch of stock in an old pile of timber, thinking my old man would have been proud of me for doing so. It took a while to figure out how wrong I was, but I think I've got the important stuff figured out now.

Atwell left the podium, taking the microphone with him. The City Council microphone squealed. Marshall Gedding adjusted the amp.

Atwell: There's nothing worth saving in this life that you can burn down. The only thing worth fighting for is love. My father *would* be proud that I finally figured that out, thanks to the woman in front of me.

Atwell kneeled in front of Fiona Lynde. The microphone was about to bust a gut and even though Marshall Gedding fussed with it, Atwell turned it off. It was okay, though, because the Council Chambers were quiet as church on Monday morning and the City Clerk could hear just fine.

Atwell took a ring out of his pocket. The City Clerk noted it was quite a bit bigger than her own, which wasn't that surprising given what the City Clerk's husband spent on it.

Atwell: Snowflake, will you marry me?

Lynde: Zamwow.

Atwell: Is that a yes?

Lynde: Frabimous!

Atwell looked desperately at Zeke Hawkins, who whispered something to Daisy Lane.

Atwell: You're killing me, Snowflake.

Lynde didn't answer. Instead, she launched at Atwell in a kiss that made this City Clerk think the two seem quite compatible. Neither of them came up for a while, which was fine because the City Council Chambers erupted in so much hooting and hollering that Mayor Finley had to use her new gavel for three straight minutes (7:19-7:22).

Eventually, Ms. Lynde indicated to the Mayor that her answer was in the affirmative.

The City Clerk isn't ashamed to admit there wasn't a dry eye in the house.

Snowflake Earrings, by Janet McMahon

(Crocheted, because Fiona thinks crocheters deserve a
Cypress Hollow pattern.)

Yarn—a small amount of white crochet cotton

Hook—1mm.

Notions—earring hooks.

Pattern (English terms used)

Finished size—3cm in diameter

Base ring: using white make 6 ch, sl st to join into a
ring. 1st round: 1 ch , [1 dc (US =sc) into ring, 3 ch] 12
times, sl st into 1st dc. (12 spaces) 2nd round: sl st into 3
ch arch, 1 ch, 1 dc into same 3 ch arch, [3 ch, 1 dc into
next 3 ch arch] 11 times, 1 ch, 1 htr (US =hdc) into top of
first dc.

3rd round: [6 ch, 1 dc into next 3 ch arch, 3 ch, 1 dc
into next 3 ch arch] 5 times, 6 ch, 1 dc into next 3 ch arch,

1 ch, 1 htr into htr which ended previous round. 4th round: 5 tr (US =dc) into next 6 ch arch, 5ch, sl st into 4th ch from hook (to make picot), 1 ch, 5 tr into same arch, 1 dc into next 3ch arch] 5 times, 5 tr into next 6 ch arch, 5ch, sl st into 4th ch from hook, 1 ch, 5 tr into same arch, sl st into top of 1st tr.

Fasten off.

ABOUT THE AUTHOR

Rachael Herron is the internationally bestselling author of the Cypress Hollow series (HarperCollins/Random House Australia) and of the memoir, *A Life in Stitches* (Chronicle). Her newest novel, *Pack Up The Moon*, is available now from Penguin (USA) and Random House Australia (NZ/AUST). Rachael received her MFA in writing from Mills College and is a 911 fire/medical dispatcher when she's not scribbling. She lives with her wife, Lala, in Oakland, California, where they have more animals and instruments than are probably advisable. Rachael is struggling to learn the accordion and can probably play along with you on the ukulele. She's proud of her dual citizenship (New Zealand and United States), and she's been known to knit.

Website: Yarnagogo.com
Twitter: twitter.com/rachaelherron
Email: yarnagogo@gmail.com

Made in the USA
Middletown, DE
15 April 2018